Death
Restaurant

(Book 2 in the ongoing series)

by

G J Bellamy

COPYRIGHT

Published by G J Bellamy

G J Bellamy
gjbellamy.com

PREFACE

Dear Reader,

Here is a very brief note because I have no wish to keep you from your story.

This book might be set in a mythical and highly fictionalized US state - let's call it Transatlantica - where, and I humbly apologize for this, stories are recorded with British spellings. Can you believe it?

So, you'll find grey instead of gray, flavour instead of flavor, and I have little to offer in defense/defence for this international outrage.

Why do this? - you might ask if you're a US reader. The answer is simple. The US is a dynamic place and is the only venue where certain elements of the story could be played out (and this goes for the rest of the series, too.) However, from my mother's knee I have learnt British English and it's the way I speak and write.

I could never pass myself off as a US national, lacking the intimate knowledge which comes from having grown up in or having travelled extensively through the US. Even if I had attempted to use US spelling and phrasing, you'd undoubtedly smell a rat and the story itself would be diminished. Neither of us would be happy with that.

Therefore, please look upon the following work of fiction as a story set in the USA but narrated and recorded by someone with a British accent.

Enough from me, I think, except to say, I hope you enjoy the story.

G J Bellamy

PS. Transatlantica is about 150 miles due East of Nantucket.

Death In a Restaurant

Chapter 1

Thursday, after 5:00 p.m.

*T*he offices of Althorn Capital Investments occupy the entire twenty-seventh floor of the prestigious Masterson Building in the very heart of the financial district of Newhampton. With a little over one and a half billion in assets under management, the company's previous annual revenue amounted to over seventy million. The costs of running the business, including the well-paid staff of fifty-three, amounted to forty-three million. This meant the five Althorn partners divided a profit of about twenty-seven million. Kirby Mayo was the only forty per cent general partner. His annual income from Althorn alone was over eleven million and he enjoyed the lifestyle and trappings that came with such a vast yearly pecuniary influx, despite which he was always thinking of ways to increase his compensation. This drive had him always looking for deals outside of the company.

No one in the office really liked Kirby - he was not a particularly pleasant man - but there were very few fund managers more successful than he or, at least, there were few with the lucky outcomes he consistently achieved.

Generally speaking, the Althorn staff had great admiration for Mayo's instincts, abilities, and acumen which caused them to treat him with reverence, but, beyond that, or because of that, he was remote from the staff and seemed merely an efficient, mechanical man with no observably endearing qualities. He was terse and direct in his speech, disliking interruptions to his work, having occasional, angry outbursts over trifling mistakes. This constituted his usual office demeanour. He was no leader of men and women. That was left to others.

With clients, however, Kirby was an entirely different being. He charmed and reassured them which was his prime objective. The promises of extraordinary profits and safety of invested capital were woven into his easy, assured flow of jargon-laden speech. Cautious, qualified investors, uncertain whether to lock in for a year the minimum capital requirement of a million dollars, often committed two or three million into Kirby Mayo's keeping by the time the meeting was drawing to a close. It was held to be a fact, by the more talkative in the staff kitchen, that Mayo could have got hold of half of Scrooge's fortune in such a way as both he and the legendary miser would have been satisfied with the transaction, and Mayo would undoubtedly have had a free lunch into the bargain.

Nola Devon, partner, specialized in merger arbitrage - the buying and selling short of both the acquiring company and the target company. Mergers were frequent enough and Nola so much had the knack of correctly predicting where share prices would go that she inevitably printed money for both Althorn and herself. A tall, thin woman with a thin face and dark blond hair, she bore a faint resemblance to a bird of prey. She was also nominally in charge of the office personnel, although she merely delegated the routine work to her several assistant managers. She, at least, was approachable and friendly towards the staff and did much to mitigate Kirby Mayo's bleak influence upon the team spirit.

Nola opened the door to Kirby's large and unusually luxurious office at five-thirty. She was the only person who never knocked before entering.

"I'm leaving now," said Nola, as she leaned on the handle. "For once, I'm actually up to date with everything. How about you?"

"Plenty to do. I've a small problem. I should be unloading an energy company that has good, long-term potential but its price has gone soft." Kirby was a large man - both muscular and well-padded - giving the impression of being more than life-sized even while sitting down. He kicked back in his tan leather swivel chair behind a large oak-topped desk which rested on two oval pillars. He clasped his hands behind his close-cropped head. Stretched out and at ease, he presented a vast expanse of expensive shirt material beneath his red-tanned, heavy-featured face, topped by its full head of grizzled hair.

In front of his desk were two more tan swivel chairs - smaller in size than the one Kirby was sitting in. Beyond the furniture of the desk grouping was a conversation area totally dominated by a fabulous, oversized sofa covered in a light golden brown material. Matching dull red rugs - thick and expensive - defined each space. An interior wall had a covering of square amber panels over which was hung a decorative abstract triptych executed in a thick impasto of vermilion and gold. Two floor-to-ceiling matte black bookcases stood behind the desk. Kirby's office would have been a show-piece except for the untidy clutter on his shelves. He had the habit of printing and hoarding materials he believed he might need. The vertical blinds - half closed against the sunlight streaming in - broke up the view of the office buildings across the street.

"What are you going to do?" asked Nola, referring to the energy company.

"Talk to someone to boost the stock and then get out."

"I guess you're going to Garland's, then?" Nola smiled. It was Kirby's favourite haunt.

"A phone call will take care of the energy company but I'll be at Garland's tonight, about seven. Why don't you come?" asked Kirby.

"I might. Jimmy is out of town. I'll be along later after seeing to the kids. It crossed my mind that you should buy the restaurant - you spend so much time there."

"Yes? I did ask about it and the hotel once. Didn't appeal to me when I saw the figures. As you know, the reason I go to Garland's is because clients meet with me there and a lot of new business comes out of our conversations. Amazing what a bottle of wine can accomplish." As he spoke, his face remained impassive, signalling nothing.

Nola nodded as she smiled wryly before leaving him to his work. As she walked away, she thought of the other reason Kirby spent so many of his evenings at Garland's and was reluctant to go home. It was his loveless marriage - loveless on his part. His wife, Rena, an affectionate, patient, trusting person, waited for Kirby in the hopes of his returning to her one day and being once more a husband and a partner. Nola knew that he had long since gone, never to return, causing Rena, unwittingly, to wait in vain.

Nola assessed their situation as coolly as she assessed the value of a company. The Mayo marriage had a liquidity crisis and was heavily short on communication and kindness on Kirby's side of the equation . She wondered why they did not divorce. She understood hopeful Rena not wanting to separate. Kirby's reasons eluded her. Perhaps, she thought, it was because of their two children.

A call came to a private number on Kirby's desk set.

"Hello, it's Morton. I'm running a little late today so I won't be there until after eight.

"That's fine. We need to get the other review board members onside quickly."

"There's a problem with one of them. I'll tell you about it later."

"Morton. You've got to make it work. There's no payoff if you don't. See you tonight."

Kirby stared unpleasantly hard at the phone for a few seconds as if he saw Morton Yates himself resting there. Trying to convince this particular group of pension fund managers to choose Althorn to generate high returns for their fund was proving to be troublesome. Morton Yates was easy to deal with - he was money-hungry and would receive a kick-back. The others were risk averse or against hedge funds on principle. Did they not realize that the minimal legislation governing companies like Althorn was what allowed hedge funds to become so profitable? Kirby had promised twenty per cent returns, net of Althorn's fees, with a commitment to use market neutral strategies to keep the risk manageable. The pension fund had not reached a decision on the company it would choose. Kirby was determined to get this seventy million asset allocation out of the teachers' pension fund.

The phone rang again.

"Tiger! Are you still slaving away in your hole?"

"Hey, Becki. Nice to hear from you. Where are you?" Kirby relaxed in his chair and smiled.

"In town, silly. I'm seeing you after dinner tonight."

"This is short notice. Had I known, I would have planned a romantic evening."

"You don't need to romance me. You stole my heart a long time ago. Actually, I want to talk to you about business - the real love of your life."

"Can you meet me at Garland's, say about ten? I'll be meeting a couple of people there earlier but I can get rid of them as soon as you show."

"I can do that. By the way, I'll have my friend, Gabbie, with me. She's nice and getting over a relationship - so hands off because she's not in the market for your attentions. Strictly business between me and you tonight."

"You never can tell what will happen. I'm really looking forward to seeing you."

"Then you'll get your wish granted around ten."

Brent Umber was in his apartment over the reclaimed machine shop he owned and which was situated near the city's centre. He was staring at himself in his bathroom mirror. 'We're not at all suited to each other,' he said to himself. He was contemplating the date he was going on this evening. The date had been arranged by the set of friends that wandered from one restaurant to another in search of novel, gastronomic delights. For Brent, this whiled away some otherwise empty hours. A week ago, Linda Roberts and he had been the only two single people at a table of twelve. Some foolish person suggested Brent and Linda go on a date together. This motion was quickly seconded, and then the word 'date' was chanted by the whole group. Under such social pressure, not to say coercion, the two singletons caved and a date was quickly arranged to quieten down the table.

It was only afterwards that Brent recalled that, although he had seen Linda before, he could not remember actually talking to her beyond, 'hello', 'goodbye', and 'pass the salad, please'. The whole group was content to talk food, wine, travel, news headlines, pop culture, and celebrity gossip. Brent barely contributed and, now he came to think of it, Linda never did. Beyond their filling in some time, Brent had no real idea why he went to such evenings.

He had been hoping a desperate hope that Linda might prove to be a kindred spirit who kept her light under a bushel. He doubted it - knew it was not the case, really - though he could not say why.

He put on a dark blue, superbly fitting, Italian, two-piece suit. Against his pale blue shirt, it made Brent look cool, relaxed, and perfectly turned out. The simple dark grey tie he carefully rolled up and put in his pocket in case there was a dress-code at Garland's. The light grey handkerchief he tucked out of sight in his breast-pocket as it had an orphaned look without the tie in its place. The hems of the suit's trousers were in perfect harmony with his expensive black shoes. Too high a hem, as some wore it, and the shrank-in-the-wash effect became evident. Too low a hem, and the wearer looked like he planned to grow into the suit - eventually. Brent preferred the look of perfection, symmetry, and harmony rightly aggregated to warrant use of the word neat.

For the drive, he was taking his seven-year-old Porsche Boxster. He very much liked the car but found it to be a little less than useful. His battered, blue Jeep was an old pair of slippers - an excellent, comfortable and familiar fit. By contrast, the Boxster was a pair of bowling shoes - excellent on the right occasion but out of place most of the time. He decided he would trade it and get... What would he get next? Something fast? Yes. Convertible? No. Electric? Not sure - maybe next time.

He was ready to go. He would pick up Linda in twenty minutes and they would be at their reserved table in Garland's by seven-forty-five by way of a walk across the park first. Brent now began to think what he could talk to her about and, as usual in these circumstances, his wits began to dry up.

An effortless talker by nature, when required to impress single women as to his potential candidacy for the position of mate, Brent became tongue-tied and wooden in his manners. Unlike some teenage boys, or grown men for that matter, it was not because of any innate insecurity about himself. His insecurity, such as it was, flowed from past events - his once having been a thief and a highly successful one at that. In his quest for a soul-mate or someone he could share his life with, the past he had firmly left behind him cast an enormous shadow forwards. Brent knew that, for him to love someone properly, he must openly tell that person all about himself. His overriding fear was that once his criminal career was known to the love of his life, she, whoever she would eventually prove to be, would reject him. He could not bear for that to happen. So, his past overshadowed the future and was expected to produce a rejection from someone he loved. The future rejection cast its own shadow back to the present day, causing him to be dull, always stumbling for engaging words to say to a prospective, future wife.

"So, you're seeing Brent tonight? I want a full report on how it goes. Tell me everything." Georgina Rasmussen had called her friend, Linda Roberts.

"I don't expect much to happen," replied Linda. She was a pleasant-looking, dark-haired woman in her late twenties.

"Oh, why's that?"

"He seems kind of boring."

"He dresses very nicely. He's very handsome, in a boyish way. Also, he has money. That's what Desmond thinks, anyway. What's not to like?" Desmond was Georgina's husband.

"Yeah, I know. But he's never spoken to me. I don't know if he's shy or what. He didn't put you up to this, did he?"

"Of course not. I doubt if he would even think of it."

"Well, okay. I'm only doing this because you guys embarrassed me so badly. I really wish you hadn't done it."

"Both of you are shy. You just never would have got together on your own. We only helped you along. Linda, it's not like you're doing anything else that's special."

"But I don't think he's my type. Besides, I really don't want to go out tonight."

"Oh, come on! He's taking you to Garlands. Anyway, let's not talk about him. What are you going to have? Something exotic?"

"I think I'll have a steak. Or a hamburger, if they have them."

"Girl, you're really blowing an opportunity here."

In the lower half of the old machine shop which served as a garage, Brent re-positioned his vehicles to get the

Boxster out from the back. His upstairs, large, two-bedroom apartment was a showcase blend of modern furnishings, a few superb antique pieces, and oil paintings from the early eighteen hundreds to the nineteen-fifties. Only one was an abstract. He liked his paintings to depict a concrete image rather than he be required to expend effort to make sense of them or they be merely a splash of decorative colour. He had just got the car out onto the street when his phone rang.

"Yo, Brent. Watcha doin'?" It was Vane - Vanessa - a girl who looked elfish, loved skate-boarding, and whom Brent had saved from a drug overdose.

"Believe it or not, I'm going on a date."

"What! What am I hearing? You're breaking my heart. I thought I was your only girl. How could you do this to me?"

"If I were your man, I'd be a nervous wreck inside a week. Anyway, how are you? How did the exam go?"

"Ninety-three per cent." Vane's career objective was to become a software engineer.

"That's fantastic! Well done, Vane. I knew you could do it."

"Yeah, well, make me blush, why don't ya? It's all thanks to you that I've come this far."

"No, this is your accomplishment. I only helped provide the opportunity."

"That's what I'm saying. Anyways, Brent, do you have any idea what it's like being a starving student? Here's me thinkin', how am I goin' to scrape by? And all the time, there's my best friend, Brent, who's loaded, just itchin' for the chance to help me out."

"I don't have any such itch. How much and what is it for?"

"Three hundred and it ain't for partying. I need some clothes, man. I can't walk round in these rags anymore. Everyone's laughing at me. See, I had the idea it would be an advance against future pay. Not that you've been giving me much work lately. You retired or somethin'?"

"I'm still in the game. It's quiet at the moment but I'll find work for you to do. What type of clothes are we talking about?"

"Oh, ya know, stuff that can be worn in class and on the street. Nothing fancy or way out there. It will meet with your approval."

Vane was eighteen and living on her own. Brent recalled a time when he was a foster child in his early teens and did not have the right clothes to fit in with his peers. He had fought at school over such matters.

"Send me a link. I'll transfer five hundred and it's a gift but don't go wild. You're a responsible woman now and I'm treating you as such."

"You are a darlin' angel. Your date is one lucky girl."

"I don't know about that. Let me know when you have your new outfit. I want a fashion show with explanations and we can do that over lunch somewhere."

"There's a new Mexican restaurant down the street from where I live," said Vane. "Supposed to be good. We could go there."

"Your choice," said Brent. "Give me a day or two's warning, though. There, you should have the link. Sorry, but I really have to get going."

"Got it. Whoa, yeah! Life is beautiful. See ya, Brent."

"Take care, Vane."

He worried about her. Knowing she could take care of herself was not sufficient to allay his fears. Vane was off drugs now and her brief experimentation that had left her dying in an alley seemed not to have affected her mental capacities in the slightest.

Brent had found her purely by chance one night as he was working on a case over a year earlier. Afterwards, when she lay recovering in a hospital bed, they had argued like screeching cat and barking dog until their warfare subsided. The dog won but received some serious, ragged scratches in the process. Vane's proud, independent spirit relented sufficiently to permit Brent to help her find some direction in life. Part of that help was the funding of Vane's education and part was he giving her work as a surveillance operative. She was good at following people and getting in places where Brent could not. Sometimes, a few from her wide circle of friends were also employed while she managed and organized them.

Despite her abilities and strength of character, Brent was always concerned she might relapse so he made her take responsibility for her actions when and where he could. It was easy for him to be involved because, as difficult as she could be at times, he looked on her as though she were his younger sister.

The Valdez residence was a newly built, custom home in the suburbs. Sylvester Valdez was in his forties. He tightly gripped a seven-page investment account statement in his hand . Seething with anger, he spoke to his friend opposite him as they sat in leather armchairs in the large and expensively furnished living room. Sylvester viciously waved the statement in the air to punctuate each point he was making.

"The market is up sixteen per cent so far this year. My investments can only manage a lousy three per cent. Why do I pay such fees? When they're factored in I've lost money. Actually... lost... money. How can these dummies lose money for me? Why am I paying them? If I had made ten per cent I'd be up a million and a half. Seriously, I should put out a hit on these guys."

"Sylvester, it's simple. Change your investment adviser," said Wilf Hahn, Sylvester's patient business associate and long-time friend.

"What about my million and a half? Who will pay me my money?"

"How is it you didn't notice before now?" asked Wilf.

"I've been busy with a few deals - you know that." Sylvester was speaking more calmly now. He flung the statement on the table in front of him. The timbre of his voice hinted that he had been cheated without his knowing. "I haven't looked at a statement in six months. Today, I decide to take some time off, relax, you know, see how things are going. I get out the statements and carefully go through them. This is what I find. I see I have been systematically robbed by thieves in suits!"

Zulema Valdez came in, carrying a tray of drinks.

"You still shouting about that?" she asked.

"Yes, I am, Zuli. I have every right to shout."

"Don't just shout. Do something about it. Besides, there's no way to get that money your investments might have made so it's no use crying over it." She handed out the drinks around the table and sat down.

"Don't push me. Not at the moment. I am so angry."

"I know, honey. It makes me sick, too, but what can we do?"

"Find someone to make up my lost money!"

"Im-possible," said Zulema.

"Well, it is and it isn't," said Wilf quietly.

"What?" said Zulema while Sylvester stared at his friend.

"There are some fund managers who can get very high returns but there's a degree of risk, you understand."

"Go on," said Sylvester.

"I don't use them myself but there are some hedge fund managers who can get twenty or thirty per cent returns after their fees are deducted."

"Not possible!" said Sylvester. "Is it?"

"Oh, yes. You have to find the right manager and, when you do and they're hot, you'll make that kind of money. They have down years as well, of course."

"What type of fees do they charge?" asked Zulema.

"Altogether, about eighteen to twenty-two or -three per cent."

"No. Too much, too much. It's my money not theirs," said Sylvester.

"That's true but think, they get you twenty points and they take twenty points, so it means they earned forty points when the market is only making fifteen at best across the board."

"So, they're that good, huh?" asked Zulema.

"Yes, if you find the right person." Wilf took a sip of his drink.

"How do we do that?" asked Sylvester.

"You'll have to do some research. See what kind of history the hedge fund has and pick one you feel comfortable with."

"How come I've never heard of this?" asked Zulema.

"Yes... this is new to me," said Sylvester.

"These are private companies and they deal only with people with high net worth and some institutions that want to improve the returns in their own funds. They don't advertise to the public."

"Okay," said Zulema. "Why don't we try one of these hedges?" she said to Sylvester. "We might make up some of that money after all."

"We could. What kind of stake do they want?"

"Half a million or more. You have to lock in for a period so they can make the money. Depends on the company, though."

"And how did you hear about this?" asked Sylvester.

"I read about them. I found it interesting. For me, I like stable, dividend income and low risk, so I never considered using a hedge fund. I'll tell you who does, though. Martin. He mentioned the name of an outfit he's very pleased with. Althorn, I believe he said. You should check with him."

"Yes," said Sylvester. He picked up his phone to call Martin. As was his habit, Sylvester got up and began to pace the room as he liked to walk and gesticulate when on the phone.

"I don't like it when Sylvester shouts," said Zulema. "He should watch his blood pressure. He worries me sometimes."

"He's always been like that," said Wilf. "He has a high threshold but when he boils over, watch out." While they were speaking, Sylvester began talking to Martin.

"Right! That's exactly right," agreed Zulema. "Then, after he's calmed down and has that cold look, that's when he's most dangerous. That's when people disappear."

"Too true." Wilf solemnly nodded his head in agreement.

They both waited in silence, listening to fragments of Sylvester's conversation from the kitchen. He came back after several minutes, smiling broadly.

"Zuli, go and put on a nice dress. We're going to Garland's tonight. The nanny can look after the children. Wilf, you want to come?"

"I'd like to but I have that meeting with the condo board tonight. I'm the president and there's the critical vote on getting our company in for the maintenance contract."

"Yes, you're right. Okay, another time."

"When do we have to be there?" asked Zulema.

"Martin got some guy named Kirby Mayo on the line. He's the big shot we should be talking to. He kinda holds court in the restaurant."

"Oh, what about a reservation?"

"No problem, sweetie, all arranged. If we can't get a table for ourselves, we can sit at Mayo's table."

"I'll call them and see," said Zulema. She stood up to get her phone from the kitchen. "What a lovely surprise. Garland's is the place to go. A real hot spot. Gotta go get ready. Bye, Wilf."

"Bye. Have a lovely evening," said Wilf. He turned to Sylvester and said, "I'll be going. Good luck tonight."

"Hey, and you, too. Thanks a million," said Sylvester. "I'll tell you one thing, Wilf, my friend. This guy Mayo is going to give me a big discount. I want my money back from those guys."

Chapter 2

Thursday, after 6:00 p.m

"*I*'m leaving now, Kevin," said Kirby Mayo to the brightest star of the small constellation of security dealers that Althorn employed. Kevin Jiang was seated at his work station. "Anything we need to discuss?"

"Ah, no. I don't think so," replied the industrious twenty-five-year-old.

"What are you working on?" As always, Kirby's face gave nothing away.

"I'm going over some research on three pharmaceutical companies I'm interested in. It's not up to date on one of them and I'm trying to get current information."

"Which one?" asked Kirby.

"Lowell-Stacey. It's a private company but they have two very interesting new drugs they're testing. Could corner each of their respective markets - if they get approved for use."

"Forward to me what you find out. Kevin, we don't usually do private equity deals but if there's a chance we can make something here, I'll consider it."

"That's what I thought. It looks that good. I was going to bring it to you tomorrow, if everything panned out the way I hoped, to see if you would be interested."

"I don't mind initiative, Kevin. I encourage it. Just make sure you don't lose focus on our core business."

"Yes, Kirby. I would never do that."

"Glad to hear it. Good night."

"Good night," replied Kevin.

When Kirby had gone, thoughts crowded into Kevin's mind as he sat back in his chair. He stayed late often in order to get ahead in his career. Not once had Kirby remarked about the early to late hours that he, Kevin, had put in. Of the last five coups that had caused an eruption of jubilation around the dealers' desks, three had been initiated by Kevin. Yes, he got the bonuses. Yes, he got recognition. No, he could not be a partner unless he brought in a raft of clients. This latter could never happen while Kirby was in power. Several dealers had left Althorn in the past to set up their own hedge funds because there was no way a partnership position would ever be offered to them within the current structure.

Kevin knew his own abilities. He was good and consistently so. His earnings track record over the last six months was better than Kirby's own. Indeed, he had achieved some of the best results Althorn had ever seen. The difficulty was that Kirby brought the clients in and retained them while Kevin never met a single one. He had come to the realization that he could go no further within Althorn.

Once, when Kevin had asked Kirby about the possibility of a partnership, his boss played him. He knew that now. Mayo had said he would think about it; said it was just possible, and that it depended upon what the other partners thought. It was never mentioned again. So, as it stood, Kevin must continue on and be expected to produce prodigious profits while knowing that, should he suffer burn out or a bad quarter, he would be shown the door or completely side-lined until he left of his own accord. In his heart he knew it to be a hard, unrelenting business. For Kevin, the business had a face to it and it was Kirby Mayo's. He could not contain his anger anymore. He threw a stapler across the room and left the office.

The air was mild for an evening in the middle of October. It had been a sunny day and, after a brief shower had fallen, the streets had a clean, washed look and the air had become balmy. The sun had set and the light from the street lamps became a diffuse halo in the air immediately surrounding them.

Brent had left his car by the side of a park. Across the park was Shepherd's Luxury Hotel. It was in this imposing and ancient building that Garland's was to be found. The hotel was one of several large edifices built on that side of the park between nineteen hundred and nineteen-thirty and which exuded a distinctive air of permanence and comforting solidity. The architects and planners had excelled themselves - each building was a remarkable realization in design and execution of the era they represented. When they were all taken together as a whole, they formed an historic gallery of achievement and good taste. It was a family of buildings rather than a field of competitors. Elsewhere in the city, soaring buildings vied to be the tallest or the most noticeable. On this elegant, tree-fringed street, the buildings were a choir of disparate parts singing the same song. The towers shouted, 'Money'; Shepherd's and its confrères quietly sang, 'Continuity'. Pedestrians on the street by the park sensed they were treading in a place of great significance even if they had no reason to enter any of the buildings.

In the park itself, the network of well-lit pathways was an entirely symmetrical grid of straight and diagonal lines.

Magnificent specimen trees lined these walkways. In places around the park's border they formed dark archways. In the more open middle, the trees were dotted here and there, interspersed with low bushes and now empty beds where bulbs waited for the coming spring or where colourful annuals in cascading patterns or waving clumps would be planted next year.

The leaves on the trees were thinning out, falling to form a carpet on the ground. There were still enough of them left on the branches to show a mass of gold or brown when near enough to the orbs of the lamps that sat atop lovely, old-fashioned iron standards that had endured through nearly a century of service. It was an unexpectedly beautiful evening for October. It was a treat of a night for lovers to walk in the park - the ones who cared not if the heavens rained or shone upon them for they carried their delight with them wherever they went.

In the centre of the park was a small, ornate fountain of four tiers surrounded by a lily pad-shaped pool. For a few hours each evening, a series of lights came on from underneath the water and hidden in trees. The sequences and colour changes were effected in soft, slow transitions so that, from one minute to the next, the ordinarily happily splashing fountain went from sunny and bright to dark and moody as the colours became sombre and the light intensity dropped. Sometimes, the water looked like lace and sometimes it looked like purple or green oil. The transition between each condition was barely noticeable. It took twenty minutes for the whole, mesmerizing sequence to be completed. Ten people could watch and each could find a different favourite fountain.

"We should get to the restaurant and go inside," said Linda, who had pulled up the collar of her coat. She and Brent walked side by side. "It's damp out here."

"Really? I suppose it is," said Brent. He wore no coat but carried a furled umbrella in case of another shower. "But the air is so lovely and soft. It's like warm velvet. Also, we haven't seen the fountain yet."

"Can't we skip it?" asked Linda. "It would be different if it was summer."

"Of course," said Brent. His voice was bright as he glossed over his mild disappointment. "If our table's not ready, we could have an aperitif in the bar, if you like."

"I don't drink much. Two at the most. Alcohol makes me woozy."

"I'm the same. There's nothing worse than a hangover."

"Do you get drunk, then?"

"No, no. Like you, I drink in moderation. I was referring to past indiscretions."

"That's good. I can't stand drunks."

"There's the fountain," said Brent, with a look of innocent delight on his face. He pointed to where the brilliant red fountain was just translating to a pale purple wash. Even from a distance, a strobe effect succeeded in making the water seem to freeze in mid-air as though lavender paint were being thrown out from the jets. "It looks amazing," he added, as his steps slowed.

"Do you think it will rain again?" Linda had briefly glanced at the light show.

"Possibly. If it's raining when we come out we'll get a taxi back to the car."

"That's a good idea." As they walked on, it crossed Linda's mind that perhaps Brent was not as bad as she had feared he would be, although why he had insisted upon walking through a park in the dark in October eluded her.

From the park side of the street, the entrance to Shepherd's presented a majestic shimmering image of welcoming warm yellow light beneath the long awning. The stately, tall man in his top hat, white-gloves, and a scarlet cut-away coat, stood out as the most obvious feature as he strode or stood upon the red carpet, waiting for the elite of the city and of foreign countries to debouch from their limousines and enter into the hotel that was worthy of six stars - the extra star having been given solely for the hotel's classically refined atmosphere.

A little distance from this illuminated mirage of the night, accented by gleaming brass and small, potted trees, one saw another awning and another red carpet and a discreet neon sign in red script that simply stated, 'Garland's'. It hung next to the short flight of wide, rounded stairs that led to a pair of tall wooden doors trimmed in brass. A doorman in a dark blue, nearly black, jacket with red facings and brass buttons stood just inside, ready to open the door wide for those who desired to enter.

Brent had visited Garland's before. This was Linda's first visit. She said nothing but her face clearly showed that she was deeply impressed by the innate formality of both the hotel and its dependant restaurant. They crossed the road and, at last, the pair of hopeful diners ascended the stairs to their destination of sublime distinction.

"That woman over there," said Linda, pointing with her as yet unused fork to a table for four that was being seated, "is in Wild Ward. She's Marianne Stark."

"I don't believe I've seen that show," replied Brent. He turned slightly to see who Linda meant. "Is it the blonde woman or the dark?"

"The blonde. She's really good. She's the number two in the hospital and she's like really down on everyone. It's because her son has cerebral palsy. Anyway, Doctor

Maverick likes her but she knows something about his past."

"Uh, what would that be?"

"We don't know yet. That's the cliff-hanger."

"Shall I go and ask her what the story line is?" said Brent, already at somewhat of a loss as to what to say to this woman he had taken to dinner.

"No! Why would you do that?"

"I'm slightly curious as to what constitutes a cliff-hanger in Wild Ward. Mysteries intrigue me."

"You wouldn't go and ask her. Not here."

"Probably not. I'm sure she gets bothered enough in public without me adding to her discomfort."

"I knew you wouldn't."

"If you insisted, I would go and ask."

"Don't put it on me. I don't want you to bother her, either. It would spoil the show, anyway."

"I always like coming here. Garland's filters out the unwashed public and so I never get bothered. Though, compared to you, Marianne, I have an easy time of it."

Galen Nash's hair was so closely cropped that he seemed to be bald. He was very tanned and nodded frequently as other people spoke. As a veteran producer and director of serialized television shows, Galen was the obvious head of the table. He had a new production in the works and, already, Marianne had been given the lead because Wild Ward was in its final season and the last show had been shot. She was to be an FBI investigator. The dark-haired woman, Bryana McDowell, was to be her antagonist - a corrupt prosecutor. The plot was to be further complicated by the fourth person sitting at the table, Cooper Fisher. Both women wanted him and he was not sure which way he was going to go.

Galen Nash believed he could get two, if not three, seasons out of this basic premise before expanding the show's horizons. Of course, the body count would be relatively high and the level of corruption would be quite dizzying. Poor Cooper had to choose between an action woman with a gun who possessed the moral high ground and the living outside of the law while working within it prosecutor who was attractively very rich. Everyone involved would be making tough, soul-searching choices while the viewer would say, 'Why did he say that?' or, 'She's so mean, she should just shoot her.'

"I don't get that much attention," said Marianne. "A few autographs, photographs, and smiling faces when I'm in public… that's about it. Though what really does annoy me is when someone asks what's going to happen next in Wild Ward. Like, as if I know until the script's put into my hand and I rehearse the lines. And, when I do know, I can get canned for speaking out."

"I've only played bit parts so far in my career," said Cooper, "so it's just friends and family who show any interest. I can see I'll have to watch what I say in future."

"It's in the contract and it's standard practise," said Galen. "What about you, Bryana? You had a long running part in the Sewer Club."

"Mainly people pointing and nudging and guys asking me out on dates. It was okay if I was with someone. But if I was out with a girlfriend then sometimes there'd be trouble."

"It's amazing how many guys come out with the exact same lines," said Marianne.

Bryana, twenty-four, and Marianne, thirty-five, were co-leads. Galen had to ensure that there was no friction between them.

"Well, you are both safe from predatory males in this place. Now, if you have any trouble deciding what you want to eat, I can make a few suggestions." The ladies had no trouble in making their own choices and all four diners had soon given their orders to the attending and attentive waiter. Once this important interaction was done and the waiter departed, Galen launched into the subject closest at present to his heart.

"Now, the first show's script is pretty much finished and it's got a real punch. I'm pleased with it. This show has staying power but we've got to get some intense acting from all three of you. The audience has to see the world the way each of your characters see it. They have to be convinced that the high-stakes moral dilemmas playing out before them are their own. Shooting will start in two weeks and I need to know how each of you is going to approach your part."

As the three actors spoke and Galen listened, he nodded and smiled. He had heard much the same before from different people at different times. His gaze wandered around the room. The smile left his face when he saw Kirby Mayo sitting two tables away near the centre of the room. The actors continued but their voices became a drone of background noise while Galen vividly recalled a past injury he had received from Kirby Mayo.

It was years ago and Galen, in his late twenties, was struggling with his new production company. He just needed a few hundred thousand to bring off a big deal and produce a short film that would end up as a series. He knew he could do it. Knew it. His small house was already mortgaged as far as it could go and he could not find more money anywhere. Kirby had been a high school friend and they met again by chance at a critical moment. Galen explained the predicament he was in and how much money he needed to get out of it. He was surprised and relieved when Kirby said he would find the money for him - promised he would, to the point that they shook hands on it. Later, Kirby told him he had found an investor and that Galen would soon meet with that investor, the documents would be drawn up and signed, and the funds transferred.

A week went past and Kirby disappeared. He did not return Galen's numerous and increasingly anxious calls. After two weeks the big deal was no longer possible. Another production company had been given the go ahead to fill the open slot. It did not take long for Galen's company to fold - causing him financial hardship for some years while his career was stalled. It was only later that he learned that Kirby had financed the successful production company's bid. Kirby had deliberately lied to him and strung him along to keep him out of the process. The series had been a moderate success. Galen knew his would have been a smash.

"How is the violence going to be treated?" asked Cooper.

These words filtered into Galen's consciousness, recalling him to the present, and he answered the question with a sudden, bitter intensity.

"I want it gritty and real. The deaths must be like slaughter and the fights are where both the good and the bad guys get really hurt. Pain. I want to see pain and suffering enough to shock everyone."

The rest of the table was silenced by this outburst until Galen recovered himself and laughed it off, saying,

"Just like that is how I want it. The violence has to be sudden and exhilarating. It has to come in with a heavy punch, create a disturbing nightmare, and then blow out again, as though it had never happened. Do you see what I'm driving at?"

Chapter 3

Thursday, after 8:00 p.m.

$\mathcal{K}$irby was present at Garland's at least two nights a week - sometimes three. On occasion, it would be a quiet night. When he saw other women it would be at other places where he was unknown. Garland's was reserved for his business affairs and every Wednesday and Thursday that was where he was to be found.

Knowing this, Will Hutchinson, another partner at Althorn who managed the market neutral strategies, entered Garland's just after eight, looking for Kirby Mayo. It was Will's responsibility to ensure that equity did not evaporate through exposure to high risk trading. When the dealers sold short, his team bought into offsetting trades. When the dealers bought, he sold options. His mandate was that Althorn should never be over extended and risk the chance of financial collapse. He was the brake to Kirby's accelerator.

"I thought I'd find you here. May I sit down?"

"Of course, Will. Anything the matter?"

Will sat down. He looked well but older than his fifty-three years. Kirby was a significantly bigger man. By looking at them, one would assume that Kirby was his superior even though he was not. While Will's twenty per cent share in the general partnership was a lesser slice of the pie than Kirby's, Will was nevertheless a partner whose voting capacity could stop Kirby in his tracks.

"I meant to speak to you tomorrow but I'm that disturbed, I thought it couldn't wait. I'll come to the point. I think we're insanely exposed in the oil sector. Opening all those sell positions after the market has already dropped - I don't get it."

"There's more down-side in this move. I'd say we're only about half way there."

"But you're just guessing. It's a fifty-fifty chance you're right. I ran the numbers. We stand to lose millions with only a modest up-tick."

"We've been here before. I'm fine with it."

"I'm not. It's not fine. This is not like you."

"Have you lost your mind?"

"No. I haven't lost my mind. Why are you shorting so heavily those two companies? I've never seen you do this before."

"You might allow that I know something that you don't."

"What do you know?"

"I don't care to repeat it. Particularly as you seem to be losing your nerve."

"Please keep your personal comments out of it. Just stick to the business in hand. What you've just hinted at is that you have inside information. You know as well as I do that we cannot have the company exposed to anything that's illegal."

"You worry too much. I'll not refer to this matter again. I suggest you do the same."

"This is not good enough, Kirby. You're exposing all the partners to unwarranted risk and, from what I infer, possible criminal charges."

"I further suggest, Will, that you go home and forget all about this. Listen, you're worrying needlessly. Just relax. In a few days we will have made five million out of it."

"No, I can't allow it. You have to stick to the proper processes. I'll have to call a meeting and put a stop to this."

"Call your meeting. Go right ahead. Now, if you please, I'm expecting someone very soon."

Will sat for a moment with a rigid look on his face. He had never been able to 'handle' Kirby - could never rein him in, and that lack of control had always been an irritation. He was sure that there had been underhanded dealings in the past. He suspected some transactions were purely manipulative and due to insider trading but he could never prove it as a fact. Now, Kirby had carelessly hinted at this latest manoeuvre being exactly what Will suspected. He knew Kirby, and knew the type of game Kirby was playing with him right now. Was he trying to get him out of the partnership? If so, why? He would need to be bought out. What was going on? No matter what it was, the concentrated short selling jeopardized the partnership and could put him and the others at some considerable personal financial risk.

"This is not acceptable. I'll shall give this matter some serious thought. I'll do something, I promise you that much."

Will got up abruptly and left. Kirby smiled to himself and gave his shoulders a little shrug. He enjoyed his games sometimes. The fish course had arrived by courtesy of a quiet and deferential waiter while the wine waiter was pouring out a glass of Chablis for Kirby.

Ten minutes earlier and nicely with a smile, Brent had asked Linda, "What would you like?" after they had been studying their menus for a minute or two. Now, he asked,

"Have you decided, yet?" He still smiled but it was harder to do. He knew what he wanted. All the suggestions he had offered her had been rejected. There was no more menu to be read.

"I like plain food," she had said, more than once. "They put sauces or herbs over most it."

"You could have the sauce on the side."

"I don't know."

"Seeing as you like plain food, why do you go on the restaurant outings to sample different dishes?"

"Oh, it's fun. I like the company and to hear what everyone has to say. I always have more or less the same thing. You probably didn't notice."

Brent decided not to reply. He was finding it difficult to talk to Linda. They were alien to one another. If Brent had liked her, he would have been stammering nonsense by now. Despite recognizing that no relationship was likely to bloom out of the arid soil of their date, he was still at almost a complete loss as to how to keep a relatively one-sided conversation going.

"What work do you do?"

"I'll have the curried chicken. Yes, it says it's mild and fragrant. That's what I'll have. Sorry, did you say something?"

"Let's order first and we can chat while we're waiting."

The truth was that Brent, being so close to his rack of lamb, was beginning to feel faint with hunger.

Their order of hors d'oeuvres, food and wines had been discreetly and efficiently taken while Linda watched with rapt attention the deft movements of the waitress. When she had gone, Brent tried again to kick-start a conversation.

"So, where do you work?"

"At a day-care centre."

"That must be engaging. Do the little ones wear you out? They have so much energy."

"No. They're okay. Some of the grown-ups... that's so funny. I said grown-ups when I meant parents. Some of the parents are like so stressed out. I could do without them."

"Yes. But you couldn't really do without them as they would not bring their children for you to look after."

"What I meant was, I could do without their attitude."

"Of course, you did."

"He has sent the fish back," said Domenic Castillo, the front of house manager. He held out the offending plate of turbot for Aden Morris to inspect.

"What? Again? But... this looks fine," said a puzzled Aden, Garland's experienced and legendary Chef de Cuisine.

"He says it stinks."

Aden took the turbot and waved it beneath his nose.

"No." He turned to bellow into the far reaches of the extensive, white-tiled kitchen. "Chris! Come here!"

"A very small man came quickly to where the potentates of the restaurant were standing with the plate of fish between them. Chris Tucker wore a lopsided white hat to mark his office of Poissonnier. Even the Sushi chef reported to him in all matters fish-related.

"Is anything the matter?" He saw the plate and the gaze of the two men.

"It's him, isn't it?!" he shouted. "That Mayo man! He dares complain about my fish!"

"Please, Chris. Let us investigate this incident in a civil manner." The calm experience of the Chef de Cuisine shone through. He was used to the eccentricities and delicate sensibilities of his staff when things went wrong in the kitchen. He needed to keep the entire operation running smoothly. The only times when there was an interruption to the flow of processes in the kitchen hall was when Aden's own sensibilities were offended. His raging fits were of cataclysmic proportions and usually ended in tears. Fortunately, for the sake of all, he had a very high level of tolerance to perceived insult and injury. The same customer, Kirby Mayo, sending back a dish because it was inedible once a week for the last three weeks, obviously meant that the customer was playing a little game.

Domenic found three forks to use. The three inspectors of the order of the fish all partook of a forkful of turbot to see if it was off.

"Fabulous, Chris," said Domenic.

"Perfection," said Aden.

"What is he playing at?" asked the Poissonnier.

"I will investigate," said Domenic very quietly and confidentially.

When the manager had gone, Aden counselled Chris.

"Forget about it. Some people are just difficult and arrogant. I don't know what this guy's problem is but he certainly has one."

"I know but it makes me so mad. I feel like I could strangle him with my bare hands."

"Whoa! Would you?" Aden was all playful and understanding smiles. "Well, I have felt like that, too. Just once or twice, you understand. However, Domenic pointed him out to me and he's a very big man. I think you would need to stab or shoot him."

Chris gave a short laugh of relief. "I'm okay now. Could you show him to me?"

"Okay. But straight back to work and no problems?"

"No problems."

The two men cracked open one of the swing doors and, at a certain angle, they could just see Domenic talking to Kirby Mayo. Chris nodded. They both returned to their duties.

It was the pension fund manager, Morton Yates, who was now in deep discussion with Kirby at the latter's table. The two men had met in order to perfect their strategy to bring the rest of the board of pension fund managers to a place where they could accept the risk of a hedge fund in a general sense. Specifically, Kirby was getting dirt on the other managers to see if there was a way of compelling them to accept Althorn as the high returns provider. Kirby saw fat fees on seventy million sitting on the table, waiting to be picked up. Morton, a long, thin, worried-looking man with a bad haircut, saw that he was essentially being asked to blackmail one, if not two, of his peers.

"I can't do it," said Morton. "He only went gambling once or twice, as far as I know."

"So, send an anonymous letter to the directors, stating he has a gambling addiction and that he should be given a leave of absence to go to rehab. Even if that doesn't work, the integrity of his professional judgment will still be under a cloud and you can use it as leverage against him. Hey, while he's away busily explaining himself to the directors, have the decision made to bring in Althorn while he's out of the office. He's hardly likely to create a fuss when his professional abilities are under suspicion. You can do it. You just need to assert yourself."

"You know, I've never liked him. Even so, I've never thought to act against him so directly."

"No one will ever know it is you. It's very, very easy. If you like, you can make it sound as though it came from someone else you don't like in the office."

"I do believe you have a killer's instinct. This is new to me."

"There's a lot of money in this for both of us. I can't help you out if Althorn doesn't get the business. You should move on it soon - this weekend or Monday at the latest. What do you say?"

It was at that moment that Sylvester Valdez chose to approach Kirby's table. Kirby transferred his gaze from the seated man he was seeking to dominate to the newcomer. Kirby did not take kindly to the interruption.

"I hope I'm not interrupting you. It is Mr. Mayo I have the pleasure of speaking with, isn't it?"

"Yes." Kirby then recalled he had arranged with someone, a potential client, to meet him. It took a second but the name came to him.

"Ah, Mr. Valdez. Thank you so much for coming." Kirby stood up. "Excuse me, but my friend and I were so deep in discussion...." Kirby gave a contrite shrug as if to finish his thought.

Kirby was taller by half a head.

"No matter," said Sylvester, who had not ceased to smile throughout the exchange. "I can come back when you've finished. My wife and I are at the table over there," he said, pointing and indicating where. "We are still eating but I wanted you to know we had arrived."

"Thank you," said Kirby. "I will be no more than ten minutes. Allow me to send a bottle of wine to your table. What do you prefer?"

"Thank you, we have wine already. I need to have a clear head. I hear you guys can be quite sharp. I will see you later."

Sylvester gave a slight bow and returned to his table.

"Well, what did he say?" asked Zulema.

Sylvester paused before speaking. He moved his lower jaw in an odd way, a habit of his, and he had an intense look as he stared into the distance. "He was pleasant. But I don't think I like Mr. Mayo."

"Oh, why? You haven't met him. I haven't met him. How can you say that?"

"I don't know. A flash of something… who can say?"

In an instant, he switched out from his abstraction and began to laugh.

"Zuli, you look beautiful in that dress. You look as beautiful as the day I married you. No, you look better, much more beautiful… but how that is possible, I do not know."

"Aw, go on, Syl, stop it. You make me blush."

He picked up her hand and held it in both of his.

"You want me to stop, uh? You don't like I pay compliments to the most beautiful woman in the world, uh?"

Archly, and in a long drawl, she said, "Once in a while it's okay." Her gaze was demurely downcast but she did flash her eyes at him once. Then he said,

"Tonight is that once in a while."

Morton Yates left Kirby's table soon after Sylvester's visit. The pension fund manager had been primed and was now, if not enthusiastic, certainly determined to remove all obstacles hindering Althorn's selection. That Morton's colleague would have his reputation harmed or destroyed did not disturb his conscience. Morton saw that it was doable and likely to succeed, therefore Morton would do it. Kirby Mayo's evident confidence in him left Morton in no doubt as to the outcome. When such a big name in the market should recognize his talents, it was the only correct response to demonstrate that he could rise to the occasion.

And, as Kirby had hinted, more than hinted really, about a job at Althorn later on and one that would pay him far more than he was earning now, it made sense to Morton to act decisively to further his prospects.

He stood outside, under the awning because of the light rain. The red-coated hotel-doorman was busy just then as several parties, leaving the restaurant at the same time, all wanted taxis. The doorman hailed one from a line of cabs that waited for such passengers. It took some moments for him to get the people comfortably into their conveyance and to receive something for his services. The two men immediately in front of Morton were talking quietly but he could distinctly hear what they said.

"... and then there was Calico Capital. He was the one that brought them down. I knew someone who worked there. The story goes, he had some kind of hold over one of the junior dealers. He fed him some supposedly hot tips. The dealer took the bait. It all went the wrong way and Calico lost heavily. It folded. 'Course, the joke was, he was on the other side of those trades."

"Why did he do that?"

"He's vindictive. Calico had beaten him out on some lucrative contracts."

"And the dealer?"

"Out of a job, no one would hire him, and he got nothing from you know who. Committed suicide about a year later. Seeing that guy in there, it reminds me of a big frog catching stupid flies. Ah, here we are."

The two men moved forward to get into their taxi. Morton walked away in the rain.

"So, your apartment is close by?" Linda had a puzzled look on her face.

"Yes, it's about a mile east of here," replied Brent.

"Then, where are you putting this garden shed you're talking about."

"That's at the house."

"Where's that?"

"In Limeview."

"Oh. That's closer to where I live. My friend, Sheena, and I have an apartment on Carston."

Linda went on to share a great deal about Sheena's life and times. After a while, Brent had to make an effort to keep looking interested. At the end of her near monologue, Linda asked suddenly,

"Do you rent out the house?"

"Oh, ah… no. I only got it this year and I've been fixing it up. There was more to do than I realized when I bought it. Still, I'm very happy with how it's looking now."

"Are you going to rent it?"

"No. I intend to live in it. That's where I'll be gardening and the reason why I need a shed. Though Eric - he's the man who's helping me set it up - he wants one style of shed and I want a different design."

"Are you going to rent your apartment?"

"No. I use it for some of the things I do. It's convenient to be downtown. Besides, I love the place. I put a lot of work into changing it from a dirty, greasy machine shop into a home - though, I've left the lower level as it was after cleaning it up. I like the early nineteen-hundreds features it has. Do you know…"

"I can't understand why you would want to live in two places. I would rent one out and make some money."

Nola arrived at Kirby's table.

"I won't stay long. I don't like leaving the children."

"Have you eaten?" asked Kirby. He called a waiter over.

"Yes. I felt I wanted to get out for a while and I like this place. So, have you been busy?"

"Moderately so."

The waiter arrived and Kirby ordered drinks for them both.

There's a potential client here who will be joining us soon."

"Oh, I see. Do you mind me sitting in?"

"No. You can help with the pitch if you want to."

"Sure. I'll play along." Nola was quiet for a few moments. "There's a reason for my coming. Jimmy and I have been discussing my leaving Althorn or, at least, scaling back my involvement. We haven't reached a decision yet. What I would like to know is, what are your thoughts? Should I make such a move?"

"That's a surprise. Is there a specific reason for this, Nola?"

"Yes. Stress. I can handle it and have done so for years. But I'm getting to the point where I recognize I need to have an end in sight or I could burn out. That would not be good for any of us."

"That makes sense. I'll be sorry to see you go. Do you have a time frame for this?"

"No longer than two years. To find a new partner, if that's what we all decide is best, would take at least three months. I'd really like to stay for another six months to a year."

"It seems to me you've already decided to leave."

"In a sense, yes. But I'm open to suggestions."

"I'll give this some careful thought. You'll be hard to replace and someone is definitely needed to take over your portfolio. I can't take it on."

Nola nodded when he had finished speaking. She could play the game, too. She had known for years that

Kirby wanted to have the majority voting position in the partnership. It was a natural condition for him to control everything. In a sense, he already did but there were constraints upon him in the shape of the opinions of the other partners. One thing she knew was that Kirby did not like to be constrained. Something else she knew and, indeed, it had already begun, was that Kirby would play his game. He would try to get her share of the partnership at a deeply discounted price. It was his nature. They had known each other for ten years and, in an instant, he had set aside any notion of friendship and had filed her away as a potential victim to be preyed upon.

What Kirby did not know was how tired she was of it all - so tired that Nola would walk away without a penny if she had to. She and her husband, Jimmy, had discussed the matter at length and agreed that a clean break sooner rather than later was what was going to happen and whatever she got for her twenty per cent of the partnership was good enough.

"There's the office administration to be considered," said Nola. "My duties are fairly light but they occur daily and it's important for staff morale that it's done properly. And you know why."

"Ha. As you have told me in the past, I'm not the easiest person to get along with. I'm sure a babysitter can be found to take care of it. Is there any of your staff who could take over from you?"

"Only Angela. But I think you frighten her. Have her make the decisions and she could report to Will for approvals. They get along okay and I don't think he would mind."

"I'm sure that will be fine. I had better ask the Valdezes over or they might think I've forgotten them."

Kirby summoned a waiter and gave a message to be delivered to Sylvester Valdez which, when received, promptly had Zulema and Sylvester walking to Kirby's table.

What surprised Kirby when they arrived, not that he showed any hint of what he was thinking, was that these prospective clients were so unlike the usually anxious or serious individuals he met. They seemed supremely happy, wrapped up and complete in themselves. Had Kirby been more reflective, he would have seen that they were in love with one another. Nola noticed it straight away, found their joy infectious, and smiled a little more than she usually did.

Kirby gave his usual discourse on how Althorn was the best choice for affluent people to realize extraordinary profits with very little risk. He dwelt on profits, profits, and more profits. It usually worked but, for once, he found Sylvester to be immune to his appeal. Sylvester, on his part, was courteous, asked good, reasonable, questions, did not argue, but he held himself aloof, as though he were mildly interested and merely doing Kirby the favour of allowing him to speak.

Zulema asked questions, too. Early on she began to direct them towards Nola. As the questions were few, and Nola could see that these prospective clients were unlikely ever to be entrusting money to Althorn, their conversation drifted into the well-being of their respective children and to the trials of parenthood. They immediately liked each other.

"Thank you, Kirby," said Sylvester, "for explaining to us what it is you do. It is very, very interesting and has given me much to think about."

Kirby was under no illusion as to how the meeting had gone. "My pleasure entirely. Should you wish to find out more, an assistant will be happy to help you."

When they had gone, Nola looked at Kirby.

"What happened there? Am I missing something?" she asked.

"A failure once in a while is to be expected. Valdez and I are not a good fit for one another."

When they reached their table again and sat down, Zulema said,

"She was nice. We could deal with her, I think."

"Was she? I heard some things she said. I think you're right." Sylvester nodded decidedly. "Him? Like I said, I could never deal with a man like him."

"Why, Syl? He didn't seem so bad."

"Why? It is a good thing you say he's not so bad. It is because in him I see a man a little bit like me. We would never get along. So, I say to myself, we will find another hedge fund and they will get our money back."

"Oh, that makes sense. You men, you always cause such problems."

Sylvester laughed loudly. "Yes, it's true. But it is also true that women, they never, ever cause any trouble at all."

"That's right! I should have a recording of this - to play for you when you forget."

"Ha!" He took a sip of his drink. "Now, my Zuli, we shall go away on a little trip somewhere. Anywhere you want to go. Anywhere you like." He waved his arm expansively.

"That is lovely… Oh, what about the children?"

"They can come, but I was thinking, just a few days and just the two of us. Think they'd mind?"

"Not if we promise them a trip to make up for it. Somewhere they'd like to go and they get to choose."

"Yes. That will be nice, too. But where shall we go?"

"Um, Paris? Or Milan? What about Rio de Janeiro?... I don't know because you ask me so suddenly, you beautiful boy."

Chapter 4

Thursday, until 10:40 p.m.

A little while later, as Kirby and Nola were discussing the future of Althorn and its place within the world of investments, a thin figure in a trench-coat approached the table. It was Kirby's wife.

"Rena! It's lovely to see you." Nola stood up and the two women embraced with more affection than that which just social custom dictated.

"I didn't think I would find you here," said Rena. She had shoulder-length light-brown hair, streaked blonde. She used cosmetics lightly and her pallor was evident. She turned to Kirby. "Aren't you going to ask me to join you?" Her voice had a fragile, glass-like brightness to it.

"Rena, what are you doing here?" asked Kirby, evidently far from pleased.

"This place seems to be your home, now. As your wife, I thought I would join you." She began undoing the coat she was wearing over her evening dress.

"No, Rena. This is where I conduct my business." Kirby softened the rejection by speaking patiently, almost kindly, to her. He stood up. "I'll get a taxi for you. I'll be home a little later and we can talk about things as long as you like."

"Kirby?" She looked a little incredulous. "No, I've come to be with you. I'm your wife."

"Yes, I know. As I said, you're leaving now." He gripped her by her arm. "We will talk as long as you like at home." He began to propel her towards the door. Once in motion, he said to Nola, "Excuse us for a moment."

"Oh, no, Kirby. Please don't." Rena looked at him. The brightness had gone. Kirby proceeded to remove his wife from the restaurant with such ease and minimum of outward fuss that it appeared almost natural.

"It's for the best. I'm sure the children miss you. This weekend, we can go and see your mother, if you like. She always likes to see her grandchildren... and you, of course. When I get home, we'll discuss everything we need to discuss."

Rena complied with his urging. What little spirit she may once have possessed to resist Kirby's will had long since gone.

Nola watched them go and felt sickened; feeling sorry for Rena and angry towards Kirby. She could only guess at the courage and effort the woman had made to try and establish herself as Kirby's wife again in this small way. It had come to nothing and Rena would be more miserable than if she had never tried.

Nola was glad she would be leaving Althorn; she almost wished she could take poor Rena with her. She decided not to wait for Kirby's return to hear the spin he would put on his actions. She would not be made to feel awkward and accept his trite, hard-hearted excuse. He would probably say his wife was ill and needed rest. Liar and bully, that's what he was.

Of all the eighty or so diners in the restaurant, the only other person who noticed anything wrong was Linda Roberts.

"There's a man over there having an argument with his wife," said Linda.

"That's unfortunate." Brent turned to see where this event was taking place but the business of the restaurant looked completely unruffled. He saw a couple walking towards the door but they did not seem excited about anything. "I must have missed them."

"No. It was those two people leaving. The big gorilla grabbed the woman's arm and pushed her along. I could see she was really upset."

"I didn't see it. I loathe that kind of thing. People should behave decently to one another. Mind you, it's also possible there may be an innocent explanation."

"Are you taking his side?"

"What? No! On the contrary, I would naturally incline to be on the woman's side. Often, there are issues on both sides, though. They can both be contributors to the situation. In this instance, we don't know what the facts are."

"I don't know. That sounds like misogyny to me."

"Linda, that is not true. What I'm saying is, you saw a snapshot. You don't know what led up to it. His action, in isolation, looked bad to you. There may be a reasonable explanation for it, such as her feeling unwell or being so distracted that he had to do something."

"You didn't see them," said Linda.

"That's true, I didn't. Let me give you an example, though, of what I'm driving at. If I saw a man shoot a dog I would immediately hate him. If it proved to be the case that the dog was rabid, then I would say he had to do an ugly but necessary thing. It's easy to jump to a conclusion but that conclusion is not always correct. As an investigator, I've had to bypass obvious conclusions many, many times to get at the truth."

"Well, anyway, I'm really surprised that kind of thing should happen in a place like this."

After that, Brent and Linda experienced together their longest silence of the evening.

There was only an interval of seconds between Kirby putting a now tearful Rena into a taxi in the rain, with the doorman holding an umbrella over them, and the arrival of another taxi containing Becki Kent and her friend, Gabbie Wright. Both of these women were in possession of large fortunes and both of them were currently free from long-term relationships. They intercepted Kirby as he was turning to go back inside.

"Well, Tiger. I didn't know you to be such a fine gentleman as to come and meet us in the rain."

"Becki! Just seeing someone off." Kirby was again all smiles and welcoming gestures. "You must be Gabbie. A pleasure to meet you."

Becki and Kirby kissed each other on the cheek. He shook Gabbie's hand. It would have been difficult for Rena to see them clearly through the rain-spattered window but the three figures were certainly illuminated under the awning. If she had turned her head she may just have seen them.

"So, you're a private investigator, then? Isn't that kind of shady?" asked Linda.

"Uh…You could say that," replied Brent, slightly taken aback. "There are definitely some aspects to the business that are not quite decent by usual standards. But

I'm not one any more. private investigator, I mean. Unless an interesting case comes up."

"Oh."

There was a long pause in which the lively noise from the restaurant made itself evident.

"What do you think of the food?" asked Brent.

"It's nice but I'd try something else next time."

"You can have another entrée, if you like."

"Oh, no. I don't seem to be hungry anymore."

"Um... do you like gardening?"

"Not really. You mean, like cutting the lawn?"

"More like growing flowers and vegetables. Making your own private space beautiful with lovely plants. It could be for others to see and enjoy or become one's own garden of delight."

"Sounds like a lot of work."

"Oh, well, I suppose it is, really. But it's worth the effort... not that I'm very good at it, yet."

"Brent? Why did you give up being a private investigator?"

"Ah, well, yes. You should find this very interesting. I did some work for someone and that led me to being invited in on a murder case..."

"Oh, stop! Don't tell me anything horrible. I hate murders."

Again, they ate on in silence.

Becki's business with Kirby could easily have been conducted over the telephone. As an investment partner at Althorn, she received a good return on the capital she had contributed when the business was launched. She wanted to hear from Kirby's own lips how the business was going. Becki intended to add another million to her personal portfolio that Althorn managed. What she could not do over the phone was see Kirby the man - see what he looked like now. She had loved him once. Then, something had happened between them and she had left him suddenly - as she subsequently had left all her lovers. They met again - several times over the years. Still, she wanted to see how he was doing now because she did think of him occasionally. Becki quickly decided that he was now past his prime. Being familiar with his ways, it was obvious to her that he lacked any originality and what he said and did were only repetitions of things she had seen and heard before. What was in the past between them should remain there, she decided.

"I've just seen an old friend of mine at another table. I'll have to say hello to her or she'll think I'm cutting her. I won't be long." Becki left the table.

"Do you live in the city?" asked Kirby of Gabbie. He was in two minds. The first was to treat this elegant, wealthy woman as a prospective client. The second was to treat her in a very different way, entirely disassociated with Althorn business practices.

"I've moved back recently after two years in Europe." The material of her wine-red dress had a faint irregular black square pattern in it. It shimmered when she moved. Kirby did not fail to notice the ruby ring she wore.

He thought of the differences between Becki and the woman sitting across the table from him. Becki talked a lot, was animated most of the time, and always mocking him a little. This woman, Gabbie, in her forties, was quiet and cool. She looked him in the eye. She was different.

"Do you prefer it here or there?"

"No preference, really. Every place has its own charm."

"I'm sure wherever you are, the place becomes more charming still."

"Then, how distraught everyone must be when I leave."

Kirby stared at her. Gabbie stared back with a tiny grin lifting the corners of her mouth. He perceived she, also, was mocking him and in a way that was beyond just her words.

"I think Becki must have been telling tales out of school."

"She's mentioned some of your ways. She calls you Tiger. I always understood you to be a dangerous man to be near - like your namesake."

"Sometimes, a little danger adds excitement to the situation."

"I'm sure it does. I'm a safety first kind of woman. I like safety for my investments and for myself."

"I think you have made yourself abundantly clear. We could discuss the weather."

"It's raining now. I'm sure it will stop eventually."

Kirby was nonplussed. He could not tell if he was being dismissed out of hand or challenged to try harder.

Gabbie, being both wealthy and attractive, had received much attention from men over the years. She had soon learned to distinguish between sincere males and opportunistic flatterers. In her estimation, Kirby was a more obvious and crude example of the latter type - one who was used to getting his own way. Her own perception, now coupled with what she already knew from Becki's chatter, only strengthened her predisposition to having no time for him at all.

"What do you like?" asked Brent.

"Most of all, I would say, I love my family. Holidays are my favourite, when we all get together. I see my brothers and sisters and all the little ones. They make fun of me because I'm late marrying but I don't mind. My great-grandmother, Nana Bet I call her, right from when I was only three years old, she's such a darling…"

She spoke of her family with some degree of animation and passion. She also took her time over the exposition of the Robert's clan.

"What about your family?" asked Linda.

"I don't actually have one that functions as a family as such. To put it in a nutshell, my father disappeared and my mother fell ill during which time I was put up for adoption. Then she died. Adoption never happened and turned into a series of foster homes. The relatives I know about can't seem to be bothered with me. To tell the truth, there's no love lost between us. That's about it for my family."

"That's awful. You don't have a family? I can't wrap my head around it."

"You really don't have to try to do that. I was pretty young when it all happened and I got used to the situation. It doesn't bother me."

"You were adopted, I mean, fostered, whatever? I don't think anything like that has ever happened in my family. There was only uncle Simon who got caught stealing a car when he was a teenager. That's about it."

Brent thought of several things to say but, looking at Linda, he decided not to expend the energy. He was about ready to call it quits for the night.

Kirby sat, silently nursing a drink. Gabbie contented herself with eating a pastry. Now, after ten o'clock, the number of patrons in the restaurant was thinning out a little. New patrons would eventually arrive in a rush of excited, talkative groups, demanding desserts, coffees, and expensive drinks. That would occur between eleven and twelve .

It had been an uneven night for Kirby. On the plus side was Morton Yates. He would surely get the job done and remove the major impediment in the pension fund decision. Becki was putting more money into her account and that meant more money for himself. Nola was leaving. He would buy her out... but at a discount.

How to do it, though? There's plenty of time to come up with a strategy there.

Will could be a problem, though. I might have to smooth his ruffled feathers. That must wait until the oil sector short positions come off. A few days at the most. Might have to get out early and miss the full drop just to appease him. I'll let him know that I took his advice to heart.

Valdez... missed that one. Unsophisticated and someone who would be hard to deal with. Not that sorry to see him go.

What possessed Rena to come here? Has to be the end of it. She cannot interfere with my work like that. She won't divorce so we'll separate. Custody of the children is the difficult part. What to do...? I think seeing them once a week will be enough for me. She'll pay for that concession, though. She'll trade everything else away for the sake of the children, no matter what legal counsel she gets. I'll string her along. Tell her we can reconcile down the road. That should do it.

This woman... How to play it? She does intrigue me. I should have handled her differently. Should have gone slow. Difficult with Becki's big mouth constantly at work. She'll be back soon. Time to mend bridges... I've nothing else to do.

"I think I may have made a bad impression," said Kirby. "I apologize for my boorish behaviour. If you like, we can talk - or we can sit in silence. I leave it up to you as to which we do. That I admire you is now an open fact between us. That you think little of me has similarly been established."

"Hmm, interesting. I accept your apology in the same spirit as it is given."

As she was speaking and looking at Kirby, there was a movement a little way behind her. Someone was sitting down. She saw Kirby's attention drift away from her face to whoever it was at the table beyond.

An horrendous blast changed everything. Things seemed suddenly to be in the air around her head. Riveted in place and instinctively bringing her hands up to her ears, she saw Kirby forcefully pushed back in his chair looking surprised. His mouth was an open O-shape and he made an ineffectual attempt to grab the edge of the table. A fraction of a second later, in the wake of a second blast, his chair flipped over backwards with him in it. Immediately, a third blast and then... silence.

Gabbie dropped to the floor. Looking around the side of the elegantly draped pale blue tablecloth she could see Kirby's outspread arm twitch, twitch and then become still. She looked away. From two or three places in the restaurant - screaming. People were screaming which seemed to announce it was over. She saw others hiding, cowering or scrambling away. She stayed where she was and counted seconds, hoping that all the damage to be done, had been done.

"Is there anything else you would care for?" asked Brent. Their inauspicious first date was coming to a close. Linda was given no chance to answer him.

Three sharp explosions shattered the restaurant's atmosphere. Chairs overturned, patrons threw themselves to the floor or crouched down, things shattered or crashed. For a moment there was silence before the screaming started. A wide gap had formed around a table near the centre of the room as people had backed away from it.

Linda began screaming in a piercing, high-register wail. Brent left her to it.

With his eyes darting everywhere and ready to dive for cover, Brent went forward as quickly as he could. He made his way around tables with cowering people behind them and stepped over living, prostrate forms. He was heading for the leper table.

As he drew closer, Brent noticed a gun on the floor. A few steps further and he reached the table. Glass and cutlery had been swept off and lay haphazardly on the thick carpet. Lying on the far side of the table, still in his overturned chair, was a man, his body twisted slightly, with arms at awkward angles, and his head to one side. His dark jacket lay open to reveal what should have been a white shirt except it was now mostly wet and intensely red with two obvious holes in the chest area. Brent saw him and went cold, the sight bringing him to a standstill for some seconds.

A large man approached as Brent was staring at the body. He looked towards the newcomer who was holding a pistol with both hands down by his side.

"Are you police?" asked the man in a deep, low voice. There was no look of the killer upon him.

"Not really," answered Brent. "Have you called them?"

"Yep." The man scanned the room and said over his shoulder, "Know him?"

"No... I think I saw the murder weapon. I'm going to secure it. If you can stay by the... body."

"Sure."

Brent found the weapon again and stood by it. He saw some people starting to leave the room so he shouted out,

"Attention, please! The danger is over! If everyone can stay where they are until the police arrive it would be a help to them!"

Most of them stopped but a few escaped to safety. Brent took a video of them with his phone as they left.

"Please, stay where you are! I know this is awful and frightening but we must all do what we can to help the authorities! Try to remain in your places! The danger has passed!"

The flow of departures halted. Brent could not blame the ones who had left. They did not want to stay and answer questions all night and some were clearly distraught, scared. He called a number.

"Hello, Brent," said Lieutenant Greg Darrow. "Haven't heard from you in a while."

"I'm at Garland's restaurant. There's been a murder. It happened about two minutes ago. You should get over here now."

"On my way. Try not to let anyone leave."

After disconnecting the call, with his hand shaking slightly, Brent quietly said to himself, "What a way to get a job."

While he waited, awkward and obvious in the middle of Garland's, he tried to notice people - memorize their positions, who they were and how they looked. Brent took many photographs. His case had begun.

Chapter 5

Thursday to early Friday

*T*he room returned to a stable condition. Brighter overhead lights came on and frightened, subdued people began to regain their feet as though rising from their graves. They would soon need to talk but first they must assess what had happened. Some decided they would see for themselves. Cell phones were now out and in use - most calling someone with a few taking photographs. Brent asked them to remain in place. Several were beginning to disregard his requests. The man with the pistol bellowed loudly in a voice that could only have been forged on a parade ground. He got everyone to stay put. Brent looked at him in astonishment. The man nodded with a wide grin on his face. It was the first sane thing Brent had seen in some minutes and he waved back. Then he thought of Linda.

"Excuse me, I need your help." Brent addressed a mature family group at a nearby table. A precisely dressed gentleman in his sixties was sitting all too placidly at a table with his wife and two adult children - a daughter and a son. The family likeness was quite remarkable. The father seemed to be at a loss as to what to do and his gold-rimmed glasses were a bit crooked. The mother seemed collected and in possession of her wits. She answered as her husband seemed incapable of doing so.

"What can we do?" she asked.

"There is a revolver on the floor right here. It is evidence and it needs to be left untouched and in place until the police take possession of it. Could you watch and make sure nobody comes near it? I have to attend to someone."

"Yes, of course. Is it...? I mean, do you think it's the weapon?" she asked.

"Possibly not. It's not my place to examine it but I counted three shots fired and I can see four bullets in the exposed chambers. If it was fired, only a single shot came from it because there aren't two empty spaces together."

"I see."

"Has someone been killed?" asked the son.

"I'm afraid so."

The father suddenly cleared his throat noisily. "Is the killer still in the room, do you think?"

"Entirely possible. Some people did leave. I counted eight who did. That gentleman over there is armed and he is watching the room like a hawk. I trust him, and the police will be here any second. I'm sorry, there is someone I need to see but we can talk later if you wish."

"They'll keep us all night, won't they?" said the daughter.

"My suggestion is that you find the first police officer you can and demand he or she take your statement immediately. I'm sorry, I must go."

"Yes, of course," said the father, who was beginning to recover his composure. "Thank you for answering our questions."

Brent left them and it was a strange sight to see - four people sitting rigidly still, staring intently at a revolver on the carpet.

He returned to his table to find Linda distraught, though she had stopped screaming.

"Why did you leave me? You should never have brought me here."

"I'm really sorry," said Brent softly. "There were things needing to be done. Now, Linda, look at me. No, look me in the eye. That's it. It is over and you are safe. Nothing more will happen. The police will be here any moment. I have more to do and so I want you to sit with a table of people. I don't want you sitting alone here. Will you come with me?" He held out his hand and she took it. "Bring your purse... that's it. Ready?"

As they started walking, the police began to arrive. The first three came in the room with weapons drawn, anticipating an ongoing threat. Brent looked over to the man with the pistol who had already placed it on a table top and put his hands behind his head. The officers approached him, keeping him covered with their weapons.

Brent got Linda to the family table. Other officers were coming into the dining room. The man with the drill-sergeant voice and pistol was being interrogated.

"Thank you for watching so vigilantly," said Brent to the family group. "I want my good friend Linda to sit with you. Like all of us, she's very upset."

"Of course," said the father with alacrity. "We're the Warners."

"I'm Brent Umber. See Linda, you're with good people now."

"Sit here," said the son, who vacated his chair to bring another one from an adjacent table.

"Thank you," said Linda, as she sat down between the mother and daughter.

"I'll be back soon," said Brent.

The private investigator approached the knot of police officers who had, by now, got the man down on the floor and had him cuffed.

"Excuse me," said Brent.

Two officers turned towards him. "Stay where you are!" shouted one of them, as he flung up his hand, signalling for Brent to stop. His pistol was in his other hand.

"My name's Brent Umber. I'm a private investigator. I'm not armed. The gentleman on the floor secured the room until you arrived. He called you in. I helped him and called in Lieutenant Greg Darrow.

The name of the detective seemed to work like a charm.

"Okay... okay. Please, just stay put for a moment." He spoke to the other officers and, after a brief discussion, one of them leaned over the pistol on the table and sniffed the end of the barrel. "It's clean," he said. They helped the man up and took off the cuffs.

Already there were other officers around the body of the late Kirby Mayo, examining him, collecting evidence, and photographing the scene. Brent and the man were asked to return to their tables. They approached one another.

"You did a good job there," said Brent. "My name's Brent Umber."

"Dan Lindsay." They shook hands. "You did good, too. I gotta get back to my wife, Brent. This'll be a long night. We'll talk later."

"Before you go... Did you catch sight of the shooter?"

"Nothing. My wife and I were too busy keeping our heads down and we didn't have direct sight on this area, anyhow. You?"

"No, I had my back to it all. What service are you in?"

"Rangers… retired." Dan grinned again. "See ya later."

"I don't think I'm needed any more." Brent had rejoined the Warners' table. "How are you doing, Linda?"

"Better, thanks."

"Good. This is a horrible business. A word of caution. It's best we don't discuss what we may have seen. You see, if we do, we might inadvertently acquire what another person has seen. We don't want to taint our own, unique evidence. You've met Linda, I'm Brent; what are all your names, may I ask?"

"This is my wife, Caroline; our daughter, Melanie; our son, Steven; and I'm Henry."

"Well, it's very nice to meet you. Were you here celebrating?"

"It's our thirty-fifth wedding anniversary. Our children wanted to treat us to a dinner before we go on our second honeymoon tomorrow."

"How lovely," said Brent, smiling all round. "Congratulations. Thirty-five years is such a milestone. Where are you going tomorrow?"

"Chile," replied Henry. "We're archaeologists, you see, and we have always meant to go back. We met on a dig there at Pukarà de Quitor."

"Excellent. You must be so looking forward to your time away together. What do you do, Melanie?"

"This is my final year of my master's degree in education."

"You must be anxious to get back to your work. The way to deal with this awful situation is to compartmentalize it in your mind. It has happened. It will not happen again. The trick is not to let thoughts about tonight bleed over into other areas of life. We are all safe now. Eventually, we will come to terms with what has happened but, to start, we should grab hold of the idea that the worst is behind us. Are you taking a degree, Steven?"

"No… I work in a bank in a real estate unit."

"So, I come and see you if I need a mortgage; and you'll give me a discounted rate?"

Steven smiled.

"I don't think they allow you to do that, do they, Steven?" asked Henry.

"Not exactly, Dad. I'm allowed some latitude in the rates but it's within a range."

"Linda and I are here on our first date and who could have anticipated that there would be all this happening. She works in a daycare centre, carefully looking after lots of little ones. Linda? Is there someone you'd like to call and talk to?" Brent had noticed that her face was pinched and white.

"Oh, yes. I should do that." She took her phone from her purse.

"As soon as is practicable, I think we should order from the kitchen. Coffee, water… is anyone hungry?"

"No, we have all eaten, thank you," said Henry.

"I think I would like a coffee," said Caroline.

"There's water over there," said Steven.

"We can't touch that," said Brent. "I'll go and see if we're allowed anything yet. Ah, here's the man I've been waiting for. As soon as he's in the swing of it all, I'll see if we can get our statement-taking started. Excuse me, I'll be back soon."

Greg Darrow had entered the room, clipboard in hand. It was apparent that he was now the senior officer present as several police officials began reporting to him.

"Right in the middle of it," said Greg. "I don't believe it. Tell me you had no prior knowledge of this."

"Honestly, it is fate alone that had a hand in my being here at all," said Brent.

"What have you got?" asked Greg.

"I have many photographs and a panoramic video of the whole dining room about three minutes after the murder. I got another one of half a dozen or so people leaving. I'll send everything to you."

"How many got out?"

"I counted eight. There may have been more but I was thinking about self-preservation for a while so I might have missed them."

"Yes. Well, you got something and that's good. Did you see anything?"

"No, nothing. Had my back to the crime scene. A family by the name of Warner is baby-sitting a revolver where I found it. I don't believe it's the murder weapon. Your people haven't seen it yet. They're over there, the table of five."

"Hey, officer. What's your name?" Greg summoned a uniformed officer to him.

"Jones, Lieutenant."

"Officer Jones, there's a revolver on the floor by that table of five over there. Please, secure it."

"Another thing," said Brent to Greg. "A woman at that table by the name of Linda Roberts was my date tonight…"

"You really know how to show a lady a good time. And?"

"She may be suffering from shock. Any medics on hand?"

"I'll get someone to look at her. Seems like there may be a few like that."

"I think the kitchen should be opened up. I'm sure the management can lay on some snacks and drinks. Also, as a personal favour and because I gave my word, can you process that table of five first. There's an older couple going on their second honeymoon tomorrow and Linda is very shaken up."

"Yeah, yeah… whatever you want, Brent. I'll take care of it."

"Dan Lindsay, big guy, ex-Ranger, he did good work in securing the room. Because he had a pistol, the first guys in cuffed him. I think he needs a big thank you and an apology."

"I'll see him myself."

"That's it for now… No, that's not it. Who is the victim?" Brent looked Greg hopefully in the eye.

"Name's Kirby Mayo, age 48. Married with two children. Wife's name is Rena. Stock market guy. I guess you saw him. Not a pretty sight."

"It wasn't. Three shots were fired," said Brent. "I only saw two wounds."

"We'll find the missing bullet. They're checking angles and trajectories right now. There are no shell casings left behind so it was probably a revolver."

"I know this is hardly the time for me to make my pitch but my services are available, if you need them."

"I appreciate that. As I said before, I can't fit you in without an approval from the brass and they're likely to laugh at me if I bring it up to them. It's just the way things are."

"I understand that. I'm sure you see how uniquely positioned I am, though. I'm a witness. I will be in the witness box when it comes to it. I can get some of these people to talk to me on the basis of equality."

"Brent…" said Greg in a patient, fatherly way that could only be leading to a negative statement. Then he looked hard at him. "I'll tell you what I'll do. If we get stalled on this case then I'll let you try a few things. But this is off the record… and just between you and me. Like no one, and I mean no one, ever gets to hear about this."

"You are a great man and I will carry the knowledge of this secret to my grave."

"You'd better. Now go and sit down and look after your girlfriend."

"I will but I believe this was our first and last date even without the murder happening."

"That's how it goes sometimes. You've just got to find the right one and hang on to her. Though how any sane woman could put up with you, I don't know."

"Your assessment is probably correct."

"You know, I'm joking, right? You did very well today. I've a lot to do so…"

"Understood. Got any paper. I have a pen. I need to write a few things down."

Greg handed him a few spare sheets from his clipboard.

It took time before the dining room was cleared. A connecting door to the hotel was opened up and the former restaurant patrons, seventy-three in number, and staff on duty at the time of the murder, another twenty-eight, were being processed by the detectives and uniformed officers who seemed to be everywhere throughout the relevant sections of the building. Garland's front entrance was now decorated with yellow crime scene tape and the doorman had been replaced by a policeman who stared balefully at a line of illegally parked media vans clustered across the street by the park.

After midnight and as they stood in the hotel foyer, Brent was intent upon installing a now quite cheerful Linda Roberts into a taxi. The process of being questioned and giving a statement had enlivened her and if she had been suffering from shock the condition had ebbed. She was now talking about murder.

"It must be so exciting interviewing everyone and finding out what they saw. I can see why you're a private investigator."

"Ah, yes… it can be interesting."

"That detective… she was very nice to me. She was really concerned with how I was feeling."

"I'm glad to hear it. Part of it is training and part is probably because she's a nice person herself."

"Yes. It's made me think about changing careers."

"Ah, has it? I understood you were well suited to looking after children."

"I like to think I am. But seeing how it works on the inside, I'm seriously considering becoming a detective."

"Are you?" said Brent, marvelling. "I think you'll find there's quite a bit of training involved. You should look into it and see what you would need to do."

"Well, I was thinking, you could teach me. You knew what to do as soon as the shooting stopped. How did you learn that? How did you get started?"

"Linda, it's a very long story and it's late. You have an early start at work tomorrow." By this time they were outside and Brent beckoned a taxi forward from the line.

"I suppose I have. I suppose I should go home. I really don't think I'll get to sleep... I'm just that pumped. So, when shall we see each other again?"

Brent was stricken dumb. Not a single thought entered his head yet he knew he had to reply. Then, two thoughts came together. The first was, tell her the truth. The second was, put her off, somehow. They had absolutely nothing in common as far as he could see, except, now, an interest in detecting, of all things!

"I will definitely help you if you plan to become a detective. As to our meeting again... We're very different people, Linda. I hadn't thought we hit it off."

"I thought we did. You're quite interesting, really. You're a bit weird sometimes but I think we can be friends because you're really sweet. I'm not sure about anything else. We'll have to see how it goes." She hugged him warmly, reached up and kissed him on the cheek. "There, thank you for a beautiful evening. I'll call you." She got into the back of the cab. Brent briskly negotiated with the driver before giving him some cash.

"Good night, Linda," said Brent.

"Good night, Brent. Talk to you tomorrow."

The cab sped away. Brent watched it go, puffed out his cheeks and let out a long breath. Had he known what Linda was doing at that very moment he might have despaired.

Once inside the cab, she immediately took out her phone. Linda knew her friend, Georgina, would be asleep by now but she was so energized - more than recovered from her earlier ordeal - she had to send her a simple text message to let someone know what was happening to her. Linda's message was this, 'Wonderful evening. He's amazing. Tell you everything soon.'

The early morning hours were now invested with boredom and resignation. The elegantly dressed patrons looked crumpled or wilted yet Brent could not tear himself away from Garland's even though there was nothing much for him to do. After he had given his own statement, he stayed out of Greg's way as much as he could.

When he tried to strike up conversations wherever possible with staff and customers he found few in a mood to chat. No one was inclined to discuss anything. They just wanted to get through it and go home. Another disappointment for Brent was that he had missed Dan Lindsay and his wife completely because they had been some of the first to be interviewed and released.

At an earlier point in time, a large, handsome man had argued loudly with Greg Darrow. He made broad sweeps with his arms. Finally, he had his last word and had stormed off with a well-dressed woman in heels, nearly running beside him to keep up because of his long, fast stride.

Statements were being taken methodically and the number of witnesses still present had substantially dwindled. There were about twenty left by two-thirty. Brent studied a few but could not make a murderer out of any of them. He wandered along a corridor and, through a slightly open door, could see a woman in a red dress, expensive and elegant. He was struck by the look on her face - it was so bleak and strained.

That could be Rena Mayo in there. How has she been left on her own like that? If it is, she must really need someone to talk to or just sit with her. Would anyone mind if I spoke to her? Would she mind if I did?

He drifted past the door once, then twice, his journey markedly shorter each time. He stopped and looked to see if Greg Darrow was anywhere in sight. He was not. Brent entered the room.

Chapter 6

Wee hours of Friday

"*H*ello. Would you mind if I join you? I seem to be at a loose end and I'd really like someone to talk to." Brent spoke softly with a slight smile.

The woman stared at him, hesitating before answering. "Uh… I don't know."

"I can leave, if you like. I can understand wanting to be alone with one's thoughts."

"That's the last thing I want. It's my thoughts I can't escape." She spoke quietly and clearly.

"Yes… that happens. Hard, isn't it?" Brent pulled up a chair and sat down opposite her.

"Did you see him?" she asked.

"I did. I won't forget what I saw."

"I can't get it out of my head. How does one deal with it?"

"Put the image in a compartment in your mind. When it tries to struggle free wrestle it back in. When the time is right, you will take out that image, stare it down, and be free from its distorting effects."

"That is a mind game. A trick."

"It is but it really worked for me. Some years ago, I had a good friend who was murdered. I, too, saw him after it happened. It haunted me badly for a long time until I settled my mind as I described.

In a way, the murder of my friend, much as I grieve over it, actually changed my life for the better. When I dealt with the issue, it became a catalyst - it acted upon me and I acted upon it. I changed and it was for the good. I could have allowed that very same catalyst to act upon me in a different way. I could have become a worse person, and I mean that literally and not in any figurative sense."

"But I was there. I saw it happen. I saw it. He was a stranger to me and yet I was the last person to see him alive. We were talking... and I wasn't being particularly pleasant... a habit of mine. Then he was shot. I sat across from him and I saw the bullets hit him."

Brent now realized he was talking to someone other than Rena Mayo but he did not know who she could be.

"I think that's worse. You had no warning and it was a horrible shock for you. I'm so sorry. I wish there was something I could do to help but there really isn't."

"That wasn't the worst... because... it was the shape of his mouth. It looked so ridiculous... Of all the things to think, why should I think that?"

"Because death is ridiculous. It is the most stupid thing I know about. The more sudden it is the more absurd it becomes. This way of thinking is a function of being... oh, I don't know... to use a trite phrase, young at heart or just young. I think older people might get acclimatized to the notion of dying. Before that, while we are young and the visible death of people is rare, a confrontation with death comes as a sudden jolt. People sometimes laugh at funerals. It's because death is absurd in itself. This being and then not being - who can treat such a sudden and permanent transition from one state to the other with any degree of seriousness when it's not among the things we normally consider? I believe you are tremendously young at heart."

"Huh. I can't say I agree... not completely. Teenagers committing suicide. Surely they have faced the reality of non-existence. They accept death as a way out of their problems."

"Perhaps. You should hear my sermon on hope but I won't bore you with it now. I will say this, the western world is not one to foster great hope for the individual. It can't do it because it focuses on money, fame, art, science, politics, and the next big crisis. If a person has no religion, no faith, what is their hope? Their children? That isn't hope. That is a deferral of hope and, anyway, not everyone has children so it's not universal. True hope must be universal and accessible to all."

"That's a little larger than everyday life hope. You believe there's a god?"

"I rather think I do, else why am I so happy and hopeful no matter what happens around me? And you?"

"Once, I did. Have you thought it might be that you're projecting and forming a god out of a happy, hopeful disposition?"

"You might be right. But, and I have considered this, I would have to fool myself at some elemental level because with my rational mind, and my emotions, and my inner being, hope springs eternal. Believe me, I do have some down days but they pass, they pass."

"I'm not like that. I have a different constitution to you."

"Describe it. I'm immensely interested."

"I feel as though I'm working through an obstacle course. If I can proceed with enough control over my circumstances that I have some peace of mind, then I am content. If I can end my days content, then I have won. It's difficult to explain."

"It could be that we're saying the same things but our inward impressions are so nebulous that many different sets of words may be used to describe them without our realizing it."

She smiled. "Who are you?"

"My name is Brent Umber. Sometimes, I'm a private investigator. Sometimes, I'm just lonely. May I ask who you are?"

"You are strange, Mr. Umber. My name's Gabbie Wright. Seeing as we're being so open and honest... I'm lonely, too. I suppose I'm also sorry for myself. You see, I came with a friend and she left me here as soon as she could because she is selfish, and, as I now realize, never has been a real friend to me, only ever an acquaintance.

The police have been trying to get me to talk about what I saw but I've been stubbornly mute until now. I did not want to speak. They sent a psychiatrist to see me but he was so dreary and long-faced, I could not imagine saying anything to him except for him to get out. He didn't stay long. Did they send you to see me?"

"Now that question puts me in a very awkward position. The short answer is no. Yet I have worked with the police in the past. In fact, I know Greg Darrow, the lieutenant in charge of this case. However, because I'm only a private citizen and a witness... nowhere near as important a witness as yourself..., he would go ballistic if he found me here talking to you.

By chance, I was in the restaurant when the murder occurred. I'm not on the case but I have the passion and drive to solve it."

"I remember you, now. You were the man shouting things. I was close by on the floor, praying... huh... That is strange. I was praying but to whom? I don't know. Let's say I was hoping... There you are again. You've blocked off all my words. I trusted... I haven't heard your sermon on trust yet... that it was all over because you were speaking. For me, you represented the end of the danger."

"Then I did something useful today. Now, Gabbie, the police do want their questions answered. I would say, get it over and done with by giving a brief, factual statement. Forget about the nuances; the police only love facts and evidence. I can't fault them in that but there is much that they miss. Give them the statement and then go home and rest. You'll need it to recover properly."

"I think I might be able to speak to them now. You've been a real help. Thanks."

"Good. You have to keep my secret, though, and not tell the police I've seen you. If you find their questions draining, just remember, you're putting one over on the police lieutenant who deserves to be fooled for not bringing me into the case officially."

She smiled. "You'd better go. They said a nurse was coming to sit with me."

"I suppose I had. Before I do, though, I have to say this - your Burmese ruby is of about the finest quality I have ever seen. Did you inherit it?"

"I did, actually. Are you a super-sleuth?"

"No, not at all. I happen to know a little about gemstones."

"Well, Sherlock, what more can you tell me about it?" Some of her usual dry, mocking manner had returned.

"May I?" He held out his hand for her to show him the ring. She placed her hand in his so that he could examine the large rectangular pigeon's blood ruby of the deepest red.

"A cushion cut ruby of about eleven carats. The steps are very slightly uneven but that adds to its beauty and authenticity."

"I was told it was an old mine cut ruby."

"Same cut, different name. Also called a step cut or a pillow cut. It's the octagonal shape that makes it appear rounded because the sharp corners are removed, like a cushion. To continue, it was mined in the Mogok Stone Tract Valley in the Katha District by Burma Ruby Mines Ltd which was part-owned by the Rothschilds - Burma now being called Myanmar, as I'm sure you know.

Dating is difficult but it's likely to be from the period eighteen-ninety to nineteen-ten. I see no occlusions but that doesn't mean there aren't any. A magnifying glass or other equipment would reveal that. It is the richest, dark red I have ever seen and has a distinct purple tinge to it. It is natural as far as I can see and has not been heat treated.

Now, it has been reset in a very nice platinum ring. I think, you probably had that done because the original gold setting had become too worn. When you got the ring back after it had been remounted, it looked different. Is that what happened?"

"Yes! How did you know?"

"They say knowledge is power. The yellow gold counteracted the purple tinge and made the stone appear to be even more intensely red than it does now. When the setting was changed to the silver of platinum, the purple became apparent again. Did you think they'd switched stones on you?"

"It crossed my mind, yes. I asked about it. Tell me, which colour do you prefer?"

"I'm sorry but, as much as I like the stone as it is now, I would choose a yellow gold setting for it. It is traditional -

the custom of the Burmese kings of old - and a ruby is prized for its deep red colour alone."

"And what value would you place on it?"

"This is well beyond what I'm used to. I'm guessing, you understand. Minimally, a hundred thousand per carat and that's wholesale."

"I see. You did impressively well. Slightly out on the date, though. My great-great grandmother received it as a gift in 1889. My great-great grandfather bought the rough stone in Mandalay, Burma, the year before and then had it cut and set in Amsterdam."

At that moment, Greg Darrow, accompanied by a nurse, entered the room and stopped dead upon seeing Brent holding Gabbie's outstretched hand as though they were a Victorian courting couple.

"Hello, Greg," said Brent. "Gabbie feels she may be able to answer your questions now." He turned to her. "Can you do this?"

"Yes, I can. Don't be annoyed with him, Lieutenant Darrow. He helped and talked me through a difficult patch."

"Good night," said Brent. "I'd better go home now, I think."

"Good night, Mr. Umber, and thank you," said Gabbie.

"Yes," said Greg. "Good night, Mr. Umber!"

Gabbie laughed.

Having been caught by Greg Darrow in the very act of doing precisely what he had been instructed not to do, Brent decided to leave Garland's before he was tempted again into disobedience.

As he walked across the park to the place he had left his car, his thoughts were surprisingly not centred on the untimely death of Kirby Mayo, nor even on the part he hoped to play in the consequent investigation. Instead, they were all of the woman he had left in the charge of the police - her eyes, her voice, the feel of her hand in his, her aura, her soul. She engulfed him. It was only when he had to fulfil the function of unlocking his car to get in it that he was brought back down to earth sufficiently to marvel suddenly at the vagaries of life and, in particular, the vagaries of the human mind.

Chapter 7

Friday morning

*N*ews of Kirby Mayo's spectacular death dominated all media the next day. The bare facts of the story were repeated frequently and, over the course of the news cycle, went from being explained as the explosive, shocking story it was, to the early acceptance stage. In this latter phase of coverage, photographs, older ones of the Kirby family, were broadcast. One old photo of Kirby became the accepted image with which to present the victim. It was of a smiling, happy family group on rocks with a sparkling sea as a backdrop. Two light-haired, preoccupied children played in the foreground. Kirby, on the right, had his arm around Rena's shoulders and she leaned in to her husband. She appeared so slight in comparison to Kirby's large frame. A few media companies were already cropping the picture so that only Kirby's face and shoulders could be seen.

Information about Mayo was being presented as soon as it was found. The in-depth articles speculated heavily on Althorn Capital Investments and what its fate would be now that it had lost its key driving force. Associated articles were presented about hedge funds as a niche industry and the absurd amounts of wealth that were gripped in their corporate fingers. The other topic of interest was Garland's. The headline that seemed to capture the mood of the event was, "Is anyone safe?", inferring that Garland's, hitherto perceived as sacrosanct, had been violated when an innocent patron had been so publicly slain.

In its zeal, the media nearly missed the homeless man, Samuel Butts, who had been murdered the same night. He received just a few, bald lines, mentioning his demise and statistically adding him to the growing homicide count for the year.

Perhaps, thought Brent as he read the report, Samuel had also sat on a rock by the sea in a happier time.

Brent was in his office that overlooked the back garden at his suburban house, having arrived there late, the morning after the murder at Garland's. He was planning his campaign against Greg Darrow's friendly refusal to let him in on the case unless there was a problem. Brent realized that it might take forever for the police department to realize there was a problem if, indeed, it ever did. He just could not accept being shut out. If Greg would not let him investigate the case alongside the police, then Brent was going to go it alone. He realized he would have to go slowly and unobtrusively so as not to disturb the lieutenant.

He needed to let the first raw emotion and energy of the event subside in the minds of the witnesses. The police would be pursuing their investigations anyway, and it would be awkward if they were to find him accessing their witnesses. He had already caused a strategic problem for himself by talking to Gabbie Wright.

The first thing he had to do was to get hold of a list of witnesses. Greg would have it and Brent needed it. Greg would not give the names to him so Brent must take them -

a tricky, delicate problem but not an insoluble one. He had in the past obtained entry into a police station to remove some very awkward evidence so the concept of raiding the police was not new to him.

A personal and very revealing cell phone, belonging to an idiot friend, as Brent thought of him, had been left next to the open door of a safe. Brent, and his friend Micky, had just spent half an hour opening the safe together. They had left the premises, pleased with their night's work. An hour later, Micky went to make a call, and uttered the fateful words, "Where's my phone?" and back they went to retrieve the device. It was crammed with personal and incriminating evidence, some of which they knew would hint at Brent's involvement in that night's escapade.

En route back to the safe, words flew like flights of daggers through the air between the two young miscreants. Great was their horror upon finding, in that same hour, the police had already arrived at the scene of the crime. However, two hours later, at 4:47 a.m., as the big clock on the wall of the detective's office declared it to be, Brent was taking the as yet unlocked cell phone out of a desk drawer and putting it into his pocket. Had Brent been caught, the phrase 'impersonating a police officer' would have been mentioned frequently at his trial.

It would be easy enough for Brent to interview the Garland's staff. They would return to their duties in the building and Brent would see them there. Topping his list of interviewees were the cloakroom attendants, the two doormen, and the wait staff. He had many photographs of this latter group which simplified matters for him. He had them on his computer screen and was writing up the notes he had taken the night before. How to get the list of customers, though? He would have to proceed very carefully.

Likewise, and with care, he could surely get at the Althorn staff and partners. To save time, he somehow needed to fast-track everything. And he needed that list.

He sipped his coffee and took a moment to look out over the spacious garden. Still damp from last night's rain, the garden looked a mess, although there was good progress being made. Paths were laid in stone. Beds of black earth had been started. The lawn was shrinking in size as areas were being dedicated to other uses. The place where the sixteen by twenty shed would go had been marked out.

Brent wondered, for a moment, why he had to involve himself in this case. He had already taken possession of it in his thoughts. The Kirby case belonged to Brent - it was as simple as that. But why? Why get in it with all the inconveniences and expense associated with his involvement when the police would probably solve it anyway? He could not find a clear answer to his question. He just had to. He hated murder. He hated the disturbing, brazenness of this particular one. Brent knew he had to help. Was he just showing off, desperate for attention? One of humanity's natural busy-bodies? Was it because he had nothing else to do and this gave some meaning, some peculiar validation for his being?

He ended by justifying his inclusion in the case on the grounds that there were people, hurt and distracted as a result of the murder, whom he knew he could help. He further thought, why was it that he felt sadness for Samuel Butts, the homeless man, but no inclination to involve himself there in his case? What were the distinctions he had unconsciously made between the two men? He could excuse himself on the basis of being present at the one event but not at the other - although he did not find the excuse entirely satisfactory.

He was certain on one point: police processes and the peculiarly focused ways of legal justice would not heal people in any meaningful way. Some would suffer for the rest of their lives by what had happened or by what they had seen. A few would suffer devastation, such as Rena Kirby, the slight, happy woman in the photograph. Brent could not imagine what she was going through. And how and when could he get to see her? - if she would even agree to see him.

Seeing a cat in the garden brought him back to the present. Eric was coming over in the evening to settle the shed design issue, bringing his home-made beer with him. There would be a war of words over the superb, golden ale. Brent would lose because Eric was inexorable in his purposes and mostly immune to counter-arguments. There was nothing wrong with Eric's design; it just was not Brent's chosen design. He knew he would lose the contest. Eric would have his choice of shed, and Brent would be happy to see the elderly gardener content. But he was going to fight him anyway. He could not let him get away with it without pushing back a little and maybe winning some small concessions. At least he could then get the needed materials ordered and the pair of them could start work on the shed on Monday. Hopefully, they would get it substantially finished before the weather interfered with the project.

His phone chimed. It was Linda's first text message of the day - others would follow. Brent read it and groaned loudly. It said, "Thinking of you. Can't stop, it's crazy busy here. Georgina says we're a perfect match."

Chapter 8

Wednesday

*T*he following Wednesday, the shed with its vertical, muted orange cedar planking was now complete apart from some interior work. The cedar shake roof was not a stylistic fit for the modern, angular lines of the house when the two structures were seen together - as Brent now realized.

Eric had wanted asphalt shingles or metal, but when he had wavered - allowing cedar shakes as being more traditional and in keeping with the garden - Brent heavily drove his advantage home and Eric conceded the point. Brent had wrung a concession from him. The consolation was that when the shed was viewed from the living room, as he was now doing, it looked fantastic. The orange newness of the boards would weather to grey and the shed would be perfect.

Brent had won that skirmish because Eric's main objective lay elsewhere. Over the beer of the planning session, Eric, in reaching for the right word properly to express himself, suddenly said,

"What's that fella's name?"

"Who?"

"The one with the mask...? You know."

"I don't."

"I used to read about him."

"Um, the Man in the Iron Mask?"

"I read that. It wasn't him."

"The Lone Ranger?"

"No. In comics, it was. I had a few of them."

"Green Lantern? Uh, Batman?"

"That's him. Batman's the fella. Now, Brent, this is what I can't remember - what did he call his belt?"

"Wasn't it a utility belt?"

"Exactly right. That's the word I'm looking for. You see, Brent, your shed has to have utility, otherwise what is the point of it?"

Eric then carefully and systematically tore to pieces Brent's lack-of-utility design choices, explaining how and where he had gone wrong.

As Brent stood recalling the conversation, admiring the shed through the kitchen window, he smiled, and turned to some items laid out on the countertop. He had already fitted the tiny camera. The business end was secure under the elasticated sleeve of his red crew-neck sweater and was connected by a long thin wire to the camera main memory and battery pack unit in his poacher's pocket. Surreptitiously pull out the camera, press the play button, and the witness names would come to Brent in a stream of video - if he could only get eyes on them. Should Greg not allow him to see the files - there were in a jacket pocket two sets of pick locks if needed. Brent could open his own locked filing cabinet in four seconds using the picks, but then he was familiar with the set-up. Even in the dark of the night before, with his eyes shut, it had only taken him six seconds to get the drawers open from pick insertion to latch release.

He donned his mid-length wool jacket. It was a severely plain, dark grey, tapered garment with a small collar and thin lapels which darted down to the topmost of three buttons. Suitable for the day because the weather had turned cooler, he not only looked elegant in it but the jacket had numerous pockets inside, including the one his tailor had euphemistically referred to as a poacher's pocket. A lot of useful things could be put in that hidden, interior pocket which was level with the small of his back.

Climbing into his old, blue Jeep, Brent knew Greg to be in his office because he had called him. When he had done so, he had noticed there were two unread messages from Linda on his now muted phone. He had hinted to her strongly, several times, that nothing would be going forward between them, that they were not an item - so please, would she stop saying they were, and, although he liked her as a friend, that was where it ended. He may as well have said the words to Eric for any desired effect to be forthcoming. Linda ignored anything she did not wish to hear, and repeatedly said that it takes time to build a relationship that will last. Brent suspected, was nearly certain, that Linda had a team of friends backing and coaching her. He wanted a word with that team. Georgina was certainly one of them.

In response to Brent's enquiry, Lieutenant Darrow had said he would be happy to see him today which statement made Brent think that perhaps - just perhaps - the Mayo case was not going as well as Greg would have liked. Soon, he would find out.

Brent exited the elevator on the fourth floor. He asked a passerby for directions to Greg's office. He found it and stopped at the open doorway.

"How's the promotion going? I like your new office." It was one of the better proportioned offices in the building and, although snug, allowed for efficiency. The new desk and chairs gave a clean, updated look to it.

"Come in and shut the door after you. The job's okay. All I hoped for but there's always something you don't anticipate. The guys treat me like management when we used to be buddies. It's a very different vibe."

"Oh, I guess it would be. That's a pity." Brent was now seated.

"I'm not crying over it. I'll tell you what I am crying about - this new chair. I can't sit in it for two hours at a stretch without getting back strain. I have to go for a walk every now and then. Somebody's already using my lovely old chair."

"Ask them to trade or you'll give them a hard time."

"Yeah, okay. I'm busy as ever so let's get down to it. I know why you're here."

"Does my coming in bother you?" asked Brent.

"The jury's still out on it. The Kirby Mayo file is stalled. Ah, before you jump for joy, this is not unusual and happens in many cases. It's almost standard that, unless we have a clear suspect at first, the momentum drops off until we get the right leads lined up."

"Yes?"

"I'm coming to it. In this file, we've uncovered at least a dozen people who have a powerful motive to murder him. I'm not talking opportunity now but solid motives because the deceased defrauded or cheated them. He was not a nice guy," said Greg.

"I haven't seen a hint of that in the media. What I've seen from them are editorials that say society is being destabilized by such public acts of violence and…"

"and… What are the authorities, meaning the police, doing about it? All through my career, I've heard often enough from supervisors about the optics of our conduct in the media. There are courses on it. As a lieutenant, I find it's a different ball game. Anxiety over the media stretches from the top down to lieutenant and it's a huge priority. The game is to get the job done and keep the media on our side. Delays in high profile cases translate into a lot of pressure for the guy who is on the lowest rung of the management ladder which happens to be me in this instance. No wonder my old boss was so bad-tempered. I thought it was just his lousy personality."

"You're under pressure, the case is stalled, and you have a wide field of suspects. What would you like me to do?"

"Slow down and you'll find out. I have three detectives working the case. One of them is a union rep. He's okay, goes at a set speed that never varies, but his real problem is that he loves filing grievances. No matter how you come into this, if you do, he would file a grievance. Long story short, you'd be out permanently in order to keep the peace. In some ways, I'm on his side. But, as a new lieutenant, I have to demonstrate I can use the resources given to me to get the job done. When I think about it in this way, the union guy is a pain because I want to bring you in to speed things up.

Last week, your getting Gabbie Wright to start talking, when she was so badly shaken, reminded me how good you are at your job. She sang like a bird after you had gone and gave me a clean statement without any relapses. I sent the nurse home.

What I'd like you to do is to speak to some of the people present at Garland's at the time of the murder and see if you can work up a few leads. You suggested it and, now I've had time to think it over, it makes sense."

"Okay... thanks. How surprising and interesting this has turned out to be."

"Yes, I guess it has. So, as far as I'm concerned, you can do some interviews but, unlike in the Songbird Estate case, it would be completely unofficial. You'd have to be willing to work for nothing and pay your own expenses."

"Hmm, I'm in," said Brent.

"That was quick."

"You don't know how I'm itching to get going."

"Union guy can't find out what you're doing. If he does, I'll disown you. His name is Otto Schroeder. Think you can handle it?"

"I'll try."

There was a silence between them for some seconds.

"Brent, if you don't mind my asking, what's it like being well-off?"

"I don't mind your asking. I honestly don't know what other wealthy people experience so this is purely my take on it. I started out poor and, in many respects, disadvantaged. What I earn is mainly investment income. I got a very big break early on. From there, I not only became prudent in what I did but I resolved to become always grateful. I said all that to say I realize that everything could easily have worked out very differently despite my hard work so I have a sense of thankfulness.

Wealth took some getting used to at first but, like everyone else, I adapted to a new situation fast enough. Essentially, I don't feel wealthy. What assets I have are not so very much when compared to many others and I don't compare myself to them. I'm content..." Brent paused before changing his mind. "No, I'm not exactly content... yet. I have just as many issues as I've ever had, only a shortage of money is not one of them."

"That's insightful... and honest. Why do you want this gig so badly? See, if it were me, and I had your resources,

I'd be thinking about vacations, a new car, and the rest of it."

"I completely understand that - you work hard every day with barely a let-up. Think about it, though. Those things, vacations and whatnot, are temporary and obvious goals - the things that money can buy that you would like now. True wealth is what enables you to be a different person, a better person. A kinder one, anyway. This true wealth could come through money but, more importantly, it comes through peace of mind. For me, money allowed me sufficient space to find some peace of mind. Instead of struggling to establish myself somehow, I could stand back and assess where my life was going.

You asked why I want this gig and, it's funny, I've been thinking over the matter recently. I want to help people and this is one way I know I can. We've discussed it before. I'm down on murder and you know why. No one has the right to bring the life of another to an untimely end. But, you know, it's the collateral damage that pains me the most... keeps me awake at night... drives me. So many other lives are so adversely affected and I like to think I can do something about it."

"Interesting. Very insightful." He grimaced and moved in his seat. "I can't stand this new chair. I really have to get another. I'll go for a walk, I think. Oh, this is my personal Mayo file. Contains report summaries, lists, and my comments."

The lieutenant slid a thick folder across the top of the desk towards Brent.

"As I have to go out for a moment, could you look after it while I'm gone? Don't let anyone take anything out of it. See, police files are not allowed to leave the office. If you should go before I get back, just pop the file into the front of that filing cabinet."

Greg smiled and got up to leave the room. He closed the door behind him.

"Good old Greg." Brent said to himself.

He took the phone from his jacket pocket and began taking photographs with it because it was a more familiar action to him. Later, when he was comfortable with his progress through the file, he tried the camera hidden up his sleeve. It worked, producing reasonable quality if he went slowly but he found it awkward to use in a hurry.

Brent went to his apartment to read the documents he had just acquired. He was so jubilant that he nearly ran through a red light on the way.

He parked his Jeep several streets away from the former machine shop. His reason for doing this was to keep the new, suburban part of his identity segregated from its urban dweller counterpart. He reasoned, should he be followed because someone disliked his inquiries, he would have a way of avoiding them and continue operations. The walk from Jeep to apartment allowed him to determine if he was being followed or not. The habit was not new to him but, having been shot at numerous times on his previous murder investigation, he was all the more diligent about security. He had been targeted then and it had made him wary enough to be vigilant and to keep up a few simple precautions.

After three hours, he had uploaded Greg's summary reports onto a computer, matched a few individuals to the photos he had taken, and was up to speed on where the police case currently stood. He crystallized his thoughts by writing his own report and annotating the lists. Brent was impressed by the sheer volume of work the police had accomplished. Nearly three hundred people had been interviewed - some of them twice. Most of these were of little or no interest, neither to Greg nor to himself.

It became apparent that Greg had organized the file so that Brent could pick up on the most important witnesses and the most doubtful ones. As to a suspect among them, Greg was reticent. However, a simple asterisk next to certain names made it clear that Greg had been having his own ideas about possible candidates for arrest. Brent agreed with the asterisked selection of names completely, although he added more as he made his own notes.

The main and undeniably ridiculous feature of the reports was that no one had seen who shot Kirby Mayo. A dining room full of people all at different angles because of the seating arrangements; restaurant staff walking about or watching the tables; a vigilant manager - not one of these scores of people had seen anything of the murderer as he or she fired the three quick shots. No one saw the weapon - since proven to be a .38 calibre revolver without a police history. No one had seen anyone suspicious entering or leaving the premises. There were no security cameras in the room and the ones outside did not show anyone of interest. It was as if an invisible ghost with a spectral revolver had done the deed. However, the bullets had been real enough, that was for sure.

Brent leaned back in his chair. Above the computer was a medium-sized panorama of a Swiss farm - Brent supposed it to be Swiss. It was a pleasant oil from the nineteen-thirties. A springtime scene, the foreground was of a hilly field studded with Alpine flowers. In the backdrop were the typical mountains one would expect to find - part snowy but not well defined, filled in with dull blues and greys. They were not important and only provided context. It was the farmhouse that shone because of its red roof, dark brown log walls and the sunlight streaming down upon it. The sky was well done, a particular cloud intriguing Brent - he could not have said why. He had his own name for the painting - he called it 'Innocence'. In his mind he went there as an antidote to some of the ugly things he had to consider from time to time.

He had just finished reading the autopsy report. The first bullet would not have been fatal if attended to immediately. It was the second one that had been. Kirby Mayo had been rocked back in his chair by the first shot, causing him to be in such a position that the second travelled obliquely - passing under his ribcage and into his chest area. The medical examiner then described the wound channel as 'eccentric' and the damage as 'catastrophic'. Brent was glad to cleanse his mind with Alpine flowers and the expectation of a small herd of bell-tinkling cows about to wander up the grassy, rounded hill.

As he stared at the painting he ceased to see it and a list of his own began to take shape in his mind, as well as strategies and tactics that addressed how he would approach strangers and get them to talk openly to him about the very evening they would probably prefer to forget. He puzzled over how to achieve, without any official recognition, the standing of confidant-in-an-instant across such a broad range of personalities and attitudes.

"How does he expect me to do this?" Brent muttered to himself, referring, of course, to Greg. The painting came back into focus again and he immediately perceived that his answer was right in front of him. He shot out of his chair and began stuffing a small backpack with the items he needed. He was going to see Nola Devon first to try out his strategy; a big risk but, if it worked, he would get access to other Althorn staff members.

When his bag was ready, he decided to put on a business suit. As he well knew, people formed impressions about people the instant they saw them. To talk to business people a business suit is a must. He selected a dark charcoal bespoke suit that was a blend of Milanese and Savile Row influences and quality but which he had obtained at a third of the price from his local, highly skilled tailor. A white shirt and a plain dark red, low sheen silk tie with matching handkerchief finished off his ensemble. What Brent found particularly rewarding was that, when he put his arm into a sleeve and held it at a little more than eye-level, the jacket effortlessly slid into place as though fitting itself to his form. This gratifying minor effect instantly produced a sense of well-being in Brent. He felt he could accomplish anything.

"I'd like to see Nola Devon, please. Tell her the matter is urgent," said Brent, as he stood at the reception desk of Althorn Capital Investments. He handed his card to the receptionist. It simply said "Brent Umber", in a clean, elegant font. His telephone number and email address were in one corner.

"Is she expecting you, Mr. Umber?"

"No. If she's busy at present, I'll wait until she's free."

"I'll see if she's available. I know she has a full schedule."

The receptionist called Nola's extension. It rang but then went to her voice mail.

"I'm sorry," said the receptionist, essentially repeating the message she had just heard, "she's not available at the moment. I have your card so I'll ask her to call you back."

"No. The matter is urgent." Brent weighed his words carefully. "The future of Althorn is at stake."

He sat down in a nearby chair to wait. The receptionist did not reply. She tried Nola's extension again with the same result as before. Brent hoped that his ominous words, coupled with the weight of Kirby Mayo's recent death that already bore down upon everything and everyone at Althorn, would have the desired effect. He waited.

Nearly a minute later, the receptionist said, "I'll find her and ask if she can see you right away." She got up and went into the office.

Any receptionist caught between the demands of an important visitor and a boss who does not wish to be disturbed has to walk a fine line. Should Brent meet Nola, he would not be dealing with someone labouring under any such ambiguity. He would need to get her onside very fast or she would send him away. If he hesitated or fluffed his lines he would sink. He tried to keep calm and stay focused on his mission. He believed he had just achieved the right mindset when the receptionist returned with Nola. This was not the situation Brent had envisaged. He had imagined a discreet conversation in a private office rather than in a public area with an audience.

Nola was in her element in her office and, although Brent did not see the hawk-like attributes that the staff recognized, she presented as a hard, cool person without weakness; a warrior of the company. He could see no trace of emotion or hesitance that suggested her mind might be troubled with too many thoughts.

As Nola walked into the reception area, she immediately fastened her gaze on the well-dressed man seated there. Young - young-looking, anyway; competent; successful; established. Not a client. Could be in the business. Not selling anything. He's here on an urgent matter. Not police, not a lawyer... what does he know about Althorn?

"Mr. Umber? I don't think we've met before," said Nola.

"Thank you for seeing me without notice. No, we haven't met. Some information has come to me that I wished to bring to your attention and that's why I'm here." Brent had stood up as soon as Nola had addressed him and they now shook hands.

At these close quarters, he noticed around her eyes a tiredness that could not be seen from a distance. She saw or felt that he possessed an intensity of purpose, that he had something to say, and that it could be important. But she also knew that one could not trust people on a handshake and was forever conscious of there being much to do.

"I'm very busy and I can only spare a little time. What is this about?"

Brent took his time answering. He looked towards the receptionist who certainly appeared thoroughly absorbed by work on her computer screen but who, he knew, did not want to miss a word of what he had to say. He turned back to Nola and said,

"It's about Kirby's death. Information has come to light. I think you should know what it is."

"I see," said Nola. Her attitude slackened. She stood down from her warrior of business stance. It was not a straightforward investment matter, then, as she had hoped. It was the other thing, the thing that would not go away. "We'll find an office where we can talk privately. This way, please." Nola showed the way. They walked side by side in silence for a few moments.

"I'm surprised by the number of employees you have," remarked Brent.

"Yes, we might have to relocate in the future because we're at capacity here."

"Would a satellite office be useful?"

"Yes, that might be the way to go…" She hesitated and then decided to finish her thought. "This office is in the perfect location. It is about the impression one makes in the market. Larger, prestigious offices make a statement about the company." She would not normally reveal that much of her ideas but the man next to her seemed easier to talk to than most men. "Here we are." She pushed a door open to let Brent go in first. It was her own office rather than the interview room she had first thought to hear him in.

As soon as he was inside, Brent noticed a painting on the wall and said, "That's very pleasant. I like the colour combinations… muted but the contrasts set them off to seem brighter. Jules Engel… I've heard of him. Usually, I'm not fond of abstracts." He turned back to Nola. "They seem to be saying something important and I never quite catch hold of what it is."

Nola looked at Brent, looked to the painting and then back again at him. She thought, Why is he wasting time?

Brent caught the look. "I know. I'll come to the point. The police do not yet have any particular suspect in mind. They have an array of suspects. I was at Garland's that night so I'm a suspect. You were at the restaurant… you are a suspect. They will continue to suspect anyone who has either motive or opportunity. I had opportunity but no motive. You have both."

"How do you know this?" Nola spoke sharply.

"I have a connection who tells me things."

She was quiet as she considered what Brent had said. She gave a slight shrug as though she had arrived at a determination. "I'll get used to their suspicion."

"Yes. But I don't think Althorn will. Already the company must have experienced a loss of business. Losing a key player will certainly have both short and long-term effects. The longer this case drags on the more likely it becomes that people will imagine Althorn might be involved in some material way, that it might be complicit. They will consider the remaining partners as possible murderers. Jealousy among the staff is easily imagined as a motive. A disgruntled client…? The list goes on. As long as nobody knows for certain, there will be a chill setting in. You will not get any new clients and, unless you have a brilliant action plan up your sleeve, existing ones will begin to melt away.

I appreciate that there is a need to transition from how things were to a post-Kirby existence and I'm sure you're doing as much as is possible. However, as long as suspicion hangs in the air, Althorn will lose business."

Nola did not look resistant to these ideas. "Shall we sit down?" she asked. Once they were settled, she continued, "We've been thinking about this constantly but, um, none of us had put it so bluntly. I see what you're saying." She was clearly still cautious - expecting more from Brent.

"I have a proposal to make. I'm a private investigator and I have investigated two murders in the past. Do you remember Sheila Babbington?"

"Yes, I do. That was only this summer. The police got it wrapped up quite quickly, I thought."

"Actually, they were stalled on it. They brought me in and, either by luck or by skill, I managed to turn it around in a few days. I can provide references from senior police officials and detectives that will confirm that I was not only paid to be on the case but that I did a more than competent job. I'm sorry to blow my own trumpet but, if you look upon me as a job applicant who is willing to work pro bono, I have to inform you of my potential. I think I can bring some skills that will solve Althorn's problems."

Nola sat far back in her chair and swivelled it slowly and slightly, left and right, as she thought it over. Stopping, she asked, "What will you do?"

"Have a free hand to talk to staff and partners with a view to establishing every person's innocence. My connection with the police works two-ways. I will tell my contact as and when I find someone I know to be innocent."

"What if you find the murderer?" she asked, sharply.

"Has to come out. The sooner the better for many reasons. The principle one for Althorn is that the matter will have been finally settled. Ms. Devon, you would know how to proceed from that point on and your damage control efforts can be more targeted. Even in a break-up of Althorn - I'm sure there is some value in transferring business to other companies."

"Very little... less than you would think." She sat forward to rest her elbows on the table. "I think the other partners should speak to you. Do you mind?"

"No, I welcome it."

"Give me a few minutes and I'll be back." She quickly left the office.

While she was gone, Brent looked at his text messages. Linda, he had learned, did not require an immediate response as long as he replied the same day. He was not sure why he had to respond but felt it wrong of him not to. He had zero romantic feelings towards her while she was essentially saying to him in various ways, love will come eventually. He knew he needed to put a stop to it but he could not see how without being offensive. Linda seemed determined to overcome any objection he might raise.

He skimmed through a few others that friends and acquaintances had sent and answered them. One interaction was with Vane. A time and day for the Mexican lunch and fashion show was proving difficult to arrange. Tentatively, they would meet tomorrow, Friday, at noon.

The minutes dragged on. Either the partners were talking together or Nola was severely absent-minded.

"Hello, Mr. Umber," said a cheery woman who had put her head in at the door. "Ms. Devon says she's very sorry for keeping you waiting. The partners are ready to see you now."

"Why, thank you," said Brent. He got up and followed her lead.

Chapter 9

Wednesday afternoon

$\mathcal{T}$he boardroom had a sweeping view of the northern end of the city and the vertical blinds were drawn back. At the moment Brent entered, the northern sector of the cloudy sky had a bright rent in it that back-lit the four figures - the four remaining partners - and caused their shape and attitude to be well-defined. Seated around the long, glass table, Nola was upright and alert, Sohil Remtulla was serious and serene, Blake Pickett seemed a mass of nervous energy and was never still, Will Hutchinson was angular, like a ladder. Hutchinson sat further away from one end of the table and, curiously, seemed to be extended full length as he sat, causing his suit jacket to be pulled in odd directions. Brent wondered where Kirby's place would have been and concluded it was where Will Hutchinson was now sitting or, rather, extending himself.

Nola introduced the partners with a few comments on what they did at Althorn and explained that she had informed them of Brent's proposal. Sohil, a twelve and a half per cent partner, was in charge of the bond and foreign exchange activities. Blake, a seven and a half per cent partner, was a veteran trader who carefully groomed and trained new traders as they were hired. Will, she explained, was in charge of market neutral strategies.

Nola asked Brent to recap what he had told her earlier. Brent did so succinctly.

"Mr. Umber," said Sohil, "I can see the value of what you intend. My concern is that, although you may be qualified to conduct the interviews, you would be doing so without oversight. The police have their procedures; who would you answer to? Who could review your work to see that it remains within the mandate that is set?"

"I would answer to you, the principals of Althorn. I would give you a report stating my conclusions and this report would also be made available to the police."

"Then we should be given the name of the person you report to in the police."

"No, I cannot give it to you at present because of a promise I've made. And, apart from that, it is the fact of your being saved from continued and continuous police oversight that is the primary benefit to Althorn that I can provide. I know you have all given statements, with Ms. Devon and Mr. Hutchinson being interviewed twice. They will be back to interview you repeatedly until they identify a possible culprit. That will not be the end of it. They are actively looking into the backgrounds of you and your staff. The investigation will extend to your client list. Until they find a candidate with sufficient motive who stands out from the rest, the detectives will widen the net to include the families and friends of all people associated with Mr. Mayo. Althorn will always be their main focus."

While Sohil pursed his lips, considering Brent's reply, Will interjected, saying,

"I don't understand. Am I to infer that you want the police to be kept in the dark about your inquiries?"

"Yes," said Brent. "Apart from my contact that Nola told you about."

"Why should we do that?"

"They wouldn't like it."

"Huh, is this illegal?" Will gave a short, mirthless laugh. "We will definitely be checking your references."

"A grey area," replied Brent, ignoring the latter part of Will's comment.

"I can appreciate that," said Sohil. "I think, if the interviews with the staff were conducted with one of us present, I would feel more comfortable with the arrangement."

"Forgive me, Mr. Remtulla, but it would not be possible for an employee to be candid with a boss present. The presence of any third party would be problematic."

"How do we know that you're not from a competitor and this is all a façade?" asked Will. His brows furrowed every time he asked a question and his tone always conveyed that he was mildly annoyed.

"You don't," replied Brent. "Nothing I can say can remove that doubt from your mind. I have no problem in signing a confidentiality agreement in regards to the practices and procedures of the Althorn business, if that would make you feel better. However, I intend to establish that I am sufficiently trustworthy to do what I say I'm going to do and nothing else."

"You had better do it soon because I have a serious trust issue… Nola, I'm against this idea."

"Will, I don't think we have explored it properly yet," said Nola.

"Five minutes, that's all I have time for."

"I have a lot to do, also," said Blake. "I have reservations but, I'm intrigued. Couldn't we set up a trial with one of us so that we can all see what you will be doing? It would give us a sense of the direction you would take."

Nola smiled, the first time Brent had seen her do so.

"I am on the spot, aren't I?" said Brent. "I can do as you propose on one condition. I choose who it is I interview."

"Before we go as far as that," said Will, "I think the trust issue needs to be settled."

"Mr. Umber," said Sohil. "It is probably best you address Will's concerns first. One thought I have is this - we hired Rowell-Scala, the PR company, and they have laid out very comprehensive strategies for us to deal with the situation as it develops. They are handling our media presence through this crisis. Bearing in mind what you have said, why can they not sufficiently handle the situation and present Althorn in an untainted light?"

"No amount of damage control can offset suspicion. There is no spin that can overcome aversion to a brand. Garland's, a brand, is open for business tonight. Are any of you going there for dinner by choice? I assume you won't. They may be busy because people will go to see where it happened. That effect will subside over time, and, I don't doubt, Garland's, like Althorn, has a PR problem it is actively addressing. However, the result is yet to be seen - the restaurant may close or it may return to normal.

I will be going to Garland's later on because my investigation takes me there. I hoped to help Althorn and, more specifically, you as individuals - and that includes your staff.

Can Rowell-Scala go to Garland's to interview people and find out information to help Althorn and, indeed, everyone involved? No. They have no idea what to do and say in the matter. They cannot find a murderer. The police? Oh yes, they can find a murderer and, most of the time, they do but they cannot help you hold your business together, whereas I'm uniquely positioned to do both. I'm a suspect, a witness, an experienced private investigator, I have a determination to discover who the murderer is and a passion to help people put their lives back together. I'm strongly motivated and I will do my utmost with or without your help."

The room was silent. Blake Pickett got up and said,

"Excuse me, I have to get back to work. If there's a vote, Mr. Umber gets mine. Nice meeting you, Mr. Umber. Hope you're successful."

When Blake left the room, Will said,

"I'm not convinced. It's all talk."

"That's true," said Brent. "Do you mind if I call you Will? I prefer to use first names, it's friendlier."

"No, Hutchinson is my name to you."

"Very well, Hutchinson. I would say that you have something to hide. Normal business practices run along the lines of hearing someone out and then coming to a decision by the end of the meeting or afterwards. You have been aggressively against me from the word go. This is a murder we are talking about. Do you realize what light you're putting yourself in?"

"I don't have to listen to this. I think you'd better leave." Will sat upright.

"You should listen because, as I said at the beginning, I report my findings to my police connection. Had you heard me out and then said you didn't want me in Althorn's or anywhere near it that would have been fine. I could understand that. What impression am I to take away from this meeting?"

In the awkward silence that followed, it was expected that Will should speak next. His eyes darted until he settled on looking out of the window.

"I put it down to the stress we're all under. I apologize for being sharp. Nola, whatever you decide, I'll go along with it. Excuse me." He got up and left the room.

"Who will you interview?" asked Sohil.

Brent smiled. "Let's do this scientifically." He took a coin from his pocket and tossed it. As he held the coin on the back of his hand, he asked, "Who would like to call?"

"Heads," said Sohil. It was tails. "I don't think it would be polite of me to stay and listen," he added. "Tell me what happens, Nola. Goodbye, Mr. Umber, or should I call you Brent?"

"Brent. Thank you, Sohil. It's been a pleasure meeting you." Brent stood up and they shook hands.

"And then there were two," said Nola, after Sohil had gone.

"Yes. Do you have any time constraints?"

"There's always so much to do. Is fifteen minutes enough time?"

"I think so. You do know that you're the leader at Althorn? You may have been beforehand but it is certainly the case now."

"I mother them. I always have. When Kirby was here… he, um, he was boss and that was it but even he left a lot of decisions to me."

"How did you get into this industry?"

"I had my career planned out since I was sixteen. I did my first trade when I was fourteen. Using some money I'd saved from my allowance, I invested a hundred and twenty dollars in a single stock and made a profit of seven dollars and twenty-three cents in just over two weeks. Liking math, I extrapolated and compounded the returns and thought I'd found a gold mine. I was hooked from then on."

"If I'd had that money when I was fourteen," said Brent, "I probably would have invested in comics, cigarettes, hamburgers and movies."

"Do you smoke?"

"Not since I was a teenager. Do you?"

"I did, once, in an effort to relieve work-related stress but when the no-smoking by-laws came in, I gave it up. I think nicotine made me more stressed, actually, overall."

"What did you do then to help relieve stress instead of smoking?"

"Diet, exercise, yoga, supplements... you name it, I've tried it?"

"Drugs?"

"No... though I got mildly addicted to the Lorazepam my doctor prescribed. I had to kick that as well."

"What do you do now? I mean, you don't seem at all stressed. I would have thought the current circumstances would be challenging."

"They are, believe me, they are. I'm leaving Althorn... not now, when it's in trouble, but later on."

"A good old exit strategy so you don't feel tied up against your will. How did the other partners react to the news?"

"I haven't told them yet."

"Oh, that's very sweet of you to trust me. I won't breathe a word of it to anyone."

"I did tell Kirby."

"Hmm... would that have been on the night?"

"It was."

"How did he take the news?"

"As I expected he would. I think he wanted to buy my share but at a discounted price."

"I see. I don't know a great deal about Kirby as a person - not yet, anyway. I've heard a few things that make me understand he was sharp, and that this was an attribute tending towards unscrupulous behaviour."

"Very much so. I could tell you a lot of stories."

"Maybe we'll come back to that later. What I do wonder is whether you knew this before you went into partnership with him."

"Implying, what? That I'm also unscrupulous?"

"I don't think you are. Somebody who saves their allowance…? I think that implies you are a highly motivated and disciplined person."

"Thanks for the vote of confidence."

"You haven't answered."

"I heard a few things about him that were… well, let's say I guess I set aside my better judgement when it was convenient."

"Did you regret it?"

"It's a situation I've learned to live with. I've never cheated anyone but this can be a savage business sometimes. I've always played by the rules. Kirby didn't. He kept his unethical practices to himself, though… to his own deals and not those run directly through the partnership. I chose to turn a blind eye to his activities and not enquire into them."

"Probably because he was so important to Althorn's financial well-being. Thanks for giving me a clearer picture."

They were both silent for a while.

"Are you judging me for that?"

"Good heavens, no. I'm not condemning you in any sense. I might do the same in your position. I can see that once you were invested in the partnership you were, in a way, stuck - committed to Althorn no matter what. Something like a marriage."

"That's the nearest thing to it. It's been a constant weight on my mind but it's easy to forget it when the partnership has done so well."

"Yes... I saw some very dry details concerning Kirby's estate and his share of the partnership. Can you tell me how it's working out in practise?"

"Each of us has life insurance on every other partner..."

"Sorry for interrupting... is that, what, sixteen policies?"

"Yes, and there are other policies as well. We are all well-funded or will be when the policies pay out so that we can keep the partnership going or wind it up, as we choose."

"Got it."

"Now, as far as I know, Rena Mayo is the chief beneficiary under Kirby's will. The lawyer who's handling the estate's affairs has been in contact with us. He more or less told us that the estate wants to keep Althorn going and retain Rena's interest in it but is concerned with how the transition will be handled."

"Has anything been decided there? You don't have to tell me but it would be helpful if I could get some idea."

"It's no secret and I think you would find out anyway. We're looking to hire someone, perhaps more than one person, to take Kirby's place. That person would come in with the understanding that there would be an eventual partnership position if he or she should perform well."

"Would you all surrender a percentage to facilitate this?"

"We've kicked it around. Much of it depends on what Rena decides."

"This must affect you more than the others."

"It's introduced a delay but in a way it makes it easier. I know two or three people who could replace me and would consider taking over my portfolio. In both cases, Kirby's and mine, it's all about how the transition is handled. If we keep profits flowing to clients we'll have no problems... as long as the clients stay with us, that is."

"I think Will Hutchinson wants to be boss," said Brent. "My guess is he'll keep his percentage of the partnership intact and increase it, if he can."

"You've got that right. He's in for the long haul. We've talked about reorganization and what that would look like but it's too soon to make a move on it."

"Do you think you could get me an introduction to Rena?"

"I might. You're pretty sure of yourself."

"I have to be. Would you trust me if I had no confidence? I don't think so. Um, are you and I on first name terms, Nola? That's a nice name."

"It seems we are, Brent. Well, I can try with Rena. She's devastated, though. You might upset her."

"Possibly. The night Kirby was murdered I was speaking with someone I mistook for Rena. I helped her a little, I think. I'll be as tender as I can."

"I'll think about it. I have some things I need to do and we don't seem to have gone very far."

"Two more minutes, that's all I need. Now, about when you saw Kirby, I think there was something you didn't tell the police in either interview with them."

"I told them everything," said Nola.

"No, you didn't. You went to tell Kirby about your plan to leave. You sat through the discussion with the Valdezes and struck up a rapport with Zulema. After that, Rena entered Garland's unexpectedly. You were happy to see her but Kirby said he had another client meeting and that he would see her at home. You stated there was a misunderstanding but Rena accepted what he said and that he then saw her out to a taxi. You also left at about the same time. Is that a fair summary of what you told the police?"

"Yes."

"Then why did Kirby bully his wife?" said Brent. Nola stared back at him. Brent continued,

"More importantly, at present, why did you cover up that aspect of the incident?"

"To protect Rena. It's in the past now and I didn't think it mattered. I thought it should be her decision to say how their marriage was going and not mine."

"Fair enough. That's what I thought you would say. Now, here's the problem. The police do not know exactly the state of the Mayo marriage. It will come out eventually because someone will say what they know. How will your statements seem then?"

"Should I contact them?"

"I think so."

"How do you know all this?"

"A witness saw they were having a dispute at a critical moment and I, myself, saw Kirby herding Rena to the door."

"What else did you see?"

"Strange you should ask me that. You are on the defensive, now. It's because you did not leave the premises immediately, isn't it?"

"Yes. I got my coat from the cloakroom then I went into the hotel and sat in the lobby."

"Avoiding the security cameras."

"Did I? Are you sure? Do the police know this?" Nola was quite agitated.

"They do. They reviewed the CCTV footage and you seem to disappear. They can't find you exiting the building at any point. Was that deliberate or a coincidence?"

"Would you believe me?"

"It isn't a question of my simply believing you. As far as I'm concerned, there is only one murderer and many innocent people. I believe you to be innocent but you have to admit it would have been possible for you to have remained in the restaurant and then to have shot Kirby. If you tell me what happened, then I can fit everything into the greater scheme of things. It is not your job to convince me of anything. It's up to me to convince myself as to who is innocent and who is not."

"I swear to you, this is the truth. I was very disturbed by Kirby's treatment of Rena." Nola became very precise in her diction. "At that point, even after having got my coat to go home, I was so indignant and angry I sat down in the hotel lobby. Then, I saw him come back inside with a woman on one arm and another walking by his side. One of the women I recognized - it was Becki Kent, an Althorn investor partner of longstanding. I stayed to spy on them, outraged even further on Rena's behalf. I went back into the restaurant and sat at the little bar by the side and watched him."

She paused before becoming more intense as she continued to speak.

"It's fascinating to watch someone you know doing something so ugly and hard-hearted. It pulled me in. He had just got rid of his wife… can you believe that…? and now he's sitting with two women, laughing and joking as though nothing had happened and I wanted…" She stopped from saying more.

"To kill him, of course." Brent finished her sentence for her. "What coat were you wearing?"

"Oh... uh, I had a brown wool trench coat and an off-white silk scarf."

"Did you put them on?"

"Well, I had the scarf over my shoulders but I carried the coat until I left... That was just after one of the women... left his table. I went back to the lobby, preparing to leave. I'd so had enough by that time. Then I heard the shots and ran out to the street to escape."

"Which woman left the table before you left the restaurant?"

"It was Becki Kent." She went quiet before asking, "Doesn't look good, does it...? Where does it leave me?"

"A prime suspect. I'll do my best to get you out from under."

"You talk as though you believe me."

"Nola, you could have shot him and then thrown away the gun. The police will have a fairly strong case against you, if they think it through. You will have helped their case by concealing things."

"I couldn't say anything... I knew my behaviour looked really suspicious. As soon as I heard that Kirby was dead, I knew they would think I might have done it. But you don't think so, do you?"

For the first time, a note of desperation entered her voice. She looked very tired now. She needed someone to be on her side.

"I'm predisposed to believe you, Nola, and if you didn't kill him I'll make sure you're exonerated. If you did, well, that's another matter. Thank you for being honest. I wonder if you would do me a favour, apart from getting me an invitation to see Rena, that is?"

"Whatever, I'm barely keeping it together here."

"Your work can wait. Let's go back to your office. I saw you had some family photographs. I'd like you to tell me about them. Also, I would get to see that painting again. I keep thinking about it."

"What, are you serious?"

"Come on, Nola. I know I've got the job, so we're just wasting time here when we could be talking about the important things in life. After we've finished, I'll see Will."

"Hold on. Like, why do you believe I might be innocent? That is important for me, you know."

"Because you wanted me to investigate and brought it up to your partners. Can we go now?"

Chapter 10

Wednesday evening

"According to your statement, you went to see Kirby after leaving the office to discuss some short positions he had opened that involved more risk than you liked."

"Yes," replied Will. He and Brent were sitting in his office.

"Why go to the restaurant to see him? It's not on your way home. If anything, it would add nearly an hour to your journey. Surely, a simple phone call, email, or text message would have sufficed until you saw him the next day, would it not?"

"As I told the police, I thought a face-to-face conversation was best. Kirby could be difficult at times and markets can move quickly. I wanted him to reduce the risk as soon as possible."

"Did he?"

"No."

"What happened to those stocks?"

"Several trades closed the next morning with a healthy profit. The rest continued to close over the next week as the prices dropped lower. We closed out the last of the positions yesterday."

"His gamble paid off, then?"

"That isn't the point. If the price had gone against us, Althorn would have been in jeopardy."

"I understand that. You see, I read your statement to the police this way. You went to see Kirby and you were angry. You had nothing to eat or drink while you were at Garland's. It looks like you came in spoiling for a fight, you got one, and you left. Kirby's death changed the dynamics somewhat but, for some reason, you did not close out the positions the next day. Perhaps you forgot?"

"You're making it sound very awkward for me. He said something that made me think differently. When I reflected on it I changed my mind."

"What would that be?"

"He hinted that he had information… a bit of news that was not available to the market. He was a very aggravating man… he refused to tell me what he knew. He liked his games." His brows furrowed.

"I'm beginning to see that side of him," said Brent. "He must have been difficult to work with."

"No, I wouldn't say that. He was very professional in every respect but he could be quite manipulative on occasion."

"Even though you were partners, you would not say you were friends. Is that correct?"

"We only ever had a professional working relationship. I have no real complaint against him except that some of his trading patterns exceeded the guidelines established for the partnership."

"I can appreciate how disconcerting that could be. In simple terms, could you explain how the profits on trades are distributed?"

"Each trader is on a salary plus commission. Depending on experience, the trader will be expected to achieve quarterly targets. Additional commissions and bonuses are given to those who consistently exceed their expected targets. Underachievers are encouraged through mentoring, training, and education to improve themselves. Continuous improvement of skills is expected of all our traders."

"What about partner income?"

"Our individual accounts are credited by commissions on net profits from our own trading activities and by net profits from the entire partnership according to our percentage holdings. Extra amounts are added for special duties. For example, I receive an amount for setting up the insurance policies each year. Nola is paid for her oversight of the office administration. Blake receives an amount for training, and so on. We get a base draw each month and can draw down more as each quarterly net profit is finalized and distributed. Of course, that's after all client allocations have been recorded."

"Then the commissions on profits from Kirby's last trades are attributed to his estate?"

"Yes, that's true."

"How do you feel about the estate being involved in Althorn?"

"Well, it's to be expected. We were careful to structure everything in the eventuality of a partner's... exit...

You know, I spoke hastily earlier. I now think it a good idea that you investigate and I mean to help you all I can. We need to get past this point to make Althorn as profitable as it's ever been, if we can come to terms with Rena and if the murderer is identified.

I do hope Rena will not prove difficult. We can buy her out but only if she is willing. The worst part is that she has a right to take up an active role. She has no experience in trading and she could appoint her own traders to run Kirby's portfolio. That would be a disaster."

"You have time to work through that scenario to the benefit of all, surely?"

"A little." Will Hutchinson began moving in his chair. He was irritated again, the furrows returning between his eyes.

"Will, your situation in this murder case is not good - not the worst but there is a modest case that could be made against you. You could have returned unseen and shot Kirby. You could have hired someone to shoot him on your behalf. This is how the police will see it. They are looking for motive and opportunity. You can come up with many counter-arguments but they are only that - counter-arguments. I want to establish your innocence and say, 'It wasn't Will'."

Hutchinson's face blanched.

"You have to find an independent witness who can testify to seeing you somewhere else when the shooting took place. Where would that have been? The time of the shooting has been fixed at 10:38 p.m.. You saw him for about ten minutes between approximately eight-thirty and eight-forty."

"I, uh…"

"Let's take it slowly. Where did you go when you left the restaurant?"

"I went for a drink at a bar around the corner, in Cusane's Parlour."

"How long did you stay there, do you think?"

"I had two scotches. I spoke to the bartender."

"That's good. Do you know the bartender?"

"I've seen him before; I've been to that bar on the odd occasion but I don't know his name."

"I'll find that out."

"You'll check my story?"

"Yes. You had your two scotches. What do you think, half an hour… more… less?"

"About that. Then I went into the park. I watched the fountains and lights."

"They're beautiful, aren't they? I only got a glimpse of them earlier that night. I really should go back… Oh, I'm sorry. A train of thought left the station. Was it raining when you were there?"

"Slightly. I had an umbrella."

"Good. I'm sure you were wearing a nice suit like you are now. Did you see the whole light sequence?"

"No… five minutes, ten at most. I walked about for a while after that."

"Very good. What happened next?" Will did not respond or look like he was going to. He writhed a little in his chair. Brent continued. "I've got you at about nine-thirty or so leaving the park."

"I went to see someone."

"Very good. Did you speak to that person?"

"Only for a moment. They were busy."

"What time was that?"

"I couldn't say. I forget."

"How long to walk from the park to this person's place?"

"Twenty minutes."

"That's about nine-fifty to ten o'clock. You can speed this up now, Will."

"You understand, don't you?" asked Will.

"Yes, I do. As I said, I'm meaning to establish your innocence and that's all."

"I went for a long walk and then I got a taxi home. I arrived about eleven."

"You have no alibi. That does not make you guilty. The person whose identity you wish to keep private may be visited by the police in any event."

"That can't happen. It doesn't cover the critical period anyway."

"It doesn't. Do you take prescription drugs for, let us say, mood disorders?"

"Several."

"You are a very cautious person. Is that everything?"

"Yes."

"You have a wife and three children. Any grandchildren?"

"Not yet."

"My choice would be family over everything else. I've never had a family. If I did, I would give my life for them. I would certainly give up fleeting forgetfulness for their sakes."

"I live my life as I choose. It's not your place to critique me."

"I'm entitled to my own opinions on my own life choices, I think. You do as you please. It's not my concern. What does concern both of us is that a case can be made against you. The charge would be murder. Premeditation could be established if there is anything that links you to a weapon, 10:38 p.m. in the restaurant, or a subsequent benefit. The last is already present in the form of an insurance policy."

"This is absurd."

"It is. Run through the facts. I know you have an analytical mind. Imagine your alibi was that of another person. Would you believe it?"

Will shook his head. "Do you believe me?"

"I can't give you any comfort. If you gave me the name of the individual you saw it might make a difference to me.

It is insufficient for the police but it makes your non-alibi status more understandable to me. You've had a scene with Kirby. It didn't go well. You're angry and want to walk and drink it off. Eventually, you get the idea to seek someone out for some comfort. This is not possible. You continue walking and then go home. You have mentioned that you had two interactions with others to substantiate this narrative. Neither are for the right time. If you remember someone else, such as a cab driver, or any person that can be traced to a location and a time, your story can be propped up sufficiently to sound convincing."

"What should I do?"

"Get a lawyer. The first thing he or she will say is that you should not speak to me."

"Are you going to the police with this?"

"Not yet. My investigation has barely got started. Lots to think about, eh, Will?"

"Do you believe me?"

"Superficially, I do. I will dig a little and see what I can find that might make a difference one way or another. I have to leave now. I'll meet with Sohil and Blake tomorrow. Hopefully, I'll see an employee or two as well. I also have a lot to do elsewhere. Thank you for telling me - it probably wasn't easy for you."

Brent stood up and looked out of the window. "Look at that, it's getting dark so early now and the clock hasn't even gone back yet. Shouldn't be allowed, should it? Goodnight."

Chapter 11

Early Wednesday night

When Brent approached the entrance to Garland's, he encountered two doormen. One was the man who had worked the previous week. The second, dressed in a dark suit rather than the livery the doorman wore, was so obviously the extra security that Garland's felt it needed to send the right message to its patrons. He was a big, heavy-set, muscular man who sized up the visitors to the restaurant in a detached, routine way. Garland's had lost a little of its distinctive cachet on its own doorstep because the two men viewed together gave the impression of bouncers monitoring a nightclub doorway. They also wore visible ID - another new initiative.

"I was here last week, Tom. A horrible business." Brent spoke to the original doorman.

"It is, sir. Our top priority now is security. You might notice additional features inside which, we trust, will not detract from your dining experience. Thank you for coming."

"Thank you," said Brent.

He had hoped to talk to Tom but it was clearly not possible at present. Tom had smiled naturally last week. This week he did not.

Immediately inside the door, Brent was required to walk through a metal detector. Two more security guards, one female and one male, selected for their clean-cut looks and politeness as well as their professional skills, held security scanners. Brent, being a single man, was given a very careful scan by the male operative. Next, he was greeted by the host.

"Good evening, sir," said the host as she smiled brightly at Brent. "Do you have a reservation?"

"I do. The name's Brent Umber and it's a table for one."

"Yes. A corner table, as you requested." She tapped the screen in front of her and, picking up a menu, said courteously, "This way, please."

Garland's was trying for a business-as-usual atmosphere only it was missing its objective. It was as if a Garland's place-setting now consisted of silver cutlery, fine china, crystal glass, and a taser. The security was a reminder of what had gone wrong.

Tanya waited on Brent. She seemed to be in her mid-twenties and had already brought him an aperitif.

"Were you here last week?" he asked.

"Yes."

"Then you will have spoken to the police?"

"I'm very sorry, sir. We have been asked not to discuss the event of last week."

"Well, of course. I can understand that. I'm only interested in your impressions and what happened afterwards. Would this help?" With his index finger, he slowly pushed across the linen cloth a folded bill with '100' visible.

"It definitely would." She put a plate on top of it. "I don't see how it can be done, though. We're not supposed to interact with the customers." Her voice dropped to a whisper as she mouthed the words, "The manager sees everything."

"Oh, that's a problem. Take the money and we'll think of a way that you're comfortable with."

When Tanya had gone, Brent looked over the whole of the room from his vantage point. The tables had been rearranged into a diamond pattern whereas before they had been more or less laid out as a grid. There were a few more empty tables and even fewer occupied seats but the restaurant's business was not too badly affected.

Even with the different layout, Brent tried to visualize and test the crime scene and sequence of events from where he sat. It became apparent to him that although the sight lines were different, two intervening tables effectively obscured what was happening three tables away. Even with one intervening table, it depended on how many were seated at it as to the possibility of a clear view of the table beyond.

The killer had sat at right angles to Kirby. It was not known if this person had turned, aimed the revolver normally, and fired, or had sat still, had the pistol between torso and arm, aimed it in whatever way could be managed, and then taken the shot. The latter method made hitting Kirby very uncertain but it did allow the shooter to remain unobtrusive, if not to say hidden, while in a wide open area.

Brent turned it over in his mind. A straight shot suggested a desperate person who could have acted spontaneously. A hidden shot would need to be practised first to decide what clothes should be worn and how to maintain the angle of the weapon for multiple shots. These were the shots of premeditation and required some level of proficiency.

While he waited for his food to arrive, Brent took out his own rough drawing of the table layout on the night of the murder. The tables were now staggered rather than in straight lines. He counted sixteen positions around the shooter's table where those seated could have seen the killer's front, sides, or back at the time of the shooting. Of these, ten had a good or direct view while the other six only had a possibility of an unobstructed view because of the angle. The police had worked on this carefully and concluded that twelve of the chairs had been occupied at the time.

The two tables best situated to see the killer was the one the Warners had occupied and another where Galen Nash and party were discussing the production of their new series. Filming had already begun on it the Monday after the murder.

Brent considered the two parties. He envisaged both tables and how they might have been behaving at the time. The Warners would have been quiet with desultory talking unless a subject came up that engaged all of them in discussion. The Warners were more likely to see the shooter as gaps in discussion would allow attention to wander. Of the four, Caroline, the mother, and Steven, the son, would have had a clear view while the other two would not.

The Nash party was more likely to be having intense, animated discussions. It was easy to imagine that three actors and a producer would provide enough clever conversation and amusing anecdotes while discussing their art for several nights at Garland's. Perhaps, though, on second thoughts, that might not be at all true. It could have been that Galen was dictatorial and the actors were being instructed and were only required to speak in turn and from time to time. Still, no one would let their attention wander too far from the table as their dinner was a business meeting.

"Your salad, sir." Tanya returned and called Brent's attention away from his diagram.

"Thanks. Had any ideas?"

"No, it's too difficult while I'm working. Here's your money back."

"Uh uh. You keep it for the moment. There is always after work. I have a few things I need to do so I can wait."

"Um, this is really awkward…"

"I get it. You choose a place, bring a friend if you need to. I'm a private investigator and I'm just looking for some information. Here's my card. You think about it. We'll talk only if you're comfortable."

"What about the money?"

"Keep it for now, as I said. I think you can find a way round this difficulty."

"Okay. I'll let you know."

Several ideas went back and forth between them but it was between dessert and coffee that a deal was struck. They would meet in Cusane's Parlour which was around the corner. This was the bar that Will Hutchinson had said he had visited. Tanya would join a small group of fellow employees going there at midnight and Brent would find her with them, as if purely by chance, of course.

Some other Garland's staff proved to be less wary than Tanya. Brent managed to elicit that the two bar staff in the restaurant knew nothing and saw nothing the night of the murder. When the shots were fired they dropped to the floor and stayed there. No person stood out as suspicious. Nola Devon's story was confirmed as far as it went. She had sat at the bar when she said she had. Nola had been wearing her scarf across her shoulders and it proved to be a useful identifier.

He also had an even better result with the cloakroom attendant, Timothy, who was blessed with an elaborate memory and who proved to be very communicative.

"That's very kind of you, sir." The man in his early sixties pocketed the bill almost as soon as he saw it. He adopted a highly confidential air and said, in a low voice, to Brent, "I'll take a break now. Just go down the side passage and I'll join you in a moment." He turned to the woman who helped fulfil the offices of the cloakroom and, speaking in a normal voice, said, "I'll be back in ten."

Once in the carpeted passageway he said to Brent, "This way, sir. I've got to have a smoke, you see. As I said, that new girl only started this week. It was Dinah who was with me last week, but, ah, she's not exactly an observant person."

They went through a door at the end of the passage that led into a long corridor which had a painted cement floor, harsh strip lighting, and was the connecting passage to numerous small rooms bearing arcane numbers in Roman numerals or, blatantly obvious words like Elevators, Laundry, and Telephone. A door at a right-angled turn led outside and the two men went through it.

Outside, a path leading away from the door was confined between two soaring blank walls, six feet apart. One wall belonged to the hotel and the other was the side of the building next door. Where the men stood was a slightly enlarged space. Over the door they had just passed through was a metal overhang that had to be sixty years old at least.

"This is the best spot in the city for a quiet smoke. Hardly any rain gets in. Never gets too hot and the wind doesn't bother you. Nice and quiet, like I said."

Brent was looking at some ancient graffiti as Timothy lit a cigarette. "How many times do you come out here in a shift?"

"Three times, that's all. The night managers turn a blind eye to it. A few of the others come here so they know where to find us if we're needed.

You're interested in that there murder. Nothing like that has ever happened here before. A man was killed in his room in the nineteen-thirties. He was a mobster so that doesn't really count. But a paying customer in the middle of dinner? Whoo, that's bad."

"I'd like to find out what you saw that night. Not everything, only the unusual events that caught your attention."

"I told the police it was a regular shift for me and quite uneventful until the shooting started. I've been thinking it over. That was a mild evening so some people weren't wearing coats. Usually, it's a coat per person when the weather's bad. That keeps us very busy but it comes in waves. Hang a coat, give the receipt, and there's another customer standing in front of you, wanting in or out. Hardly have time to breathe.

It's like this. I've been doing this job for so long I could do it in my sleep. I divide the customers, in my mind of course, into little groups. There's the ordinaries. They just want to drop off or pick up. There's the talkers and they've got a lot to say. Directions to this… what time that…? can I ask you something…? and on it goes. I like them. They make the job interesting because I like helping people. Then there are the time wasters, selfish people… I have words for them but they don't bear repeating. There's always one every shift who's complaining about this or that. What for? Doesn't change anything. That night there weren't any and that was nice."

"Then everything was quiet and unexceptional?"

"It was, it was. A steady flow - busy, but no surges the whole night. When it's quiet like that, I don't have so much to think about so I take to noticing more. What I notice is people. I look and say to myself, there's someone who should check their coat but maybe they're not staying long so there's no point. What are they up to?"

"Did you serve a woman about ten o'clock?"

"We were both on and, let me see, I handed out a white faux fur - nothing special. She was suburban. Dinah who was on that night, she had a brown woollen with a white scarf, both very good quality. I couldn't tell you the time but the brown woollen didn't put her coat on and went back into the restaurant.

"Did you see her again?" asked Brent.

"I did. She went into the lobby. I don't recall seeing her after that."

"Is there anyone you specifically saw after ten o'clock."

"Male or female? Because there was a man, wet through on account of the rain. He had no coat so I thought, car's broken down most likely. Then I got busy and didn't see where he went. Oh yes. There were two women in grey trench-coats but they weren't together... came in two minutes apart. One lady was standing by a pillar and I thought, oh, I hope you don't stand next to each other, because their coats were so similar, you see, and I know how people hate that, especially the ladies. Neither of them checked in their garments."

A waiter came out of the door for a smoke and said,

"Hey, Timothy. How's it going?" He nodded to Brent.

"Very well. Quite a busy night, considering," said Timothy.

"It's okay. I reckon we'll be back to normal in a month," said the waiter.

"You think so? It's my belief the security guards are putting people off from coming in. It could take much longer than a month."

"Hope you're wrong about that. We've got the holiday season coming up." He sounded gloomy.

"I'll go," said Brent. "You've been very helpful…"

"I've finished here so I'll walk back with you. It's getting chilly out now, isn't it?"

They walked back together but, despite Timothy's incessant speech, Brent learned nothing else that was of use to him.

He sat in the lobby and considered the introduction into the narrative of a wet, coatless man and two women in near identical trench-coats. He had not seen them mentioned in the file Greg had left with him but then it did not include the detailed witness statements, either.

Chapter 12

Late Wednesday night

Cusane's Parlour was a large Irish bar and grill establishment. It revelled in all things Irish although the owner, Brent learned, was a second generation Polish man. The barman's name, though, was Pete Flynn and his grandparents still lived in Dublin. He and Brent chatted amiably beneath a sign of white Gaelic script painted on green that read Éirinn go Brách, which means Ireland Forever. He told Brent he remembered Will Hutchinson, though he had not known his name, because he was the man drinking Scotch whisky, by himself, in an Irish pub when he should have been drinking Irish whiskey or, in Gaelic - uisce beatha - water of life.

The occupants of the bar were quite varied by type but unified in purpose - to talk, laugh, and enjoy themselves. It being late Wednesday night, the place was only half full. Brent surmised that a quiet group of five were evidently employees gathering together after their late shifts had finished. They proved to be from Shepherd's or Garland's because he saw Tanya come in and join them while he was sitting in a booth. When she looked round, Brent waved to her and she came over.

"Thanks for coming," said Brent, as he stood while she settled herself. "Is there anything I can get you?"

"Um, you're having Guinness. I'll have one, too, thanks."

Brent went to the bar. When he returned, it struck him as funny that he was now serving his waiter.

"Will that be all, Madam?" he asked.

Tanya smiled uncertainly and Brent slid onto the booth bench opposite her.

"You don't mind talking about last week?" he asked.

"No. I think it helps me. I'm not too bad, like thinking it will happen again or anything. It's better to talk it out and get it done." She took a careful sip of her drink so that the creamy froth did not stick to her lip.

"How was your shift tonight?"

"Could have been busier… I like to be busy and it's not just for the tips."

"You mean the fifteen per cent service charge?"

"You don't get so much from that because all the staff share in it. It's the extra ones. You can't count on them but they're decent when you get them. Something I wanted to ask you. You're a private eye, how can you manage to eat at Garland's? Does it pay that well?"

"No. Without going into a long explanation, I'll only say that investigation is also a bit of a hobby with me."

"Oh, I see." She was quiet and it was clear to Brent that she was trying to pigeonhole him in her mind.

"Were you looking after the section of tables where Kirby Mayo was sitting?"

"No, that was Felicity."

"Perhaps you can introduce me to her?"

"I can't do that. She's really bad and hasn't been to work since. We think she has PTSD."

"Oh, I'm sorry to hear that. I'll not trouble her, then, since the police have her statement already. Perhaps you can help me understand the seating arrangements." Brent took out his grid-style diagram, unfolded and turned it right way up for Tanya to look at. "It's looking scruffy now so excuse the notes and arrows. I was sitting about here tonight. This is the table where the victim was. It's funny, despite the subsequent rearrangement, that table is in more or less the same position. Here's a pencil. Mark the tables you had with a T and those Felicity had with an F."

"Okay. Oh, I've still got my hair up." She removed a clip, let her hair down, and bent over the diagram. She took the mechanical pencil and quickly filled in the letters. Brent noticed her very dark, curly hair had golden-brown highlights.

"There." She lifted her head, smiled and handed the diagram back to him.

"Let's see. Oh, you were some distance away. Who had the section with this table in it?"

"That one? That was Ted's. What's interesting about that table? Was it where the killer sat?"

"That's what the police say. Any chance you noticed someone there."

"I wish I had but I didn't. My job is to remain focused on my own section and nothing else. Naturally, I see some things going on around me but I would say it's mostly what the other servers are doing that I notice. Job's a bit competitive in some ways. You always want your own section to do better than the other sections.

Anyway, I said all that because Ted is the kind of guy that if everyone has a lousy night, he didn't. If you got a big tip, he got a bigger one. You get a local celebrity, he gets an international celebrity. He's that kind of guy. I'm not jealous - it's just a fact. So, I kind of keep an eye on him. I looked over just before the shots were fired. I didn't see him and, honestly, I didn't notice anything strange. It all looked normal."

"People like Ted occur in all walks of life. Your manager, Domenic, he doesn't encourage rivalry, then?"

"No, not at all. He emphasizes team-work and that's how we're trained."

"How long have you been working at Garland's?"

"Nearly two years. I like it. I'm permanent part-time and work three shifts a week. If I need to, I can usually get another shift. Domenic's pretty good about that although it's Josie who works out the schedules. She goes insane if people mess with them once they're done."

"Ha, I can just picture that." Brent was tempted to ask a little more about Tanya herself but realized he should keep to his mission.

"When the shots were fired, where were you?"

At that moment, the Irish-themed music that had been playing unobtrusively in the background was cranked noticeably louder, causing Brent to turn and look. Pete was smiling and then began singing. He was joined by a loud, boisterous chorus of ten, congregated around two small tables pushed together. Unfamiliar with the song, Brent turned back smiling to find Tanya singing quietly along. She sang in tune. It appeared that half the bar knew the song and had joined in. Brent did not know the Irish tune or the words but suddenly wished he did.

After it had finished, other singalongs were played but it was only the party of ten who knew them so they were singing much more quietly to themselves.

"Are you Irish?" asked Brent.

"No. That first one is a favourite here and I've learned the words because everyone else seems to know it. It's a lovely song."

"It is very lovely." Brent thought to ditch the investigation and just talk to Tanya instead.

"I'm sorry…"

"Oh, yes! When the shots were fired I, uh, I know this sounds ridiculous, but I was carrying a Piña Colada on a tray to a customer and so I knelt down slowly so as not to spill any. I can't believe I was so stupid!"

"My goodness, what dedication you have. You would deliver a drink through flying bullets? I think you should receive a medal for courage. Does Domenic know about this?"

"No. I've only told you because I feel such an idiot for doing it."

Brent was silent. He had two things cross his mind from opposite directions and collide somewhere in the middle. The first made him angry. Innocent people were in fear for their lives because a psychopath took to shooting in a public place. As he was dealing with that and doubling his resolve to find the killer, the second thought hit him. It had a different effect. Tanya trusted him beyond his payment for information about what she saw and what she knew. She had told him something she was embarrassed about. Brent believed he knew what that meant. Once again, he wished he was far removed from the case. He thought he had better get on or he might become tongue-tied.

"I think that says a lot about you and all of it good. But, um, while you took cover, did you notice anything around you? I'll rephrase that, what did you notice?"

"My heart was pounding. The shots were over so quickly that I thought it might be safe to look and see if there was anyone coming towards me. I had a quick look and then got my head down again. Someone was whimpering and complaining but most of the people were quiet. I could see one of my customers; she's a very nice lady and she looked terrified. I was, too, so I thought to wave to her and she waved back. Then, after what seemed an age, someone started shouting. I couldn't take it in at first so I peeked over the top of the table again... oh, that was you, wasn't it? I knew you looked familiar but I couldn't place where I'd seen you before. You were wearing a blue suit."

"That's right. Ah, when you looked over the table when the shots had just been fired, did you see anything... anyone?"

"There was someone moving; I noticed the movement out of the corner of my eye. I didn't see anyone, exactly. It was more like I was aware of someone being there."

"Please show me where you were on the diagram." He produced the document again.

"I was here in my section and the table was between me and where the shots came from, which I think was about... here." She put her finger on the place. "Wow, that's not exactly where the killer's table is. Oh well, perhaps I'm wrong about that. But I did see someone around this area... moving away from...well, from the crime scene."

"Here, mark the place and the rough direction you think he or she travelled." Brent offered his mechanical pencil to her. She took it and filled in the details.

"This is such a nice pencil," said Tanya.

"Keep it," said Brent.

"But it's your pencil and it's expensive."

"I hardly use it." It was his favourite.

"That's very nice of you. I accept." She looked pleased and clicked the pencil a few times while staring at the lead.

"I think I have intruded on your personal time way beyond our original deal. I think I should..."

"No, Brent. Like everyone, I could do with extra cash but not for what I know about this murder. It's too important, it really is. I feel I need to do something personally about it, no matter how small my contribution. Talking this through helps me and, if I can help you in anyway, it will mean a lot to me."

"Very nicely said. Okay, so the phantom was just behind a table of actors and such..."

"See what I mean? In Ted's section, of course."

"And you only get a lowly private eye."

"I didn't mean it like that. Besides, you hardly look lowly. Look how you're dressed. I pointed you out to a friend and she said, 'Don't let Marty see you with him, he'd be so jealous.'"

"Marty is your boyfriend, I take it?" Brent felt himself deflate.

"Yes. I've completely forgotten to text him."

"Yes, do that. If I were him, I would be anxious to hear from you."

While Tanya sent a text, Brent looked at the diagram again. The phantom's exit direction could have been through the kitchen doors or into the hotel lobby. There was no saying which. He also wondered if the killer had remained in the room.

The evening ended. Tanya went home in a cab which Brent insisted he pay for. Eventually, she had accepted. Brent also went home. He was glad he had so much yet to do because he found he really needed to keep busy just now. Even while he was trying to forget Tanya, he was remembering another woman in a more intense way than he ever had before.

Chapter 13

Thursday

*B*rent got up after four hours' sleep. It was 6:30 a.m. and raining. Not exactly feeling fresh, he was, at least, focused again. Flat yet focused. He worked on a list of things to do and people he had to interview. That evening he would be back at Garland's with the tasks of getting into the kitchen and of interviewing Domenic, the manager.

As he drank his coffee, Brent realized that he had nearly lost his objectivity in the case. Had Tanya been unencumbered by a boyfriend, whose wretched name was Marty, he would have sat in her section again to pick up wherever they had left off; whereas, from a professional standpoint, he needed to be in Ted's area to gather new information. As soon as he could, he would book a table. The trouble was, the tables were all for four or six in Ted's section. Brent was now so familiar with the seating arrangements at Garland's that he could get a job as a host. A table of four… who to invite? Anyone but Georgina and that crowd. He'd work on it and think of someone.

While he was thinking, another woman came to mind and it was not Tanya or Linda, and he lost nearly an hour thinking about her. It was not the first time this had happened in the past week and neither would it be the last time.

His list of interviewees began with Dan Lindsay, the ex-Ranger, and his wife Eileen. Ex-military - he guessed they would be early risers so he would see them first, if possible. The Valdezes had some interesting comments logged against their name in Greg's reports. Sylvester had a criminal record but most of it old and none of a serious nature. Petty things.

As Brent knew, the man had the sort of reputation that got linked to many crimes but he was never brought to book for any of them. A little bit like himself, Brent thought. Also, he had done some work way back when for Sylvester. He doubted he would remember him. The Valdezes lived further out, on the fringes of the city in a new sub-division. He would see them after the Lindsays.

Becki Kent and Gabbie Wright lived close by each other in the same exclusive neighbourhood. If they were not out of town he would need to see each of them separately. He put them down for Saturday, knowing he had to spend the best part of tomorrow, Friday, at Althorn because that office would not be open at the weekend. He intended to see as many employees there as he could, as well as to interview the two partners, Sohil and Blake.

I have to maintain the pressure on Will Hutchinson to get that withheld name from him. Why does that seem so important...? Perhaps I just want to annoy Will. Then there is Nola herself and, more vital at the moment, her getting me an interview with Rena. That will be one tough interview to do.

Galen Nash. Nash, Nash, Nash - how to fit that group in? Some or all of them could be more resistant to seeing me than most. There again, they will be filming on location on Monday. I suppose I will have to crash the set somehow. Surely one of them saw the murderer? Marianne Stark… I can't remember if I've ever seen her but I know the name. I've never heard of Bryana McDowell and Cooper Fisher. Should be interesting. I can't really see them as suspects. Neither does Greg. I should talk to him today but I need to have something for him. I haven't got very far yet.

The Warner family? Ma and Pa will not return from Chile until Sunday. Should be no difficulties about seeing them or Melanie and Steven and that all could be left until next week. Who else to see? Oh, yes, Domenic at Garland's.

How to see Domenic and get him to talk? What reason would induce him to answer questions? That could be very difficult. And who was the guy in the rain-soaked clothes? Greg Darrow might know. Vane! Oh, my dear Vane. I promised to take you to lunch!

Brent was annoyed with himself because he had given his word to Vane to take her out and make a friendly fuss of her new wardrobe. He also had said he would get work for her and he had not. Brent had been looking forward to their lunch together, too. He was about to pour another coffee when a thought, a beautiful, luminous thought came to him. Several perplexing strands came together into a manageable whole. It put a smile on his face.

He sent off a text to Vane, saying, 'Get back to me asap - like immediately! I have work for you and two skater friends with smarts. Good money and interesting stuff - clear your schedules.'

Brent saw the overnight text message from Linda Roberts - "Hi. When shall we meet this weekend? Luv u."

Brent replied, "Sorry Linda. Busy until end of next week at least with important investigation. I might be out of town. We'll talk when I get back."

He was so happy to be solving problems and putting distance between himself and Linda. He felt he had to harness some of the sudden burst of energy and renewed interest in life that had descended upon him. Brent had a short, intense work-out with free weights. He even went downstairs into the garage-section of the old machine shop that was his city pied-à-terre to scale the rock-climbing wall he had installed - something he had not done in a little while. He used the wall to keep his climbing skills honed in case he had to break in through an upper story window.

"Come in, Brent," said Dan Lindsay. Brent had called ahead and the Lindsays had said they would be happy to see him.

"Thanks. Sorry it was on such short notice but I thought, hey, you're a military guy, you're probably up for anything at any time."

The inspiration for Brent to say this was the Lindsay's small bungalow which was so extraordinarily neat and well-maintained and the small front garden which was already being prepared for the coming winter. An inspection by anyone, military or otherwise, would find nothing to fault.

"No problem," said Dan, with a smile.

Brent was invited to sit down in the living room. He sat down and put his bag next to the armchair from which position he could easily see Eileen moving about in the kitchen. Dan sat opposite him on the couch. Between them was a low coffee table with a top of rich, dark, figured wood.

"Hi, Brent," Eileen called out. "I'm making coffee. Would you like some?" She sounded bright and cheerful with a warmth to her raised voice.

"If it's no trouble, thanks," said Brent.

"How do you take it?" asked Eileen.

"Black, one sugar, please."

"Mine's the same," called out Dan.

"You don't have to tell me. Hey, Brent, if he cuts himself, he bleeds coffee."

Dan smiled and gave a short shrug. It was a relaxed and familiar gesture. He spoke in a low voice, "She's worse than I am."

"I know you said something," called Eileen. "Don't believe a word he says. And don't you guys start talking until I'm there."

Brent had hardly needed to read the police summary that stated they were both ex-military, in their fifties, both sergeants, and both decorated for bravery during tours in Iraq and Afghanistan. He was taciturn and she was forthright. Both were friendly and relaxed and looked fit and well.

Eileen came in with a tray, carrying the coffees, some plates, and a heaped basket of muffins. She put out coasters on the table and set the mugs down on them.

"Help yourself to a muffin. There's blueberry, carrot and walnut. I baked them this morning."

"Go ahead, Brent," urged Dan. "They're really good."

"I'll have a blueberry, I think." Brent put one on a side plate. He sat forward in the armchair. Dan and Eileen sat close to each other on the couch. He got the impression that if he was not present they would be cuddling. Eileen kicked her slippers off and tucked her legs up on the couch.

"Good coffee," said Brent, after carefully sipping the very hot beverage.

"Yeah, Eileen has it down to a fine art." Dan took a sip also.

"I know I was a bit vague on the phone," said Brent. "The reason for my visit is in connection with the murder."

"We thought it would be," said Eileen.

"I'm looking into the case. I normally do private investigation work and I've worked with the police in the past but I do not have any authority in this particular matter. I'm acting as a private citizen on my own account and not for anyone else. I do have a well-placed connection in the police department who is not entirely unaware of what I'm doing. I will be discussing my findings with that person."

"Okay," said Dan who nodded. "I get you." He looked at Eileen.

"Why are you investigating the murder?" asked Eileen.

"I had a friend who was murdered some years back. The police could not get evidence enough to have a clear suspect, let alone bring anyone to trial. I took it up and I found out who did it but I could find no solid evidence, either. I became a professional investigator after that. I'm telling you this because my friend's case ignited a passion in me and it changed me. I learned the skills I needed and I know in the Mayo murder I can put them to good use. I was there as a witness and I feel personally involved."

"I can see that," said Eileen.

"So, you ask questions, we answer them, and if there's anything useful you give it to the police?" said Dan.

"Yes, that's it exactly."

"Isn't that duplicating the police work?" asked Eileen. "We saw Lieutenant Darrow on the night. Then Detective Schroeder came round yesterday. We told them the same things because that's what we saw."

"That's part of their work, particularly when the case has slowed down which this one has. They go back and check and recheck statements, looking for variances. A witness might remember something differently or add a new fact. A suspect might stumble over a lie."

"Are we suspects?" asked Dan.

"No more than anyone else is. Less so, for some reasons. You see, the police are at the stage where there are about forty names known to them who they cannot rule out as possibles. You are on that list but let me reassure you that there are a good few individuals who have some, let's say, peculiarities in their behaviour that night. You are not on that shorter list."

"Makes sense," said Dan. "What do you want from us?"

"I'll not go over the ground the detectives have. That's their job. I want to know if you saw anyone or anything unusual while you were in the restaurant. If you don't mind my asking, why were you at Garland's?"

"It was the anniversary of the day we first met," said Eileen. "We always go somewhere special to celebrate."

"That's nice," said Brent. "I'm sorry your special occasion ended the way it did."

"What we don't understand is why someone would choose the middle of a busy restaurant. Did they want to get caught?" said Eileen.

"That's what one would think. It's turned out that they were either very lucky or very clever because no one saw the shooter. At least, no one knows they saw the shooter but someone must have. Perhaps many people did."

"You're looking for odd behaviour," said Dan. "The shooter would want eyes on the target for some time before taking the shot. There would have to have been an exit plan."

"Probably several," said Eileen, "if he was at all professional."

"How were the shots grouped?" asked Dan.

"The first wounded Kirby Mayo, the second killed him, and the third missed but travelled low, ricocheted off a pillar before hitting a wall. A .38 calibre snub nose revolver was used. The police reconstruction has it that if a target was set up in the place of the victim there would have been a twelve to eighteen inch grouping. The first two being about six inches apart with the third being the outlier."

"From what distance?" asked Eileen.

"Eighteen to twenty feet. You should know that there are two theories as to how the shots were taken. Like this... aiming directly, or... like this... hiding the shot."

"That's like a movie scene," said Dan.

"Nobody in their right mind would take aim and hope they wouldn't be seen," said Eileen. "It has to be the covered position. Is there a name for that?" She looked to Dan.

"Yeah, you just christened it."

She slapped his shoulder playfully and smiled.

"See, Brent," continued Dan, "to me, it looks like this person knew what they were doing and had some skills. That's a pretty good grouping for a trick shot, under pressure, while trying to remain concealed. You'd have to have eyes everywhere or someone to spot for you."

"What do you mean spot?" asked Eileen.

"Think about it," replied Dan. "Let's assume it was a professional job. The shooter has to stay focused on the target. He can't be watching all around himself, waiting for the moment when there's no one nearby or looking at him, and then line up the target. There's no way that would work. Now, If there was a lookout - a buddy on a radio - at the right time he or she says, 'take the shot', then the shooter, who's ready, can take it with a good chance of not being seen. One thing I don't get is why choose a revolver? An automatic with a silencer would be my choice but then, that's harder to conceal."

"Yes, it would stick out too far," said Eileen.

"The police say a revolver was used so that no shell casings would be left behind," said Brent. "My theory on it is, I think it possible a revolver was chosen because everyone would hear the blast and dive for cover. That would give the killer a second or two... perhaps more, to start his getaway. As soon as he is a table or two away, anyone who sees the killer will believe it's a bystander heading for the exit. They might even have followed him thinking it's a good idea to get out immediately. In those first few seconds, no one knows if a mass murder has just begun. It's all confusing and chaotic."

"That sounds possible," said Eileen. "But it might have been a crank who just fired normally and got lucky."

"That's exactly right. The police are looking for two killers in the sense that the shooting positions require two different personalities."

"You found a weapon," asked Dan. "Was it the one used?"

"No. It was fully loaded. It was .38 calibre snub nose with all the numbers filed off. It dates to the early eighties. What you just said about a spotter has got me thinking. That is a definite possibility and it goes a long way to answering the question of how the killer managed to remain anonymous."

"This is interesting," said Eileen. "We didn't see anything. Our table was against a wall and we weren't oriented to see the... what do you call it? Crime scene?" Brent nodded. "Yeah, so I don't think we can help you there."

"We were talking when the shooting started and we naturally hit the deck immediately. Training kicked in." Eileen nodded in agreement with Dan's statement.

Brent took the first bite from his blueberry muffin. "Mmm, this is truly superb."

"You like it?" said Eileen who wore a gratified smile. "I never know how they're going to turn out."

"Brent, they always taste good even when she burns them."

"I do not burn them! It was just the once when I forgot to put the timer on. He won't ever let me forget it. Just ignore him and, please, have another one."

"I would like to but I had a good-sized breakfast."

"Then you must take a couple with you." She was out of her seat, in her slippers, and off to the kitchen in quick, economic movements. Eileen returned with a fresh paper bag. "Take what you want and as many as you like."

"Hey, not all of them!" protested Dan in mock horror.

"Silence, soldier. Ignore him. I can always make a fresh batch. It's my day off. I work part-time at a veterinarian's."

"That must be interesting," said Brent.

"I love it there. It's not like work; it's more like a social group for me."

"That reminds me," said Dan. "I should get going. I've a couple of jobs to finish up today."

"I'm sorry for keeping you. You should have said. We could have met when it was more convenient for you."

"No problem. I'm a self-employed carpenter. Construction mostly."

"He's so modest," said Eileen. "Just take a look at this coffee table. He made it all by hand."

Brent first examined the hand-rubbed wooden surface and then got down to look underneath. He spied some well crafted joinery - the mortise and tenon joints were as nearly precise as machine cut ones.

"You have some serious skills, Dan. And an eye for beauty."

"There you go," said Dan to Eileen. "He means you."

"Oh, do stop it," said Eileen with a smile that said he did not have to stop at all. "Just listen to him. See what I have to put up with? He spent ages on that table."

Brent smiled, too. Dan did not like direct praise; it embarrassed him. What Brent saw was a man at peace with himself and content in his marriage. Eileen was every bit his equal and counterpart. Perhaps she had taken a few rough edges off him. She had probably gone through her own changes. The two of them had grown closer and survived the rough parts together. That they loved each other was undeniable. They had exactly what Brent was looking for.

"I'll be going now," said Brent. He got up. "Thank you for your insights. If you do happen to remember anything new, here's my card so you can call me, although I think that's unlikely because you're both trained, astute observers in so many respects. It's been an absolute pleasure meeting both of you."

"Come by any time you like, Brent," said Eileen.

"Take care, man, and good luck," said Dan.

At about ten o'clock, Brent had to take a chance on the Valdezes being in. The phone number the police had in their records was no longer in service. Brent assumed that it was a deliberate move and not because of a shortage of money. He was made certain of his assumption when he drove up and parked his old Jeep in the street in front of the house. Theirs was the largest in a sub-division of large houses. Five new cars were parked on the forecourt of the four-car garage. The security camera system was a top of the line Falconview.

He rang the bell and heard a loud chime. Brent was surprised when the door was opened almost in the same second by Sylvester Valdez dressed in shorts and a t-shirt. He was eating an apple.

"Who are you?" He took a bite out of his apple. He looked beyond Brent to his old Jeep and then back again.

"My name's Brent Umber. I'm not a police detective. I'm investigating the murder at Garland's."

"So?"

"You were there that night and I was hoping you could spare me five minutes."

"I don't think so."

"You know you're a suspect."

"I know."

"I can clear your name."

Sylvester went quiet and chewed slowly.

"How would you do that?"

"I can get the police off your back by proving you're innocent."

"How much you want for this?"

"Nothing."

"Nothing! Ha, that's a good price. Let's see if I got this straight. You knock on my door when I'm busy. You're investigating a murder but you ain't police. You say you can clear my name when it don't need your help and you're doing it for free. You a nut?"

"Many people would say so. I know your reputation. I know who you are. I did some work for you once... a long time ago."

"That's what you say, huh? You say you know me, huh? I don't remember you."

"There once was a warehouse and it had very expensive luggage in it. Someone needed it moved but they didn't have a key. I may have been asked to help in that scenario; I don't really remember it to be honest."

"Ha, yes! I heard that old story and there was a skinny kid with a big attitude in it. Come in, Brent Umber, I remember you now."

Once inside in the massive hall, Sylvester directed Brent to the kitchen at the back while he started bellowing upstairs - his voice filling the air.

"Zuli! Come down! I want you to meet someone!"

"What!?" Her voice sounded quiet and distant.

"We have a guest!"

"Who is it!?"

"You'll see!"

The kitchen was huge and had every conceivable labour-saving device in it. What Brent liked about it was the rich blue and green patterned tiled floor and the appliances that had been custom painted in a blue to match.

"Sit at the island. Can I get you anything? You want breakfast?"

"I've eaten already, thanks, and I'm fine. I like your tiled floor - very effective."

"My brother-in-law imports tiling so I got it from him. Looks nice." Sylvester sat down opposite Brent on a high stool with a low back to it. "You filled out a bit since I saw you last. That was a funny night but let's wait for my wife, Zulema. We weren't married back then."

"Oh, hi. I thought you'd be in the front," said Zulema, as she entered the room. She was beautifully dressed in expensive clothes over which she had a long, gauzy garment in brilliant reds and blues that she could wear because of her dark complexion. She looked uncertain because Brent was in the kitchen.

"Zulema, this is Brent Umber."

Brent got up, went to her and shook hands. "I'm very pleased to meet you. My sincere apologies for dropping in unannounced. I did try calling."

"Nice to meet you." Zulema looked puzzled.

"I changed the phone number," said Sylvester, "to stop the cops bothering us. Zuli, I gotta tell you a story. Sit down, honey."

When the three were seated around the kitchen island, Sylvester took up the narrative.

"Do you remember my telling you the story of when I helped myself to some high-end luggage? Like Vuitton and those other brands?"

"I remember," said Zulema, "and I gotta nice Tumi from that upstairs. I don't remember the story, though. I don't think you told me it."

"What! I didn't tell you! Now, listen. It's a good one. Me and three other guys, we get to hear of this big shipment of the best quality luggage there is. We're led to believe that the warehouse, this long warehouse, is a piece of cake to get in and out of. We check it out on a Wednesday night and yes, there is nothing for us to worry about. So, about one in the morning on the Saturday, the four of us start driving in this big old truck. We're gonna back it up to the dock and load it to the roof. One of the guys is going to get us in - he's to deal with the alarm system and the locks. He says the system is easy, easy - he can do it blindfolded. We get there and what! They installed a new, state-of-the-art alarm system in the last two days. Our guy says he can't do it and doesn't know the system. He says we have to bail. Like, bail? That's all wrong.

The next morning I work the telephone to see if anyone's available. Nothing. No one. Finally, someone says a friend of a friend knows a new guy who might have the chops. I says, okay, get him for me. Long story short, one o'clock Sunday morning we're rolling again. Now, there's this mouthy kid, nineteen, and he's saying, "I'll get you in no problem, Mr. Valdez. It'll take me five minutes, Mr. Valdez." He tells me not to worry. Okay, I think, but shut up will you? He's the only one talking and we all had about enough so I tell him to be quiet. I think he's showing off and is going to make a mess of it and then I'll have to teach him a lesson.

Zuli, was I wrong. He does it in four minutes like he's the guy who installed the system. He even climbs up a tower like a monkey to get to a junction box. When he's finished, I tell him to go watch out the front while we're busy with the forklift. The warehouse is long with two driveways, one each side, so he has a hike.

Half an hour inside and we're all done and the truck is loaded to the top. Not one more piece could we get in it. Then this kid comes running back saying there's a private security guard doing the rounds in a car and it could come our way. I make a quick decision and say leave everything as it is and we go. So we left the doors open and only had time to switch the lights off. Just as we're about to scoot, we hear the car coming down the driveway. The kid gets out, points and says go. So we head out on the other driveway. Literally, Zuli, we're on opposite sides of the building. And the kid waits for the guards at the shipping doors and starts running around to lead them away from us."

"And you all got away?" asked Zuli.

"Not yet we didn't," continued Sylvester. "The guards have called the cops and a nearby cruiser is right on scene only two minutes later, can you believe it? We hear sirens in the distance and everything. They had to be searching the area. If we're on the road they'll pull us up for sure and that would be it for me.

Then right out of the dark the kid is on the cab step and he made us all jump. Like my heart is right in my mouth. He's pointing at something ahead. It's a narrow driveway between two buildings where all kinds of trucks like ours are parked. The kid is gasping for air because he's run all the way. We pull him in and he says go down the alley and cut the engine. I trust him and I do what he says.

Another long story short, the four of us spend the whole night there with the cops driving around looking for us. They gave up and we fell asleep. Four guys in a cramped cab all night keeping their heads down because of the cops? We don't smell so good when the church bell woke us up in the morning but we all got away.

Now, Zuli, guess who's the kid who kept your husband out of jail?"

"I don't know, Syl. Who is it?" Zulema knew very well what the answer was but she would never spoil her husband's story.

"This is him, sitting right here. Brent Umber, my friend."

After the story, they all talked about many things such as how Sylvester and Brent lost sight of each other and how they had both switched to legitimate or, mostly legitimate, businesses until they had brought themselves up to the present day.

Before they got to the discussion of the murder in the restaurant, Brent checked his phone and saw that Vane had responded by text message, saying, "Two smart dudes and one genius girl ready to roll. Call me." And, for once, there was no message from Linda.

Chapter 14

Later Thursday morning

"*T*he police have been to our house four times, Brent," said Zulema intensely, holding up four fingers before her face. "It's too much, too much. We did nothing." She waved her hand as though sweeping the police away.

Zulema had instantly accepted Brent as her friend after hearing Sylvester's story. Brent, on the other hand, had used his former acquaintance with Sylvester as his way in to get information. When he had heard his earlier escapade recounted he had cringed inside and wanted the blue and green tiled floor to turn into a sea and swallow him up. He was ashamed but he could not show it or mention it in front of the Valdezes.

"You see how they are upsetting my wife?" said Sylvester. "I cannot have this."

"It's difficult," said Brent. "They're obviously coming after you because of your past."

"I know, I know, but we're innocent in this murder." Sylvester rubbed his chin.

"Who interviewed you at Garland's?"

"A uniform, I don't remember the name. But they kept us so late," he said.

"His name was Rick Winton," said Zulema. "Then we saw Lieutenant Darrow - he only asked a couple of things…"

"I got so mad with him! Sorry, Zuli. Winton whatever had referred us to see a detective immediately. Everyone else is going home and we're kept waiting… Why do we have to stay?"

"It's your record," said Brent. "They fixed upon it and Darrow was backing his officers. That's what they do."

"Yes, yes… go ahead, Zuli."

"Thank you. So, finally we left. Next day, Detective Claire Knight came to the house. She was okay. On Sunday, it was Detective Schroeder. He asked a few questions. Then he calls back. Next day he comes and stays for a long time. Then he calls. Let me see, two more calls, the next day. Then Syl disconnects the phone. Then the detective is back. We haven't heard from him yet today."

"Brent," said Sylvester, jumping into the brief pause, "he keeps asking what is my business, what am I doing, you know? It's not about the murder. He's after me. Can you believe it?"

"I know someone who's on the case," said Brent. "I'll see what I can do, though I can't promise anything."

"That's nice. It will be a real help," said Zulema. "He came in the evening once, right at dinner time. It upset us all. I had to explain to the children and it was hard. They don't understand what's going on and we haven't told them about the murder. The detective is here and their dad is getting mad. What do I say to them?"

"I'm sorry to hear this." Brent paused to see if any more would be said on the matter. "Okay, I have a few questions but I'll just recap the night to see if I'm missing anything. The reason you went to Garland's is because you were thinking of investing at Althorn Capital. A conference call through a friend got you set up with Kirby Mayo. You managed to get a table and arrived a little after eight when you immediately ordered dinner. Later, but before nine, Sylvester approaches Mayo who is in conversation with someone. The purpose is just to let him know you have arrived and as soon as he's free you'd like to meet him. A little after nine, Mayo sends you a message asking you to join him which is delivered by a waiter. You go almost immediately and join the table where you find Mayo's associate, Nola Devon, already seated. Mayo gives his sales pitch, Ms. Devon adds some comments to it and then there's a Q and A session. This takes about thirty minutes. You were back at your own table at nine-fifty because that is when you ordered dessert. You remain at your table until shots are fired. Is that more or less everything?"

"Yes, we sat talking. It was a lovely evening," said Zulema.

"Did you decide to invest with Althorn?"

"No, we did not," said Sylvester. "That man, Mayo, he was all wrong for us. We found someone else."

"I see. In what way was he wrong, if you don't mind my asking?"

"Sylvester didn't like him. He says they would fight with one another over commissions."

"That's right. I'm a stubborn man, sometimes…"

"Oh, oh, oh," said Zulema.

"I admit it, yes… but I'm a lot better than I used to be."

"Used to be! Brent, I can tell you stories that you would not be-lieve."

"He doesn't want to hear about that. So what? I had a temper and would dig my heels in. Not any more."

"Only sometimes," said Zulema.

"Alright, you win. Sometimes! You see this Brent? You see what can happen to a man when he's married? He can't win."

"Are you married, Brent?" asked Zulema.

"No, I'm still looking for the right person."

"Shouldn't be hard for you," she said.

"It's that old car of yours. Buy a new one and the ladies will take notice."

"I'm planning to get a new car and perhaps one lady will be pleased with it. I'm keeping my old Jeep, though. Um, I have a plan of the seating arrangement at Garland's. Could you take a look at it and show me where you were exactly?"

Brent took a file out of his bag and showed them the diagram. They had been seated at a table for two on the opposite side of the restaurant to Brent.

"I suppose you didn't see anything when the shooting started, being so far away?"

"No," said Zulema. "We knew what to do and down we went. But it was over so quick."

"It's a weird hit. I mean, shoot someone in a restaurant like that? You're going to get caught. What do you think, Brent?"

"Same as you - it seems incredible that anyone would think it could be done and got away with. However, the fact remains that there are no obvious suspects. There are lots of people with motives, though, apparently."

"Do the police think we have a motive?" asked Zulema.

"Not that I can see. They're fishing at the moment."

"Yeah, and Schroeder wants to pin it on me."

"He won't, though. He's just an annoyance. Did either of you see any person who stood out for any reason? Like they shouldn't have been somewhere or they looked tense, behaved oddly?"

"No." Sylvester shook his head slowly as he thought.

"All the people looked nice, behaved nice. Wait, wait, there was that guy who looked a mess. He was all wet, like from the rain."

"I didn't see him."

"He was close to our table for a second and then turned and walked away. You must have seen him."

"No. I was only looking at you... the whole night."

"Yes, you were, you sweet boy. He's so romantic sometimes... sometimes."

"Ha...ai... ai..." Sylvester was laughing. "Hey, Brent, you're my witness here. I can't win."

The conversation wound down and no further information of importance came out. Brent left amid promises on all sides to keep in touch and with Brent repeating that he would do what he could about Detective Schroeder.

After Brent had gone, Zulema and Sylvester returned to the kitchen.

"He seems very nice. Very polite... listens well. I can't understand why he's not married."

"Who knows? He's doing alright for himself. I don't know."

"Maybe he's a shy boy around girls."

"He's old enough to have grown out of that. He's not a teenager."

"I know... but it's such a shame that a nice boy like that can't find someone."

"You know, Zuli, I feel very sorry for Brent, yes, I do."

"Oh, why?" Zulema looked puzzled.

"He's looking for something he can never, ever find. He has no hope."

"What are you talking about?"

"He's looking for the one perfect woman and I've already found her."

Brent drove away but stopped again before he had left the subdivision. He stared into the distance and thought over what he had witnessed over the course of the last two interviews. Two very different couples had worked out the way through all the twists and turns of being attracted to each other, desiring each other, committing to each other and the binding of themselves together. The first blush of romance had passed but both marriages had achieved the working relationship that endures over the years. Humour, Brent noted, was important. Their shared experiences had piled up to form an unbreakable bond of devotion. It took time. A strange thing, this set of internal feelings called love. It begins quickly, grows inexplicably, and becomes a spirit in the hearts of men and women.

The Lindsays were friendly between themselves with a ready welcome for outsiders. Reserved Dan was frequently thinking how to compliment his wife in his bashful, jocular way. It meant she was high in his affections. Eileen was proud of her man - the coffee table proved that. Their relationship had an even, peaceful flow to it - like a lazy summer river.

The Valdezes had a more dramatic dynamic to their relationship. Zulema admired her strong-willed husband. She could never control him but she knew how to stand up to him. Sylvester worshipped his wife but not in any monomaniacal sense. Their relationship was more like the sea - tempestuous or placid, always with waves - the result of some external force upon it, and always, always there.

Brent could not clearly envisage his own future but he was more than encouraged. Zulema knew everything about Sylvester's past and did not judge him for it - that was obvious. That her judgment was biased was also obvious. It was possible she had her own criminal history, although not according to the police records. That Zulema accepted the fact of her husband's criminal career demonstrated that there were women in the world, nice women, who might also accept him, Brent. There was hope after all and his regretted past might be accepted as a wretched phase that would not be repeated. Someone came to Brent's mind and he wondered if she would listen to him.

Deciding he had brooded long enough and was neglecting the case, he remembered Vane's message and called her back. They worked out a place to meet. Brent and three skateboarders were going shopping.

Chapter 15

Thursday afternoon

*A*t one o'clock in the food court of a mall, a table was made to look untidy by Zack, 17, who slouched low with his head right back, Mason, 19, who sprawled, face on the table, because he had only woken up half an hour earlier, and Vane, 18, whose attention was locked into the screen of her phone.

Brent saw them from a distance and was not surprised. It was about what he had expected, although Zack's extraordinary mass of dark red curly hair was a sight so surprising one would never expect it. Brent joined the teenagers and sat down at the table.

"Hi, Brent," said Vane, looking up from her phone for a split second before she shut it off. "This is Zack, and that's Mason."

The last named raised a hand and opened a sleepy eye. Zack said "Yo" and stared at the newcomer.

"Okay, guys, I take it you're interested to hear what the deal is. So, what do you want - the money and conditions first or the mission?"

"Money, man," said Mason, who struggled to get himself vertical in his chair.

"Mission first," said Vane.

"That's the right answer, Vane. You get a bonus of fifty bucks. There you are." He handed her a crisp banknote. Mason and Zack both sat up straight. "Now, if you two do not pay attention you can leave and I'll find replacements in this food court."

"What's the mission?" asked Mason.

"There's a TV production being shot on location this coming Monday. They'll be on-site at six a.m. and ready to work. So will the three of you. Late shows and no-shows will not be tolerated and will be fired immediately. I'll pick my own replacements. Vane is in charge. She is your boss. You talk to her and she talks to me. If I change the instructions she will tell you what you have to do. In the event she has to track someone, you can call me directly if anything arises while you're working. Everyone understand the management structure so far?"

Mason and Vane said, "Yes"; Zack nodded.

"I didn't hear you, Zack."

"Ah, yeah, sure."

"Good. There are four people you will be keeping under observation. Three are actors and one is the executive producer and director. I'll give you information sheets and photographs in a minute. What I want is eyes on these people. The director is likely to be wherever the cameras are in operation. The actors will come and go as they play their parts in scenes. When they stop for breaks so do you. Now if anyone does anything a bit weird, goes off set, or otherwise looks stressed, watch that person instead of another. I'm not interested in any of the acting for the production; it's unusual personal behaviour I'm looking for. You are keeping them under surveillance and that's all.

The shooting finishes on Friday morning so that's when you'll be finishing up unless there is some overtime available because of a change in circumstances. Okay, questions?"

"It might be hard to get close," said Vane.

"Yes. Get friendly with Security, if possible, but don't try and get yourselves onto the set unless there's a very good reason for it, such as a really bad argument, a security problem, or something like that. My idea is that you're there every day and so you become part of the scenery. It should seem like this is where you normally hang out and they happen to be filming close by. Got to be natural. So, sit around and talk, skate a little but don't draw attention to yourselves. We'll scope out the area on Sunday. You hang around and take photos and make notes of anything you see that's out of the ordinary. So, everyone on board with this?"

"We just be ourselves and you pay us to watch these people... that's what you want?" asked Mason.

"Correct. Keep eyes on them. Make a note of anything unusual."

"Some places, Security wants us gone just because we're skaters," said Zack.

"Try not to react. Comply with their requests and be friendly. If Security is difficult we'll work around it by other methods."

"Don't get me wrong, Brent. Who expects skaters to be out at six in the morning?" asked Mason.

"When we survey the site, we'll set up several positions so that you're not in one spot all the time. First thing in the morning...? stay well back and don't crowd them."

"You guys good with this?" asked Vane. They both answered her in the affirmative. "Okay, Brent, what's the remuneration?"

Brent smiled inside. Vane had to study for her courses and it was beginning to show in her language.

"Expenses. Fifty a day each in advance for food, drink, and travel. Remember you may be following someone. I'll give Vane a three hundred dollar reserve in case you have to take cabs. You'll get a new phone each and I expect you to start each day with both your own and the new one fully charged. Don't have two phones in your hands at the same time.

Pay. You get a hundred dollars a day for every day worked. Plus, at the end of the week there is a bonus of a thousand each. Miss a day and you're gone and someone else gets your money.

A few more conditions. You're a team and you'll be working as such. So, after the first hour, two are on duty which means no social media or games, while the third has down time. That's when Vane can do some work on her courses online, if she likes. You change each hour. You cannot be zoned out by social media, music or games. From time to time, do some skateboarding but no showy stuff. If anything happens you're all on it and have to divide your duties to cover what needs to be done. Vane will be reporting to me daily. You all have to put in the work and I'll know if you haven't because I'll be dropping by occasionally. Are you all on board?"

Agreement was universal.

"Now for the weird stuff. We are at this mall because tonight all three of you are going to Garland's restaurant which is high class and exclusive. You're getting complete new outfits including overcoats and shoes with a budget of eight hundred each.

Mason and Zack, I'll help you select your outfits. All of you will go to a hair salon. Zack, if you don't want a hair cut it does have to be tamed somehow. Vane, I'll set you up at a nice store and the staff will help you out in choosing what you need.

The reason for this is that I have to work tonight. You'll be providing me with cover so you need to look the part. This is a separate mission. If you don't want in, you can still go next week. Oh, yes. You'll get a free meal, keep the clothes, get a ride home, and have two hundred each in your hand when the meal's successfully over. What do you say?"

Vane was dropped off at a smart-looking store into the care of an experienced sales associate who instantly took her under her wing. Brent explained where they were going and the simple, elegant look he thought would be appropriate. He left them to it.

It was easy for Brent to help Mason. The nineteen-year-old had naturally conservative tastes and chose a very dark grey suit. The young man was torn between a white shirt and bow tie and a dark blue-grey shirt and dark tie. In the end he chose the bow tie which, Mason admitted, was an item he had always wanted to wear.

Zack was the reverse. He immediately gravitated to the loudest check sports jackets and intended to match it with a pair of heavily striped dress pants. He tried them on while Brent was finishing up with Mason, who was now looking prosperous and respectable.

"Wow, Zack!" said Mason. "You've got to be kidding, right?"

Brent turned and found himself in complete agreement with Mason. Looking at Zack, only the occupation of circus clown could come to mind. Recovering from the shock, he said,

"Ah, Zack... I see you like to make a bold statement. That's not the effect I'm looking for, though. It's about blending in with the surroundings... the mission dictates it." That's what Brent said. What Brent thought was, He'll put me off my dinner.

Eventually, after several abortive attempts, Zack arrived at a selection and would be wearing a mid-blue jacket with a noticeable, but not too obtrusive, orange-red, wide check pattern over dark grey trousers. A white shirt and a tie of a muted orange and white geometric pattern on a black background completed the ensemble. He could not be missed in a crowd but at least everything worked together, complemented his hair colour, and he looked kind of cool in an off-beat way. Zack's hair seemed wilder than ever against the dressier clothes. Brent hoped the hairstylist would wrestle it into shape - anything that was a recognizable shape.

Overcoats, socks, and belts were added to the bill which Brent then settled. He left them in a shoe shop while he went to see how Vane was getting along. He found her trying on her ultimate choice - a rich turquoise, satin dress that he could find no fault with and thought suited her perfectly. She was so visibly pleased with how she looked in the mirror, as she toyed with a filmy, cream-coloured shawl. Vane looked grown-up.

"What do you think, Brent? Does the shawl go with it?" asked Vane, when she saw him in the mirror.

"I think it does. You look beautiful. It's a very lovely dress and I really like the colour."

Vane smiled naturally and without restraint. Her eyes showed her joy, also.

"It's missing one little thing," said Brent, frowning as he considered Vane's reflected appearance. "I might have the fix for it, though." He stepped behind her. "Put your head forward."

"What are you doing?" asked Vane.

"You'll see... and lift your hair out of the way."

He took something from his pocket and fastened it around her neck. He stood back. It was a princess length strand of Akoya pearls, graduated in size, and possessing extraordinarily high lustre. They glowed white-cream against Vane's skin, and had rosy pink overtones in their glow where they lay against the dress.

"Oh, my goodness. They're fabulous," said the astonished sales associate.

"They're on loan for tonight," said Brent. "These are yours on your graduation day but I thought this evening would be a good opportunity..."

Vane was speechless and motionless for a moment, except for a hesitant touch of the pearls. She then impetuously hugged Brent as a little girl would hug her father.

After they had parted company, Brent went home to put his notes in some order and to write up his reports. He felt lazy, despite having so much to do. Tomorrow would be spent at Althorn Capital, interviewing people - from bemused juniors to crusty partners. He had to keep on top of the workflow because tomorrow he would be inundated.

He read a text message from Linda. "I totally respect that you're busy. Just to say I'm thinking of you."

Chapter 16

Thursday Night

"*M*y soup's cold, man," said Zack.

"It's Gazpacho and it's supposed to be," said Brent, who was wearing an immaculate light grey suit.

"It is? How weird's that?"

Zack's hair had been restrained after it had been washed and dried. The stylist had repatriated the corkscrew escapees into the main mass by using some of her secret formula for such things which was kept in an unmarked bottle. The main mass she tied into a thick, wide pony tail by means of a length of purple paracord that Zack produced from his pocket. Should a newcomer ask any waiter in Garland's where the guy with the hair was sitting, the waiter would still instantly know who it was and point to Zack.

Brent, to ensure he enjoyed his meal, had laid down simple rules of etiquette that he thought skateboard-loving teenagers could adhere to. These were:- no swearing, no shouting, no shoveling of food, no slurping, and no speaking with a full mouth. He had to add no slouching after the fact. Once the initial warning had been given, fines for infractions were on a sliding scale beginning with five dollars for the first, ten for the second, and so on. Zack was down fifteen because he was a slurper. Mason was already down fifty when he finally understood what it meant to break the first rule. He 'so what' laughed off the first few five dollar infractions but stopped laughing shortly afterwards when he realized what it was costing him. After that, things continued pleasantly.

Vane had become lady-like in her ways and, although they were foreign to her, she managed naturally graceful movements which made her look the part. Her normally elfish appearance had vanished. She looked lovely not least because she felt lovely, and had matured to the point where she could give the impression of being a young woman who was used to dining at places like Garland's. She touched her pearls from time to time. Sitting across from Brent, Vane smiled at him often. Also, she had committed no infractions.

"Guys, you know why we're here, right?" she said.

"Yeah, Brent's investigating a murder or something," answered Mason.

"Yes. It happened right here in this restaurant."

"No way! Where?" said Zack, who turned round in his chair as if expecting to see a corpse.

"Two tables away from us," said Brent, "but let's not disturb the people sitting there. What you might find interesting is that we're sitting at the table closest to where the shot was taken."

"Oh, Brent, how could you do that!?" said Vane.

"Pure chance. I had to get in this section because I've got to talk to the waiter. He was on last week when it happened. Do you want to move?"

"To a different table…? No, it's okay. I was surprised, that's all."

"I'm glad you brought the subject up, Vane. Any of you, how do you think I should approach the waiter to get him to talk about what he saw? There are some difficulties involved."

"If it was me," said Zack, "and you asked, I'd just tell you. It's a really big deal. I'd want to tell everyone."

"He will have repeated the story to the police a few times. He's probably sick of it."

"I don't know," said Mason. "Couldn't you, like, pay him something?"

"Yes, that often works," said Brent. "How much do you think is appropriate?"

"Uh, twenty bucks? How long would it take?"

"Let's say ten minutes max."

"Yeah, I'd say twenty."

"That's a good estimate under normal circumstances. But this guy is used to getting big tips. There are a lot of wealthy people in the room."

"Fifty? A hundred? That makes it difficult. Like, he might think you want him to talk so bad that he'll hold out for a big price," said Mason.

"From what I know of him I think that is quite likely. So, if I'm to get him to talk without any problems, I have to pay him some serious money. Agreed?"

They all agreed.

"The next problem to solve is where can we talk. He's not allowed to talk with the customers beyond his service duties. The manager would notice him."

"Then, you'll need to see him on a break or after work," said Vane.

"That's right. I'll have to find out where he would be most comfortable. The next potential problem is that he might have reasons for not wanting to talk to me. What are they likely to be?"

"Maybe he just wants to forget about it," said Mason.

"I think, if he's upset, he'll tell you he is, right up front," said Vane.

"That's possible."

"He might be on the assassin's team," said Zack. "Like, the waiter sets it up, gives the killer the signal and gets out of the way."

"C'mon, that's not how it happened," said Mason, derisively.

"No, actually that is a solid theory and a real possibility," said Brent. "Zack, your fines are forgiven."

Zack looked surprised and then, animatedly, with fists raised, said, "Yesss!"

"What? We can wipe out the fines? Ah, cool," said Mason.

"Let's assume," continued Brent, "our man has a guilty secret. He will either refuse the money and not talk or he will accept the money because he wants any opportunity to strengthen his alibi and would get the cash as a bonus. Either way, you see, it proves nothing. Now, according to his statement, he was in the kitchen when three rapid shots were fired and did not see anything. This was corroborated by other witnesses. He also states that he did not see the shooter or notice anything unusual about this table. You've got that…? So, how do I test to see if he's telling the truth?"

"Kidnap him?" suggested Mason.

"I thought of that but if he's innocent I'm in trouble."

"Wow. Would you do that?" asked Zack.

"Let's stay focused," said Brent.

Vane, who had been quietly listening, interjected, "You have to break his alibi or catch him out in a lie."

"Yes. How do we set that up?"

"Like a trap… oh, there's gotta be a way," said Zack, enthusiastic and excited.

"If he was involved," said Vane, "he'll have a weak spot. He'd feel guilty. If he feels guilty he'll show it if you, uh, challenge him."

"Very good. How can I challenge him in a public place? You see, here in the restaurant we have the upper hand and he has to behave himself. Outside, he can just walk away and we won't find out anything."

Brent waited but no more inspiration was forthcoming.

"I'll write him a note. What should it say?" asked Brent.

"We know everything," said Zack. The others laughed.

"Mason, is the waiter in sight?" asked Brent.

"Uh, he's taking some food to the table behind you."

"I should be quick, then."

Brent took out a pen and a small notepad. He wrote a note and tore it out. Then he put a folded fifty dollar bill on the table and placed the note on top of it. He put his hand over them.

"Mason and Zack. You two talk about music or something. Don't look at him at all but keep him in your peripheral vision. Vane, you call him over. When he arrives, be pleasant and say, 'This gentleman wants to speak to you.' Then just start playing with your food or phone. We all good? Okay, Vane."

Vane put her hand up and attracted the attention of Ted, the waiter. He came over immediately. Zack and Mason were talking quietly about bands they had seen and liked.

"Yes, ma'am?" said Ted.

"The gentleman wishes to speak to you," said Vane with a smile.

"Yes, sir?"

"You're Ted, aren't you?"

"I am, sir."

"Please read this." Brent handed the note and bill to the waiter. Ted read the note and hurriedly put both note and bill into his pocket.

"I... er... will be back shortly, sir. We can speak but I need a moment. Thank you." He gave a slight bow and left the table.

"What did the note say?" asked Mason.

"The police suspect you. Talk to me."

"I am so going to be a private investigator," said Zack.

"That's very clever, Brent," said Vane. "But you thought he was hiding something before you did all this. Like, you knew."

"I didn't know. But this is the third time I've been here in just over a week. The first two times the service was impeccable. Tonight, Ted has only been doing an average job and, reputedly, he's the top waiter here. Could be anything that's putting him off his game but I got the impression it was our table because he seemed quite engaged with the people at the next one. That means it has to do with us or this table. I'll find out."

"This is why you invited us?" asked Mason.

"Partially that's the reason. This is a table for six and I would feel very weird sitting here by myself. I would also annoy the manager who I cannot afford to annoy. You see, we have a more difficult task ahead of us. I have to persuade the manager, the chef de cuisine, and assorted sous-chefs to let us, at least two of us, go into the kitchen while it's operational and talk to people. Kirby Mayo, the man who was killed, had sent back a plate of fish. I need to know why he did that and how the staff reacted."

"Um..." said Mason. "Could one of us pretend we're, like, interested in becoming a chef or opening a restaurant?"

"That is a very good idea because it's what I plan to do." He looked at the smartly dressed young man who was evidently pleased with himself. "Your fines are cancelled," said Brent.

"Whoa!" said Mason.

"But... but, I expect courteous and professional behaviour from all of you. Courteous means that you treat every person you meet with equal respect and that level of respect is a high one - it's how you would like to be treated by others. Professional means that you get the job done well, even when you don't want to do it."

"I hear you," said Zack.

"You weren't courteous to the waiter," said Mason. "He might be innocent."

"I thought I was. I said please. If he does prove to be innocent I will apologize to him. You must remember, I'm looking for a murderer here. Which reminds me, you can't go off the program I set for you. It could be dangerous."

"I think you handled him fine," said Vane. "Thanks for showing us how you do it. Like, who knew?"

"Thank you for the vote of confidence. Who wants to be a chef?"

"We've been watching Domenic Castillo for about five minutes now. What do you make of Garland's manager?" asked Brent, who was now sitting next to Vane.

"He must be in his forties," said Vane. "Maybe fifties? It's hard for me to say. He moves around a lot, got some energy. Talks to a lot of people. He notices things... nearby and across the room. He doesn't miss much. See, he did it again. He saw a hand up at the back and he's sent a waiter over immediately."

"If he was working the room when Mayo was killed, do you think he would have seen something?"

"Like, we can't stare at him because he'll see us so we're kind of peeping at him, but I would say yes, definitely. You saying he saw the killer?"

"He might have - only Domenic was in the kitchen at the time of the murder. It seems many people were in the kitchen who normally would not have been. If they had all been where they normally are, any of them could have seen the killer. I find that very curious. Someone made a suggestion the killer had an accomplice. A spotter."

"That's creepy. It's so cold and calculating," said Vane.

"Yes. Back to Domenic - what do you think of the man?"

"He looks wealthy. That suit looks the same quality as, well, yours. He's got a deep tan and thick hair that's been cut recently. He takes care of himself and likes to be outdoors. Smiles a lot but not like a goofball. He has one face for the staff and another for the customers. That's it! He's like a showman or an orchestra conductor - someone who controls everything and everyone."

"Yes, I agree. He doesn't seem to do anything but he makes sure everything happens at the right time. You know how we just paid Ted, the waiter, to get him to agree to talk to us? Well, if Domenic were offered money like that, would he accept it, do you think?"

"I doubt it. He doesn't look like that kind of guy. How much would it take?"

"No idea. Any large sum would make him suspicious. A small sum and he would dismiss it. Then, let me ask you this. Do you think he's a kind man?"

"I suppose so. I don't know, really. How can you tell?"

"Imagine yourself asking him a question. If you were to ask, 'Can I see inside your kitchen?' - what would he say?"

"Oh... he would say, 'I'm sorry, the kitchen is busy now.'"

"Yes. If we showed real interest, he might say, 'Come back tomorrow when we're not busy.'"

"Yeah, he looks like the kinda guy that might say that. So, is it off?"

"Not yet. Imagine saying this to him - 'I'm an investigator working on behalf of Mrs. Rena Kirby whose husband was killed last week. She is very distressed. I know you're busy, but there was an incident about some fish last week. Is it possible we can briefly talk to the persons who prepared his food? Mrs Kirby wants to know in detail what her husband was doing during the last moments of his life. It would bring her some peace of mind to know. Sorry for such an odd request.'"

"Did she say that?"

"Well, no, but she will want to know every last detail she can be told. Besides, I will tell her about the fish on Sunday when I see her."

"You're seeing her? I can't get my head around how bad she must be feeling."

"She's taking it very hard. I've only spoken to her on the phone so far."

"If you said all that, our dude would say, 'Please, come into the kitchen.'"

"Think so? Shall we give it a try? We've got one shot. Zack and Mason aren't needed for this."

"I'll do it but I don't think you need me."

"You increase the likelihood of his buying the story by at least fifty per cent."

"How do you make that out?"

"If it were just me he might think I'm a reporter. You are too lovely and youthful for him to make that assumption about you. We just need a reasonable excuse for your being present and he will be most helpful, I think."

"Brent? Supposing Zack was with you? What would you say?"

"Honestly, can you see Zack getting past him? Or Mason?"

"Like, no, definitely not."

"There's your answer then. Once we're in, there will be several parties in play. I can only keep one or two under observation. As I'm asking questions, watch what the other people are doing and that's not only people in the group but people further away, too. Facial expressions are very important, especially if they think they're not being observed."

"What are we looking for, exactly?"

"One of them could be a murderer. More likely, one of them could be the spotter. I don't know but I hope at least to clear some or all of them - that's the manager and the three waiters who were in there at the time of the shooting as well as any staff involved in the fish incident. That's five or six people I should think."

"You're gonna have to work fast, babe. Do I get a speaking part or do I stand around like a dummy, staring at people's eyebrows?"

"Sure you can. We'll rehearse the lines once we've got the cover story down. We can't both be speaking at the same time, though. We have to work as a team. One of us has also to watch the waiters coming in to get the food or to return plates."

Chapter 17

Thursday night

"*E*xcuse me, Mr. Castillo. We know you're a very busy man and we apologize for interrupting you," said Brent.

"Oh, not at all. Please, do not apologize. What may I do for you?"

"My name is Brent Umber and this is my assistant, Vanessa."

"Pleased to meet you, Mr. Castillo," said Vanessa.

"Ah, Madame, the pleasure is all mine. I hope you have enjoyed your dining experience?"

Vane had still been reeling from being called 'Ma'am' for the first time in her life by the waiter. To hear the manager's cultured, slightly European-accented voice addressing her as 'Madame' took her aback a little more. She rather liked it, though, and replied confidently,

"Oh, thank you, yes. The service was impeccable and the food wonderful."

"Madame, you honour us, thank you. Now?" He looked brightly and expectantly from one to the other.

"It is concerning the tragedy of last week," said Brent. "I've been asked to look into the matter on behalf of the Mayo family and Althorn Capital. Of particular concern are Mrs. Mayo's interests as she is deeply wounded by her loss."

"I cannot imagine how awful it must be for her. We, too, are suffering but it is as nothing by comparison. She has our deepest sympathy."

Vane looked deeply sympathetic and solemn.

"Mrs. Mayo is receiving little comfort from the police," said Brent. "As you can appreciate, she has a strong desire to learn more of the night her husband died."

"Very little comfort, Mr. Castillo," said Vane.

"Yes, I can see how that would be."

"There seems to have been an incident over some fish which Mr. Mayo returned. For some reason, this troubles her disproportionately. She would like us to inquire into the matter and provide her with a full report. I don't doubt she will fix upon some other minor detail at a later date but it is the question of Mr. Mayo's fish, at present. Would it be possible, do you think, to allow us a few moments with the person, or persons, who prepared the fish?"

"The fish...? I'm sorry. You have surprised me. It is an unusual request though one that is easily accommodated. Please, step this way."

"Thank you," said Vane and Brent, together.

The temporary firm of BU&V Associates was in. Phase one of the mission was complete. Vane was having trouble with her mouth - a grin was trying to break out.

In the kitchen area, the retrial of the turbot was being conducted with the questionable fish in absentia. It had been partly consumed, the rest had been discarded.

"I tell you, there was nothing wrong with it," said Chris, the Poissonnier, in an elevated voice that made it evident the wound to his pride had been re-opened, causing personal offence and irritation to flow out.

"I have eaten the same dish here recently," said Brent. "I found it to be superb. The turbot was perfectly cooked and melted into flavourful flakes upon the tongue."

"I'm very happy to hear that. Thank you. And that particular Pacific turbot which Mr. Mayo had was also excellent," said Aden Morris, the Chef de Cuisine. "I tasted what was sent back and the customer had no cause for complaint. No cause at all. I permit nothing to leave my kitchen that is not of the highest quality."

In the silence that followed, each gaze, one by one, transferred to Domenic Castillo. He was expected to speak.

"I had to speak to Mr. Mayo," said Domenic, primarily addressing Brent. "It was not about the food, you understand? The turbot was the third such return." The manager turned to Vane. "Please excuse me for mentioning this." He returned his attention to Brent. "Mr. Mayo was a very frequent visitor to Garland's and always sat in one of the centre sections . More than a month ago, he began to talk to a waiter who had recently joined us. She told me that at first he was quite pleasant but over several evenings he was making suggestions to her that were becoming more offensive. She came to me and explained what was happening. It was an awkward situation. I immediately had another waiter, a man, take care of Mr. Mayo's table.

I had him flagged in our reservation system that, in future, Mr. Mayo would only be seated in a section where a male waiter could serve him. Immediately after that, he began to send food back, complaining it was substandard. The turbot was the last of three such instances."

"That must have been a difficult situation for you," said Brent.

"Extremely so. I attended him after each incident. He was reasonable and we confined our discussion to the subject of food. On the last evening, however, he became very unpleasant. I was on the point of asking him to leave, or, at least, not to return to Garland's if he was not going to be happy with our excellent fare, when the host approached, escorting a male guest to Mr. Mayo's table. It was untimely, and I decided to speak to him later."

"That was awkward," said Brent.

"It was. For me to have to speak to a regular patron and ask him to leave? This is terrible. I have to be discreet and avoid any disturbance to the other diners. It is my duty to prevent them being upset due to another person's bad behaviour. Also, it is my duty to protect my staff."

Brent quickly looked at Vane.

"This makes it hard for us," she said. "We have to report back to Mrs. Mayo and I don't see how we can do that under these circumstances."

"Excuse me," said Aden. "Do you need us any longer?"

"I'm sorry. Thank you for sparing us your valuable time," said Brent. "You have been very helpful. I always enjoy the food when I come here. This is my favourite restaurant."

"Well, we thank you, Mr. Umber. We try our best," said Aden.

"Goodbye," said Chris. The two men returned to their work.

"I can feel your concern," said Domenic, speaking to Vane. "It strikes me that you need only say to Mrs. Mayo the barest details and not bring out the whole history. Surely, it is best not to add to her misery?"

"That's what I'm thinking," said Vane. "She did ask for a full report from us, though."

"I'm often put into delicate situations," said Domenic. "I find that I must do and say what leaves people feeling comfortable. When someone is unreasonable I have to be diplomatic and patient with them. With Mrs. Mayo, I'm sure someone with your experience can inform her without disturbing her."

"What would you do?" asked Vane.

"Me?" Domenic look pleased and surprised by her question. "I think I would say, Mr. Mayo did not find the food acceptable because, although it was good, it was not according to his taste as the waiter who served him was not the one he had usually and so his desires were not adequately communicated."

"That is so clever," said Vane. "You've, like, covered everything and said nothing."

"I think we can use that," said Brent. "Mr. Castillo, you've been extraordinarily helpful in accommodating us. We've taken up more than enough of your time."

"I'm glad I could help you." They all shook hands and began to leave the kitchen together.

"We haven't had dessert yet and I'm really looking forward to something special," said Vane.

"Madame, I used to be a Patissier, and, if I might suggest, the Tarte Conversation is quite exquisite or, if you prefer, the Mille-Feuille is crisp and light…

Vane and Brent went back to their table. Mason was on his phone and Zack was away from the table.

"Okay, time for the debriefing session. What did you see, Vane?" asked Brent.

"Chris shows everything on his face. Like, he was very angry and had trouble keeping it in. Do you think he's insecure?"

"Might be. Do you see him as the killer or as a spotter?"

"Can't be a spotter because he's in the back all the time. A killer? He looks like an ordinary guy... I can't imagine it."

"It's hard to visualize. You have to understand that almost all killers just look like ordinary people. Unless they belong to a gang that marks itself with signs and tattoos to intimidate, they will look like anyone else. The big thing to remember is that a killer, after the fact, works at looking normal. They want you to believe they are innocent, they have no motive, and their alibi is true. Often, they give themselves away in working too hard at looking normal."

"Well, Chris didn't do any of that. He might have hit Mayo but he wouldn't plan to shoot him. That's what I think."

"I agree. That's how it struck me. What about Aden?"

"No... He's out. He's, like, totally open and it's all 'my kitchen' with him."

"Might he be a suspect if Kirby Mayo died in his kitchen?"

"Oh, yeah. Totally."

"Domenic?"

"Really? He's so nice. His manners are beautiful. Even better than yours."

"Huh, I know where I stand, now."

"I didn't mean it like that, Brent. I really didn't. You're nicer."

"Thank you. Domenic is quite a subtle man. He would be capable of working out a plan and executing it. One thing stops me from considering him as Kirby Mayo's killer. Have a guess what it is."

"I didn't see him," said Mason, who had been listening closely, "so I've got no clue."

"Come on, Brent, I can't think of anything."

"He would never kill him in his restaurant because it would disturb the diners. It is the last place he would choose. Besides, he has no reason to commit murder and, for the same reason, he would not be the spotter for the killer."

"Of course!" said Vane. "I should have thought of that... Did you see Ted?"

"I did and I hoped you did, too."

"He was the only one of the waiters or of anyone in the kitchen who took notice like it meant something to him."

"Right. That's good. I'll be meeting Ted when his shift ends. Let's get him over to order desserts... Where has Zack got to?"

"Here he is, on his way back," said Mason. "What's up with him?"

Zack sat in his seat and was visibly bubbling with excitement.

"Guys! You will ne-ver guess who I've been speaking to in the lobby..."

Brent put the three teenagers into a taxi and sent them home. He had fulfilled all his promises and they went away jubilant and happy. Vane had returned the pearl necklace to Brent, saying that they might go missing in the apartment she shared and that she would have to kill someone if they did. She had thanked him... more than thanked him.

"If you weren't so much older than I am," she said privately to him, "I would make you love me."

"I do love you as my sister."

"You know that's not what I mean. If you were, like, twenty-two or something, you wouldn't stand a chance."

Brent smiled. "Think we'd get along?"

"Most of the time. You know, you've made it really difficult for me."

"How's that? What have I done?"

"You haven't done anything but any guy I meet I'll be comparing to you. How's that for a problem to make it hard for a girl? You've been so nice to me all the time and in so many ways but, you know, Brent, letting me help in a real investigation - that was, like, so special. Goodnight, brother." She kissed him.

"Goodnight, Vane. I couldn't have a sweeter and more fascinating sister."

Brent watched the taxi pull away until it was out of sight. He turned and headed to Cusane's Parlour to await the arrival of Ted.

The waiter, Ted, had himself under control as he and Brent stood at the more secluded end of the busy bar. It helped that the waiter was no longer under Domenic's watchful eye. After he had introduced himself, Brent watched the man down half his beer and visibly relax, preparing to speak.

"You said the police are on to me. I haven't done anything wrong!"

"I'm sure you haven't."

"What's bothering me is how you come to know so much. You're not with the police."

"No. I'm a private investigator but I hear what's going on in the case. You had communication with Kirby Mayo. There's something you're keeping back and it makes you look suspicious. You tell me what it is and I'll make sure the police don't bother you."

"How can you do that?"

"I have friends in high places."

"I don't know. What happens if I don't tell you?"

"I'll find out what it is eventually. Before I do, I'll make sure the police make your life a misery."

"I'll lose my job if you do that."

"That's preventable, isn't it? You only need to tell me what it was."

"Looks like I have to trust you. I've no choice." He drained his glass.

"Would you like another?"

"Yeah, sure."

The bartender served another drink to the waiter. When they were alone again, Brent said,

"Let's have it."

"Okay. Mr. Mayo was a good tipper. Always. That night, he asked me to get some information for him on another customer. He gave me three hundred and said for me to make sure I got what he asked for."

"What time was this?"

"About eight-thirty. A guy named Hutchinson had left the table, then there was the deal over the fish. It was when I was serving him trout as the replacement. Said he'd seen someone he was interested in. It was a party of four. Marianne Stark was one of them."

"She's plays the lead in Wild Ward, so I've been told. Continue."

"That's right. Well, it wasn't her but the older guy at the table he wanted to know about. Trouble was, they were in another section."

"Whose was that?"

"Felicity's. She's off sick… really bad. I'm sorry for her."

"Yes, me, too. How are you handling it?"

"Okay. Made me sick when I saw him but, uh, you gotta get over stuff and move on."

"You do. Did you get any information?"

"Yes. I, uh, asked Felicity what she knew. She said she had overheard they were doing a television show and they were discussing how they would play the parts. Said they were getting right into it but she could never stay long enough to make out what they were talking about exactly.

So, I got Felicity to let me serve them their desserts. They hadn't ordered so I thought I would stand back and listen for a while before going over the dessert menu with them."

"Did Felicity cover for you?"

"Yes, she did. She spoke to Mayo. I think that's what has made it worse for her."

"What about the manager? Does he mind you switching sections?"

"We often switch to help each other out when it's busy. He encourages it. Where was I…? Yeah, so, I go over and listen in and then ask a few questions about the upcoming show and that. I smooth-talk them a little and find out some things. I bring their desserts and find out a bit more. I don't push them… can't. I only want to earn the money I've been given and keep Mayo sweet.

I wait a while and then go back to my own section. I gave Felicity fifty bucks for her help. Then I went to see Mayo. Told him everything I'd found out which wasn't much. He seemed pleased so that was cool."

"What did you say to him?"

"That they were starting to shoot a new show called Two-Way Street Beat next week. Some of it was going to be shot on location, some in a studio, but they'd rented an old building as a permanent set. They seemed real happy about that but I didn't find out why. The guy Mayo was interested in was Galen Nash. I found out later he's a big shot producer/director. I'd never heard of him. Anyway, Mayo sends a message over to Nash. It was, 'Best wishes for the success of your new show'. Sounds harmless so I go over and deliver it. This guy Nash, he's all kinds of smiles when I say it to him but when I tell him who it's from his face goes bright red. I mean, it was like the colour of a beet. He waves me away. I say, 'Thank you, sir,' and get out of there." He gulped some beer down.

"So that has made it very awkward for you. The money, an upset customer, and a guy playing a game who gets himself killed later on."

"Exactly my point. I'd lose my job if they found out."

"I'll keep your secret," said Brent. "This might fit in with some ideas I have but I don't see how it plays into the murder investigation. If the police should start to probe you about this, tell them the truth, otherwise you'll end up in worse trouble. But I believe I can divert the police away from you so that you'll not be under suspicion. However, that does not mean they won't come back to question you again of their own volition."

"Three times already. I'm getting used to it... always the same questions in a different order."

"What about your serving of Kirby Mayo? And anyone with him?"

"Nothing unusual with him or any of the visitors at his table. He always ate well and drank a lot of wine. He usually dined alone and then people came to see him. Not much is made from the food from his table but he always ordered a lot of wine. The people who met him sometimes had an appetizer, or a dessert, cheese, or whatever. Garland's made good money on the wine, that's why he was always allowed to have a prominent table for four."

"Did he get drunk or anything close to it?"

"If he did, I didn't notice."

"Is that everything?" asked Brent.

"Yeah, I think so."

"Here's my card. Call me if you think of anything more."

"Sure, okay," replied Ted.

As Brent left the bar, Ted read the business card first before putting it and the hundred dollar bill accompanying it into his wallet.

Chapter 18

Friday

*I*t was a little after nine when Brent reached Althorn. Nola introduced him to such staff as could spare the time during trading hours and who had a closer connection to Kirby than others did.

These numerous, brief interviews yielded nothing in the way of a lead. Brent spent most of the time repeating the same reassuring lines about his being there to help resolve some of the issues Althorn Capital was facing. Most interviewees responded well to being allowed to express themselves on the subject. The PR company had begun conducting similar interviews but theirs lacked the substance that Brent's incorporated. He asked, "Who do you think killed Kirby?" and that question produced a wide range of speculation that almost every employee was eager to expand upon. Unfortunately for Brent, the speculation thickened his file of notes but did not advance the case.

Later on, the intense trading business of the day subsided and everyone was winding down with very few orders being placed. The traders had mostly switched to administrative duties to clean their desks for the weekend. The cheerful woman Brent had seen before escorted him to Blake Pickett's office. A conversation with Blake got interviews set-up with two of the top traders but Brent had to wait to see them as they both needed to get some work finished up.

Talking to Blake Pickett gave no indication of his possessing any animosity towards Kirby Mayo. He presented himself as a pleasant, soft-spoken, authoritative man who knew the business and knew how to get the best from his traders by patiently mentoring them. Brent was given no sense of Blake's possessing driving ambition, bitter resentment, or any other strong emotion or overriding thought that could lead to his wanting Kirby Mayo dead. If anything, the reverse was true. Blake very much wished that Althorn could return to the way it was and was anxious that it would move into the post-Kirby era without difficulty and with new blood restoring the partnership's prospects.

Having some minutes to spare before the first of the two interviews, Brent thought to talk to Sohil but was unsure where to find him. He knew where to find the cheerful lady.

"Excuse me. Cheryl, isn't it?"

"That's right. How can I help you?"

"I was hoping to speak with Sohil for a few minutes."

"Of course. He's in the bond department. I'll show you the way."

They went through the reception area as it was the most direct route to the separate department which was on the other side of the floor Althorn occupied.

"What work do you do here, Cheryl, if you don't mind my asking?"

"Client communications. I keep up our media presence, write the newsletters and organize promotional programs, among other things. I'm working on a golf tournament for next year but I'm not sure how it will go because it's our first and well, you know what happened - it makes a difference to everything."

"Yes, I suppose it would. It's a good idea, though. I think a social event like that would make an impact and say, 'We're moving forward'."

"That's what I hope but I can't help worrying about the turn-out."

They arrived in the bond department. It was as if they had crossed an invisible frontier into a different land. The lively excitement and continual movement in the trading area was completely absent, replaced by a solemn, quiet atmosphere. Employees looked very serious. One man, having a pronounced look of resignation on his face, appeared to be thinking to himself, 'What more can go wrong?' If the trading area had the air of a house throwing a birthday party, the bond department was a funeral home.

Cheryl spoke to a man sitting at a workstation close to Sohil's office. The partner's door was closed. He pointed to a small office that served as a conference room where another man was sitting, looking at his phone.

She returned the few steps to Brent. "Mr. Remtulla is on an important call. If you could wait a moment, he shouldn't be much longer. There's another gentleman waiting but he won't take a moment, so I'm told. Would you like to wait?"

"Yes, I can wait. Thanks for your help, Cheryl."

Brent entered the office and took a chair. He and the seated man nodded to each other. After about twenty seconds, the man spoke.

"I thought I recognized you. You're Brent Umber… a private investigator."

"I am. I'm sorry, but have we met before?"

"No. I saw you at Garland's restaurant. I'm Detective Otto Schroeder."

"Pleased to meet you," said Brent, and stretched out his hand. The detective shook it.

Brent was actually not at all pleased to meet him right at that moment. Schroeder, the union representative and detective, was the last person he wanted to meet.

"Can I ask you what brings you here?" said the detective.

"Althorn has engaged me to help with their PR problem."

"Ah, I see." He was silent for some seconds during which he was clearly turning the matter over in his mind. "Why would Althorn hire you when you're a witness to the murder they'd like to put behind them?"

"I approached them. I thought I could combine the civic duty of helping the police enquiry with an employment opportunity. I'm here to look into the backgrounds of a few of the personnel. If I were to find anything, I would send the information on."

"Hmm, so that's how it is... You can't be interfering in a police investigation. There are penalties for that. You'll have to watch what you do."

"I have no intention of interfering with anything."

"Let me see... who's interviewed you so far?" Schroeder consulted the police database through his phone and scrolled through until he found Brent's statement. "Got right involved, didn't you...? Saw nothing... Looks okay... on the surface."

"How's the case going? Do you have a suspect yet?" asked Brent in as cheery a voice as he could muster.

Schroeder ignored him. "So, tell me... what do these people here think you can do for them that the police can't?"

"Establish the innocence of the partners and employees so that their business doesn't suffer unduly."

"We do that by finding the murderer."

"Absolutely, but that might take time during which Althorn suffers a slow bleed in prestige and loses business."

"Hmm, that concern is not part of my job. Yes, I can see why they would take action. It seems odd they pick you... What were you doing at Garland's?"

"Trying to impress someone. It didn't matter in the end."

"Do you go there regularly?"

"I haven't in the past. Detective Schroeder, I didn't kill Mayo and I don't know who did. If I find any valuable information would you like me to pass it along to you or to somebody else?"

"To me."

"Good."

Sohil came in just then and, before he spoke, Brent said,

"Detective Schroeder was here first. Will you be long, Otto?" He used his first name as a way of annoying the detective.

"Just a question or two." Schroeder gave Brent a cold look.

"Then I'll leave you alone. I'll wait in the reception area."

"Certainly, Brent, and thanks," said Sohil.

"Hi, Greg. It's me." Brent had called Lieutenant Greg Darrow.

"Solved it yet?"

"You wish. I'm finding it slow going but I'm working at it. A couple of things and a bit of bad news."

"Give me the bad news first."

"That's what I always say. I bumped into Schroeder in a back office at Althorn. If I had seen a mugshot beforehand I might have avoided him. I hadn't so I didn't. He recognized me, though. Didn't like my being around."

"What did you say?"

"Told him the truth which is that Althorn has engaged me to provide evidence that no employee or partner was involved in the murder."

"That's a tall order. You pretty much have to find the killer to do that."

"I know but people imagine things and some would naturally think the crime is related to the wealthy company. I convinced them at Althorn that if I can demonstrate that certain people are innocent they'd find some relief. Trouble is, by the second meeting I'd got three possibles."

"Sounds like you're deep in the weeds. Anything else?"

"The Valdezes are out as far as I can see. So are the Lindsay's. Now, Schroeder is giving the Valdezes a hard time; probably thinks they deserve it. They probably do but not for murder. Can you steer him away?"

"That guy is such a time waster. I told him already to leave them alone. Valdez would never pull a stunt in public. Anything else?"

"Security cameras. I have information that a guy caught in the rain came in after ten and entered the restaurant. Then he turned round and walked out. He was noticeable because he was so wet. Any idea who that was?"

"No, I'll look into it."

"Two women, very similarly dressed in grey trench coats, came in separately but close together after ten. They didn't check their coats. That's everything."

"Made a note. I don't get told everything and these may have been checked already. Worth checking again, though.

Okay, my man, please keep out of Schroeder's way. He's not a dummy and if he sees you in the wrong place again he'll come after you and he's tenacious."

"Thanks, Greg. I'll keep my eyes open."

No more than ten minutes later, Brent was seated in front of Sohil in the latter's office.

"Detective Schroeder seemed more interested in you than he did in the case. Do you know him?" said Sohil.

"We've only just met. He's having difficulty with the concept that a private investigator is going over similar ground to his own investigation. I believe he thinks it should be a police only affair."

"I can see why he would think that. How can I help you?"

"I'm interested in your relationship with Kirby Mayo."

"Not much to tell there. Of all the partners we had the least to do with one another in our professional capacities. Most of the bond business is with small institutions and where this department intersects with the hedge fund strategies is when we park clients' cash to earn interest before and after the trades are executed. Also, we run the foreign exchange desk. Much of that is automated."

"I see. So the cash is made to work all the time."

"Exactly. This is junior level work, so Kirby never had anything to do with it. The reverse is also true of his work - I had nothing to do with it. I had little reason to see him more than once or twice a week. I have no interest in what he does... er, what he did, I mean. I understand bonds and find them reassuringly predictable... most of the time."

"It sounds almost like two separate businesses. What attracted you to the partnership?"

"I had my own company but it was very difficult to get new clients. At first I saw the partnership as only providing a cost-sharing benefit to me. When I considered it, I thought that a more prestigious address might give a boost, in addition to the small increase in business from Kirby's and the other partners' clients.

What convinced me in the end was that Kirby Mayo seemed to have the Midas touch. He had a good track record and seemed driven to make a success of the future partnership. I thought, 'Why not?'. If the hedge fund business of Althorn grew exponentially, it would lift my bond business with it. That is exactly what happened, and well beyond my expectations. Institutions come to me directly now and high net worth individuals like the diversity they find in Althorn. Some of them have more traditional investment accounts, which include bonds, alongside their riskier portfolio allocations."

"What about your personal dealings with Kirby?"

"Always professional. Always courteous. He was never a man I could warm to. I'll give you an example. My daughter got married last year. I invited him to the wedding but he made his apologies and did not attend. He sent a very generous gift accompanied by a letter containing some tender sentiments. It surprised me when I was shown it. The next business day we were in the office together; he never asked once about the wedding."

"Sounds like he had thoughtful, kind feelings but never cared to vocalize them."

"Could be. That was my take on the matter. Unless it was for the purpose of bringing in new business, he was not a sociable man. Anyone in the office can tell you that. Fortunately, Nola has more than made up for it. Very efficient, very pleasant to deal with… she is such a nice person."

"Then I take it, she came to your daughter's wedding."

"Oh, yes. Nola is a friend of my daughter and was quite involved with the preparations. Brent, you have no idea how insane they go over such things as a piece of fabric or the choice of a photographer. The uproar in the household… it was truly amazing… and expensive." Sohil suddenly looked glum.

"Do you have another daughter?"

"I have four daughters and only one of them married. Do you have children?"

"Not yet and not for some time to come, I think."

"Well, children are a blessing. The love they can give you is very special. The love you give them changes you inside. But my goodness, it is unbelievable the amounts of money they require."

Brent smiled. "How often did Kirby talk about his children?"

"Very rarely. He had photographs of them and Rena in his office. One had to assume he had normal affection for them. I don't really know. What I do know is that things were not good between Rena and him. I don't know the details. I think Nola understands more but it is not my business."

"You met Rena?"

"Rarely, and more so in the early days. A devoted wife I would say but I only ever met her socially in large gatherings."

Brent nodded. "Did Kirby and Will get along?"

"Professionally they did and for most of the time. They are oil and water. Will is much more cautious in his approach to investing in the market. They are, or were, both necessary to the partnership's success. Will took Kirby to task on occasion. He would get annoyed and Kirby would simply dismiss him, making Will's arguments ineffective. I think Kirby listened and modified his actions sometimes but he would never allow Will the satisfaction of knowing he was in the right."

"Is there anyone you know, or are aware of, who might have been motivated to kill Kirby?"

"I have thought this matter over carefully. There are a few names the police have now - individuals Kirby harmed financially. Those incidents were outside of the partnership so I have no direct knowledge of what transpired. Also, he had extra-marital liaisons… there may be something there. I really don't know."

"Rena Kirby is a suspect. Do you think she could have murdered her husband?"

"Truthfully, I just cannot even imagine her committing murder. No, it seems impossible - but you never know."

"I want to thank you for answering my questions. I have to see a couple of employees in a few minutes."

"Go right ahead. I'm sorry I couldn't help you more than I have."

"You have helped. I build up pictures in my mind of who the players are. The murderer and the victim may occupy the foreground but I cannot make sense of them unless there is an adequately filled-in background with the proper context. You have helped me visualize the setting."

Carmela Xanthopoulou was the third-ranking trader who was also an employee. She made it quite clear to Brent that she wished to be elsewhere and knew nothing that could be of any use to anyone. As far as she was concerned, Kirby was dead and she was sorry but life goes on.

"How did he treat you as an employee?" asked Brent.

"He focused on business, just business. He had no time for holding people's hands. He expected professionalism. That's what I liked. He could smell out a profitable deal - it was an instinct with him."

"Did he train you at all?"

"Gave me some direction on a few deals. I had some experience before I joined. Blake helped more with showing me how they do things here."

"What do you think of Blake?"

"He's a nice guy. Smart. Knows what he's talking about."

"And in comparison with Kirby?"

"Not in the same league. Blake is successful three trades out of five and Kirby four. The difference between those two is night and day."

"Where do you stand in comparison, would you say?"

"Three point three and getting better all the time. I really have to go now."

"That's given me some useful insight. Thank you, Ms. Xanthopoulou."

She nodded, got up and left the interview room.

"You wanted to see me?" asked Kevin Jiang.

"Sorry to keep you after hours. I'll be as brief as possible. Please, sit down."

"I often stay late so I do not mind."

"Thank you. My name's Brent Umber, by the way. As has already been explained to you, this conversation is in strict confidence and I do not report anything to the partners except those things that will help the company as a whole move forward through this difficult phase. My job here is to see what needs to be done and clear the name of Althorn of all taint.

Um, what do you do when you stay late?"

"Research and analysis. We have a research department but if I identify a stock that has potential I have to double check to satisfy myself that I'm making a good call."

"I invest a little," said Brent. "I'm very cautious and research what I can but you guys take it to a level that is way beyond me. You must have nerves of steel."

A little modest laugh escaped Kevin. "You do get conditioned to risk-taking but it takes some time. Analysis is the key component for me. If I traded by instinct I would lose too often. Instinct is where you think you know the future. It opens the door to pride. You cannot be proud in this industry. You must have knowledge and experience and the ability to apply what you know in an objective manner."

"I think I understand. Would it be like an early successful string of trades in, let's say, a rising market, leading one to believe that all one's trades will be successful going forward?"

"That is exactly my point."

"How would you characterize Kirby Mayo's style of trading?"

"He successfully traded in a large number of diverse scenarios. His assessment of market moves was extraordinarily precise. Mr. Mayo was very good at quickly assessing a company's prospects, determining its worth, and predicting the way it would move in unusual circumstances. Such catalysts could be headline news, market news or proposed changes within an industry."

"Did he have any faults in his style?"

"Yes. We all do. Sometimes he was impatient and I have seen where he closed a trade before the move. He did do his own research but was more accepting than I am of the research department's findings. That might not be a fault in him… perhaps it is my overly analytical mind that makes me less trusting of other people's work. Sometimes, he relied on… subsidiary lines of information."

"That is a very coy way of putting it, if I understand your meaning correctly."

"You understand me. He had skills beyond the market place. He could attract clients and keep them. I think he had a network of associates and they would give him information he could use. My guess is supported only by the observation that he would buy or sell an obscure company and a week later he had a large profit."

"Did you, by any chance, look into these trades?"

"Yes. But only a few times. I went over the research that would have been available to both of us and could find no obvious reason for him to have placed the order. The first time I was only thinking to learn about his strategy. After that, I knew the truth."

"Did you mention this to anyone?"

"No. It would only have ended my career at Althorn."

"Yes, I suppose it would. Now that he's gone, do you feel better about the situation?"

"I don't know. If he had not been murdered I might. Mixed feelings."

"How did you get along with him?"

Kevin hesitated.

"He was not friendly towards anyone. He was always precise and to the point about work."

"If Blake Pickett had occupied Kirby's position how would you have felt about that?"

Kevin was eager to discuss Blake.

"Blake understands people who trade. He is an excellent manager and very approachable. He spends time discussing our concerns. All of us, that is."

"Then Blake had an open door policy and Kirby a closed one?"

"That is over simplified but summarizes the situation correctly."

"You give me the impression that you are in the business for the long haul and so, I wonder, if you have any ambition about setting up on your own one day?"

"Of course. I do not have the people skills to attract clients or institutions so I would need to align myself with people who can. I see myself doing what Blake does now. I could train people to trade effectively.

I do like trading, Mr. Umber, but it is quite stressful. I feel I am expected to be at the top of my game every day. I strive for that but I know that I cannot achieve it indefinitely. Part ownership of a corporation would give me two things. It would give me more control over what I do and it would also give me the responsibility of others who work for me. As the head of a team, I could take the early enthusiasm of the new traders and show them that there is a way for them to participate eventually in profits through shares in the company. Should I wish to reduce my role or retire, I could do that by surrendering control to the next generation."

"Yes, I can see how that stress could be tough on a person. I like the idea of your exit strategy and can see how it would work. You've been very thoughtful about this. Does Althorn offer anything similar to employees, like a junior partnership?"

"No."

Brent paused for a moment. "I don't speak for Althorn in any capacity but might there not be an opportunity here? Kirby's forty per cent could eventually be split up. For example, an experienced trader might be allowed to take charge over some of the existing portfolio while another person is brought in as a business development manager."

"It is a fluid situation and there might be developments as you describe. Nothing has been mentioned to me... if I'm the trader you are referring to."

"It's early days but it will be settled soon, I'm sure. If you were offered a partnership and the terms looked reasonable, would you accept?"

"Yes, I would."

"You know, delving into Kirby Mayo's past, I have come across some very disturbing features. You may not have been aware of them. Have you ever known him to manipulate or control anyone? Lie to them, even?"

Kevin re-positioned himself in his chair and then became still again. "I cannot recall off-hand. Let me see... like any office there have been a few incidents and a couple in which Mr. Mayo was involved... they were minor in nature. I do not think he did as you suggest. I would absolutely have to say no."

"So it puts beyond question that he ever manipulated you?"

"Absolutely. No question. I cannot recall anything of that nature."

"I'm glad to hear it. Okay, supposing he lied to you about something and you weren't aware that he had till much later?"

"What do you mean? "

"Okay, let's put it this way... I'm looking to find out if he insulted or slighted you in some way?

"No, he didn't," answered Kevin.

"Let's try looking at it another way. Were you a threat to him? Did you jeopardize his career? I mean, I've seen some of the results both of you have had recently. You're the number one producer. I think you were a threat to him.

I doubt he liked the feeling, although he benefited by your success. What I want to know is whether you felt he was in your way and/or whether he resented you as a competitor?"

"Mr. Umber," Kevin said nervously, "I can't speak for Kirby and I have no idea what his thoughts towards me were, but, for myself, I am a professional and very focused - too focused to play the office politics game."

"Of course. I hadn't mentioned office politics... you did. Seeing as you've brought it up, let's address it. What you're asking me to believe," said Brent, "is that, having proved to yourself that Kirby was employing unethical and probably illegal tactics in his trading practices, you, with your fine analytical mind, were content to work for such a man whom you also outperformed, and he was content to have it so. Kirby Mayo was a vindictive man, or so I'm given to understand. You were a threat to him and he would therefore be prone to manipulating you for his own ends. You're saying that nothing like this happened. There were no incidents between you. You have in mind to be a partner here. If not here, then elsewhere, where you would have more control in running things. Kirby indisputably ran things here."

Kevin looked aghast. "What are you saying? That I had a reason to kill Kirby?"

"I didn't say that. I'm sure you're holding something back and I want to get my job done. If you'd tell me what it was I can move on. I won't repeat it to anyone else."

"There's nothing to tell. I have ambition but there is nothing wrong with that. Kirby was a dominant man. I discovered that as soon as I arrived here. I am not holding anything back. I have not done anything."

"Probably not," said Brent who smiled. "I think that is all for now. Thank you for being most co-operative, Kevin."

"Thank you, Mr. Umber."

Kevin got up to leave. He looked far from comfortable with the way the conversation had gone.

"Enjoy your weekend, Kevin."

Brent was writing some notes in a ring binder when Nola Devon entered the room.

"That's so sweet. I haven't seen a binder like that since college." She sat down at the table.

"Ah, a little foible of mine. Everything gets typed up eventually but I can express myself faster and more freely with a pen. How are you?"

"Doing well enough, I suppose, under the circumstances."

"I've checked your story and I can report that there are no holes in what you told me."

"But… I'm not off the hook?" she asked tentatively.

"No. I am now, however, highly disposed to believe everything you say."

"That sounds like a definite maybe."

"Better than that, I think. You're here late, aren't you?"

"Nothing unusual. My husband is looking after the children. That means I can avoid the worst of the rush hour and keep my work up to date without my mind being elsewhere."

"Teamwork in marriage. That's the third time today I've come across the phenomenon."

"Is that so? Does it have a bearing on the case?"

"No, it's just something pleasing I've observed."

"I take it you're not married?"

"Sadly, I'm not. No little children are waiting for me."
Zack, Mason, and Vane crossed his mind but the thought
seemed ludicrous and so he dismissed it. "Did you manage
to contact Rena Kirby?"

"I did. She might see you but she wants to talk to you
first on the phone. I think she's tired of talking to the police.
We can call her now, if you like."

"Can we do it on speaker-phone?"

Nola nodded as she punched in the numbers on the
extension. The phone began ringing. A weak voice
answered.

"Hello?"

"Hi, Rena. It's Nola."

"Hi, Nola…"

"Brent Umber is with me. He's the man who wants to
come and talk to you."

"Oh, yes."

"Hello, Mrs. Mayo," said Brent.

"Hello," replied Rena.

"I would very much like to meet you in person. Would
you mind if I did?"

"I don't know. Why do you need to see me?"

"I'm a private investigator, as Nola probably told you,
and what I really want to know is what Kirby was like.
There is no one better placed than you to tell me about
him."

"I don't know. Why do you want to know about him?"

"I'm trying to find out the truth. You see, a lot of his
business associates are under suspicion because the police
do not have a prime suspect. I strongly believe that if I
could talk to you and learn more about Kirby, I can help
the police direct their inquiries more effectively because I
can establish who is innocent. Any little nuggets of
information from you might really help me."

"Is this true, Nola?"

"It is. And he promises to be very respectful to you."

"I see. That's reassuring. Mr. Umber? I'm not sure I can agree to this because Kirby..." Rena stopped suddenly.

"Um, would it be that Kirby might not like business matters being brought to his home?"

"Why, yes. That's exactly it," she replied, surprised.

"Do you think he would have made an exception in this case?"

"Uh... yes, I think you're right. He probably would."

"Then, there is no real objection against my coming to see you?"

"I suppose not."

"I can come to your house tomorrow or on Sunday. Which would you prefer?"

"Sunday morning, I think... about eleven? Would that be okay with you?"

"Eleven will be fine. Now, is anyone staying with you, like a friend or relative?"

"An aunt is staying with me."

"And will she be there on Sunday?"

"Yes. Her name's Marjorie."

"Excellent. Then I'm looking forward to meeting both you and Auntie Marjorie on Sunday at eleven. Or do you call her Auntie Marj?"

"She's Aunt Marjie."

"I'd better get her name right or I might be in trouble."

"She's very nice. You'll like her."

"I'm sure I will. Until Sunday, then. Goodbye."

"Goodbye, Mr. Umber. Are you still there, Nola?"

"Yes, I am, Rena."

"I think I can talk to him."

"Yes, I think you can."

"Thank you. Goodbye, then."

"Bye, Rena. Bye."

Nola and Brent looked at each other when the call was disconnected.

"She's very fragile," said Brent. "I'll not upset her. My questions can wait until another time, if necessary. I'll just sit and hear her out."

"That's probably the best thing you can do. Don't bring Althorn into it. The business can survive for a bit longer. Let her make her decisions in her own time."

"I think you're right…. Sad, isn't it?"

"Very sad. That was insightful of you to guess that she's still mindful of Kirby's habits."

"It's because she has yet to accept the fact of his death. She will eventually… after the funeral or later than that. It will be a gradual process, anyway."

"The funeral's next Friday," said Nola in a flat tone.

"Is it? I shall go. I hope to be closer to the truth by then. In fact, I'm hoping to *know* the truth by then.

This is the very thing I hate most about murder. The victim is laid to rest but those who loved the victim are doomed to limp on and on, carrying the pain of the crime for years until they find some way of accommodating it in their lives."

"I've been coming to that realization. It's made me look at my life more closely. I think I've deferred too much for the sake of my career. It's crowded out sympathy for others. I won't say I regret my choices but I do regret missing out on some important things and pushing others into a very tight schedule. It won't be this way for much longer."

"Makes sense to me. I'll wrap up here for now." Brent began to pack away his things.

"Have you made any progress?" asked Nola.

"Yes, I have. I've obtained insight into the operations here and at the same time found no widespread animosity towards Kirby. I've a few interesting leads to follow up... Nothing concrete as yet."

"Who is it?" asked Nola, her eyes riveted upon Brent.

"Actually, it is who are 'they'. Like yourself, there are others who might fit the profile of this murderer but probably do not. Just as I haven't mentioned your name to them, neither will I mention their names to you... At least, not at the moment.

Nola, it's only a process. Like a police investigation. You don't really want me to explain. It would cause you to go through the ugliness of suspecting a co-worker unnecessarily, one who is later proved to be innocent. It might sour existing relationships and taint them going forward. Be assured, it will all be in my report except I will not disclose, uh, personal matters that are unrelated to my mandate.

"I understand. You're wrong about one thing. I would very much like you to explain."

"Oh, I know. If I were you I would find me very annoying about now."

Nola laughed. "It's not as bad as that. I'm just curious, of course."

"I can say this much. I think the staff here is in good shape overall, when everything is considered. Some of them might have been a little subdued but no worse than that. Have you noticed anything?

"Not person by person so much... The office is definitely quieter than it used to be."

"I'm sure it will pass in a week or two... Well, that's me done for the day." Brent closed his bag. "Goodnight and thank you for trusting me enough to give me a chance at this."

"I should be thanking you… It's odd because, in a way, we're both on probation. You're still an unknown quantity and I might be a murderer. We both know ourselves but we do not know each other. Goodnight, Brent. I hope you are as you appear to be."

Brent checked his phone. Linda's message said, "I've been so busy this week. I'm meeting some old friends over the weekend. I so wish you were going to be there."

Chapter 19

Early Saturday Morning

"*P*hil, how are you? It's Brent." He had called an old friend, a car dealer.

"Hey, man. Staying sane?"

"Most of the time. I'm in a hurry. I need a car that's going to look good in front of a $20-million mansion."

"Well, you know, you're in luck. I have a real beauty but boy, if it got a scratch, you and I would not be friends any longer."

"Really intriguing. What have you got?"

"Okay. It's a red Bentley GT coupe, three years old with low mileage. It is a thing of beauty. That should do you."

"That's absolutely perfect."

"Yeah, well, there's a catch."

"Oh. Let's hear it, then."

"If you damage it in any way, shape, or form, you bought it at full price. No friendship deals here, buddy. Not on this unit."

"But I'm a safe driver, Phil. I don't intend to hurt your car."

"Nope. Words won't make me feel as comfortable as your promise to buy it would. I trust you, Brent, like family.

And, like family, you'll try and take advantage of my good nature."

"How much?"

"Hundred and forty-five."

"Ouch… You know I'm hooked, right?"

"Just say it then, Brent."

"But a damaged car is not worth full value, you know."

"I never knew that. I must have been an idiot my whole life. Try again."

"It's like this. I'm in the market for a new car and I've a Boxster to trade. If I agree to this, you get me into the car of my choice but you absolutely do it on a razor-thin margin."

"Let's set the deal out. You borrow the car and pay one-forty-five if you so much as breathe on it. If the car is returned in its present pristine condition I get you another car and I make what, like, twenty bucks on it? That sounds like a great deal - for you."

"Show me a legitimate invoice and we'll say a thousand on top. How's that?"

"That's better. I can do that for a friend. We all clear now?"

"Yes. I promise to buy the Bentley for a hundred and forty-five thousand if it gets damaged. I haven't even seen it yet and I must be crazy."

"You are. I'll get some plates on it so it looks like you own it. After someone?"

"Yes, whoever's responsible for that murder at Garland's."

"Interesting, interesting. Come on over and your car will be ready."

It was nine o'clock and Brent was standing, looking out of his bedroom window, in his architect-designed house. Later, he would meet Becki Kent and Gabbie Wright, in that order. He was dressed in what he thought was an excellent and comfortable combination of clothes for the day. Instead of dressing up to the social circle he intended to invade, he dressed down. Clean faded jeans, clean black training shoes, a new sunset red-orange knitted top, over which he wore a favourite bomber jacket of worn, brown leather. Dressing down was a relative term. He had paid approximately eight hundred for his ensemble and had achieved a look often aimed for by top fashion houses. Had he purchased their wares to emulate his outfit, he would have been out about seven thousand. The one concession to name brands was a Breitling watch which Brent did not like because it felt too clunky. It did look impressive, though. He added an antique carnelian signet ring.

He was looking good. Brent had been feeling excited about the car. He had ramped himself up for the interviews to come. Now he was lonely and staring out of the window. He thought of many people and many things. What he wanted was someone he loved to say to him, 'I know you can do it. Come back safe to me.' There was no one to see him go and no one to see him return. The house was spacious, elegant, and comfortable, but it was so empty sometimes. No one filled it for him.

He sighed to himself. Putting on some cologne, he thought of how he would approach Becki, a woman he had never met who lived in a wealthy neighbourhood, and gain admission to her house. The challenge would normally absorb his interest. Today it did not. He put his distraction down to the fading away of the year, the bare trees, and the weak gold light that passed for sunshine yet barely warmed the air. At least it was dry.

Brent wanted to take the Bentley onto a racetrack and flat out make it roar around the circuit. He had never driven a car that suggested it had available such unlimited reserves of power. At low speeds it drove itself. He was fascinated by the slightly irregular hand-stitching on the thick, luxurious seats, the mass of expensive metal knobs, and the surprising level of attention to detail found everywhere. The car was an obvious, eye-catching metallic red - not so different to the carnelian he was wearing. He liked the colour but he noticed people staring at the Bentley. He would never buy one because of that but was thrilled to be driving it for a while.

Becki Kent's house was one of a half dozen highly valuable properties she owned around the world. The sprawling villa in Cannes was her favourite. The large apartment in New York was her springboard for the most dynamic aspects of her social life. She owned a mid-sized hotel in London and a stay there was a rest in a hideaway in the middle of town. Greg Darrow's note on Becki put her estimated net worth somewhere between four and six hundred million.

The colonial mansion that Brent observed would have been valuable wherever it had been built and it was extravagantly valuable because of the area in which it was located. The problem with it, Brent thought, was that it had been built too large to begin with in the nineteen-twenties and had been added to since. The original symmetry had been degraded by the additions. It had all the right features but it said, 'location, location, location' instead of 'elegant charm'. Not for the first time, Brent was encountering an expensive property in an expensive area that had somehow completely missed its architectural design objectives.

More importantly for the moment, the house had a high electronic iron gate and he would either have to see to it in broad daylight or wait for someone to go in or out. He needed to drive up to the front door.

A little after ten, a pick-up truck came down the driveway to go out. He guessed correctly that it was a gardener who had been busy with the fall clean-up of leaves and was taking a load away. The gate clanked and then slowly began to slide open. The old pick-up rolled out and the red Bentley rolled in.

He parked on the driveway in full view of the house. He looked the façade over to identify and count cameras. The system was old enough to be replaced. He climbed the stone staircase and rang the bell. The porch was too shallow to be functional beyond keeping the rain off someone on the doorstep. If Brent had a porch, he thought to himself, he would sit in it and watch people go by and say hello to some of them. He could not remember the last time he had seen anyone doing that.

The door was opened by a foreign maid in her thirties. Filipino he thought.

"Good morning," said the maid pleasantly.

"Good morning. Is Becki in?"

"Oh, she's, um, she's not available."

"Yes, I know what she's like. Probably not dressed yet." Brent leaped with sudden alacrity through the door and the maid had no time to close it on him. He brushed past her. "I'm terribly sorry, please excuse me," he said. Then he shouted into the depths of the house, "Hello, Becki!? It's me, Brent."

He knew he had been heard because the faint noise of a chair scraped on the floor came from somewhere towards the back of the house.

"What's your name?" asked Brent of the maid.

"Patty."

He took out a business card and a pen and wrote a note on the back. It read, 'Don't blame Patty. I pushed past her. Re. Lead on Kirby's murderer.'

"Well, Patty, my sincere apologies for being so rude to you. But it's very important I speak with Becki immediately. If you give her this card I will explain everything when I see her. Where shall I wait? Here?"

"No. You can go in there." Patty directed him to a large room at the front of the house. She was uncertain what to make of Brent. The way he had called out made her think he was a friend or even a family member. She disappeared with the card.

Brent went into the unlit room. It was sparsely furnished for its size with a few side chairs, a sofa, a small cabinet of curios, and no table. By contrast, the walls were covered with at least fifty paintings of different sizes. Squeezed into one corner was a small Utrillo. It was charming in itself but the delicate colours of a Montmartre winter street scene looked anaemic because of a large impasto cityscape in bright new acrylics hanging next to it. The room puzzled Brent. It was more like a haphazard warehouse for art than a decorated room in a home. The only use which came to mind for such a room was that cocktail parties might be held there.

"Patty, who is it?" Becki Kent was sitting in the breakfast area. A man was preparing food in the kitchen for lunch. A tall, young woman was leaning against the casing of a double width archway between the two rooms, typing a message into her phone.

"His name is Brent Umber." Patty handed the card to Becki who then looked at both sides.

"Says he has a lead on the murderer. Is he from the police?" asked Becki.

"I don't know. No, I don't think so. His car is too nice."

"He must be a neighbour, then. Why's he here now?"

"Do you want me to see him?" asked the young woman. She spoke with a European accent that was hard to place.

"Would you, Bobbie? I'll go and put my face on." She got up. "Why don't these people call?"

"You wouldn't answer them if they did," Bobbie said languidly, as she left the room.

Brent heard Bobbie coming towards him while he was looking at a painting.

"Good morning," he said when he saw her. She was dressed in a loose black polo neck over black jeans.

"Hello. Is it a habit of yours to shout in other people's houses?" said Bobbie, as she approached. She came to a stop a little closer to Brent than he would have expected of a stranger.

"No, I never do it, as a rule. I'm sorry for disturbing you like this."

"You have disturbed us. Why are you here?"

"To see Becki."

"She doesn't know who you are."

As she spoke, she transferred the steady gaze she had directed at Brent's face to the window and the red Bentley outside.

"I know Kirby Mayo was a friend of hers and I have important information about his death that I think she should hear."

"I suppose she can spare a minute to hear what you have to say," said the woman, looking back at Brent.

"Thank you. And your name is?"

"I'm Becki's personal assistant."

"Right, right. I have to ask, this room, what is it used for?"

"Parties."

"That's what I thought." Brent smiled. "What about the paintings? There are so many of them."

"You might be a thief for all I know."

"I used to be but I gave it up."

"I think I'll call the police."

"You can if you like. There's enough for me to look at here until they arrive."

Bobbie moved away. "Technically, you're trespassing."

"I am, in a social sense. Not yet, in legal terms."

Using her phone, she searched the internet. After some seconds, she said,

"Private Investigator."

"The address is out of date. I only work on cases that interest me now."

"Who are you working for?"

"Myself and the public good."

Bobbie folded her arms and gently tapped her phone on one of them a few times.

"What is this information you have?"

"I can only share it with Becki at present."

Bobbie left the room without saying anything more.

"I'm told that you're a private investigator," said Becki. "My assistant is concerned that you are here to gather information. I'm inclined to agree with her."

Becki was dressed in a pale mauve woollen dress and wore heavy, gold jewellery.

The setting of the empty party room gave a dislocated feel to the atmosphere. The lack of furniture left the impression that everything had been cleared out of the way for a battle. Becki was accompanied by Bobbie.

"That is exactly right. I'm working on the case and I gather information from everyone I meet who is connected with it. I'm building a picture in my mind of how the murder of Kirby was committed. I understand you were there that night."

"Not so fast, Mr. Umber. I don't know that I trust you at all. In fact, I don't trust you. You come into my house, shout your head off at me, saying you have information. Now you tell me you're collecting information. You'd better leave."

"I will do that if you insist, but… First, I can justify my presence here but I was reluctant to do so to your assistant. Second, I do have insights into the case that I really do think should interest you."

"Then you had better go ahead and justify yourself," said Becki.

Both women stared at him uncompromisingly.

"When asked who I was working for, I said it was for myself and as a civic duty. That's true. I omitted to say that I am also commissioned by Althorn Capital to do what I can to clear the partnership's name by establishing that there is no connection between the business and Kirby's death."

"I see. Go on," said Becki.

"The object is to insulate Althorn from the inevitable conclusion the public will draw that a business associate might have killed him and that Althorn itself might, in effect, be harbouring a criminal. The loss of business could become catastrophic to Althorn.

I have interviewed the general partners but you are the only investment partner and I urgently need to talk to you about the case."

Becki pointed quickly to the phone in Bobbie's hand, saying, "Get Nola Devon." Bobbie accessed the number and walked away out of earshot as she waited for the call to connect.

"Why did you not contact me first?" asked Becki.

"Partly because I have a lot of people to see, my schedule is so fluid as well as so crammed and I need to move quickly, and partly because I have the suspicion you would direct me to your lawyer which is what you have done to the police after giving them your initial statement."

"Yes, I would have done that to you, too. I do not want to see the police again."

Bobbie returned and handed her phone to Becki.

"Hello, Nola…? Brent Umber is standing in front of me. What can you tell me about him?"

The room was silent for over a minute. Brent looked away. He caught sight of the Bentley and wondered what the car's top speed was and where he could personally experience it.

"Thank you. How are the children…? and Jimmy…? That's good. Goodbye"

She handed the phone back to Bobbie.

"Nola has a high opinion of you. Thinks you're trustworthy."

"I'm relieved to hear it," said Brent.

"You still have to prove yourself to me but… we might as well do that in comfort and I hate this room."

The three of them were now seated in what once would have been a drawing room but was now called a lounge. It had changed very little from one designation to the other. Fine-grained pale wood panelling from the early nineteen-twenties had darkened with age and had acquired the soft glow that only age can produce. The rectangular room had a moulded ceiling patterned with three large concentric circles which were repeated in the design in the thick long rug that lay upon the parquet floor. The rug had a cream ground, the circles were rose-pink and the border was a series of patterned bands of the same pink, mixed with sky blue and yellow ochre. This room had comfortable covered chairs and sofas in a variety of pastel patterned blues and pinks - enough for twenty. They were arranged in conversation groups, with the main group centred around the fireplace.

A black lacquered grand-piano with its lid open occupied one bright corner. The light came through the white gauzy drapes of two windows and glowed pale gold in the October sunlight. These were flanked by heavy, lined curtains of an old pink satin, as were all the other windows. Antique occasional tables supported a variety of old lamps which were covered in the same pink material of the curtains and were finished in old-gold braid and tassels. The paintings - all of them old - were chosen for their decorative colours and slightly sentimental themes. A woman had chosen for the room, Brent thought, but she had not designed the house. He wished she had.

They seated themselves by the fireplace. The chairs were very comfortable. Becki sat in what appeared to be 'her' chair while Brent sat on the edge of a sofa. Bobbie sat at the far end of the same sofa. Brent would have to turn his head from one to the other.

"Who decorated this room?" he asked.

"My grandmother," said Becki.

"It's lovely. It has such a warm, welcoming feel to it."

Becki had been a beauty and would still be one if she had not had such a hard look in her eyes. It was as if she were drilling into a person to extract what she wanted. Even though she had been reassured by Nola, distrust seemed to dominate her attitude, and now she knew what the situation was with Brent, a degree of contempt was becoming evident in her voice.

"You haven't forgiven me for my intrusion, have you?"

"No, and I'm not likely to unless you tell me what you know."

Brent turned his head. Bobbie was staring at him.

"I still don't know your name?" asked Brent with a smile.

"Never mind her," said Becki. "You came to see me."

"That's true. I'd rather go through life being polite than not. You want me to get on with it and so I shall.

Becki, you were in the dining room the night Kirby was killed. You say you didn't see anything unusual because you were busy talking to a friend. As far as your statement goes that let's you out as the killer and helps Althorn in so far as the investment partner is exonerated. The problem is, I have an issue with your statement."

"Ha! What do I care what you think. Anyway, you said you knew who the murderer was."

"You see, Becki, you set up a meeting with Kirby Mayo. Part way through, you leave to sit at Amy Feinstein's table. She's a friend who was at Garland's with her husband and they both corroborate your statement. Minutes later, with you safely out of the way, Kirby is shot and killed. This makes you a suspect with an alibi."

"Is that it?" asked Becki. She had a slight smile.

"Far from it. Next, we should consider Gabbie Wright. You bring her along to the meeting with Kirby. She is at his table when the shots are fired and she sees Kirby die right before her eyes. Quite understandably, she goes into shock from what she has seen. Knowing she was in shock, you just left her, providing no comfort to her. That wasn't very friendly of you and it adds to the suspicion."

"Don't you think I was in shock? Do you know how much I've suffered?" She tapped on the arm of her chair.

"Actually, no. I can't tell that you're suffering at all. You apparently didn't suffer the night of the murder because of the clear, coherent statement you gave the police. I see no sign of you suffering now. But your friend was certainly suffering."

"That's up to Gabbie. I wasn't going to babysit her. There are nurses for that. As soon as I knew one was coming, I left because I wasn't needed. Call me callous."

"Very likely you weren't needed but it looks bad for you."

"Is that all? I'm innocent and my lawyers will take care of everything. You're a real idiot." She crossed her arms defensively.

"I won't dispute that fact but I wonder how you picked up on it?"

"How could I shoot Kirby when I'm at a table that's completely out of the line of fire?"

"Simple. You didn't. You gave the signal to this nameless lady on the sofa next to me. The signal was to say that no one would see her shoot Kirby. She shoots, everyone dives, and she escapes in the confusion."

"That's ridiculous," said Bobbie.

"Leave him to me," Becki said in a sharp voice. "You have come into my house and accused me and my assistant of murder. Do you think…"

"Becki!" Brent shouted. "I did not accuse you. I laid out a case against you. If I can do that so can the police.

Throw me out if you like but you'd be foolish to do so. It would be better if you had me on your side. You wanted a conflict here. I didn't. Play it all however you wish. It makes no difference to me. If you're involved in the murder I will find you out and, if I don't, the police will. If you're not involved, as you say, why are you fighting me?"

"Don't ever talk to Ms. Kent like that again," said Bobbie.

"You're just as bad," said Brent turning to her. "You think you're above everyone else and can get away with playing games. Do neither of you realize how suspicious that makes both of you appear? There is a murderer about somewhere. He or she may have had an accomplice. Why, oh why, are you two signing up for the parts?"

In the silence that followed, Brent realized that both women were angry enough that they would be unlikely now to relent and tell him anything. He got up.

"You have my number. If there's any information you can give me, I'll be pleased to hear it. Goodbye."

A block away, Brent parked the Bentley. His recent interview had not gone wrong exactly but it had not gone the way he had hoped. He had interviewed many hostile people in the past and always came away feeling he had failed as a communicator. He had come to understand, through his own experiences and those of others, that this hostility was inevitable according to some fixed percentage. It seemed to be about one in five. If he had official standing in the case it would have gone a lot better. He would not have needed to push his way in. Becki and no name would have been required to answer his questions - the ones he had never got to ask. Still, he had learned a lot.

He took out his ring binder and began writing notes while all the raw thoughts, observations, and impressions were still fresh in his mind.

Chapter 20

Saturday around noon

*H*e travelled another block to Gabbie Wright's house. It was after eleven now. He was counting on a better reception here and he knew it was not just for the sake of his investigations that he was counting upon it. He stopped and looked before driving in. The gate was open and there were a number of cars parked in the driveway which meant she had visitors.

He wondered whether, in the same way as owners are sometimes said to look a little bit like their dogs, houses might reflect a little of the householder. It was true of poverty and prosperity and scruffy and tidy comparisons but beyond that? He was not sure.

The house he now observed was a marvellous gem of mid-nineteenth century craftsmanship and design in warm orange brick. Having three above ground stories - the top possessing three dormer windows, it appeared to have been placed on a pedestal. The verandah was supported by Ionic columns and was the width of the house and deliciously deep. Two large windows with twelve lights each were on either side of the double doors and five more the same size were on the second floor. Light could flood in during the day and flood out in a blaze at night. Perfect symmetry, proportion, and care were the hallmarks of this home.

Since the gate was open, Brent drove in and parked. All the other cars and SUVs were new and some very expensive. Under the porch he rang the bell. He noticed a new security camera but, for once, he did not feel inclined to survey the system.

A maid answered the door.

"Good morning, sir," she said.

"Good morning. I think Ms. Wright is probably too busy to see me now. If you would give her my card and ask her if she could spare me a few minutes, I would greatly appreciate it." He wrote a note on the back that said, "I'm investigating the case for private reasons."

"She's not expecting you?"

"No. I can wait out here."

"I'll take the card to her and see what she says, sir," said the maid, politely.

She disappeared into the house, leaving the door ajar.

Brent walked along the porch and surveyed the street. What a sense of accomplishment, he thought, the original owner or any of the subsequent owners must have possessed to look out on such a neighbourhood with such a house behind them. The house had stood in its place for over a century and a half and it would, if allowed, still stand for that span of time again.

The door opened. Gabbie stepped out.

"Admiring the view, Mr. Umber, when you should be finding the murderer?"

"Hello. I am, actually. It deeply impresses me with a sense of the longevity of the place. You must love it here."

"I do. I often have a wisp of a vision and the street is suddenly crammed with carriages and horses instead of cars. Please come in. It's a little chilly out."

"I'm sorry, of course." He now noticed what she was wearing. Her special occasion dress was very long, black and silky, overlaid with artistic mauve and warm pink irises on long dark green stems. Once inside, he said,

"That is a very beautiful dress."

"Oh, this old thing? It's just something I wear around the house." She smiled at him and at her own joke before gesturing towards a small reception room or reading room for Brent to enter. Once inside, she shut the door behind them. He would normally have studied the airy space for its classical elegance and exquisite furniture but, for once, he was not interested in those things.

"I'm not intruding, am I?" asked Brent.

"Very much so. However, I hoped you would come."

They stood facing one another, each going through that split second estimation of another person. Brent saw a lovely, elegant woman, in every degree composed and self-assured. Her colour had returned since last he saw her. Gone were the strain and confusion caused by seeing a man die right in front of her eyes. Her dark, straight hair that came down to just above her shoulders was now in perfect order instead of being dishevelled. Gabbie's steady gaze was not uncomfortable because it held no threat. She was forty-two, according to the police records.

"A celebration?" asked Brent.

"It's my nephew's birthday. He's thirty-one and still believes they're important. I'm fulfilling my role as auntie today and giving him a birthday luncheon."

"I'm jealous of your nephew in so many ways."

"How am I to take that?"

"Ah, yes. I see. It was in the sense of family that I meant, and this house and... I'd better not say any more."

"And me as your auntie?"

"I have thought of you a great deal since we met and it was never once as an auntie."

"Hmm, this is interesting. Is that your reason for coming here today?"

"Yes, but not entirely. I'm also here about the case. But mainly I wanted to find out how you're doing and if you needed my help at all."

"Please, Mr. Umber." They both sat down in the armchairs she had indicated. "This attention is quite flattering," she said when they were settled.

"Why's that?"

"Because it is sincere."

"That's one of the qualities I admire about you. Your directness."

"Well, we are progressing, aren't we?"

"Eventually, I hope to make my meaning plain but only when I feel more sure about you," said Brent.

"This sounds very serious."

"I am being serious. Often I'm flippant which would be a foil for your mocking; I'm sincere, you say, which is a counterpart for your directness. We both want honesty. And we are both facing loneliness."

Her eyes dropped for a moment. "You caught me at a weak moment."

"That's true. I would add that the weakness you speak of was a result of your strength, of your resolve to deal with your emotions on your own, of the defences you have become used to putting up to protect yourself. It was only a further strength, not weakness, that finally allowed you to drop your usual defences. You dropped them because you wanted help. I've made the assumption, rashly or wisely, and I don't know which it is yet, that you wanted my help."

"Let's say that's true. Will that help you come to the point?"

"It will. In the same way you wanted my help then, I want yours now. Right at this very moment, if you asked me, I would tell you my whole life history. You cannot know how important that would be to me. It is not the baring of my soul alone; it is doing so to a woman I believe I could come to love. In fact, I know I am on the brink of being in love with you.

It's strange. I hardly know you, Gabbie, but I trust you. I really do think you would hear me out, hear all about my past life, and not judge me... perhaps... you would accept me. That I can speak to you now, in this way ... it's something I thought I would never be able to do with anyone. I wanted to talk to you because I believed you would understand. But if I did tell you of these things I would feel then as though I belonged to you."

"My, how serious you are. l can see that much. Brent, for now you must keep your secrets. If you tell me them... as you say, you will have gone too far."

"Sadly, especially since seeing you in your beautiful home-surroundings, I've come to realize that - but only because there's a reason why I fear it would not work between us. We are in the same mountain range but you are stuck on one peak and I on another."

"Is it because I'm older than you?"

"No, not all, Gabbie. Far from it. It's because we have lived very different lives in such different spheres. I might not be happy in your world and you might not be happy in mine. It's more than that, though... If it did not work out between us we could lose all hope. I know I would and I could not bear that."

Gabbie sighed before saying, "It's odd how one's mind dictates what one will think about. You made me forget a murder. Instead, I've been thinking about you ever since that night.

I imagined, if we had met fifteen years ago, I would have loved and stayed with you. I see the differences between us but, back then, we would have worked through them... through everything. I'm not sure I could do that now. It's undeniable that something kind of magical happened between us when we first met - and during the days that have passed since then that spark of magic has created something that's smouldering and ready to burst into flames. But you're right, there is no certain future for us. That is what you want, a future that is certain. I'm not sure it's what I want so I don't know if you could find what you're looking for with me. So it might be better to damp it all down and never allow it to blaze.

Brent, right now, if you insisted, I think I might say yes to whatever you proposed but if you did insist you would cease to be the man you are at this moment. Are you still sure of me now?"

"Yes, because you're so honest and straightforward."

"That is such a relief to hear. I thought... it doesn't really matter what I thought. Like you, I have secrets I would like to tell to someone... to you in particular. Likewise, I would tell you if you wanted me to. You need for us to have this understanding because you have to ask me something awful about something I'd rather forget. Is that it?"

"It is such a shame that these things are intertwined..."

The door opened.

"Here you are! Oh, sorry. I didn't know you were busy."

"Come in, Alicia. This is Brent Umber."

They said hello to each other.

"Alicia's my sister and it's her son David's birthday today."

"It's a pity I will not be staying to meet David but many happy returns of the day to him," said Brent.

"Thank you. The cake's arrived," said Alicia to Gabbie. Alicia then left, shutting the door quietly behind her.

Gabbie turned her attention back to Brent. "I think I can guess. You want to ask me what I saw when Kirby Mayo died. You're wondering if I'm strong enough to relive that experience. You feel awful because you've come to my house during a family celebration. You don't wish to hurt me. Brent, please ask your questions."

"Thank you. I was thinking, if we were sitting on that sofa, I would be able to hold your hand." He took his jacket off.

Gabbie smiled and went over to the sofa. Brent sat next to her, held her hand and slowly and gently stroked it for some moments. He barely noticed, and certainly did not comment on, the sapphire and diamond ring she was wearing.

"Now, I need to know what happened in the minute prior to his death. I'm not interested in his death and we need not go there. It's only the brief period before it. You're sitting at the table. He's talking to you. What is he saying?"

"We had been quiet for a while because he was becoming objectionable. Nothing bad, you understand, but it was obvious where it was going and I put a stop to it. He didn't like that.

During the silence, I was wondering when Becki would return. I was trying to make a pastry last so I could keep my hands occupied. I was taking smaller and smaller bites to make it go further."

"Did you hear anything around you. Or behind you?"

"I was lost in my own thoughts... I heard someone laugh behind me."

"A friendly laugh? Which side?"

"It was friendly... although, maybe a little forced and on the left, my left."

"That was possibly from a table of actors. Um, did you notice anything in your peripheral vision?"

"No... nothing. I was either keeping my eyes down to avoid Kirby or looking into the distance into a neutral zone."

"I see. Did you notice anyone in these neutral zones?"

"I saw Becki. I thought she was coming back but she didn't. Waiters... no one in particular."

"Around you, were there any smells, such as a dinner, a scent, something burning?"

"A faint smell of lemon, I remember that."

"Now, what was the sequence of events? You say you were sitting in silence for a while, how did the conversation start up again?"

"That was Kirby... he had a change of heart and apologized for being... what word did he use... that's it, 'boorish'. It sounded quite Victorian and I nearly said something. He apologized, said he admired me, and he believed I thought little of him. He gave me the choice of restarting the conversation on this new and improved footing. I replied that I accepted his apology... and added a little of my usual barbed wit..." She squeezed his hand. "I really wish I didn't do that. It's how I keep people distant but it's such a habit now I do it with family sometimes when I don't mean to."

"I know. I try to be cheerful with everyone I meet but sometimes it's an act. We all hide ourselves in different ways, with different coverings... Were you aware of any sights, sounds, or smells while he spoke?"

"No. Hearing him speak was somewhat better than the silence that had been prevailing but... Why, by the way, are you so interested in smells?"

"I'm wanting to impress you with how thorough I'm being. Did you hear any hard or metallic noises?"

"No. If you mean the gun, no."

"The conversation has ended. What next?"

"I was... wait a minute. Don't say anything more."

Gabbie sat up and let go his hand. She unstrapped her shoes and pulled up her long dress a little so it did not crease when she put her legs up on the sofa. She rested her head on his chest. "I want to hear your heart," she said. She got comfortable and gave her hand back for him to hold. "If someone comes in you must ask me to marry you and I will say yes, otherwise, what will they think?

You want information and this is the critical point you've been driving towards. I'll only tell you what you want, if you accept my condition. If we married it might be awful, worse than we imagine, but I'll risk it and so will you, despite all our fine words. There, what do you say?"

"I love challenges," said Brent.

"I know you do. Your heart is racing a little but I knew you liked challenges and interesting situations before today."

"How did you know?"

"You had no idea who I was and yet you came and spoke to me to be kind to a stranger despite the fact you weren't supposed to. Then, you held my hand for so long... you no longer cared if the lieutenant caught you. I understood that to mean you liked me."

"And I thought I was clever."

"Yes, I'm a clever girl and now I've got you trapped. The trap is a reasoned one. I have yet to begin to love you but I know I could very easily. I can't decide what to do next and neither can you... not really, you can't. So, let's leave it to chance. If anyone walks through that door in the next half an hour our fate is sealed for us."

"And if they don't?"

"We will both be sad and not see each other again because it is not to be. Fate will have decided. But I will know there is a man in the world whom I could have loved and came very close to doing so."

"Okay, I agree. I will ask you to marry me if someone comes in here in the next half an hour. As time is so short for us... this is so weird... I want to tell you just two or three things. First, the car I drove up in today is borrowed. Second, I'm quite comfortably off and could support you in a very pleasant suburban lifestyle... don't laugh... I also have a well-appointed apartment over an old machine shop in a rough, industrial area. I renovated it myself."

"I like the sound of that. We could spend our honeymoon there. Go on, one more."

"If we had met years ago, I probably would have stolen that ruby ring of yours that you were wearing the night we were at Garland's. However, far from that being the case, when we met the other day, all I became interested in stealing was your heart. Since then, what I want is for us both to be happy. At peace anyway."

"You were a thief? Are you still one?"

"I was but I made myself break free from that life. I was never caught. I had found early on that I hated stealing from people so I switched to businesses only. There's much more to tell."

"Your heart was beating really fast while you were telling me that but now it's back to normal. Poor Brent. I think you've been paying for your past. It does sound exciting, though. Could you have broken into this house?"

"Yes. Now you have to tell me a secret. Only one, though."

"There are fourteen family members on the other side of that door and some of them remember this. When I was twenty-one I became a political activist. I would go to all types of protests. I made my family miserable by telling them they were capitalists and destroying the environment. I remember one screaming match when I was saying that all wealth, including theirs, should be redistributed. They had no idea what to do with me. Said I must have been indoctrinated or on drugs.

What they don't know is that I had a severe crush - I mean I had it bad - on the local organizer. I was only hanging around hoping he would notice me. I wasted nearly a year on that guy… I think it was his wavy hair… Anyway, I threw myself at him and he hooked up with someone else and then I left the movement. My family still doesn't know I was in the movement only because of him."

"He was an idiot."

"He was a good speaker, could rally the troops, and had some interesting ideas. I saw him a few years back and his hair was not what it used to be. He works in retail banking now. So much for the revolution or whatever it was we thought we wanted… Brent, you should continue with the questions now."

"Yes, okay… Um, you've just replied to Kirby. What were you both doing at that moment?"

"We were looking at each other. I can't speak for him, of course, but I was trying to guess what he would say next. I thought he was employing a different strategy. Becki had told me a lot about him. I knew he was only ever interested in a woman for two things. One of them, if she had any money, was how he could get hold of it. The other was the usual one.

We were looking directly at one another. Then, there was a slight noise behind me of someone sitting down or standing up so they had to be at a nearby table... I don't think it was the nearest one. He saw who it was and stared at them for, I would say, two or three seconds and then..."

"Stop. If you're going to say what I think happened next you don't need to."

"His mouth? Well, I was going to. What you said to me before worked even though it sounded stupid at the time. You have no idea how I've been thinking - Brent said this, and Brent said that. Thinking of you has got me past it all and so quickly, too... Do you think it's only gratitude towards you that I'm feeling?" She sat up and looked at him.

"I can't answer that. Might be."

"No, I don't think it is." She laid her head down again. "It's beyond that now. You have a good heart. Go on."

"In those few moments, did you get an impression?"

"I don't want to make more of it than it is but I think he recognized who it was. He had an impassive face unless he was smiling or laughing. He smiled when he turned on the charm and laughed at his own jokes or when rebuffed. At all other times you couldn't tell what he was thinking. I might be biased but I thought he was always calculating what served him best. To say he had a face like a mask was close to the truth but it sounds too melodramatic. When he looked away, there was a fleeting emotion as if he had seen an old friend, but it really was fleeting. I might be reading that in, of course."

"From what you say, could it be that he had a look of recognition and then closed it down immediately because it was not... I don't know... appropriate?"

"Could have been that. That is everything."

"Thank you. That's been very helpful."

"I guess you have to collect all these little details to get at the truth."

"Yes. In a confusing case like this anything could be useful."

"Why did you borrow a car?"

"My run-around is an old Jeep. I never thought, for some reason, that you would mind that but it seemed to me that I needed an expensive car to visit someone else, as though I were a neighbour, to act as a calling card. It worked. I visited Becki before coming here."

"Did you!" Gabbie sat up quickly. "Do tell. How did you get into the fortress?"

"I got through the gate when a gardener was coming out. I parked the car ostentatiously and rang the bell. A very pleasant maid answered. I managed to, well, leap past her, with apologies for being rude, and then proceeded to bellow, 'Becki, where are you?' types of things."

"No! That is so rich." Gabbie held her hands up to her chin and her mouth was open in smiling surprise. "You have got to tell me everything that happened. Leave nothing out."

Brent began to tell the tale and, as Gabbie subsided a little, he put his arm around her shoulders as he worked his way through the narrative.

When he had finished, Gabbie said, "Now I can tell you something, Mr. Investigator. I've known Becki for years. We went to the same prep school. She was three years my senior. She was very attractive, had many friends... I was a bit jealous of her because I was so gawky by comparison - but she was nice to me, although I recall she was pretty mean to some girls.

Don't interrupt." Gabbie put a finger on Brent's lips as he was about to speak. "I'm coming to the interesting part and you need to write it down."

Brent took out a notebook and pen and they resettled themselves.

"We lost sight of one another after that but we had mutual acquaintances. She had to be about twenty-three and we all knew she was having serial relationships. That's when Kirby Mayo's name first popped up. Rumour had it that he was the love of her life. But then, out of the blue, they split up. And she went away somewhere... Europe but I don't know where exactly. Am I going too fast?"

"No. I'm keeping up."

"Several years elapsed and then she came into her wealth... Two inheritances very close together. Her grandfather died and then her father died shortly afterwards. Neither grandmother nor mother were alive and so it all came to her, she being an only child. I'm not sure of the timing but Kirby, who's married by this point, starts seeing her again and they pick up where they left off."

She paused while his note-taking caught up.

"Only it's an intermittent, as well as clandestine, relationship while she's in town here. Kirby obviously had no qualms about cheating on his poor wife but he didn't want her to know about his extra-marital activities."

"When would you say this began?"

"I got most of this from Becki herself and she wasn't really giving me dates. It's come to me as more of a series of reminiscences over time. Anyway, it was during that phase of intermittant relationship with Kirby that Althorn Capital got started and Becki put up money to finance the business. That's all I know of that. She was still involved with Kirby, off and on, but there were others as well.

After that, I get the idea that they were apart for some years - Kirby built up Althorn into a thriving business and Becki flitted about, globetrotting all over the place. Then, probably due to her financial involvement in Althorn, they saw each other again. I don't know when, but somewhere in all this there was a moment when she began to dislike him. When that was I have no idea. She might speak fondly of their early days together but then there could be a real change when she mentioned him again - as though she could hold two types of Kirby in mind at the same time."

"My guess," said Brent, "is that she really loved him all along but was hurt by him somehow. Kirby Mayo was not a nice man and this comes from multiple sources. It's possible she thought she had been manipulated by him. That might have occurred after Althorn was started."

"I don't know," said Gabbie. "That sounds plausible."

"How did you two meet up again?"

"About three years ago, she started staying here more frequently and spending less time in Europe. We met socially and it was just when my marriage was falling to pieces because of my own cheating husband. I wouldn't say she helped me through it but she did provide a diversion that was useful to me. We took to going to a few places together on our own. Friendly, but more in the sense of keeping each other company. She started having parties at her house. A real mish-mash they were. All types of minor celebrities, politicians and socialites, including yours truly, who thought they might be missing something important if they stayed away. What's interesting is that I recall Kirby being invited to at least two or three parties but he never came." She stopped abruptly. "I'm building a case against her, aren't I?"

"I'm afraid so. Do you want to stop?"

"I would never have told these things to a police detective. What will you do?"

"I have to be sure which person is the murderer. There are other candidates... some I've yet to meet. They may have compelling motives, too. This is the most detailed picture I have of anyone so far so it does put Becki in a class by herself. Do you know if she can handle firearms?"

"I never heard her mention it. But it couldn't be her because I saw her in another part of the restaurant."

"You did. She might have had time to get in position. Is that possible?"

"I suppose she could have. I don't think she did, though... Let me tell you the rest, not that there's much more. Just recently, she was in Europe for some months and returned two weeks ago. I'd only seen her once before the night we went to Garland's. She appeared to be her usual self, which is interesting, outspoken, generally optimistic, self-centred, and a little bit spiteful sometimes. I know people who are far worse without being entertaining - Becki is always entertaining.

On the way over to Garland's she seemed to me to be apprehensive but that all disappeared when we met Kirby outside. Then she was all gush and innuendo again. I thought I was going to be the chaperone who was about to fail in her duty." She paused. "Something that's puzzled me... what was Kirby doing outside waiting for us? He said he had been seeing someone off but he had a guilty look on his face."

"I should think he did. He had just had a low-key but nasty row with his wife in the middle of the restaurant and was pushing her into a taxi to send her home. She had come to see him and he had told her to leave and go home."

"No! How awful is that? Do you know, he was smiling and kissed Becki right afterwards. What a disgusting creep."

"Yes. That's about what I think."

"Why are you looking for his murderer, then?"

"As vile as his behaviour was, did he deserve to die for it? And whoever took it upon themselves to dispense such summary justice had no right to do that and should be prevented from ever doing such a thing again."

"I knew you would say that kind of thing."

"What is the name of Becki's assistant?"

"That's Bobbie. She's a strange woman in some ways but quite pleasant to talk to. I've wondered why she stays with Becki. She has a degree from the Sorbonne - I don't remember in what, though. And you accused her of pulling the trigger, did you? Do you really think she did?"

"I don't know. Why would she? Becki might have paid her money to do it but why in the restaurant? Why would anyone choose to do it in a restaurant?"

"Can we stop talking about the case now?" asked Gabbie.

"Yes. We're at fifteen minutes over our half hour. Would you like to make it an hour?"

"I think so. Fate seems to need all the help it can get today."

They sat back on the sofa and Brent put his arm around Gabbie again.

"We're like children tossing a coin and making it best of three when it doesn't come out right."

"Yes. After all these momentous things, what shall we talk about?" she asked.

"What types of art do you like?"

They chatted about small things for some minutes. Comfortable and relaxed, one would have assumed they were already married until it came to the final minute. That was when they fell silent, each alone with their own thoughts.

"Time's up, isn't it?" asked Gabbie.

"It is." He looked at his watch. "An hour and two minutes."

"Sometimes, one's family can be so unreliable. Usually, at least three of them would have knocked on the door by now. Ah, well, Brent. In some other life-time." Gabbie put her shoes back on.

They stood together and kissed. With an effort, he left her in her lovely room and went to the door to let himself out. He went, wanting her to call him back. She had watched him leave, wanting him to turn back and say, 'When will I see you again?' Both told themselves it was for the best.

The front door closed. Gabbie stood at the window watching Brent go down the stairs. He knew she was watching. She knew he would now turn and wave. She waved back. The door of the room opened.

"Has he gone?" asked Alicia. She stood next to Gabbie. "The food is all ready. Oh, nice car. Who is he?"

"He's a stranger. Alicia, you cannot imagine how close you were to having a new brother-in-law. If ever that man and I meet again you almost certainly will. This is a secret you have to keep."

"You mean, you and him? Is this true? You've got to tell me everything later! Right now, we've got a birthday party to get going."

Chapter 21

Saturday Evening

 $\mathcal{T}$he Bentley was returned to Phil without incident. Brent went back to his house which was as empty as when he had left it. In his office, he spent the afternoon eating sporadically, typing up his notes, and adding to his report, although he was not sure who would ever read it. He had never worked so slowly or been so distracted before.

He looked over the list of people yet to see. The Warners - as suspects they did not figure in his calculations; as witnesses, though, they were very well placed. He would phone them but not today. The Two-Way Street Beat TV show - they would have to be scheduled and he needed feedback on their movements first. The man in a damp suit and the two women in grey trench coats - a call to Greg was needed on Monday. Rena Mayo scheduled for tomorrow - that might be a long session. Who else? He had no one else.

He had started a list of likely candidates for killer, or killers. It was a very short list. Becki Kent was out in front. Will Hutchinson was second and only because he had not told Brent everything and he had no alibi. He believed all that Nola Devon had said but she, also, had no alibi. Kevin Jiang was definitely hiding something - but he was unlikely to be shooting his way into a partnership position.

It was Becki who stood out. Becki and Bobbie. Could it be that Bobbie was Becki's daughter? She played the part of an assistant but why was she in the room when Becki was interviewed? Why was she so protective of her employer when the gloves came off? Who was her father...? Kirby, of course. Bobbie would be the right age... born in Europe, maybe? Rebecca and Roberta? He could not give this to Greg yet. Something more was needed. Where was the evidence? Where were the witnesses?

It was nearly five when there came a noise at the patio door. It was a faint scuffling sound being repeated rapidly. Brent went to see what it was and saw a large ginger cat up on its hind legs, scratching rapidly and meowing, staring up at the handle area. When it saw Brent, it took to pacing up and down a few steps. It was obvious the cat wanted to come in.

Brent opened the door a crack, putting his leg in the opening so that the cat could hear him but not get past him into the house.

"Go home, boy. Where do you live?" Brent tried repetitions and variations on these themes without success. It started raining and Brent shut the door and closed the curtain. He was not a cat person and had never had a cat. He went back to work which at that moment primarily consisted of sitting in a chair, staring at a list, and getting nowhere. The rain came down harder and the cat was scratching at the back door again.

When he could stand it no longer he opened the curtain. The light was almost gone outside and there was the wet cat, still meowing.

"Alright. You can come in on the following terms. You stay in the kitchen on a blanket until I can find where you live. Then you go home. You get food, water, and a place to sleep while I'm looking. Oh, yes, and you do your business outside. Do we have a deal?"

The cat meowed so they appeared to have come to terms. Brent opened the door, the cat shot in, his name would eventually be Monty, and he was soon eating tuna.

The cat did come to live permanently in the kitchen on a blanket in a basket and, being an outdoor person, did most of his business outside. Brent put up some 'Cat Found' posters but the weather took them down. He posted online but nobody answered. Over time, milk, toys, treats, a scratching post, favourite food and a favourite chair in the lounge were added to the contract on Brent's side. On Monty's side, he added occasional fleas and required trips to the vet, the most dramatic of which being when he had half an ear disappear after a fight. The only divergence from the usual arrangements made with a cat was that Monty was rather aloof and would not be stroked more than twice without his claws coming out and teeth being sunk in. What he did do to make their cohabitation tolerable was that he made answering noises when Brent spoke to him.

On this particular Saturday evening Brent was blissfully unaware of what the future held otherwise he probably never would have opened the door.

At about eight, the cat wanted to go out and, after Brent opened the door, it disappeared into the night. Brent assumed he had discharged his duty and that this was the end of the matter. He went back to what he had been doing which was thinking of Gabbie.

He had been supremely happy for more than an hour but since then the time had been punctuated with pits of agony and ended in a bleak and spiritless blanket of depression that felt like it would last forever. Often, he had thought about returning to her. His thoughts became merciless and, he reasoned, she would think he was after her money. She would think less of him. She had already forgotten him. He had made a fool of himself.

He saw Gabbie's name in lists and reports and he saw her in his mind. Her last name was Wright and he found with slight embarrassment the pun rattling around in his brain that she was right for him. This was quickly chased away by the grim thought that he was undoubtedly wrong for her.

Their decision had been to stay apart. He had said, out of his own big mouth, that they would not be happy. He had cursed the hour and the day with his own words. He had let slip away from him the woman, the very prize, he had been seeking for so long. And what did he get as a consolation? A wet ginger cat, and even he had now left him. Fed up and dispirited, he decided to go out for a drive. He would go and see if Will Hutchinson was murdering someone. And, if Hutchinson was not slaying anyone, Brent felt he might slay him for being so stupid and pompous.

There was no good reason for Brent to be sitting in his Jeep at nine o'clock on a Saturday night, staring at someone's front door. He had intended knocking on the Hutchinson front door just to annoy Will. He could not say why he wanted to do that but in his present volatile mood it seemed better to annoy Will than to leave him in peace. The man was having an affair. The man was cheating on his wife. The man was betraying the vows he had made when he had married. The man had subverted for himself 'Till death do us part' into 'Until I get bored'.

What made people who were once in love lose that love? Wrong expectations of each other and of what a marriage should be or should look like? Brent did not have the energy to run through lists in his mind as to what all the probable causes were that could wreck a relationship. Odd word that, wreck.

The few things Brent had read or heard about why a marriage ceased to function had all agreed that a breakdown in communication was an ominous sign. 'He never talks to me; He doesn't understand me; He ignores me' seemed to be on one side of the equation. The other side was, 'She's always talking; She expects me to be a mind-reader; She's too tired all the time.' Those were some of the issues that presented themselves.

He thought over what might go wrong between himself and Gabbie.

Talk. Brent would talk to her about anything and everything whenever she wanted. She might even have to tell him to stop talking so much. If they lived on a desert island she would probably have to say, 'Brent, please stop talking. We have to get some sleep because we're up early tomorrow to harvest coconuts.'

Understanding. No problem there. He would want to know everything about her - even her thoughts in real time, though that might be a little claustrophobic if required too often.

Lack of attention. Impossible. It was just impossible for Brent to accept this.

Always talking. She was not like that.

Mind-reader. Yes, that could be an issue from time to time. She could easily hold something back, expecting him to know what it was. If she did, it would likely be the one thing he feared. She would be seeing clearly that it was over between them and she would not say it. Why over? Why? There need not be a reason for that.

Lack of romance. They would do things together. He would be attentive. He would surprise her with things she liked. He even thought to show her how to break into a warehouse for laughs - if she wanted to, of course. They would compensate the owners for any inconvenience.

He came to a decision and got out of the Jeep. The Hutchinsons lived in a suburban house, comparatively modest when measured against Will's multi-million dollar annual income. It was in a small, typical sub-division and the Hutchinson residence looked as though it might have been the show house for the original development.

Brent walked up the driveway. He could hear some sounds coming from inside that hinted there were visitors. No matter. He was intent upon getting the name of the person Will Hutchinson was shielding and upon trying to fix the Hutchinson marriage - if it was at all possible to fix. He considered the possibility that the Hutchinsons had an open relationship which, if they did, he need bother himself no further.

He rang the bell. *Should be interesting*, he thought to himself.

"What are you doing here?" said Will Hutchinson sharply upon seeing Brent.

"Have you got a lawyer yet?" asked Brent. "You're going to need one."

"I'm not discussing this with you. You're fired." He spat out the last words but in a low voice so that his guests would not hear.

"You didn't hire me. Are those friends or neighbours visiting?"

"None of your business." Will angrily tried to close the door but could not because Brent's foot was stopping him.

"The police have already begun making discreet inquiries about you. Soon, they will be interviewing your family and friends. Then they'll cast a wider net and canvas this whole neighbourhood and many of your business associates. You are the prime suspect as far as they're concerned and they'll take their time and do a thorough job. They'll talk to many hundreds of people about you in connection to Kirby Mayo's death. On paper, you're the man. If they think you did it with an accomplice they'll assume it was the person you're shielding."

"They do not know about... that person." He was still combative.

"I do and you're trying to slam the door in my face. Way to go, Will. Even if I don't tell them, they will find out because they'll keep you under surveillance, tap your lines, monitor your internet traffic and cell phone usage. You'll know they're getting close when they get search warrants. How do you see all this presented in the news with your face front and centre? Althorn will be dead and buried even if it eventually turns out that you're innocent and you will be ruined. You need to ask me in now. Put me off and I'm going straight to the police so they can fast-track your file."

The belligerent man visibly deflated as Brent spoke. He looked worn and resigned by the end. "You'd better come in," he said.

"Thank you," said Brent as he entered. The hall was pleasantly decorated with off-white floor tiles, oak staircase and trim, white walls and a modern chandelier that was on a low setting. The pieces of wooden furniture he could see were a mixture of antique and expensive reproductions. An attractive oil lamp converted to electricity made a pool of warm yellow light where it sat on a finely grained table.

"Where shall I go until you get rid of your guests?" Brent whispered because he could clearly hear the guests talking in the living room off the hall.

"Go through to the kitchen where there's a breakfast nook. Please excuse the kitchen - it's in a mess. I'll be a few minutes."

Will had reverted to the typical apologetic householder caught unawares by an unexpected visitor. This was the first behaviour Brent had seen from him with an endearing quality to it.

The nook next to the kitchen was hardly nookish, being quite a large area with a big table around which six people could be seated comfortably. Here, evidence of older children was to be found. Shoes on plastic mats, the fridge obliterated by notes, photos, and magnets, stray and forgotten objects that should be with other school things or in a closet. Brent suspected it was a continuous battle to keep the place moderately tidy. The presence of guests had suddenly overwhelmed the kitchen with dirty dishes and the like and only the guests' departure would allow the clean-up to begin. It was a home.

A woman came into the kitchen through another entrance. She was bringing away another pile of used crockery and utensils from the dining room.

"Oh, hi," she said. The house was configured in a way that she had to be aware of Brent's arrival and yet she showed surprise. She did so by pulling her head back slightly but sharply as if to show Brent how surprised she was - undoubtedly because a stranger had invaded her home at such a weird and inconvenient time. Her adolescent gesture said - 'Like, this is not what we do.'

Instantly, Brent could see the schoolgirl in her. Even at forty-four with three teenaged children, he could readily picture her at fourteen with braces.

"Hello. You're Lucy. My name's Brent Umber. Can I help you with the dishes?"

"No, no. Why would you do that?" She smiled a smile which said 'That is weird'.

"Just trying to be helpful so you can attend to your guests. What did you have?"

"Baked chicken with sweet potatoes and oranges."

"That sounds interesting."

"Um… like, do you want some? There's plenty left over." She sounded uncertain because she was uncertain of Brent's status in the house. She spoke a little like a teenager. Brent thought she was picking it up from her teenage children.

"If it's no trouble, I wouldn't mind a small taster."

"Oh, sure." Now she knew what to do with Brent. Somebody wanted food and she knew how to feed them. It was clearly a continual requirement in the house.

Brent got up and went into the kitchen.

"Quid pro quo," he said. "If you're going to feed me I have to earn my keep. I can't sing for my supper because I sing flat but I can load the dishwasher."

"You don't have to do that."

"I insist. Do you rinse everything first before stacking or just put it all in?"

" It cleans off most things. Scrape the heavy stuff into the bin in that cupboard."

"I had a dishwasher in an apartment once and I literally had to wash everything by hand or the machine got clogged and the glasses came out streaky. I don't miss that beast."

"We had one like that once. It just would not die and like I so wanted a new one. The one we got after that was really good. Cleaned everything but the pointy bits kept breaking off."

"Ah, the tines."

Lucy was making up a plate for Brent. There was more than a taster on it.

"Is that what they're called? The money they wanted for new racks was ridiculous."

"Isn't that like everything, though? What looks like a ten-dollar part costs two hundred to replace, and if it's electronic just forget it and buy new."

"I know. It's what everyone says. Then it's new phones for the kids or new clothes. Always something."

She put the completed plate in a microwave and got out cutlery and a fresh place-mat.

"Do you want some wine with it? It's a Chardonnay," said Lucy.

"That will be perfect, thank you."

She quickly set a place at the table in the nook. While she was there, the microwave chimed.

"Leave that; your food's ready. You didn't really need to... Oh my goodness, you're so quick."

"I used to work in a restaurant."

"You should teach my kids how to do that. Here you are."

"Let me dry my hands... there... thanks. Why don't you sit with me and tell me about your children."

"But, like, we've got guests."

"Your friends?"

"Will's... and mine. You're a friend of Will's, right?"

"Come and sit down and I'll tell you something really interesting. Bring a glass with you."

She hesitated. "Okay, why not?"

They sat at the table together.

"This is delicious. All the flavours combine so well and the chicken is perfect."

"Thanks." Lucy smiled.

"Cheers," said Brent. Lucy replied, 'Cheers', and they clinked glasses.

"So? What is this interesting thing?"

"I'm a private investigator and I'm working on Kirby Mayo's case."

"Oh, really? I've been thinking about that such a lot. Uh…"

"Yes, I know. It's hard to know which question to ask first. Do you know that the murderer sat in the middle of a crowded restaurant and fired and not a single person had so much as a glimpse of him?"

"It's not possible! You'd think many people would have seen what happened. Somebody had to have seen something."

"That's exactly what I think. But, there it is. No one's come forward to say that they saw it happen or noticed the killer escaping."

"Maybe they were in disguise and kind of blended in. Oh, I know! Like a waiter."

"That would be a perfect disguise. You should join the police department - you'd make a good detective."

"Yeah, I wish."

"No, seriously. Why don't you try?"

She sucked her teeth. "Because I'm too old."

"Oh, no. You don't look old at all. You look lovely."

"Can I remind you that my husband is in the next room?"

"I haven't forgotten. We are here and you are still lovely. And you could do that job. In fact, you could probably do anything you put your mind to. You could run a restaurant for instance. Put this delicious chicken on the menu and you'll have to beat the customers back with a stick."

"Me? Run a restaurant?"

"Certainly you could. I saw you put everything together for this plate very efficiently. You just need to organize and scale up for thirty or forty diners."

"I have thought about it from time to time, I must admit."

"There you are, then. Your children are teenagers and they'll be going in different directions sooner than you'd probably like. There's your opportunity to do something for yourself."

"I... I don't know."

"Will would finance it, wouldn't he?"

"Don't even go there."

"I see. In a few minutes, you, Will, and I shall indeed be going right there because we have some important things to discuss. I want you to know that, while I will be objective, I am on your side."

Sounds of people getting up and moving about came from the next room.

"I think they're leaving... I'd better get back to our guests."

Lucy sat at one end of a four-seater settee and Will was at the other. Brent had entered the living-room first and, recognizing the lay of the land furniture-wise, had made sure he had sat in Will's favourite armchair. They sat opposite him.

"Would you like a coffee or a tea?" asked Lucy. "It's no trouble for me to get it."

"That's kind of you but no thanks," replied Brent.

"Lucy doesn't have to be here," Will said to Brent. "She won't mind." He smiled at his wife. "I'm sure you have something to do, don't you?"

"I kind of thought Lucy would be interested in hearing about the affair you're having," said Brent. He waited for an explosion, a reaction - anything. Instead, there was nothing.

"She knows all about it," said Will. He was looking satisfied with himself.

"Good. Lucy, what is this person's name?"

"I don't know. Will's never told me."

"Will, last chance now. What is this person's name?"

"I don't think I want to tell you. I've thought about what you said and it's not going to happen like that. I'm innocent and I trust the police to find the guilty party."

"Well, I tried. I will forward my report to the police as it stands."

"What does it say? You said you would submit it to the partners first."

"The report is incomplete and there are comments on people other than yourself which you cannot see at present. You're not helping me at all. I don't know, I'm beginning to think you killed Kirby Mayo.

I came to you privately and you would not answer my questions. I suggested a lawyer and you haven't hired one. I've come to you now with your wife present as a witness that you need actively to do something in the situation. You've refused to do anything at every turn. Why?"

"Is this true?" asked Lucy. "I mean, you could be in trouble with the police?"

"This man is just causing trouble. Don't worry, I'll take care of it," said Will.

"How is he causing trouble? It sounds like he's trying to help us," said Lucy.

"What is it now? You suddenly know better than I do?" said Will, aggressively.

"She does," said Brent. "Lucy, what time did Will return home that Thursday night?"

"Thursday…?"

"Eleven p.m., you remember?" Will loudly interrupted Lucy, talking over her.

A long silence followed.

"Like he said." Lucy parroted what was required of her.

"What construction do you expect me to put on this?" asked Brent.

"The correct one which is that I was home by eleven so I could not have killed Kirby."

There was not much left for Brent to say. He knew Will would not tell him the truth about the person he was concealing. That area was not to see the light of day and Will was confident he could keep it that way. The stock-broker was so obviously lying. More amazing, he expected his lie to be believed. Not exactly believed - accepted, and then forgotten. It was quite fantastic, really. His manner was odd, also. Will was adversarial until challenged, then he would collapse. Having collapsed, he would then become increasingly belligerent once more until he negated his former acquiescence.

Brent looked at Lucy briefly and supposed the Hutchinson marriage was only a co-existence - a trap of habit and unquestioned attitudes. He would like to hear her story if she would tell it. Did she see others? Would Will allow that? No and no, Brent decided. The Hutchinson marriage bed was pushed up against the wall. Lucy was trapped against a hard surface. The selfish man on the open side controlled all her movements.

Why the apparent lack of money? The home was prosperous but not a wealthy one. Will's after tax income had to be two or three million. The maintenance costs of this suburban house and its family of five accounted for a fraction of that amount.

"If there's no more to discuss?" said Will, his tone suggesting Brent leave.

"One more item. Are you going to retire when Althorn fails?"

Will was not merely silent - he was stricken dumb but without shock, as though he had caught sight of something that he did not recognize and could not interpret.

"I wouldn't mind much if it did fail," said Lucy quietly.

Will looked at her and then back to Brent. "Tell him."

"Are you sure?" she asked. When he did not answer she turned to Brent and spoke as if her husband was not in the room.

"Let me just say something first, Brent. There is no way this guy could commit a murder. I know him and he's not violent. He'll shout at someone and walk away in a huff and get all moody but he won't do anything to them. It's not his nature.

Now for what Will wants me to tell you:- He's obsessed with not having enough money to retire on. He budgets for everything to the penny and everything else he makes goes into pensions, investments… you name it. It's like a reverse gambling addiction. It really is. He can't stop himself.

When we were first married, we agreed that's what we would do - put everything into investments and then leave the rat-race. We had this big target of twenty million and he calculated all the future values of money and how we could get there. I thought it was a cool idea. We budgeted for children, for this house… dishwasher repairs, everything. I didn't realize that he had, like, lost sight of the goal after a few years and was saving for the sake of saving because we never talked about it much. It's what we did and I was used to it.

It was five years ago. We had an argument, more like a disagreement really because the passion had long gone. It was about money. It was then I understood something was wrong... like, really wrong. I was so focused on the kids that I hadn't noticed that I had stopped loving him. I remember what he said, 'You and I have a retirement plan and we must stick to the agreement.' I might not have noticed then if he had said 'our agreement'. He said, 'the agreement'. That was more important to him than anything else. The weird thing was, when I sorted it out in my head, I realized I didn't care.

We discussed divorce. He said he would agree to a divorce if we reach the original target for retirement money for himself as well as for me when our assets came to be divided. When we hit twenty a piece we'd go our separate ways. We're at thirty-two million and change so it's only about another three years max.

He's really good with the kids. It's me he treats like garbage but I don't care. I'm doing this so the kids have a normal life growing up. He does treat me with respect in front of the children because if he didn't, he knows I would destroy our little plan and we would be done and finished.

He sees women to meet his needs and I put him on a strict budget for that because that is not going to delay the program." She turned to Will. "There's one you really like and it's she who you're protecting, isn't it?"

"Yes," said Will.

"Yeah, so, that's how it is. Nobody knows; not friends, not family, not even the kids... you're the first person we've ever told. Just so you know, if I was seeing someone he'd get jealous but not because he loves me. It would be his wounded pride. Could you imagine it? I mean, if he got jealous enough to try to win me back or blow up our deal?

All this would have been for nothing and I'm just not having everything ruined.

Anyway, I can put love on hold for a while longer. As soon as it's over I'm back in circulation. Just another three years at the most and then we are done. We both really want that day to come. Isn't that so, Will?"

"Yes. Lucy has stated everything I would have told you if she had agreed to it. I'm keeping the name of the lady to myself. I care about the children and don't want them hurt in any way in this matter or at any time. I was here at eleven that Thursday, wasn't I?"

"He sure was," said Lucy.

"Now that you know, what will you do?" asked a rather subdued Will.

"Well... I could never have guessed this scenario. I'll keep my word and not disclose any of this. In my report, I'll say I met Lucy and she confirmed your alibi and leave it at that. You've got to realize that, unless they arrest someone else pretty quickly, the police will check into your lives. As I've said, I'm surprised you haven't already heard from them."

"We'll be ready when they get here," said Lucy.

"I have to add," said Brent. "If I had found Lucy was being victimized by you, I would have done something to help her."

"I sensed you might," said Will. "I nearly panicked when I came to the door and found you there but, I know Lucy, so I calmed down. It was our friends being here that worried me."

"Don't forget the boys," said Lucy to Will. "They're at a friend's house and need a ride home," she explained to Brent.

"Yes, I should get them now. I'll see you next week, Brent. Goodnight." He got up and left the room.

They waited while he put on a jacket and went out to the car. When he had gone, Lucy said,

"That was nice... what you tried to do. It's good to know you would have been on my side - but, as you now see, my marriage is a hopeless case and a lost cause. I'd ask you to stay for a coffee but you can't be here when the boys return. Trish is at a slumber party."

"What would happen if you met the right person before the day? Just curious."

"They'd have to wait and I won't cheat. Trish is only fourteen. We get on really well, so, she'll be seventeen and I think at that age she'll be able to handle the divorce. The boys will be nineteen and twenty, so they'll do okay. Besides, they'll still be seeing their dad. Teenagers... they'll probably not notice anything until we move out of this place."

"Thank you for telling me everything. I had Will highly placed as a suspect."

"I bet you did. He's hopeless at lying. I've always seen right through him. But he's so stubborn and he has this irrational fear of being poor in his old age. That's what this is all about. I didn't clue in for years. I thought we were saving for our future."

"Did you love him?"

"I must have. We had some very nice times together and he was good to me. But I lost all feelings for him and I can't say how it happened only that it did happen slowly, over time. Like, it might have been my fault but I don't care enough to go back and analyze the past."

"I'd better be going," said Brent. They walked to the front door. "Goodnight."

"Goodnight and thanks for loading the dishwasher."

Chapter 22

Saturday night to Sunday morning

*A*s Brent was getting into his Jeep, a heavy-set man in a raincoat and walking briskly approached him. Brent did not recognize him at first.

"Mind if I get in?" said Detective Otto Schroeder.

"No," said Brent.

Once seated inside, Schroeder said, "Drive round the block and park fifty yards from the house. I don't want to walk back to my car or be seen with you."

"They're under surveillance?"

"Yes."

"Nice way to spend a Saturday night."

"Yeah. The officer watching the place ran your plates, saw a name he recognized and called me."

"Am I that interesting, to bring you out?"

"No. I want you to tell me what you've got on the Hutchinsons."

"It's simple enough. Lucy says Will came home at eleven on the night. She's absolutely clear on that point. It's a thirty minute drive at the best of times from here to Garland's. He can't be shooting Mayo at ten thirty-eight and be home at eleven."

"Uh-huh. Wife testifying for her husband."

"Still pretty hard to break unless you have other evidence."

"Not yet. What was he doing after he left Garland's? Pull up over here."

"He sticks to his story of having a couple of drinks in a bar and then going for a long walk until he went home in a taxi. I verified he was in Cusane's Parlour until about nine-fifteen but nothing afterwards."

"We did that. Leaves him an hour and forty-five. Take off a thirty-minute taxi ride and that leaves an hour and fifteen minutes for him to kill Mayo. We can't find the driver of the cab company he gave us."

"It doesn't put him inside Garland's. You need a witness in there."

"I know. That would solve a lot of problems."

"Wouldn't it just? What's your take on Will Hutchinson?"

"I think he had a grudge against the deceased. He dropped hints without knowing he was doing it. The thing that bugs me most about him is why does he live here? It's a nice neighbourhood. My place is three blocks away and this is the area my wife and I can afford. He makes twenty times what we do. He could live in a much bigger place in an exclusive neighbourhood."

"Maybe they're saving everything for a rainy day."

"There is that. Do you know they've got over thirty million socked away? Why not spend some now? I mean, does he want to be buried with it?"

"Detective Schroeder, why are you so chatty tonight?"

"I want information. I checked you out. Some people in Belton say nice things about you. So does Lieutenant Darrow. Is he feeding you?"

"Aw, come on. I'm not falling for that one."

"Right. I spoke to him. Reading between the lines I'm sure he is. Normally, I'd have a serious issue with that but I decided, if you tell me what you know, I'll let it pass."

"That is what I said I would do... I wish I had something concrete. It's all hypothesis at the moment. With the Hutchinson's, I'm dropping them down quite low on the list of likely suspects. I don't see Valdez involved, either, despite his reputation."

"I'd like it to be him. He wouldn't do it that way, though. He's got a temper but he's got enough self-control, I think, not to be so stupid."

"It's not the Lindsays..."

"Thought of them, did you...? Yeah, guy with a gun in the area. Securing the area makes for a good cover story. He's got sniper training - he'd choose that method but, unfortunately, he has no motive and no connection with Mayo or Althorn Capital."

"The other three remaining partners at Althorn seem unlikely to me."

"Nola Devon has no alibi."

"I've spoken to her several times. There's no motive. Don't tell this to anyone but she wanted out of Althorn because of life issues, stress, that kind of thing. She had only told Kirby Mayo that night that she wanted to leave. The other partners don't know yet. She wants to keep it quiet so that Althorn can survive. If she leaves now, down goes the ship. She's the one keeping it all together."

"She doesn't have an alibi."

"Alibi! Her lack of one is her alibi. She got annoyed with Kirby over how he treated his wife. That's no reason for her to pull out a revolver and kill him. It was she who got me into Althorn which is the last thing she would do if she was the murderer."

"Yeah. It's all wrong, I guess. Anyone else?"

"There are a couple of others... I don't want to say anything about them until I've checked on a few things. I'll let you know when I've got more. Oh, yes. Gabbie Wright is not involved in it at all."

"Okay. So, you think we're wasting time here with Hutchinson?"

"I wouldn't say that. He's not important to me at the moment... You can tell me something. Have you spoken to Rena Mayo yet?"

"I haven't. She's been interviewed a couple of times. We can't get much out of her because she's falling to pieces. I feel sorry for her but, hey, I have to keep an open mind. Their marriage was going nowhere, you know what I mean?"

"I do. I hope it isn't her. I don't know, I get a bit sentimental sometimes and I haven't even met her. I've cast her in the role of the grieving widow."

"No room for sentiment in this game. So, here's the deal. You feed me and I'll feed you with what I can. I'll let you know if you're to steer clear of anyone and you back off from them immediately. You okay with this?"

"Yes, I can do that."

"Here's my card. Call me if you get anything."

"Are we officially on first name terms now?"

"Sure, Brent."

"Thanks, Otto."

They shook hands and the detective got out of the Jeep.

The blue Jeep pulled into the driveway. The outside automatic light over the garage came on. Rain came down with the wind that stripped leaves from trees to plaster them flat on the interlocking paving stones. What had seemed like an inexhaustible supply of leaves two weeks earlier when they first turned colour was now more than half gone. It was nearly November, that desolate month which gave nothing to this region of the world except a threat of winter and damp, chilly air, stealing all the while a little more light from the sky, making the days a dismal grey and the nights a forlorn, moist black.

Inside the house, Brent switched on lights and closed the door behind him. He usually loved the proportions of his house and was pleased with the renovations he had undertaken and completed. He felt no pleasure now.

At eleven-thirty, with the day, as counted by a clock, nearly gone, he did not feel like he was in a lovely house and definitely not in a home. He felt he had entered a large space which sheltered him from elements but diminished him. He had been working on that which made him feel most alive, most useful, and now in the house he felt dead and useless. Brent had wealth but it did not look at him with a cool steady gaze. He had plans but he could not speak them to the well-shaped ear he had seen earlier. He had questions but no soft, cultured voice would suggest an answer. There were things that puzzled him but no quick mind was present to cut through to the obvious. Usually independent and resourceful, he seemed to have become suddenly dependent on a certain person acknowledging and reassuring him and she was not present. He had said he was on the brink of love, on the very edge of it. Had he now fallen over the brink? He certainly felt lovelorn and it hurt.

A crow neither flies at night nor in a straight line but if a bird could have been persuaded to do both, seven and three quarter miles in a south-southeasterly direction would have had it depart from where a man lay, painfully wide awake, stretched out on a sofa with an arm over his face and the lights off, and arrive at a house, a pretty house, normally full of light, which had but a single lamp burning. Next to the lamp sat a woman.

The birthday celebration had been a success though it had been hard for her to get through it. Serving staff had cleaned everything away scrupulously but she had wanted them to leave the mess and just go. Her sister had not had opportunity to quiz her about the stranger and the woman was glad she had not needed to explain - not now, not today, anyway. She wore a thick white bathrobe, had cream on her face, her hair in a band, and she had teased out a strand to twist and twist again as she stared at nothing. She might have cried, if she were the type to cry. She smiled occasionally, but it faded as soon as it appeared. Getting up, she switched off the lamp. As she walked, lights came on automatically and she ascended the stairs to her bedroom. Gabbie carried her phone in her hand just in case there was a call. If the call did not come, then tomorrow she would go away if she could think of somewhere to go - not that it mattered where she went.

About one in the morning, Brent was in his kitchen, drinking some water. A rapid scratching came at the patio door. He put the glass down, pulled the door back, said, "Oh, it's you," and the meowing ginger cat walked in.

On the way to the Mayo residence the next morning, Brent stopped at a supermarket to get some food and supplies for the house which included cat food. Having never fed a cat before, Brent had never paid attention to the pet food aisle. He stared at the array of food and could not understand what it was he was supposed to buy so he looked at the keywords. *Senior, kitten, adult, nursing mother, diabetic... uh, he's a tom cat so that makes him an adult. Fancy, gravy, chunks, pâté... what is all this? Dental, bone growth, maintenance... Hairball? Finnicky, fastidious, farm-fresh, supreme, organic, grass-fed, chef, surf & turf... trout? Cats get trout?*

"Oh, excuse me. You have a cat, right?" Brent asked an elderly lady who was pushing a cart and looking at bags of dry cat food.

"Yes. I have five cats."

"Five! Wow. Um, what do you feed them? You see, I've taken in a stray, temporarily you understand, and I need a few days' worth of food until I can, uh, return him to his owner."

"I get whatever is on special and if they don't eat it they go hungry. That bag of kibble down there is a good deal."

"Thanks very much," said Brent as the woman wheeled her cart away.

Brent picked up a bag of the kibble.

"Excuse me but I couldn't help overhearing what she said. You mustn't get those biscuits. They have a high ash content."

"Ash? There's ash in these biscuits?"

"Yes. It blocks the urinary tract. Specially in males. Very painful for them. You would have to go to the vet."

"You mean the cat would go to the vet?"

"That's what I said. You should get this dry food, and then wet food like that, or that, or this one is very good. You need to understand your cat's needs and provide a selection to see which he prefers. There's a lot of information in the nutritional facts on the label but you kind of have to interpret what's being said because a lot of manufacturers lie."

"They do?"

"Well, it's more like extreme marketing and it depends on who the target group is. You have to be a savvy shopper. Don't forget the treats and a toy or two."

"He's only staying a couple of days but he eats like a pig. Could you just put what I need in my cart, please?"

When Brent left the checkout he realized that what he had paid to feed a cat for three days, although the kibble would last longer than that, equalled a month's wages in some countries.

The Mayo house in off-white faux stone with natural stone details was of a class and type that one would expect to find in the possession of a wealthy hedge-fund manager. It had been constructed on its ravine lot about four years earlier and to the best standards. French design lines were evident throughout the modern construction.

Upon passing through the real stone archway with double iron gates, one came to stand on a glossy paved courtyard with a large-scale design of a sinuous, complicated pattern in black stones woven into a field of variegated red stones. The miniature complex was comprised of three distinct buildings - the house itself and two mirror-image garage blocks on either side - enough for sixteen vehicles. These accommodated visitors' vehicles and the construction standard was such that they were uniform with the house. Any ordinary person would have been happy to live in them. The white garages themselves had mid-brown wooden doors that suggested horses and not cars. The rooms above were staff apartments and roofs were capped by dark grey tiles which had a distinct blue cast to them. The courtyard had to be a sun trap in summer.

The white stone house itself was not massive but, instead, was an absolutely symmetrical two storey residence with nine large windows, double doors, and a semi-circular portico over the entrance. This latter had a small balcony on top of it, accessed through the central

French windows of the second floor which functioned as a door. Shaped evergreens stood in narrow beds beneath the first floor windows. Large black urns in various places suggested they would again contain the brilliant flowers of summer. Those flowers would be red if Brent could have made the choice. All in all, although he preferred older style houses as a rule, he was impressed by this one. What he was yet to discover was that, at the back of the house, all symmetry was lost to function.

There, the land fell away and the house had four soaring stories sheathed in glass. On one side was an indoor swimming pool in its own long white building. On the other was a multi-level complex of different-sized octagonal patios in grey wood, descending the ravine and having wide stairs down - sometimes up - connecting the various sections together. Between the two, a path descended, linking the house to a small outdoor swimming pool with its pool house and, further down, lay a tennis court. A party of three hundred in the garden could find space to talk or saunter about without feeling crushed together.

Once inside, Brent was disappointed by what he could see. Everything was tastefully appointed with expected colour schemes combining with white walls and carefully placed lighting. The furniture was good - very expensive - and nothing could be faulted. Brent felt the interior was close to saying 'office'. Decorative items were few and large, selected for form over detail and colour. The artwork tended towards being generic and uninspiring. The one item that had any power to it was a massive black and white framed print hanging in a lounge at the front of the house. It was of a tiger, stalking through tall grasses, its gaze intent upon unseen prey.

"Good morning, Mr. Umber. You're right on time."

"Good morning. I apologize, I've only heard you called Aunt Marjie. May I call you Marjie? You can call me Brent."

"That's what friends and family call me." She looked puzzled by his familiarity.

In her late sixties, and wearing little make-up, Marjie had opted to keep her hair its natural grey colour. The style of it was dated - waved, full, and descending only to her jaw line. It suited her. She wore a plain, navy, woollen dress with a pale pink cardigan over it. A simple string of pearls and a pair of black, low-heeled court shoes completed her outfit.

"I want to keep my meeting with Rena as informal and low pressure as possible. I will not ask her any difficult, direct questions. This will be more in the nature of a chat. If we use first names, I think she will find that more comfortable."

"Then by all means," she answered readily. "You'll find Rena this way." Her shoes clicked very slightly on the floor as they began to walk towards the back of the house.

"Where are the children?" asked Brent.

"They're upstairs with their nanny. I thought it best to keep them occupied."

"I agree. I'd like you to stay for as long as possible or come back from time to time if it is not. Do you mind?"

"No. I know something of the state of their marriage. Rena has confided in me so I think very little will come as a surprise." She said this in a matter-of-fact tone.

They entered the large room - a section of a larger, open-plan area. The vertical blinds were pulled all the way back and, from a distance, the glass wall revealed only an unbroken expanse of clouds unrelieved by any trees or buildings because the ground dropped away so close to the house. It gave the impression that Rena, draped with a blanket and seated in a deep armchair with her feet resting on an ottoman, was in the club-room of a massive, yet future, airship. She was nearly parallel to the glass and her head was turned away.

"Rena, dear," said Marjie, "Brent Umber is here to see you." Rena turned to look at him.

"Hello. Please don't get up. You look so deliciously comfortable," said Brent.

"Hello. I'm sorry I haven't dressed to meet you but…"

"That's fine. If I had known, I would have brought my dressing gown."

"Would you?" she asked, non-plussed. "Please, sit down."

"Oh, yes." He chose an armchair directly opposite her. Marjie sat some distance away but could easily join the conversation if needed. "This chair is so comfortable!" Brent exclaimed with a beaming smile which the two ladies found quite disarming.

Now that he could see Rena properly in the daylight, he saw how pale she was. Her light brown hair was tied in a pony-tail. Over her pink matching sweatshirt and sweatpants she wore a pale blue robe. By the side of the ottoman was a pair of fluffy white slippers. These fluffy, comfortable, domestic items underscored how un-homelike was the rest of the house. Rena's apparel was intimate and cozy - the rest of the house was anything but those things. It made Brent think that if Kirby had been a bus driver, he would be alive and both he and Rena might even now be in some smaller, cozier house, enjoying peace and a little happiness.

"My goodness, you and Aunt Marjie look so alike." Brent looked from Rena to Marjie and back again. Rena smiled.

"My sister, Rena's mother, and I," said Marjie, "could almost be taken for identical twins except there's a two-year gap between us. My daughter, Kate, is so like Rena you would think they were twins."

"Has that ever caused confusion?"

"Confusion?" asked Rena.

"One of you being mistaken for the other."

"No… Well, once. We played a trick on Kate's boyfriend… but that was so long ago…" Her voice trailed away.

"You're not allowed to leave me hanging like that. What happened?"

"It was a silly joke she and I played when we were sixteen. We were at a party and the light was dim. I pretended to be Kate. But when I got kissed, Kate got annoyed. We laughed about it afterwards, though."

"Was she angry with you?"

"No. It was her boyfriend not being able to tell the difference between us that made her really mad. I didn't know he was going to grab me suddenly. It was so funny."

"Did you know this story, Marjie?"

"Yes. Daniel, then Kate's boyfriend, is my son-in-law."

"Did Kate and Daniel know Kirby?" asked Brent, who had turned back to Rena.

"Of course they did."

"Did they get along well together?"

"Yes… I think so."

"You sound hesitant."

"I suppose I am… I couldn't tell what Kirby was thinking most of the time."

"Oh, I see. He didn't talk much, then?"

"He used to… years back."

"And you knew what he was thinking at that time?"

"It was better… It took me a while to understand him. He changed after we were married. He had swept me off my feet… stupid phrase, that. Before Robin was born he was devoted to me."

"Robin's your eldest daughter?"

"Yes."

"Does she look like you?"

"A little. I can get you a photograph," said Rena.

"I'll find it," said Marjie, immediately getting up.

"Thank you," said Brent to Marjie. "Rena, you were saying that Kirby changed after you were married. How did he change?"

"He became very serious…like, all the fun went out of him. He started working longer and longer hours and went away at weekends sometimes. Kirby spent some time with Robin but he really didn't seem that interested. He certainly had less time for me."

"Maybe family responsibility changed his outlook on life."

"That's what I told myself but I couldn't help always thinking it was more than that."

"Here you are," said Marjie who had returned with a photograph album and handed it to Brent. "She has many albums but this is the best historical one."

"Thanks." Brent got up and took the album over to Rena. He knelt down beside her chair and rested the album on the arm. "You give me the guided tour. If all you beauties look alike, how can I hope to tell you apart?"

Rena smiled. She turned the pages and gave explanations of time, place, event, and person. It covered a period after Rena had married up until the time of the birth of her son, Mark - a period of roughly nine years.

Knowing what he knew, Brent could easily track the changes in the relationship - almost from page to page. At the beginning of the album, Rena was a slender, smiling girl and Kirby was a big young man, often laughing. They both stared out at the world together. Each successive page gave evidence of a progression - or, rather, a regression. Kirby laughed, then he grinned, then there came a longer period filled with slight, photogenic smiling, and finally, at the album's end, Kirby seemed only able to manage a very forced, thin smile, if it could be called a smile at all.

After Mark's birth, there was one photograph where Kirby had a completely blank and emotionless stare. The contrast between the earlier and later photographs was so stark that they might as well have been of two different people, one of whom had ceased to exist long ago.

Rena matured by the second page. From then on she maintained a happy, bright appearance which was similar across most of the pictures. By the last few pages, however, a wistful, uncertain note had crept into her features and attitude. Instead of looking at the camera, she was most often looking elsewhere. She smiled less frequently and with less openness. Several had her looking at Kirby. Brent put the album back on the table, and sat down again.

"Do you know how much this has told me?"

"I know. It's right there, isn't it?" said Rena.

"There must have been reasons for his changes."

"All I knew was that I wanted him back. Why did he change?"

"Do you think it could have been his work?"

"He became so hard and calculating… I think that was how he was when he traded. I suppose so. Huh, I've thought about it enough… you'd think I'd know by now."

"Rena, you do know."

"You mean his work affecting his personality?"

Brent was quiet and she searched his face rapidly for an answer, for a sign of what he knew. She saw it, not that Brent signalled it in any way.

"Yes. I know he saw other women. I was probably the last to find out. Aunt Marjie, I haven't told you about... some things." She was beginning to break.

"Oh, dear. I did wonder. My poor girl." She hurried to Rena's side and hugged her. They both started crying as Rena told her aunt of Kirby's infidelity and how she had tried to get him to come back to her but had waited in vain. Rena cried freely. Her speech became distorted as her mouth tried to frame words about his lies and indifference, and her repeatedly crushed hopes over Kirby's repeated affairs. Marjie struggled to remain as composed as she could while failing to do so.

Brent watched them for a moment and heard a little of Rena's admission of total failure in winning Kirby back. He got up and walked away to give them some time. He stood in another section of the open-plan area and looked through the glass wall at the vista. By standing, he could see the sprawling patios below - the height making them look like an artist's rendition. Further away a boundary line of tall trees marked the top of a steep slope which descended to a creek at the bottom. The big sky dwarfed everything including what skyline there was.

Looking from an oblique angle, he could see towards the south the towers of the financial district massed in a clump. The buildings seemed small, manageable, as though they could be picked up and moved if necessary. A gap in the clouds allowed the sun to touch them - steely-blues, gold, greys, browns. The clump of financial storehouses looked out of place, as if it were no more than a picture cut from a magazine and pasted onto the real world.

He hated what he had to do next. He must go back and press Rena in her present fragile state for any information he could get. Brent would have to make her say words she did not want to say but which would give him understanding. Primarily, he must clear her from the Suspect List, though he could not see her in the role of killer at all. Next, he must gain insights into her private life because they might give some indication as to who could have killed Kirby and why. Finally, and of least importance to him, he must find evidence the police could use. What Brent wanted to do instead was say, 'There, there,' and out-bawl Aunt Marjie.

Chapter 23

Sunday afternoon

"*I*'m sorry about that. I'm better now." Rena was sitting up, Marjie was sitting in Brent's chair, Brent was sitting on the ottoman. They formed a smaller, more intimate group.

"I can't talk about that anymore. I'm not ready."

"We don't have to," said Brent. "There is a matter that does have to be discussed. Your movements on that Thursday night. Do you feel able to go over them?"

"I gave a statement."

"I know. The police will want to go over it again, too, to see if you remember anything more."

"Do they think I killed him?"

"They have to keep an open mind. Rena, you left Garland's in a taxi at 9:51 p.m. to return home where you went to sleep about midnight. Next morning, the police notified you about seven-thirty. You collapsed and had to be taken to hospital. They discharged you in the afternoon. Those are the only facts that have been established from your statement.

I'm not here to challenge any part of what you've told the police. If you can tell me, I'd like to know what you saw and heard from the time you entered the restaurant until the time you rode away in the cab."

"How can that help?"

"I don't know yet. It's possible you saw something that could be useful. Did you recognize anyone there? Was anyone staring at you or at Kirby? Did anyone do anything strange?"

"I'm reliving that last time I saw him so often... Nola was there. She saw how he treated me. She's a friend but she couldn't stop him. Who could? He always did what he wanted... I don't remember anyone or anything unusual. I went to be with Kirby and he turned me away. That's what happened."

"Did you foresee that possibility?"

"No. I don't think so. All I thought was that I had to try. What else could I do?"

"But, in the back of your mind, you must have had an idea it might have ended badly?"

"It was a public place. I thought he would have no choice. We'd sit together and we would talk and then he would laugh like he used to... I had hoped he'd agree to our going to marriage counselling. That's what I was going to ask him to do."

"I see. If you had been able to talk together and the subject of marriage counselling came up, what did you intend doing if he refused to go?"

"I think... I think I would have left."

"This visit of yours to Garland's was a last-ditch effort, then. Did you intend to divorce him if it didn't work out?"

"Never. I could never have done that."

"Would he have divorced you?"

"He'd never spoken of it... If he had made up his mind to do that, he would have done it."

"Kirby walked you away from the table and out of the restaurant to put you in a cab. Did you argue?"

There was a long pause before she answered. "Brent, you're bringing me to a point where something did happen and it's something I can't hide any longer. I'll tell you and Aunt Marjie what I haven't told the police.

When the taxi pulled away I turned back to look and she was kissing him. I knew it was her. There was another woman with them…"

"Who is she?" asked Marjie.

"Rebecca Kent… He's been infatuated with her for years. I found out about them because once he left his laptop open on an email from her. I couldn't believe what I was reading… but it seemed it was all in the past, like it was years back. Then I began to put it together that he was seeing others, that she had just been the first of many. I thought… it… was over between them. But maybe it had never been over. No surprise he sent me home when he was expecting her at any moment. What a stupid fool I've been but, hey, I miss him, despite everything." She tried to smile but began crying again instead.

Brent left them a little while later. It was impossible for him to find out at that moment if Rena had continued on home in the cab, armed herself with a revolver, gone back to Garland's to shoot her husband, and then once more returned home. She certainly had had enough time to do it but could she? A twenty-minute drive each way between house and restaurant gave her a seven-minute window to walk in, fire three shots and leave. It was possible and she certainly had sufficient motive but was it likely? Rena need only have kept quiet about seeing Becki and the immediate motive for a crime of passion would have remained hidden. If, indeed, she had shot Kirby, then everything Brent had just seen this morning was an act and, if so, why negate all that the act had achieved by needlessly volunteering information that supplied her with a motive? This sequence of facts was sufficient to convince Brent of Rena's innocence but, since none of the detectives had witnessed his interview with her, they would not be able to view this new information in the same light. It was, therefore, evidently another matter that Brent would have to keep back from the police.

Vane was in the front passenger seat talking to Brent. In the rear seats, Mason and Zack had ear-buds in and eyes locked on phones. They were heading to the place where they would set up their surveillance post the next morning.

"What happened to that woman you were seeing?" asked Vane.

Brent hesitated for a moment, thinking she meant Gabbie.

"The one you went on the date with? She must have loved it - she got a murder along with her dinner. Beats roses and a box of chocolates any day."

"It's not something to joke about."

"Who said it was? Yeah, well, I didn't mean it like that. Just me talking. I'm glad I wasn't there to see it. So, how'd she take it?"

"It's very complicated."

"Come on, bro. Ya gotta tell me."

"I'll tell a little but what I want to know first is which is your real voice. You sounded like a lady, a professional lady, and now you're back to skater-girl. Which one is you?"

"Yeah, I'm a chameleon. I can adapt. I'd have sounded like a real idiot talking like this and wearing pearls at that place. If I talk properly 'round these guys? They'd give me ... a hard time."

"They can't hear you now," he said.

"That's true. Come on, Brent. Don't be so annoying. Tell me what happened."

"Very well. Her name's Linda and the date was a complete failure. We're such different people... We have literally nothing in common. I tried to tell her about the Sheila Babbington case and she said, 'Stop! I hate murders. Don't tell me anything!' Something like that, anyway. But there was much more to it."

"Then the reason why you look so sad is nothing to do with her?"

"No... Do I look sad?"

"To me you do."

"It's because there's a ginger cat at my house and I have to find its owner."

"That wouldn't make you sad... Fine, if you're not going to tell me."

"One day I will."

"Is it to do with the case? How's it going anyway?"

"It is to do with the case and I hope we can clear these TV show people so that it doesn't become more confused than it is already."

"Do you have a suspect?"

"Yes. There's no evidence, just a hunch. I seem to be muddling through it without any energy. I used to have so much energy. I wish I were eighteen again."

"Yeah, well, I wish you were, too." Vane put the back of her hand up to her mouth while her elbow rested on the door. She was smothering a laugh.

"Why?"

"You heard me... You know I like you."

"Are you referring to what you were talking about the other night?"

"Wow, Brent, you are so slow."

"But…" Brent felt his face become warm. He had assumed this awkward subject had been dealt with. "Look… you're not serious, are you?"

"I do believe you're blushing, Brent." Vane laughed harder - tears were beginning to form in the corners of her eyes.

"Why are you laughing? You're laughing at me, aren't you?" He had no idea what next to say as Vane began convulsing with laughter. Brent began laughing, too - so much so he had to pull over to the side of the road.

"Are we here?" asked Mason, leaning forward. "Are you guys okay?"

"What's so funny?" asked Zack.

Vane answered with difficulty. "It's just a joke between brother and sister."

"You two are related?" asked Zack. "Like, I had no idea."

The set was to be located in and around a 1910-built building which was situated on a side-street. Inside the building, Bryana, who plays the rich, conniving prosecutor, has her offices. The ornate exterior of the same building was to be used as a backdrop for many scenes throughout the series. One of these was to be an intense shoot-out which leaves the male lead wounded or dead in the season's finale. Who will get to him first to hear what will probably be his dying words? Will it be Bryana or Marianne, super-cop, who has accidentally shot him during the fire-fight? Coincidentally, Marianne will pretty much hit everything she aims at but, for this one time in the series that she misses, poor, conflicted Cooper takes the errant bullet. Can you believe it?

Service trucks, trailers and cube vans necessary to next day's filming were already parked in a line in a wide one-way alley, out of sight of the actual film set. Cars to be used as props had arrived. Police 'no parking' notices had taken out a swath of sorely needed weekday parking spaces. Security personnel, the location manager, and other staff were already at work. Brent parked his Jeep two blocks away after having first surveyed the area around the set.

Brent gave Vane summary reports of Galen, Marianne, Bryana, and Cooper. He also gave her photographs that could be used to get an autograph if a quick cover-story was needed. The weather was forecast to be fine and dry for the next few days, although the end of the week held a chance of rain.

They found a few locations where either the set or the parked vehicles could be overlooked but not both. There was another area near the junction of the side-street and the alley that was perfect for observation of both areas but had no cover. One place there caught the attention of the teenagers.

"What a sweet spot!" said Zack.

"Do a kickflip!" said Mason.

The three skaters were on their boards instantly and heading for a loading area at the back of a building next to the intersection with the side-street. Within a couple of minutes, Brent understood why a slightly crumbling commercial loading dock with a concrete pad, a concrete ramp, stairs, and round metal railings was considered to be 'sweet'. The three teenagers began doing some amazing tricks.

Vane was surprisingly good. Brent realized he had never seen her skate before. Mason might have an edge on her in skills but he was not 'dialled in' to some of the tricks he was attempting and so came off as the most amateurish of the three. Zack was in a league by himself. Smoothly and effortlessly, he made the board do whatever he wanted it to do and did it so gracefully, without any apparent effort. They skated for a few minutes longer before Brent called them back to the mission.

"You can use this area sometimes but it's too exposed and obvious. You can't do proper surveillance while you're skating. It's one or the other."

"I still don't get what we're supposed to be looking for," said Mason. Zack nodded.

"One of the four people whose photos you have could have pulled the trigger or could have assisted someone who did. If so, that person will have this on his or her mind and it might show in behaviour and actions. Eventually, I have to talk to each of them to find out what they saw, if anything."

"Okay. So we watch and follow if they look out of line," said Mason.

"That's about it. Do you want to eat now? How about that Mexican restaurant you mentioned, Vane?"

"Sure," said Vane.

They walked back to the Jeep. Brent and Vane lagged behind a little.

"Where are we at?" asked Brent.

"We're brother and sister, like you said."

"Awkward, isn't it?"

"Yeah. I'll get over it. I can't help my emotions... You know what's really weird?"

"What would that be?"

"It's that I can talk to you about it - a little... anyway. It's like you're my best friend as well as everything else."

"I'm honoured and I'm really sorry if I've done anything to mislead you."

"You haven't. Not intentionally."

They were quiet for a while until Vane said,

"I really love skateboarding and the life that goes with it but, I don't know, I guess it's coming to an end sometime. A lot of the people I hang with think they're cool. They've got attitude, but they're immature, really. If you hadn't come along when you did I'd be dead, for sure. If you hadn't helped me afterwards, I'd be trapped. You've shown me a way out. Oh, yeah. How are my pearls today?"

"Safe and waiting for your graduation day."

"I'm gonna do it, you know. You just watch me."

Chapter 24

Sunday evening

*B*rent called Andy Fowler, sometimes known as Deadpan. He is the type of person who at a social gathering is the guy who sits in the corner and does not say anything and whose name and face cannot be remembered. Deadpan, on the other hand, could, among strangers, recount afterwards what everyone had said and in what order, produce simple drawings of what they looked like, could tell everyone's age to within two or three years, accurately estimate income and educational background, and know who disliked whom. If pushed, he could guess at what medication certain people were taking, what psychological problems they had, and if they were unfaithful to their partners. Under his very bland and insignificant exterior was a very dangerous man. He could so easily blackmail people. Instead, he turned his talents to surveillance and hired his services out along with those of his shadowy network of associates.

"How are you, Andy?"

"Very well, thank you, Brent. And yourself?"

"Personally, I'm okay. I'm investigating the murder at Garland's."

"That sounds interesting."

"Yes, it's interesting. I was there when it happened. At the moment, I hope you can help me sort out the mess."

"Happy to oblige. What would you like me to do?"

"I need four or five people watched."

"Before you go any further, a few of my associates are already on assignments so if you could prioritize the list it would be much appreciated. It's busy at the moment, you see."

"Right. First is Rebecca Kent who is usually called Becki. I'll send you her details and a photo - likewise for the rest of them. Probably living in the same house as Becki is a young woman in her early twenties named Bobbie. She is Becki's personal assistant. I don't know anything more at the moment. No photo for her yet but I'm working on that. University educated, has a trace of a European accent - I'm thinking France, Italy, or Switzerland. She has long, dark brown hair, is about five-ten in height, has a lightly tanned complexion and dark brown eyes. Athletic looking but no distinguishing features. I'm going to follow up on her. The address is one you'll need some kind of cover to watch."

"That sounds like it could require three operatives or more. Start tomorrow, I take it. How long for?"

"A week minimum. We'll review it after that."

"Next?"

"Will Hutchinson. Works at Althorn Capital. He's a possible suspect. Says he has an alibi but won't provide the name of the person who could substantiate it."

"Ah, I see. This person, male or female?"

"Don't know but I'm fairly sure the person is female. Hutchinson needs only be tailed from Althorn to wherever it is he goes. Probably there's a pattern to his visits with Thursday nights being almost a certainty."

"Very good. Next?"

"Kevin Jiang. He's hiding something about his relationship with the deceased, Kirby Mayo. The man is clever, ambitious and very focused on what he wants to achieve. I think Kirby may have been in his way.

All I need from you is where he goes, who he sees - background stuff really. I'll talk to him again after you've accumulated some information on his movements."

"That leaves one more."

"Nola Devon. Not much of an alibi but I'm almost certain she's innocent. I want some insight into her family relations. I need to verify my assumptions if I can. She will be outside of work hours, too. She's definitely the lowest on the list of priorities, so if you can't get to it, no worries."

"I'm not sure I can help on that one," said Andy.

"Send me all the information you have. I can start Ms. Kent and Bobbie tomorrow. Mr. Hutchinson… Tuesday, I think. Mr. Jiang by Thursday. Ms. Devon… I won't have anyone available until a week today unless I take a person off the first job."

"That's fine. Defer Nola Devon for the moment. This is going to take longer than I had hoped it would."

"If you don't mind my asking, are you working for yourself?"

"As far as you're concerned, yes - but Althorn Capital has invited me to assist them."

"Okay. I'll probably do the gas company van routine at the Kent household. Runs a little expensive but it works well."

"No problems with that. There's one issue I have. Should any of your associates be spotted, I need to be informed at once. They would all immediately suspect me of having them tailed and I would need a heads-up that some damage control was required."

"Of course, Brent. I only have an A team. There is no B team. I'll look into Bobbie, personally. I have to warn you, though. If she's a foreign national, I don't have the resources to investigate her in her country of origin or any place she stayed for an extended period of time. I can recommend a few names depending on where it is."

"No problem, Andy. Um, do you have a moment. I'd like to tell you about something I've set up today."

Brent then explained to Andy the surveillance he had established at the film set.

"That's a good idea. The cover makes sense. The risks I see are that you have three hastily trained operatives and, as we know, teenagers can be unpredictable at the best of times. Rotating the positions is good but I don't like it that they're in view of the targets all the time."

"I know. I thought I'd take a chance. How would you have handled it?"

"Probably would have rented an office to set up a surveillance post for the film set. I'd have wanted another post with a view of the trucks. Then I would have had at least two or three walking in the crowd and they'd have to be rotated daily. It would have been expensive to do. At least five people on site at any time."

"That's about what I thought. What's more, the likelihood of getting anything useful from this exercise is very low."

The cat was comfortable in the kitchen. Brent was in his office doing his best to send the cat home. He was printing off fliers with which to plaster the neighbourhood.

When the printer stopped, he sat and thought about how complicated his life was at this moment. He had a big, empty house with a stray cat in it. He was on a case that was difficult and might never be resolved. He had Linda

Roberts, daycare worker, pursuing him although she had now gone silent and he did not know what to make of it. He had met a potential soul-mate, Gabbie, only to decide they must pass like ships in the night which had left him feeling as though he had fallen into the dark sea to drown while waving goodbye to her. In between those two, he had met Tanya, waiter, who Brent found so pleasant that he wished to forget all else in her company. That momentary excitement had soon been quashed by discovering she was already seeing someone. Then, like a broad, ragged streak of orange paint across all his thoughts - Vane had a crush on him. He rarely got headaches but he had one now. He went to the bathroom cabinet to get a remedy for it.

Before eight, Brent, armed with his fliers, a stapler, and a tape gun, went out in an attempt to resolve one of his issues. He had printed off more than was strictly necessary and so ended up farther away on unfamiliar streets. The houses were smaller, two- and three-bedroom bungalows and cottages, built between the thirties and seventies with no two being identical.

He came to a house with a streetlight outside. The lamppost would have been a perfect place for one of his fliers if it had not had so many garbage containers beneath it. A woman came out of the house, dragging a big cardboard box.

"Here, let me help you," said Brent.

"It's no problem, I can manage," said the woman. One of the flaps ripped and came away in her hand.

"Could you hold these for me?" said Brent, who had run up to her.

"That's very nice of you," said the woman. She took hold of the fliers. Brent put the stapler and tape gun down on a step.

"It's a bit early for a spring clean. What have you got in here, a body?" said Brent, as he lifted the box.

"No, I'm moving out."

"Oh, that's a shame when I've just met you. Do you think they'll take this?"

"I hope so. I don't know what else I'm going to do with it."

Brent carried the box and the woman walked to the curb with him. Brent put the box down. The lamppost light illuminated both of them. The woman, whom Brent thought was in her late sixties, held out the fliers to hand them back to Brent.

"Lost a cat? Let me look… Hey, this looks exactly like my cat, Monty."

"No, I found one. Is he your cat?" asked Brent, hopefully.

"No. Monty died five years ago. This one is so much like him. I don't believe it."

"You would remember if you had seen a cat like this?"

"Sure. But I haven't." She sighed deeply and looked sad.

"Is anything the matter?"

She puffed out her cheeks and blew out a long breath. "Plenty, but there's nothing to be done. Sorry, don't mind me. Thank you for your help."

"Is there any more I can bring out for you?"

"No, that's about everything. Thank you. Goodnight."

He watched her walk away. He was suddenly overcome with an overwhelming sense of loneliness and of desolation for the burdened woman. His heart contracted with sorrow for her without knowing why.

"Excuse me. My name's Brent. I live a couple of streets over. I can't let you go in without knowing if I can help you. Please, talk to me about it, will you?"

In the half light, she faced him. In a flat monotone, she replied,

"Alright, I tell you. My husband was sick for a long, long time before he died. We had to put a mortgage on our house. When he died, his pension, it stopped. I work part-time as a cook in a restaurant but I can't get more hours. I have a small pension but it doesn't go nowhere. If I don't sell my house the bank will foreclose. I got very little equity in it. There, you wanted to know. I told you."

Brent had been listening intently as she spoke. Even in the uncertain light he saw that the house needed repairs. There was no money to fix it up and the woman standing before him did not seem the type who could undertake such things. When the house sold, it would be for well below market price. He thought her to be first or second generation Italian.

"I've been toying with the idea lately of hiring a housekeeper," said Brent. "Probably involves cleaning twice a week although I keep things very tidy. The housekeeper would buy food and supplies for my house and she could add her own groceries to the bill... I'd pay for both. If she could make a few lunches and dinners for me that would be perfect.... Yes, and we'd have dinner together once a week - if she wanted to, that is. Do you think fifteen hundred a month would be the right amount to pay the housekeeper for those duties?"

"I don't know what to say. Are you offering me a job?"

"Yes, I suppose I am. What's your name?"

"Maria. But, ah, you don't know what my cooking is like."

"That's true... I know, we'll do this." Brent took out a pen and a card and began writing his address down. "Call me tomorrow and name an evening you can cook a dinner for me - for both of us. That will be your try-out. It can be at your house or at mine.

Now, you'll need an advance because you probably have to get a few things so, here's some money for those. If you think this is all too weird, just put the money back in my mailbox. If you want to cook the dinner, you can bring a friend or family member with you. Should it not work out you keep the change." Brent held out the card enclosed in five folded one hundred dollar bills.

"I don't know. I'm all confused." Maria looked at Brent's face. He looked honest even in the bad light. She knew that if he walked away without her taking this money an opportunity to stay in her house would have slipped past her. It hurt her a little to take charity for that is what she felt it amounted to. Maria also realized that she had little choice, considering the way the world was and her age. She further realized that Brent had disguised the charity with some degree of sensitivity to make it seem less obtrusive, less harsh. She would be dependent upon him, a stranger, going forward. At least, Maria reasoned, even if it did not work in the longterm, she would be doing a lot better for a while, and he looked like a nice boy. "Okay," she said, as she took the card and money. "I'm gonna make you a dinner you will never forget!"

Back at his house, Brent contacted Greg Darrow.

"I'm sorry to say, Greg, that progress is slow. I might have more by the end of the week."

"You must have a hunch."

"I do but it seems too fanciful to me at the moment. I'm checking on it and as soon as I have anything you'll have it. That brings me to another problem."

"Which is?"

"My new best friend, Otto Schroeder. I met him outside Will Hutchinson's house. Hutchinson probably has an alibi but he's being difficult about it."

"You'll have to be more specific," said Greg. "I have so many open case files it's not funny. I don't go over the cases in detail unless a detective brings it to me with a problem or a decision has to be made."

"Hutchinson's a partner at Althorn. He has a motive, which is an insurance pay out. He wasn't on the best of terms with Mayo. He appears to have had opportunity - unless he gives out the name of his lover. That's what I'm working on acquiring so I can get him off the suspect list. He's a difficult person to deal with."

"I remember him. I saw he had time unaccounted for in his statement."

"Well, Otto has surveillance on him. That's the problem. Otto wants me to report to him directly. I said I would - to keep him happy. What do you need to keep you happy?"

"I don't mind you doing that," replied Greg. "He came to talk to me about you. I could tell he was fishing but he didn't seem annoyed. By all means, talk to him. But when you think you've got something tell me first. Can you do that?"

"Certainly. He thinks we talk to each other anyway."

"See. I told you he was a good detective. Just keep him off union matters and he's a decent guy. Cross him, and he won't let go. That everything?"

"Yes. Sorry to bother you."

"That's okay. Had some family over today and they've only just gone. Couldn't get rid of one of them but you don't want to hear about that. Goodnight."

"Goodnight, Greg." Brent put his phone down. The cat was at the patio door. Brent let him in. Tomorrow, the neighbourhood would see the posters.

"Do you want something to eat?" asked Brent. The cat meowed that it did.

Chapter 25

Monday

As soon as he was awake and had a coffee in his hand, Brent began scouring the internet for a photograph of Bobbie. He managed to find one and forwarded it to Andy Fowler.

After that, Brent contacted an agency based in the United Kingdom. He asked them to track Becki Kent's movements in the last two years to provide some information on her and her assistant. He forwarded a list of Becki Kent's European properties and several photographs. Brent told them what it was he was looking for and they said that it should be no problem and that they should have the information in a few days.

Text messages from Vane at the film set told Brent that the three skaters were cold and bored. They had observed a lot of activity while an outdoor scene was being set up. A car had reversed into and totally destroyed the key light set up at the entrance of the building. This brought out Galen Nash who shouted at everyone. By nine, the actors had yet to appear.

After nine, Otto Schroeder called while Brent was in his home-office, studying his stock portfolio and making some investment decisions.

"I interviewed a guy yesterday by the name of Morton Yates. He's a pension fund manager and not a friend of Mayo's. Don't like him. He's hiding something."

"What makes you say that?" asked Brent.

"He didn't come forward to give a statement. We had to find him on CCTV footage and track him to his car to get his plate number. A couple of witnesses mentioned in their statements that he was in the restaurant just prior to the time of the murder. That's what got us looking. They noticed him because he was soaked through with rain. A waiter remembered him talking with Mayo earlier in the evening. Yates tells me he went for a walk to a coffee shop only to return to talk to Mayo again. He sees Mayo is busy and so leaves in a taxi. Yates says he didn't notice anything unusual."

"From what you say, it seems he got wet because he was anxious to discuss something important but it was too private a matter to do so in front of someone else. Probably legitimate but it's also possible to read a possible motive to murder into it."

"I'd agree with that normally but he was too jumpy. He's the kind of guy who wants to know what you know before answering anything and then looks relieved when you don't talk about the thing he's wanting to keep hidden."

"All right," said Brent. "Let's take it from Mayo's perspective. Yates has gone and Mayo doesn't expect to see him again that night. Why? Because he's undoubtedly mentioned to Yates - or Yates would just assume - that he has a full roster of meetings with various people that evening. Now for Yates's perspective. Yates might have come back on the off-chance that he would find Mayo between meetings. However, when he finds that Mayo is indeed talking to someone else, Yates doesn't want to disturb him. If it had been really important, he would surely have stayed, letting Mayo know that he'd come back and would wait till he was free.

"Okay," said Otto. "What else?"

"Yates, returning unexpectedly, decides his talk can wait until the next day or whenever. Is Mayo even aware Yates has returned? Difficult to say but he probably isn't otherwise he would acknowledge Yates and ask him to wait for a while. Therefore, what we can be fairly certain of is that Yates knew he was not expected and Mayo was unaware of his return."

"That's hypothetical. It sounds reasonable but maybe Mayo sees Yates and ignores him. Go on."

"Okay. We have a Pension Fund Manager and a Hedge Fund Manager discussing what? Sports? Celebrities? Cars? Kirby Mayo used Garland's as an office. Yates was there to discuss business. This is after pension fund hours so, we are probably safe to assume, they were having a chat about how Althorn could get business from the Pension fund and Mayo was wining, dining, and, probably, bribing Yates. That's a bit of a stretch but let's make that assumption. Mayo stays in Garland's. Yates leaves. Have they come to terms or not? If no, Yates would probably not return. If yes, he might. The reason Yates returns to see Mayo is because he now envisages something will go wrong with the deal. Althorn won't get the business and Yates won't get the commission or whatever it should be called.

Something occurred or Yates thought of an impediment after he left and he's a little desperate to see Mayo. Yates will risk getting soaked by rain and entering a prestigious restaurant looking like a drowned rat to talk to Mayo as soon as possible. Why? He's money hungry and he doesn't want the deal going south but he needs Mayo to speak to him - reassure him on some point.

Mayo is busy. Yates realizes he looks like an idiot and forces himself to go home. He will contact Mayo through means other than a face to face."

"All that's possible," said Otto. "But let's say Yates has learned something and is running back to kill Mayo. Maybe his nerve fails him. Then, a bit later, he has a second crack and puts a couple into Mayo."

"Okay, let's say Yates is gunning for Mayo for some reason. Let's go through it. Yates has foreseen a problem - we have no idea what it is. He goes back to Garland's and, because he cannot approach Mayo, decides to shoot him on the spot. Why would he do that? What could possibly have been Mayo's action to bring about such a reaction from Yates? A crime of passion? Yates does not figure in Mayo's personal life at all so, no, that's impossible. Has Mayo cheated or stolen from Yates in any sense? It's possible, but we have no evidence that this is the case. In fact, it's the same for any other potential reason we can cite.

Who is Yates? A guy who got caught in the rain. Did he have a grievance against Mayo? Quite likely. Did he shoot him in the heat of the moment? No - unless he waited around for an opportunity to do so later. I can assure you, Domenic Castillo, the manager at Garland's, might have overlooked Yates for a minute or two but not for any longer than that.

The same for the wait staff. If Yates had been working up his courage to shoot Mayo many people would have seen him. Yates stood out because he was soaking wet. If he then nervously stood and pulled a pistol to aim at Mayo from two tables away a dozen people would have seen him. Therefore, it is impossible for Yates to shoot Mayo in such a deliberate fashion. If he had shot Mayo spontaneously that would make sense to me but that wasn't how it happened. If he premeditated to any degree, it does not. Yates, as interesting as he is because of whatever it is he is hiding, did not shoot Mayo."

There was a long silence on the other end.

"Yeah, that sounds about right," said Otto. "If those two were dealing under the table I'd say that's about the level of anxiety Yates was showing. I still have to check him out, though."

"Of course, you do. There are a couple of things I'd like to ask you," said Brent. "Is there anyone in either Mayo's or his wife's family who might have a motive?"

"No, not really. The house, contents, and about half the money goes to his wife, the rest goes into a trust for his children. There are a few small other bequests in the ten to twenty thousand dollar range but that's it. He had a brother he wasn't close to and who gets one of the bequests, a small amount. And if any of them had a personal score to settle I haven't seen it yet."

"So no candidates there. The other matter concerns two women who came into the hotel after ten o'clock. Both were wearing grey trench-coats and neither checked in their coat. Know anything about them?"

"There were two? I know of one because I saw her on the tape. She was staying in the hotel and has an alibi. You saying there was a second one?"

"Yes. Talk to Timothy in the cloakroom. He saw them both."

The conversation ended shortly after that. Brent was puzzled as to why Otto had called him. There seemed to be no reason other than the detective's acceptance of him as a professional investigator.

One fact in the case pointed to something but Brent was baffled as to what it meant - a fully loaded, and therefore unused, .38 calibre revolver had been found on the floor of the restaurant. The murder weapon had been the same calibre and type. Why two revolvers and was there a connection between them?

He had gone through various permutations of who could have killed Kirby Mayo - from a single assailant, with the second weapon being unconnected, to as many as three or more people consisting of assassins and spotters. This last arrangement seemed absurd. Also, to murder someone in a crowded restaurant seemed absurdity in itself.

"Good morning, Greg," said Brent. "Got anything more on Nash and the actors you can give me?"

"Hi, Brent. What kind of thing?"

"Background details. I've pulled a few things together but it's mostly useless - social media gossip and incomplete biographies."

"I don't think we're looking at any of them. Their statements agreed and they all give each other an alibi and say they didn't see anything. Why the interest?"

"Suppose one of them is lying and did see the killer but he or she is not admitting to it. I have to find out who that person is and how they're involved."

"Let's see what I can find for you in the database. Takes a moment... You getting along with Schroeder?"

"I seem to be. I had a surprise call from him this morning. He was quite chatty and let me air one of my hunches about a witness."

"I like to see you guys playing together nicely. Here we are. Got a pen?"

"Yes."

"Fisher, Cooper, 28, actor. Born in Germany, family name Trucco but that's because he was adopted by a Swiss

Family and lived in Geneva. Came here when he was nineteen to finish his degree and pursue an acting career. Has worked at numerous temporary jobs. Returns to Switzerland on average twice a year. Got a small part in his first movie at the age of seventeen after making a connection at the Locarno International Film Festival... where's that?"

"That's in Switzerland on Lake Maggiore. The south end of the lake is Italian territory. I have his film career from the internet."

"Good. Nothing much more. Got a drunk and disorderly when he was twenty. Next, Bryana McDowell, 24, actor and singer... Brent? There's more here than I thought. Can I send this stuff to you? I don't see anything interesting and you probably have most of it already."

"Oh, please do. I didn't mean to take up your time like this."

"Okay. I'll send it on."

"Thanks. Bye."

"Hello, Mr. Umber?"

"Hello, is that Maria?"

"Yes, it is. I was thinking about the dinner. Would you mind Wednesday evening?"

"That would be fine. I have to warn you, sometimes I get called away on business but, at present, I'm free at that time."

"Okay. Um, I don't know if I want to cook here or there."

"Whichever you prefer. My kitchen is fully equipped. Perhaps you would like to start the dinner at your place and finish it off here. That way you can get a feel for this kitchen."

"Uh, okay. I can do that."

"Are you bringing anyone with you?"

"I don't think so. I walked past your house. You have a nice place, Mr. Umber."

"Please, call me Brent."

"Brent? How will I get the food from my house to your house?"

"I'll come and pick you up."

"That's good. That sounds perfect. If you could do that at six o'clock, we can have dinner at seven. Is that okay with you?"

"That's perfect. I'm very pleased you decided to give it a try. I'll get the table ready. What will the dinner be?"

"Can I keep it a surprise? I'll bring everything that's needed so you don't have to worry about a thing. It's going to be good."

Brent called Henry Warner and it was part social call and part inquiry. Yes, Henry and Caroline had enjoyed their trip to Chile - it had brought back many old memories and they had made many new ones. Yes, the family was all doing well and showing no signs of trauma after the murder happening so close to them. No, he saw no reason why Brent should not interview any of them - the police already had done so several times. No, they had not remembered seeing anything unusual at the adjacent tables.

Andy Fowler called to inform Brent that the surveillance vehicle was in place. After that call, Brent had nothing to do. He reviewed the case as he understood it. A definite picture was forming in his mind. He could not help ascribing to the person who had fired the shots an intense, powerful urge to destroy. The problem as he saw it was that no one he had spoken to so far possessed any such trait. He wondered if he was mistaken as he tried the fit of person after person into the role of killer.

Brent was at a loose end and had to wait for useful news to come from Vane or Andy Fowler - if it ever did. This waiting with nothing to do but think had him in a nervous state. He needed an outlet. More interviews would follow later in the week but, for now, he needed to divert his mind and channel his energy into a productive area. What he needed was some excitement. Within ten minutes he had thought of two things to do, with the first naturally leading to the second. He began to plan each of them meticulously. In the afternoon, he would go out and get the advanced fieldwork done on these projects - after he had visited Vane, Zack, and Mason.

The filming of the outdoor scenes was in full swing by the time Brent arrived. The early afternoon sun lit one side of the street, requiring various light diffusers, reflectors, and shades to be used as well as lights. Dressed in jeans and a hooded sweatshirt, Brent mingled with a loose knot of people grouped on one side of the yellow 'Do not cross' tape which cordoned off the side street where the filming was to be done. A uniformed security guard stood on the other side of the tape. With the ebb and flow of the busy main street, the knot of people continuously grew or shrank in size. There was not much to see from that distance - a ring of lights, a few people within the lights, and a lot of people beyond the lights, moving around. Brent waited to see a scene taken. It was over in thirty seconds and it looked like nothing had happened.

A building on the corner overhung a raised pedestrian area. Brent saw Mason there, leaning against a concrete pillar. He was holding and staring at his phone. Brent phoned him. He watched as Mason answered his call unaware of Brent's proximity.

"It's Brent. What's happening?"

"Hi… I'm watching Nash doing a street scene. We think Marianne is inside the building doing a different scene in there. We can't get close to that set. Vane's watching a dressing room trailer - Bryana's in it. Zack's talking to a security guard. The guy checked us out earlier but he's cool. He used to be a skater. Not much happening. To be honest, Brent, I think we're too far away to see anything useful."

"That's okay. Keep at it. Talk to you later." Brent called Zack. "Hi, Zack… just say things like yeah and sure while I speak and don't make eye contact with the guard. Get a clear photo of his ID and send it to me. Can you do that?"

"Yeah, sure I can."

"Would your man take a bribe?"

"No… he ain't like that."

"Can he be persuaded to let you on set?"

"Uh-uh. No way."

"Do you see any way on set without being detected?'

"I don't think so."

"Okay, thanks."

"Yeah, hang loose."

Brent left the small crowd and walked around the block to find Vane. He called her as he went.

"Hello, Vane. Whereabouts are you?"

"Hey, Brent. In the alleyway watching a door as though I ain't… whoa… as though I'm not watching a door."

"I'm close to you at the west end of the alley. Can you leave easily?"

"Sure."

Brent saw Vane walking towards him from the other end of the alley. He thought she looked confident and self-possessed. She had changed a lot in the year or so he had known her. From a scruffy, angry girl, she had become a young woman, a hard-working student, and a good friend. It was an odd relationship they had - each feeling responsible to and for the other. It was so easy for him to talk to her. Vane did not know it but Brent valued her very highly and, in a strange way, depended upon her. On paper, their friendship would have had the status of mere acquaintanceship. In reality, he needed someone to care for and she needed someone looking out for her. They each fulfilled those all-important roles for each other.

"That's a beautiful jacket. You have good taste."

"This is what I got with the money you gave me. You like it, then?" She started posing to show off her jacket. Vane looked happy.

"Very much. It's functional, stylish, and suits you perfectly. Now, as important as your wardrobe is, we do have a case to think about. What's your assessment of this stake-out?"

"Honestly, I don't think we're going to get much while they're on set. We can't get close enough to the actors. Everyone's so busy, like moving around, disappearing into the building, or a vehicle. Nash is always like in the middle of everything and he's always working."

"What happened at lunch?"

"They got food from a truck. Some sat around outside but most went into the building to eat."

"Did you notice anything happening between the actors?"

"Not really. I saw Bryana and Cooper talking together for a minute. They both laughed about something. That's it."

"Thanks. I have an idea. Why don't the three of you put on a show? Wait until Nash is passing so he can see your skills. I want him to notice you."

"You think he might use us in the show?"

"It's a remote possibility. He or someone else might come over and just talk. That's when you try and get onto the set as a visitor."

"Okay. We can try."

They chatted a little longer before Brent left and Vane took up her surveillance post again.

In the evening, Brent ate a solitary meal. No one called him about anything. No news had come in about the case. When he had finished, he lay down on the sofa as his mind ran over the details of the murder in the restaurant. From the characters in and around the drama he tried to construct a narrative that would fit the details. Nothing fitted without being forced. What was it he did not know? he asked himself. He tried the 'five whys' approach but became sidelined and it ultimately failed.

Kirby was shot in a public place - why? Because it was the only opportunity that presented itself to the killer.

Why was that the only opportunity? The killer could not approach him privately.

Why not? Because the killer had limited time… Because a public statement had to be made….

Interesting… a public execution for a public crime, or a private crime? One or the other… private, I think. What had Kirby done? Numerous double dealings in business…? That doesn't warrant a deliberate public attack… that requires a hit or a private killing.

The reason for his murder has to flow out from a relationship…. Rena? She doesn't fit the profile at all but then it's very easy to build a case against her. There's no intense passion or spent passion that I could see. Rena suffers from resignation to her life with Kirby without a hint of any vengeance being sought. Could be an act but I doubt it.

Becki? Why would she? She and Kirby had always had a convenient arrangement over the years which did not demand fidelity to one another. She seems to lead a full and busy life apart from Kirby - seems, really, to have got past Kirby altogether. She would not shoot Kirby like that. If he had offended her somehow, she might stab him on the spur of the moment. She might even hire someone to dispose of him but she would not kill him like that in a restaurant full of people, putting herself in such jeopardy.

Was there another affair and another woman…? There seems to have been quite a few but none that lasted any time. If there was another, it would need to be more recent and more intense… within the last few years. I suppose the police will sift through those. I haven't a clue.

Either Nash or Stark could have murdered Mayo. McDowell and Fisher are too remote because of their age. Not one of them could murder Mayo without the others seeing them. 'Excuse me a moment, I have to murder the man at the next table - please don't mention it to the police.' However, how is it possible they did not see who sat down at the empty table? Are people really that unobservant?

Why is it I want to have the woman in the grey coat holding the revolver? I really feel it could be her… in the absence of any concrete evidence pointing elsewhere.

The cat was scratching at the back door again. For a moment, Brent could not recall if the cat was in or out. What he did know was that not a soul had responded to his posts or flyers.

Chapter 26

Tuesday into Wednesday

*A*ndy Fowler called at eight in the morning. He reported that nothing had happened at the Kent residence the day before beyond the usual comings and goings.

Brent went to his home gym. He worked out to exhaustion on all his exercises and then took a shower.

Later, he called Nola Devon. He informed her that he hoped to have some definitive reassurance for her by the end of the week. She informed him that Rena Mayo was intending to keep her partnership share alive after the will was probated and so the executor was now actively seeking two individuals to take over Kirby Mayo's position at Althorn - two who would work well with the other partners. Nola believed, in some way, that Brent's meeting with Rena had precipitated her decision.

"It was as though she had got past a barrier," said Nola. "I suppose you can't tell me what was said."

"No, I can't. I'd like to but… professional ethics and all that kind of thing. She did get past an issue, though. I hope she heals properly."

"Yes. It couldn't have been much of a life for her. I'm glad she's taking an active interest in the partnership for her own sake as well as everyone else's."

"Yes. Would Kevin Jiang be able to take over Kirby's portfolio?"

A hardness crept into Nola's voice, indicating to Brent that he was overstepping the mark in delving into the inner workings of Althorn. "Why do you ask?"

"He seems competent. I was impressed by him. Sorry if I'm interfering."

"No, it's not interfering. He's about the best trader we've ever had but that is also his limitation. He can't schmooze the clients. We need someone who can. Kevin could run the portfolio; he's already doing some of that work. We need someone to expand the business. That will have to come from outside."

"I just thought I would make the observation that, maybe, since Kevin's and Althorn's interests are already aligned, he, as a known quantity, would be a good and safe bet."

"I'll keep it in mind. Is there anything else?"

"Not at the moment. As soon as there are any developments I'll let you know."

"Hi, Brent. You will never, ever guess what happened." Vane sounded very excited on the phone.

"You got an autograph?"

"No. That's nothing. You'll be wanting my autograph."

"Um... let me see... you got a part in the show?"

"Yes! We did some tricks this morning like you said. Then Galen Nash, he's such a cool dude, he saw us and said he wanted us in a scene. This afternoon, we'll be shooting it. Guess who's got a speaking part?"

"Let me see... would that be you?"

"Yes, yes, yes! It's not big or anything but I get a couple of lines. Yeah... No... Like, whatever."

"Do you? What do you say?"

"I just said it. Yeah, no, like, whatever. I know it's not much but it's a start."

"It certainly is. Well done for getting inside and congratulations on the part. What about the others?"

"I'm so glad you're not angry. We all get to do a few tricks. Zack and Mason stand behind me when I play opposite Marianne Stark. She's running around looking for some guy and stops by us in the street to ask which way he went. The part was going to be played by a window cleaner but they wrote us into the script instead. Said it added depth and colour. And we're getting paid for it, too!"

"This is wonderful. I'm really pleased for you. You'll remember that you're on a mission, I hope?"

"Of course, Brent. That's the whole point. I was thinking that I'd get chatting to a manager or two and they'd let me hang out on the set for the rest of the week. I'll act like I belong and won't get in anyone's way. I can only watch where the scene is being shot. That leaves Zack and Mason to cover everything else. You okay with that?"

"Couldn't be better. Break a leg."

As soon as he was off the phone, Brent forwarded photographs of the film set security guard's credentials he had received from Mason to a lady named Maude. She was an expert in replicating things like passports, driver's licenses, and security clearances. For a job as simple as the one Brent was requesting, Maude could provide him with same day service.

It was not until eight in the evening that anything of significance happened. It occurred while Brent was wondering what Linda Roberts was doing. Despite his prohibition on any contact between them because of his workload, he found her to be a distraction anyway. Not to hear from her was almost as bad as hearing from her. He was failing to understand what was going on between them.

Andy Fowler called.

"Well, Brent. This must be the fastest piece of work I have ever done for anyone. Hutchinson left his office at six p.m. and took a taxi straight to a condominium. I'll send you the information I have. Hutchinson owns a place there but a woman by the name of Karlee Smith rents it from him.

Now I can't go as far as to say she actually pays any rent but this place is clearly his alternative home. That information came from a security guard who knows both of them by sight and has made some assumptions.

You'll like this part; the security guard says he remembers seeing Hutchinson the night of Mayo's death just before ten o'clock because he said hello to him and was ignored which was why he remembered the incident. Said he looked rattled. The guard went on his rounds at ten-thirty without seeing Hutchinson again, which he would have done if your guy had left in that half-hour.

What Hutchinson may not be aware of is Ms. Smith sees someone else at the weekends. You'll see it in the report. I can go further in this matter if you like."

"No, I think that's sufficient. If I need to establish an alibi for him I now have at least one credible witness and possibly two. There's no way Hutchinson could have got back to Garland's in eight minutes, in time to commit the murder. Thanks, that's good work."

"It goes like that sometimes. Nothing of interest at the Kent residence yet. I can start someone on following Ms. Devon tomorrow instead of Thursday."

"Yes, please do that - only promise me you won't find anything."

"Well, I hope I don't, then. One thing this line of work has taught me is that the world is so full of surprises nothing surprises me anymore. Goodnight, Brent."

Andy sent the report as promised. It consisted of three terse, factual paragraphs and no more. Brent now knew why Hutchinson had not wanted to reveal who he was with that night. The man knew himself that he had a rock solid alibi and, if push came to shove, he would be forced to divulge it. However, the reason for his reluctance to clear himself was now apparent. It was not that Hutchinson cared that his wife knew of his adultery. It was not that he was gallantly trying to preserve the other woman in the affair. It was because he possessed real estate his wife knew nothing about. Hutchinson obviously did not want it included in their inevitable divorce proceedings. Judging by the address, the condo was probably worth about   a million - a small amount when compared to the Hutchinson family's total wealth but it was a mean and grasping, dishonest act by Will Hutchinson, nonetheless.

Brent was up early Wednesday to beat the rush-hour traffic on his way to the film set. He was successful in avoiding the worst of it but had to park in a lot four blocks away from the set. It was still well over an hour before the late October sunrise and the air was cold, close to freezing. He walked past the stairs of a subway station entrance as a small but steady stream of commuters emerged from below onto the sidewalk. Brent joined the flow, walking with them.

As he approached the street where the set was situated, Brent slowed and looked at the lights. They were filming a night scene involving several cars. He did not stop to watch because no one else was stopping. When he was clear of the area, Brent stopped by the wall of the corner building and sent out a group text message to the skaters, asking for the nearest to come and meet him. Mason was by his side within a few seconds.

"I saw you from across the street," said Mason. "Wassup?"

"They're shooting outside that building. What's inside?"

"It's Bryana's office set on the seventh floor. They're shooting most of the time in there. Security's tight, man. There's a cop right outside the elevator door. You won't get in."

"You might be right. What does Bryana or any of them do when they're not on set?"

"Like, they all rehearse. They read the script together or chill out. There's one guy who goes to sleep whenever he can but he's weird 'cos he does it so his face don't get messed up. You know, the make-up, right? At lunch they all kinda relax. The rest of the time, it's go, go, go."

"How was your session?"

"It was cool. I had a blast. But I gotta tell ya, Brent - Zack was like flying. His tricks were so good they got him doing a whole bunch more than they'd planned for the scene."

"I'm glad for all of you. How did Vane manage with her lines?"

"She's so sassy. She made up some stuff and they're keeping it. Oh, how'd it go?… Yeah, yeah. Marianne is all breathing hard because she's been running after this dude. She comes around the corner and the dude's just gone and she says,

'Did you see which way he went?' to Vane.

So Vane says, 'You want me to catch him for you?' when she's supposed to say, 'No.' Now they're both off script.

Marianne says, 'Girl, you don't have the training or experience.'

So Vane says, 'Try me, sister… When I catch him, you'll tell me where I apply to become a cop.'

'You're not gonna tell me?' says Marianne.

'Whatever. He went that way.' Vane points and Marianne rolls her eyes and takes off running. Then cut. Galen Nash just loved it."

"I have an idea why she went off script… What impresses me is your recall. Have you got any career plans?"

"Career? Like, no. I do whatever I want."

"I'm not sure how long doing what you want takes but when you get tired of it you should think about focusing your talents on your future."

"I've got plenty of time for that."

"Yes. Right now I have to talk to some of those people who are so very busy. I think I'll get closer to them."

Chapter 27

Later Wednesday morning

*B*rent, with his newly forged security credentials around his neck, walked past the yellow tape, saying, 'Good morning,' to the guard who was watching him quizzically. Once inside, he located Nash - he wanted to see him first. An action scene was being set up and the producer-director was talking to a couple of assistants. On the back of one of his cards, Brent wrote the following message: 'Help me catch Mayo's killer. I need 3 minutes.' He waited for an opportune moment to approach and hand the card to Nash. The director looked at Brent before taking it. He read both sides of the card before calling to someone.

"Annette! Take over here for a few minutes." The assistant director nodded.

"Who are you and what's this about?"

"I'm an investigator. Someone at your table had to have seen the murderer but they're keeping quiet about it. If it wasn't you, then one of your stars is withholding evidence. When you're halfway through the first season, how will that breaking news affect ratings and the future of the show?"

"That's a good point. You're not with the police?"

"No. I represent the interests of Althorn Capital. The surviving partners are anxious to maintain the reputation of their business. That can only be managed if the killer is found."

"Look, this sounds like lawyers should be present. We've had the police interview all of us three times. They promised to keep away while we're shooting. I can't have any actor upset about this. Can't it wait?"

"It could. I'll tell you what I want. All I need is to interview your three actors in a group, to find out what they saw and heard in the two minutes prior to the shots being fired. That's it. You can be in the group, as well."

"A re-enactment? What happens if you find what you're looking for?"

"I'll know who it is who's holding back. Then either the police or I will talk to whoever it is privately. If I talk to that person, then, if it is possible, I can protect your show just as I'm protecting Althorn's interests. If it's the police… they'll go by the book."

"I don't think we can do this, Mr. Umber. You spook just one of my actors and it will affect the quality of their work. I can't afford for that to happen."

"I understand. Tell me, what was the seating arrangement that night? Who had their back to Mayo's table?"

"That would have been Cooper."

"Is there any reason why you chose that particular table?"

"I didn't. It wasn't my dinner party."

"Oh. Whose was it?"

"Cooper's. He was taking Bryana and Marianne to dinner and then asked me to join them after he had booked the table."

"I see. Where did the rest of you sit?"

"I was on Cooper's left, Marianne was opposite me, and Bryana opposite Cooper. Look, if you're going to ask me if I saw anything, the answer is, I didn't. We had finished eating and were talking. Marianne was making a suggestion about her part and then the shots were fired. I dropped to the floor. That's all there was to it."

"Did you see if anyone else at the table noticed anything before the shooting?"

"I don't think so. You mean, whether they were staring at someone?"

"Yes. Do you recall anything like that?"

"Only Bryana. She's got a lot of energy so she never really sits still and is very aware. She looked around the room a lot but she was engaged in the conversation the whole time. Marianne is very graceful and very focused but completely unaware of what is going on around her. A clown on stilts could stand next to her and she wouldn't notice."

"What about yourself?"

"I guess I'm somewhere between the two of them. I saw Kirby. You probably know he played me for a sucker some years back. I had a lot of animosity towards him but that has mostly gone now that he's dead. I'll be straight with you, I'm not sure I care whether the killer is found or not."

"I can appreciate that. You were at school together, then later, he let you down over a financing deal. The possibility remains that someone at your table saw someone or something critical. They're either deliberately suppressing what they saw or they're unaware of its significance. It's likely to be the latter. What they witnessed may mean nothing or it might be crucial to the case. The police will come back to haunt you until they can close the file. What do you want me to do?"

"I don't know. I don't like the re-enactment idea. If you could talk to them quietly like you have done with me, I guess it's okay."

"Thank you. I'll be as unobtrusive as possible. Oh, yes. Two things. Did you see a woman in a grey trench-coat?"

"No."

"Last thing, I promise. Cooper - how was he at the table?"

"He's a very quiet, unassuming guy. Good manners. He sat still but was very aware. He's the kind of guy you don't have to work at to convince of anything so you don't tend to look at him that often. I can't say I noticed what he was doing. You know, you wouldn't think much of Cooper as an actor until you'd explained what he's to do in a scene. Then he delivers just the way you want it. Definitely one of the easiest actors I've worked with and that's saying a lot."

"Thanks again, Mr. Nash. I'll wait until they're not busy to talk to them."

"Sure. Look at that. I told them not to put the car there." Galen Nash walked away to plunge back into the intricacies of the production.

Brent went inside the main building and up to the seventh floor. At that early hour the security guard was inclined only to glance at Brent's tag, nod, and say nothing.

Several rooms had been turned into permanent sets for all the office interior shots. The smallest set was for Marianne's office, the largest for Bryana's. The production goal was to complete each episode in sequence as far as was possible. It was always an unwritten production goal that script rewrites in future episodes should not force completed scenes to be retaken.

Bryana was having her make-up done on set. When she was finished, the make-up artist removed a paper towel tucked into the top of Bryana's clothing. The setting for the upcoming scene was a carpeted corridor. Bryana, with long black hair cascading over the shoulders of an expensive business suit, was to come stomping quickly and angrily along the corridor, carrying some thick file folders. She was to turn into an office and approach a colleague quietly working at his desk. The hurling of the folders onto his desktop was to be accompanied by a brief, angry, sarcastic monologue, beginning with, 'Who do you think you are!?' The corridor shot was completed in two takes. The setup for office interior shots was underway when Brent managed to get Bryana by herself for a moment.

"Hi. Galen said I could speak to you. It's about the murder of Kirby Mayo. I'm investigating it. Here's my card."

"I'm in the middle of a scene."

"I know so I'll be quick. It's the moments just before the shots were fired that I'd like you to try to recall. What were you talking about?"

"Like, there was Marianne saying how she felt she needed more challenges in the domestic life of her character… to make her more sympathetic."

"Okay. You were sitting facing Cooper. Did you see anyone at the table behind him?"

"That's where the guy died. From where I was sitting I could see a woman in a dark red dress at the table but nothing more than that, really."

"Did you hear anything behind you?"

"I kinda sensed someone sitting down but that's all."

"Good. Do you think Marianne noticed anything or anyone around her?"

"No. She was talking a lot so, no, she couldn't have."

"What about Galen. What was he doing?"

"He looked like he was going to sleep most of the time. He smiled at me and then said to Marianne if her character came across as too sympathetic the plot would lose some of the tension it was trying to build between her and me. He said he wanted a fine balance, yada, yada."

"What about Cooper? What did he say?"

"He agreed with Galen. I can't make that guy out. He was like in two places sometimes. When I spoke to him he was totally listening but it was like he was looking through me and not at me. At the time you're talking about, I can't say I noticed him doing anything special. He sits very still and you sometimes forget he's there."

"Did you see a woman in a grey trench-coat at any time?"

"No. Can't say I did."

"Thanks. You've been very helpful and I'm sorry to have disturbed you."

Brent waited around to see the file-throwing scene. The first take of the medium distance shot was very convincing. After two takes, the set was changed to take close-up shots of Bryana in action, followed by shots of her colleague at the desk. Brent left before those were started to find Marianne.

He contacted Vane to warn her he was on the set and that they should not acknowledge one another. He instructed her to ignore Bryana from now on.

Marianne was in make-up. This was in a trailer which had become the relaxed, social hub of the set. Inside there, it was not possible for Brent to talk to one of the co-leads without several pairs of ears hearing every word he said.

He waited outside. Brent was more than surprised when Zack came out of one of the doors. The skater saw Brent, smiled before realizing they should not be seen speaking to each other. Zack quickly walked away. Brent sent him a message,

"What?"

"It's cool. Chillin' with friends."

"Have you got another job?"

"No. On mission. Learned a lot. Nothing useful. OK?"

"Yes."

At about seven-thirty, Marianne came out and went immediately into the costume trailer. Brent had to wait again. He saw Cooper Fisher in the distance but decided to stick with Marianne and intercept her before she headed onto the set.

When Marianne emerged from the costume department she was wearing a long insulated coat against the cool October air. The coat was open and revealed her set costume consisting of a bullet-proof vest, conspicuous under a dark blue, mid-length jacket and over the top of a white shirt, with jeans and sneakers to complete the uberly active detective ensemble.

Brent saw a set manager-type coming towards her. Brent got in ahead of him.

"Excuse me, I'm an investigator. I need to talk to you about the Kirby Mayo murder. Galen has approved it. It won't take a minute." He handed her his card.

Before she could answer, the manager approached and was already speaking before coming to a halt.

"Ms. Stark, the scene starts in ten minutes. Your props are ready."

"Marianne will be there on time," replied Brent abruptly.

"Okay," said the manager who left them alone.

"Sorry about that. It's important we talk."

"I guess it is. So talk fast, because I have to be in the zone, like right now."

"The two minutes before the shots were fired, I think you were explaining how you thought your character should have more challenges in her domestic life to make her more sympathetic. Sounds reasonable to me."

"Yes, I thought so, too. In this business you have to ask for ten things to get one."

"While you were speaking, did you notice anything or anyone around you?"

"No. I was concentrating on what I was saying."

"Makes sense. So, did you see anyone sit down at a table near you or a woman in a grey trench-coat?"

"No, to both."

"You were sitting opposite Galen. How did he seem to you? Do you think he noticed anyone?"

"Not Galen. He looked sleepy but he was listening. He nods his head slightly. As long as he does that you know he's taking in what you're saying."

"What about Bryana?"

"She doesn't sit still. I like her but she made me jump when she dropped her knife on a plate. She was listening but I was really directing everything I said to Galen."

"Why did she drop her knife?"

"She was playing with it and I think it just slipped out of her hand. That's weird, you know. The sound of the knife made me jump but when the firing started I was really calm and did what everyone else did, like it was a rehearsal."

"That could be because of your training or it could be because you're a cool-headed person."

"Ha! You've got that wrong. I lose it sometimes and it's tears or rage and nothing in the middle."

"Really? You surprise me."

"Obviously you're not a fan of mine otherwise you'd know. Brent Umber, are you with the police?"

"No. I work privately. I'm looking after Althorn Capital's interests in this case. I thought the simplest way to do that was to find the murderer."

"I hope you do. I love Garland's but I'm never going back there."

"Would you go back if they re-branded the place?"

"Same place, different label? I don't know. Strange how the mind works but I probably wouldn't. I was too close to the event."

"Cooper Fisher must have been sitting on your right. How did he seem to you while you were speaking?"

"He's a very nice man but he does this weird thing with his eyes sometimes. Like he's looking right at you, and then, without moving his head, he's looking somewhere else."

"That was what he was doing while you were explaining your point?"

"I don't know. I only glanced at him a few times to include him in the discussion so I didn't really notice but I think he must have. Maybe he was tense with Galen being there, I don't know. It's a big part for him. Why all this interest in Cooper?"

"No real reason beyond trying to determine who could have seen the killer and at what point the killer was seen. I think that's everything. Thank you."

"Well, that was easy. The police aren't too bad but they make a bigger deal out of it than you just did. Gotta go now. I have to shoot some bad guys."

It was not possible to get close to Cooper as he was on set and acting. Brent would have to wait until lunch. He decided to sit out the wait at a café across the street.

Although the place was fairly busy he got a two-seater table. He looked at his phone for messages. Several had come in and he dealt with them while sipping a coffee. He was engrossed in one from the U.K. detective agency and was about to open an attachment containing a preliminary report when a woman asked,

"Is this seat taken?"

"Ah, no…." Brent looked up to find it was Gabbie Wright talking to him. "How did you…?" Brent jumped out of his seat. "Please, sit down."

"Thank you. Apologies for making you jump." She sat down and put her coffee on the table.

"Don't apologize." Brent sat down. "I don't think you're here by chance."

"No. I've turned private investigator. The day after our last discussion, I began thinking about the case from your perspective. I wondered, what would Brent be doing now? Interviewing and trailing people. I became fascinated with both the case and your part in it. I didn't do much more than that until I noticed a gas utility van parked outside of Becki's house - I pass her place frequently. On Monday, I took no notice of it. But it was there yesterday and today. That made me suspicious so I circled around and watched it for a while from a side street. Bobbie came out of the house to her car. As soon as she was on the road and a hundred yards away, a car pulled out and, I believe, began to follow her."

"That's very good," said Brent. "Would you like another coffee or anything else?"

"No, I'm fine, thanks. I somehow guessed it was you behind that. I was also relieved to know that I was not under surveillance. Anyway, I couldn't imagine it was you sitting in a van for hours on end so I wondered, what you would be doing at this moment. I remembered a news story about a television production and the people in it being at Garland's on the night. I did some research. Once I got here, I asked myself, where would be a good place to stake-out the film set? And here I am."

"How clever you are. You would have made a fine investigator. And now you're here to tell me something…. something I probably don't want to hear."

"And I don't want to say it." Gabbie took Brent's hand in hers. "I couldn't phone you… I wouldn't have got the words out properly… and email would be ridiculous. I'm going to Europe for a while and I wanted to say goodbye before I went. There's more to it than that, of course. I'd like us to keep in contact. I want you as my friend."

"Yes, that would be nice. Now, Gabbie, if on your travels you find someone, you know he'll have to meet with my approval, don't you?"

"Quite possessive, aren't you? That will work both ways."

"Of course it shall. Though I cannot foresee meeting anyone else I could ever…. I wonder if I should tell you. I had a crazy idea. I imagined that, just the once, you and I together would break into some business. Not an easy place, a moderately hard one. I'd show you how to disable cameras and motion detectors, and pick locks so that it was you who was breaking in and I would be your accomplice. Once we were inside, we'd go into the warehouse and, using chalk, we'd draw a huge, beautiful heart and put our initials inside it. Then we'd leave and set everything back as though we were never there…. It's so funny, I've even been scouting out places and I found one that looks perfect for such a raid."

"You're really serious, aren't you?" She looked astonished.

"Gabbie, you have no idea of the fear, the rush of adrenaline, and the sense of triumph it can produce. It would have explained my past to you better than my mere words ever could."

"I can't see myself ever doing such a thing… though the heart is a different matter. Clever of you to think of a way to express the fleeting nature of our… is it love? Infatuation? Need?"

"All of the above. When do you leave?"

"This Friday. I'll send you all my links. I'm quite active on Facebook. I think that would be the best way for us to communicate and stay in touch."

"I'm so glad you came," said Brent.

"I'm glad I did. I've been very lonely but I think I'll be alright now." They leaned across the table and kissed. Gabbie got up and left the café.

Brent sat staring out of the window. A few minutes later his phone gave an alert. He opened the link, logged in, and accepted the friend request immediately. Brent posted on Gabbie's Facebook page. It was a very tender message and yet entirely suitable for public scrutiny. Gabbie responded on Brent's page with a post that was equally tender. He sat quietly, wrapped up in his own thoughts for a while, not heeding the noise and bustle around him.

Finally, with a great sigh as he dismissed from his mind what might have been, he returned to the email from the U.K. detective agency. Brent opened the attachment which contained the preliminary report. Much of the information was routine and of low value to him. The huge surprise the report contained was buried in the small section on Bobbie, whose last name was Mueller. There he saw a single word which resolved some issues and suggested so much more. Brent was now getting close. He knew what he had to do.

Chapter 28

Wednesday continued

*G*uessing rather than knowing when lunch would be called on the set, Brent returned a few minutes before twelve. He hung around the lunch trailer for a while but, when it became apparent it was not yet "lunchtime", he strolled over to watch what was being filmed. The scene he saw being shot was of Cooper Fisher talking to Bryana in front of the entrance. Their discussion was heated and angry - particularly so on the part of Bryana's character. Her demeanour and gestures indicated Cooper was acting like a complete idiot which, if he were, might cause one to wonder what she saw in him or what the script writer was thinking when he wrote. Perhaps, Brent amused himself by thinking, the writer had thought that the smart woman who has everything going for her needs also to have an idiot in her life. However, he concluded that the dialogue had to have been more nuanced and it was just that he could not hear it. The take was finished and it was deemed to be a good one. It was now lunch-time for crew and cast.

"Hi, I'm Brent Umber." He had intercepted Cooper as he was walking away from the set with two crew members.

"Bryana told me about you," said Cooper. He was about the same height as Brent. They wore similar clothes and were close enough in age that they looked like friends.

"You've been busy otherwise I wouldn't intrude on your lunch-break. I need a few questions answered."

"You guys go ahead; I'll catch up with you." Cooper spoke to the other two. He and Brent slowed to a halt.

"What do you want to know?" he asked, turning towards Brent. The two men stood facing each other. Cooper was tanned with light blue eyes and wore a perpetual stubble of two-days' growth. He would have a thick beard if it were allowed to grow in but clearly his character was meant to look so importantly busy and rugged that there was only time and need to shave every third day.

"You were sitting with your back to Kirby Mayo's table. I'm wondering if you overheard anything that was said?"

"I noticed a few people joining his table. I was aware that they were talking but I did not hear what they were saying. Our table was in conversation most of the time and the tables there were widely spaced."

His natural voice was clear, very precise, and quite low - with only the merest trace of an accent. This identified him as both educated and a foreign national without giving a clue as to where he was from.

"I'm very interested in the few minutes before the shots were fired. Let me see, Galen would have been sitting on your left… no, on your right." Brent used his hands to lay out the positions at the table.

"That is correct."

"What was he doing?" Brent watched Cooper's eyes.

"He was doing what we were all doing which was listening to Marianne make suggestions about her character's development over the series."

"How was he sitting? Did he reply to Marianne?"

"He was very relaxed. He sat low in the chair. He has the habit sometimes of closing his eyes while listening. He let her speak but made a few comments."

"What sort of comment?"

"Oh, he was concerned that if Marianne's character was overly sympathetic it would destroy the dynamic tension between the main characters. He agreed with a few suggestions she made."

"How did Marianne react to having some of her ideas rejected?"

"She is a professional and she wants the show to be a success. I do not think Marianne was upset."

"What did Bryana say? She was opposite you, I believe."

"Yes. She said very little. The conversation was between Marianne and Galen."

"Did you agree with Galen?"

"I did. We must work as a team."

"Was Marianne upset by your agreeing with Galen?"

"No. I do not think so. I was polite. I stated that, as the series progressed, undoubtedly her character would develop in the way she wanted but if that development came too early then we would have a problem. Bryana's character might become a caricature only…. I'm not expressing myself well. Galen said that they must be both equal and opposite - both flawed and problematic, with good qualities and driving ambition but with their ambition running along different tracks. Behind these façades, they have gentler and kinder characteristics. It is about the balance between the two women."

Brent noted the earnest sincerity in Cooper's voice. He had watched the actor's face and had not seen the eye-shifting habits the two women had mentioned.

"It sounds like Bryana was not so engaged in this conversation as the rest of you."

"Yes, maybe. She listened. Just as it is for me, this is an important role for her. Perhaps she thought she should tread carefully in such a topic."

"But you didn't?"

"No. For me, I must express my opinion on this matter for the good of the production."

"Who was sitting behind Bryana?"

"There was a table of five people earlier. No one came after they left."

"One person did."

"I did not see that person."

"But you had to. The way the tables were positioned you had the perfect opportunity to see the killer sit down at the table and take the shot. The bullets passed behind Galen's back and hit Kirby Mayo at the next table. Then, if you didn't drop to the floor like everyone else did, you would have seen that person leave… or join another table."

"No. I saw no one."

"You did. Was it a male or a female?"

"I tell you, I saw no one."

Brent sensed that if Cooper were acting he had not anticipated this line of questioning in the script.

"I think you did. The sight of the killer may be buried in your subconscious. You are repressing important images that will identify the killer. You might be doing this because of the horror of the murder. I want you to act out those few seconds for me. You need to relive the experience so that we can get to the truth. Cooper, you have to dig deep, otherwise you will always feel guilt."

"Guilt? Why should I feel guilty about anything?" The pitch of his voice became higher. He no longer looked at Brent directly. His eyes began to shift.

"You are already beginning to relive that night. You are seated at the table and, from your position, there is a gap between Bryana and Galen which allows you a narrow but unobstructed view of the killer's table. Probably while Marianne is speaking, someone walks up to the table and sits down. You see that person clearly, possibly wearing a grey trench-coat or having one over an arm. Within seconds, shots are fired. I presume you hid as everyone else did. You need to describe who it was you saw for the police to have a chance of capturing the killer."

"I have no idea what you are talking about! I saw no-one. No one! This is over." Cooper walked away. Brent watched him go. Quietly, he said to himself,

"Oh, Cooper, but you did see her." Brent then called Andy Fowler.

At five minutes to six, Brent was pressing the doorbell of Maria's house.

"Hello, Maria."

"Hey! You're right on time. Everything is in boxes. Watch the big one, it's heavy and it has the wine in it."

"My goodness, there's enough here to feed an army."

"Ah, it's not so much. Besides, you can have the left-overs for lunch."

Once they had arrived at Brent's house, Maria took over the kitchen and forbade Brent entry to it.

The table in the dining room was ready. Indeed, this was the first time Brent would use the dining room for its intended purpose - he preferring to dine out than cook for himself alone. That was one of the problems with not having a family - there were never enough people to make using the dining room worthwhile. It was a good-sized room, being some twenty feet square. The walls were painted a warm mocha colour with large white crown moulding and wainscoting three and a half feet high. The ten foot ceiling was white with a large rosette from the centre of which was suspended a chandelier with six lights. This hung so low over the table that, when the lights were dimmed in the evening, the table became the focal point, intimate and cozy, and the spacious airiness of the daytime room was forgotten.

On the dark-stained hardwood floor was a thick rug with a dark ivory field and an intricate geometric border in muted reds, browns, and black enclosing a sparse pattern of small hexagons scattered across the field. On this stood a Jupe table - a circular table that when closed sat six comfortably but, when rotated slightly, opened out like a flower to reveal hidden jointed panels. These, when extended, expanded the table to seat twelve people. Brent had become fascinated by the mechanism and had purchased the new table for its excellent craftsmanship. It was closed for this evening. The glowing, figured walnut grain was hidden beneath a white table-cloth. Upon the table cloth were two place settings of Royal Crown Derby in the Broadway pattern - a white ground with a black and gold geometric border. The flatware was Christofle - Perles design - which lay on dark coffee-coloured napkins. The thin-walled wine glasses were by Micahel Aram. A set of Taylor King chairs, upholstered in Tuscany yellow fabric, ringed the table.

Brent had chosen everything in the dining room a few months earlier, including the mirror and paintings. Everything worked well together but there was no feminine touch to it. The table's centrepiece was half a dozen late chrysanthemums in a low glass bowl; the flowers were dark red and gold and had come from the garden. It was all 'his' with no 'hers' and so he never used the room.

"Okay, Brent. Are you sitting down?" Maria called from outside the room. "First course - the Aperitivo." She came in carrying a large tray full of tantalizing promise; a decanter and glasses, surrounded by luscious and colourful edibles, as well as a crusty Italian loaf and butter. Maria had dressed up. She was wearing a plain dark blue dress and a considerable amount of jewellery. Because of her dual role of chef and diner, she was also wearing a very festive white and yellow apron.

They sat facing each over Camparis and a small bowl of olives and sections of oranges .

"You got a beautiful room here. Everything is so nice."

"Thank you. Do you need help in the kitchen?"

"No, don't worry. It's all ready. Just so you know, I cooked everything except I didn't make these olives and a friend did the dessert. Everything in between is me. Okay?"

"That's wonderful."

"Now, you want me to clean twice a week?"

"Yes. It would only be to run the vacuum round and dust. There's not much to tidy up. Most of the rooms aren't used. Sometimes my office gets messy but you had better leave that to me."

"What about the kitchen and… how many bathrooms you have?"

"Two. If you could do the kitchen floor when it looks like it needs it and the downstairs bathroom. I'll do the upstairs one."

"Oh, alright. What about laundry?"

"I'll do that."

"You like Campari?"

"I do. It has a refreshing taste."

"It prepares the palate. Take your time and I'll bring in the next course."

"Here we are... Antipasto. Beef salami, Italian cheeses, marinated peppers, olives. We're gonna need more plates. Where do you keep them, honey? In that cabinet?"

"I'll get them."

"No. I'll get them when I need them. You just sit and enjoy."

Maria cut the bread on a wooden board. A few crisp flakes of crust fell on the table cloth.

"My mother always cut the bread at the table. To me, it says family. You like the crust?"

"I do. Thanks."

She offered some bread and passed him the butter. Then she poured a glass of Valpolicella for Brent and for herself.

"This bread is wonderful. It's still warm!"

"I'm glad you like it. I baked it this afternoon."

"Did you? What, you made it yourself? It's delicious! I could live on this and the wine."

"Ha... My husband, Dino, he used to say the exact same thing."

"Next course - Primo. It's tomato and basil penne."

"It smells fantastic," said Brent. Maria smiled.

She set down the bowl. It looked good. Although the presentation was not that of a high-end restaurant, the penne looked very inviting nonetheless. For Brent, this was the critical moment. If the pasta was horrible, Maria would not be able to cook for him. If it was bland, they would have a month's trial. If it was acceptable he would wait to see what the rest of the meal was like before committing to anything.

Maria served out the food and set a plate before Brent. She returned to her chair. She quickly took a forkful but, before eating, she anxiously watched Brent put a forkful of penne in his mouth. She waited a few seconds without saying anything. He took a second forkful as she tasted some of her own.

Not able to contain herself any longer, she asked,

"How do you like it?"

"Maria, you have a job."

"I do?"

Brent saw tears well up in her eyes and then overflow.

"I'm sorry," said Brent.

"No... it's okay. I'll be back in a minute." She left, dabbing her eyes with a corner of the apron.

The Secondi was Chicken Francese with a lemon butter sauce. A Santa Margherita Pinot Grigio accompanied it as did the Contorno di Fagiolini alla panna, the delicious Italian rendition of creamed green beans. The dessert was a Tartufo of chocolate and vanilla ice-cream with dark cherries. They finished up with some cheeses and then came the coffee. Maria made coffee better than Brent did although she used his coffee and his equipment. By the end of the meal, Brent was stuffed full and very, very content. Maria, who had quickly recovered from her emotional outburst, was thoroughly happy. Neither of them stopped talking.

They discussed many things. Maria spoke of her husband frequently. Brent explained what he did. Soon, they were reviewing the Mayo case. Brent laid it out objectively and described the characters involved without bias.

"So, who do you think did it?" he asked.

"It was not the wife. No, no. If this was on the TV, by now I would be very suspicious of the actor. He didn't shoot but he knows who did. I agree with you - I think it's the woman who did the shooting. Yep. Gotta be."

"Could there be another player? Someone we don't know anything about?"

"Like a mystery man? Maybe. That's the kind of thing some shows do to you. Then it's some guy you saw in the first episode but forgot all about. What's the matter?"

"I've got no evidence only a theory."

"Yes, that's hard. Like, supposing you accuse the wrong person? Then what?"

"Then I mess up people's lives because I'm not clever enough."

"Nah. You gotta do it. Don't get yourself down…. You gotta do your job. If you make a mistake, hey, it's an honest one. These people will all live. Besides, the police have to know so they do their own inquiries. Let them worry about all that. It's not your problem." She used a butter knife to emphasize her last point. Maria liked her own bread.

"What's that noise?" asked Maria. "There it is again."

"That will be the cat at the back door."

"This I gotta see." Maria got up and went to the kitchen with Brent following.

She opened the door and the cat came in.

"He looks a bit like my old cat but he's bigger. You hungry?"

The cat circled the kitchen floor between Brent and Maria before coming to a decision. He started arching and rubbing his back against Maria's legs. Brent was totally ignored.

"Oh, what a sweet boy you are," said Maria. "Come along, Monty. Let's get you something nice to eat." The cat followed her closely. Every time Maria was to come to Brent's house in the future, Monty would always follow her wherever she went - although he did not care for the vacuum cleaner.

Chapter 29

Very late Wednesday

*I*t was after ten p.m. when Brent called Greg.

"I hope I'm not disturbing you," said Brent.

"No. What have you got?"

"I know who did it and how it was done but there's no evidence unless someone breaks down and starts talking."

"Can you tell me who it is?"

"They're on the list. That's the problem - there's more than one person involved. There's an individual I need to interview. If I can, and the person is co-operative, I believe I can get the whole scenario. The problem is that person is unlikely to want to talk to me. If I give everything I have to you now, I'm sure you won't get anything from anyone involved. They might confess they might not. So, I feel I have a slim chance of shortening the whole process and of finding definitively where the guilt lies. I know, it's not making much sense."

"Well, Brent. I can see that this is important to you. I don't know. I could act as though we never had this conversation but I have a conscience. You have to give me a little more."

"There are some names on the list. One of them is guilty. One or two might be guilty or might be innocent but know something - I won't understand what the situation is until I've spoken to them some more. If I give you all the names, one or two will be charged and possibly convicted but they need not be if I can speak to them first."

"Ah, I see. One of those deals. An unwitting accomplice type of thing."

"That's close to it."

"I'm going to bed now. Give me the name - better still, give the name to Schroeder - by noon tomorrow. Goodnight, Brent."

"Pleasant dreams, Greg."

A single associate of Andy Fowler was keeping the Kent residence under surveillance from her parked car. She could contact Brent directly to inform him immediately upon the return of the occupants. At ten thirty-five, Becki Kent and Bobbie Mueller, both of whom had just returned, were at home, and Brent was apprised of the fact.

Soon afterwards, Brent parked his car on a side street. He got out and began walking. The air was damp and cold. There would be a frost overnight causing the remaining yellow leaves to fall faster and render the trees bare. It was dry at least.

At the gates of the Kent residence, Brent scaled one of the eight-foot high, stone pillars, and dropped down neatly on the other side. As he walked silently along the darkened driveway, the nearly full moon only managed to glimmer through thin, low cloud. There was a single, soft-lighted room at the front but, in the darkness, the rest of the house had taken on the appearance of old army barracks or a prison.

Brent was not entirely sure he was taking the right course of action in coming at all. He had to try - that's all he knew. He had not driven up to the gates because he was sure he would have been refused admittance and the gates would have remained firmly closed against him. Even in knocking on the front door, as he was about to do, he realized there was only a small chance of gaining entry.

He had even thought of breaking in (of course, he had!) but it made no sense under the circumstances. If he could talk to Becki on her own that would be ideal. He had hoped she would have got home first and he could have seen her while Bobbie was still out. That was not to be - they had arrived back together. With a deadline of noon the next day, he had to talk to Becki tonight.

Another house, another doorbell, a different reception. Earlier that evening, Maria had been all smiles and nervous anticipation when she had opened her front door. Later, when she 'got the job', her attitude shifted subtly, transforming her from nice neighbour into something more like aunt, friend, and confidante. Brent liked her. Brent also liked her cooking. Maria had the habit of calling out from wherever she was to wherever Brent was, always beginning with the words, "Hey, Brent!" He rang the bell.

Bobbie answered the door. She stared hard at Brent.

"I know it's late but it's important," said Brent.

"I guess you want to see Becki."

"Yes. This is her last chance. She needs to see me."

"You'd better come in." She opened the door wider to let him pass.

After he had been admitted, Bobbie turned and walked across the vestibule with Brent beside her. She showed him to the lounge he had visited before. He waited there for nearly ten minutes before Bobbie returned with Becki. They both looked sullen as they sat down. All three of them sat in the seats they had occupied before.

"Well, we all know why I'm here."

"You have no evidence," said Bobbie.

"That's true. I only came because, if your mother is innocent, I think I know a way of protecting her. If she is not, then my visit is a wasted one."

Bobbie gave a quick glance at Becki before turning back to Brent. "She is innocent."

"I'm glad to hear that."

"What do I do?" asked Becki.

"You have two choices. You, Bobbie, and Cooper continue as you are and keep silent. Tomorrow, I will give your names to the police. Maybe you can tough it out, maybe not. You have to assess your chances. If one of you fails, all three of you will be convicted.

An alternative is that you, Becki, go to the police and tell them your story - I'm assuming that what you would say would exonerate you. If I hear your story first I can tell you what I can do to help you. It won't be much and I might not be successful. If it were just the police, it would be fine, but then there's the District Attorney's office to consider. I don't know anybody there."

"Would money make any difference?" asked Becki.

"No. Even if you paid me off, someone would join all the dots eventually. I happened to do it faster than the police this time. In a way, Becki, this is the best you can do with such a bad hand."

The two women looked at each other. Bobbie got up. "Tell him everything," she said. She turned to leave the room.

"You're not going to do anything, are you?" asked Brent.

She stopped. "No. I'm not like that. I will go to the police to surrender myself. Maman and Cooper will never be mentioned by me. I will go to prison, be a model prisoner, and then be free again. We will talk later, Mr. Umber."

After she had gone, the silence was awful.

"When you were here before," asked Becki, "did you know it was Bobbie?"

"No. When I accused her of possibly being the killer it was only to provoke both of you to be more forthcoming. It was a coincidence. But it stuck with me."

"This is so bad. The whole thing is a horrible nightmare. You've got to understand that I had no idea Kirby was going to be killed.

He and I loved one another. This was before he married. When I say love, I mean he meant everything to me. Everything. I thought the same was true for him. I became pregnant. Naïvely, I thought we would marry. When I told him, do you know what he said? He said, 'You have to get rid of it.' Those were the first words out of his mouth and each one hurt me so badly. He made it all my fault, my responsibility. It broke my heart. Our relationship was over.

I told him I would have an abortion. It was crazy. I still loved him even though he had hurt me like that. I went away but we stayed in touch. What he didn't know was I gave birth to a baby girl in Geneva. I named her Roberta and gave her the last name of Mueller which was the last name of one of my nurses. I gave a fictitious name for the father on the birth certificate.

I'm not a motherly kind of person. After a few weeks, I put Roberta … Bobbie … up for adoption. By chance, one of the nurses I had met was looking to adopt. Her name is Vittoria Trucco and she wanted a big family. She, and her husband Tommaso, had a daughter of their own, Mika, but after she was born, Vittoria couldn't have any more children. When I met them, they had already adopted Cooper, a German boy. We started talking about Bobbie. The Trucco's liked the idea of another daughter. Bobbie was a sweet little thing but … ah, well … I wanted to keep her hidden from Kirby. Don't ask me why; I can't explain it.

The Trucco family never had to worry about money again. I got them a nice family home on Avenue L'Ermitage in Geneva. It was arranged that I would see Bobbie twice a year for a week or two at a time and she was told I was her aunt.

This arrangement worked. I was happy with it. Bobbie grew up a nice, normal girl and the Truccos treated her like their own. All three children went to the University of Geneva and enjoyed student foreign exchange programs. Mika is a doctor now."

"What ages were they?" asked Brent.

"When Bobbie was a year old, Cooper was five, and Mika eight. They were all very nice children, together and separately." Becki seemed inclined to stop speaking.

"How did Bobbie come to live with you?"

"Yes … she, ah, she is very clever. At about age fourteen she had worked out that she and Cooper were adopted. The first I knew of this was when she confronted me on her fifteenth birthday. She flat out said, 'You are my mother so do not lie.' What could I say? Bobbie, Vittoria, Tommaso, and I had a discussion and it pretty much all came out. Cooper still did not know he was adopted. The Truccos were forced now to speak to him about his being adopted even when his biological parents had died in a car accident.

What none of us knew, although there were signs if we had noticed them, was that Bobbie and Cooper formed some kind of a bond between them. I might have thought it was like 'us against the world' but it wasn't that. It was much more than that. This was my fault - at least, I exacerbated things. I couldn't help myself and told, as a means of self-defense, how Kirby had spoken to me about my pregnancy. I didn't understand that Bobbie internalized it and grew to hate Kirby. I honestly had no idea.

I told you she was clever. She's manipulative, too. At some point, and she admits to it herself, she decided to kill Kirby. The problem was, she included Cooper in her plan. He would do whatever she told him to do. It was as though she had some kind of hold over him... Before you jump to any wrong conclusion, they were not lovers. Anyway, her cause became his cause. If she had said forget it, he would have.

Bobbie was twenty-one when she finished university. I asked her what she wanted to do. She said she wanted to live with me. What was I to think? In some ways, I deeply wanted that. But how could I now have a twenty-one-year-old daughter appear out of nowhere? It was Bobbie's suggestion that she become my personal assistant. I agreed and she got a good salary. She lives here but has her own apartment."

"Did she do this to get close to you or to get close to Kirby?" asked Brent.

"It was both. We do have a mother-daughter relationship. I am so wounded over this. I can't cry yet but I will soon. I know it. Anything's better than this sick, fearful feeling I have all the time.

Cooper was working here and Bobbie wanted to be close to him, me, and, although I didn't know it, Kirby as well.

For three years you couldn't, I mean, I couldn't, tell anything was the matter. It was about a month ago that I found her looking at a photograph of Kirby on her computer. This started a long discussion. She knew I had loved Kirby over the years... that we had an on again, off again relationship despite his being married. We discussed it all. It was good for me to talk to my adult daughter about this. It took a lot of pent up feelings away. It ended by my telling her that I thought if I saw him a final time, I would know where I stood once and for all. I didn't think I had any love left for him but I would know for certain if I saw him again.

Bobbie said she had never seen Kirby. She suggested my meeting him in a public place and that she would get to see him - she didn't want to meet him or have me accompany her; she said she just wanted to see him in the flesh. He wouldn't know who she was. She said she needed to do that to get closure. I agreed, of course. I thought it would be helpful for both of us. We would both see him and move on for our different reasons.

What I didn't know was that Bobbie had designed a test. She told me all this after she'd killed Kirby. She had vowed to herself that if I still loved Kirby he would live. If I did not, he would die. It was a simple decision for her.

When Garland's was suggested as the venue, Bobbie got Cooper involved. I knew where Kirby always sat in Garland's and Bobbie relayed this information to Cooper, who reserved a table next to Kirby's. Bobbie planned the whole thing, including scouting out Garland's ahead of time.

I took Gabbie with me on the night for moral support. She's nice, and I regret leaving her like that, but by then I was certain Bobbie had shot Kirby and I was in no state to talk to anyone." Becki finished speaking.

"Could you tell me how it was actually done?"

"Oh, yes. Bobbie wore a black skirt and white blouse very similar to the waitresses in Garland's. Her idea was that a customer would think she was one of the staff, but the staff would see her as a customer. She went there wearing a long coat. When she was inside, she took her coat off to blend in. She had arranged that Cooper would act as her lookout... which you guessed and that's changed everything."

"I knew it would," said Brent. "I got to a point, before speaking to Cooper, that I felt sure it was Bobbie who had fired the shots. Perhaps I convinced myself. However, I knew she would have needed an accomplice. In getting some background information, I found the name Trucco popping up in two biographies and that Bobbie and Cooper had both grown up in Geneva. It was too much of a coincidence for them both to be in Garland's. I knew about Cooper being adopted and I guessed at Bobbie being adopted, too. I was more certain when your own travel dates and destinations were factored in. The only plausible answer that made sense to me was that Bobbie was your daughter and you had put her up for adoption. It was easy to surmise that Kirby was the father."

"Yes. Bobbie said you would be trouble. I freaked out when you accused her. She didn't seem to care. You heard her just now.... Nothing seems to touch her. She'll do what she says she'll do."

"Do you know anything of the final few moments?"

"Ah, she waited for me to leave the table. Bobbie says she knew I felt nothing for Kirby by leaving the table and by the way I acted around him. If I had known what she had in mind I would never have left that table."

I'm not sure where exactly she was but she sat down at an empty table close by and where Cooper could see her. He gave her a signal that the manager was not looking and she fired. She's very good with a pistol and has won competitions in the past. I suppose she was training even back then."

"Did Cooper thoroughly understand what it was that Bobbie was about to do?"

"I haven't seen him since so I can't say. He might not have."

"Do you think it's possible he believed that Bobbie was going to pretend to wait on Kirby's table so that she could get close to him without her father knowing?"

"I object to the word 'father'. He was never that."

"I agree but in a legal sense he was."

"It makes a difference if Cooper knew, doesn't it?"

"A huge difference."

"He didn't know anything... and I think I mean that."

"If that's everything - I'll need a few words with Bobbie now."

"Please try and keep Cooper out of this. It was a unique circumstance."

"I understand."

Bobbie and Brent faced each other inside the front door.

"Before I came here tonight, Ms. Mueller, I was fully prepared to give three names to the police. Tomorrow, by noon, I will hand in two names. That's the best I can do unless you turn yourself in first. Ask for Detective Otto Schroeder."

"Thank you. I will be there at ten in the morning. One more night in a comfortable bed is not to be missed."

"May I ask one last question about what you did in Garland's...? Why in public?"

"I studied him. He was an evil, controlling man and all his petty evils were private or hidden. What better than a public death to atone for them?"

"Would you kill anyone else?"

"No, I don't think so. I have no reason. In self-defence I would as anyone would."

"Goodnight," said Brent.

"Goodnight, Mr. Umber."

After he went out of the front door, she pressed a button to open the driveway gates for him to exit the property.

Chapter 30

Thursday

*T*he first thing Brent did in the morning was to call off all Andy Fowler's operations. He and Andy came to terms on what Andy was owed to date and Brent thanked Andy for his help. Vane, Zack, and Mason he left in place on the set. He knew they were really enjoying themselves.

No matter what he did, Brent found everything pointing to twelve noon. That was when he would call Schroeder. He rehearsed what he would say to the detective. If Bobbie Mueller had not surrendered herself to the police then Brent was duty-bound to speak of her and Cooper. Should she have surrendered, he would see what progress was being made.

Cooper Fisher ... Brent could not be sure if he was knowingly involved or not. Half his thoughts had Cooper, in possession of the discarded revolver, a potential assassin up to his neck in the murder plot. The other part of his mind had Cooper involved in varying degrees from complete dupe to foolish accomplice. Only Bobbie could definitively say which was the true situation and that closed-mouthed, controlled woman would not say anything she did not wish to say. Schroeder would have a tough time with her. Bobbie would control the narrative.

Phil, the car dealer, called.

"How are you doing? There are a few vehicles I can get hold of that you might be interested in."

"Hello, Phil. What have you found?"

"A couple of Mustangs, a Corvette, and a BMW M4 coupé. You interested in any of these?"

"I like Mustangs… and Corvettes. I think I'd pass on the M4. I'm not sure. Got anything with four doors?"

"You should have told me that upfront. There is one nice, quick car I can get. Low miles and under a year old. It's a black Porsche Macan Sports. Four doors with a hatch. All-wheel drive. But didn't you want out of Porsche?"

"I don't know what I want exactly. How much is it?"

"We said a thousand on the invoice… let me have a look here… Fifty-two and it's yours and that's a very good price. There's plenty of warranty left. You want it?"

"I haven't seen it." As they had been speaking, Brent had called up some photographs online and liked what he saw.

"Trust me," continued Phil, "these are nice… Drives like a sports car but it's roomy enough for a daily driver. Good in the winter, too. I've driven them before. You'll have no complaints. If you don't like it, I'll buy it back at the invoice price."

"Okay. Can I get it tomorrow?"

"Let me see… yeah, you can. It'll be in the afternoon, say two."

"I'll be there."

On top of satisfying the urge to get a new car for himself, Brent felt good about having just solved a problem that had arisen. Maria had not been able to afford a car for some time. Now she would go shopping twice a week in a shiny, black Porsche.

By eleven, Brent could think of nothing but the upcoming phone call. The future fate of people's lives hung heavy upon him. No matter who deserved what in the way of justice or punishment, the permanent alteration to people's existences was a depressing outlook. Bobbie was dealt with but it was not easy. Cooper, the willing, ardent actor, might be handcuffed and yanked from the production set, headed for a life behind bars. All those careful scenes taken by Galen's cast and crew would be for nothing. Another male lead would be found with Cooper being excised from every shot. If, somehow, he came out of it unscathed, the sister of his formative years would nevertheless be behind bars. It had to affect him. The loss of manipulative Bobbie in Cooper's life would do what to him? Brent had no idea.

Becki would also suffer, was already suffering. He had not liked the woman because of their initial meeting. He could not agree with the life choices she had made as they seemed purely focused upon herself. Still, they were her decisions to make and, if he lacked sympathy, he could at least acutely feel something of that pang of awful emptiness that would blight her latter years. She was not deserving of that. Her money could not compensate for any part of the wreck that had occurred. He imagined there would be few people who would feel really sorry for Becki and wondered how her relationship with Bobbie would hold up when bars and the memory of murder separated them.

Rena was well out of it, Brent could not help but think. This was not the way her failed marriage should have been resolved. However, it had been resolved for her and in a year or two she would be better. It was difficult for Brent to put himself in her place because he did not think the way she did. He could not imagine existing on hope alone for the resolution of a marriage. It required small actions as well as larger ones to improve a relationship but, when it came to the point where it could be seen that there was nothing more to be done, hope, he felt, was too short a plank to bridge the gap.

He called Nola Devon.

"Hi. I can't say too much but there should be some news today or very soon and Althorn is in the clear. Could you mention this to the other partners, please?"

"I'll do that. That's such a relief…. You know who it is?"

"Yes, I do. I've known for a few days but there's so much I can't say right now. The picture's fuzzy as to when the police will make a statement. They might leave the announcement until after the funeral. It depends how confident they feel about the information they receive."

"Okay. Am I right in thinking that you were instrumental in getting this resolved?"

"I can't say anything."

"I'll take that as a yes. Are you still going tomorrow? It's at eleven."

"Yes, I'm going. I've become so involved in the case that it will be like a decompression."

"I hope it's like that for me as well. I know you can't say anything now but would you mind giving us all an explanation of what you did and how you did it at some time in the future?"

"I can certainly do that but it should be understood that I cannot repeat everything I know."

"Oh, yes, of course. I suppose there might be some embarrassment if you did. Anyway, Brent, I get the impression that we are very much in your debt."

"I'd rather you didn't think that. You all helped me immensely by being so accommodating. You, Nola, were particularly helpful in that you trusted me enough to give me a chance. None of the other partners would have done that."

"You know why that is?"

"Er... I don't."

"Brent, I should imagine that a lot of women trust you because you are so open and have integrity. You don't have hidden motives."

"That's not strictly true about the hidden motives."

"You do realize you just proved my point? I think if I asked you what your hidden motives were, you'd tell me. Then they wouldn't be hidden."

"Oh, I see what you mean.... It's just the way I am."

"Don't change. I'll see you tomorrow."

Finally, the clock on Brent's computer got to twelve. He called Otto Schroeder's number. Would Bobbie have kept her word and turned herself in or would he be compelled to give her name and Cooper's to the police? Either way, he knew he could not let on to the detective about the extent of his involvement or his precipitation of Bobbie's confession without there being the serious risk of implicating Becki as an accessory after the fact.

"Brent. We've had a real development this morning," said Otto.

"What's that?"

"A woman walked in and confessed to killing Kirby Mayo. We're processing her now."

"She's not a crank or anything?"

"No. Her name's Roberta Mueller. She brought in the murder weapon in a plastic bag. The .38 revolver had three shots fired and her prints are all over it. Haven't got the final report from ballistics yet but it looks like it's going to be a match. This is the crazy thing... she murdered her father."

"That sounds very, very sad."

"Yeah, it is. Patricide. I've never had one before. Anyway, I'm busy right now. Thanks for your help... you were doing good. This confession has saved us all a lot of trouble."

"Yes, it has."

"Why were you calling?"

"Oh, you know, just to see if you had any news."

"Yeah, I should have called you but I've been right in the thick of it."

"We might work together again some time."

"I don't mind if we do. You never know what's going to happen next in this game. Gotta go."

"Goodbye."

Brent knew that the lunch at the day-care centre where Linda Roberts worked would be finished by one o'clock. He called a few minutes afterwards. It was a day for tying up loose ends.

"Hello, Linda? How are you?"

"Oh. It's you. Listen, Brent, I have to tell you something. I've been waiting 'til the end of the week like you said but I have something important to say."

"Do you?"

"Yes. We can't see each other again. I'm going to be totally honest with you. It's not you because you're quite a nice guy. There's someone else."

"Is there? Who's the lucky man? Do I know him?"

"His name's Terry and we used to date years ago. He came back to town last weekend and we met by chance at a mutual friend's place. I knew immediately that he was the one for me and that it wouldn't work out between us."

"Yes, I think you're right."

"Then you're not mad?"

"Not in the sense you mean. Linda, I'm happy for you. I hope you and Terry have a long and happy future together."

"You're not, like, upset?"

"Ever so slightly, but we did only have the one date, you remember."

"Okay... cool. I was worried that you'd fall to pieces. Seeing as you're not going to do that... okay."

"Have the police been bothering you at all?"

"No. I haven't seen them. Why do you ask?"

"They caught the murderer. The case should be closed soon. It was a woman in a grey trench-coat. She came in and acted like a waitress and then shot Kirby Mayo."

"Oh, yes. I remember her. She had the coat over her arm, actually."

"You mean, you saw her?" Brent was incredulous.

"Yes. I didn't see her shoot or anything. She was very tall with black hair and dressed like the servers. Looked like a model or something. I thought she was meeting someone and had arrived early. I remember thinking she had made a big mistake over what she was wearing. You know, like, she shouldn't have been wearing that outfit. Anyways, she sat down, let me see, two tables away from where the guy was shot."

"Did you tell any of this to the police?"

"No. They didn't ask me."

"Phone them immediately and tell them what you've just told me."

"Do I have to? They've caught her."

"Yes, you do. If you don't, I will, and that will look bad on you. Linda, I don't mean to be rude, but you are an absolute... sweetheart, and you need to talk to them now."

"You weren't gonna say sweetheart, were you?"

"No. Call them, please, and I'll send you a wedding gift. Open up the registry and I'll sign up for something expensive. Just get this done."

"Oh, all right, I will. It would have been a big mistake going with you. You're such a bully. Goodbye."

"Goodbye."

Chapter 31

Friday

*B*rent slept well. When he awoke at five o'clock, he lay in bed, lazily looking into the dark and wondering if it was really necessary for him to get up. The choice lay before him. He could either be depressed because the case had ended or feel alive because there were things to be done. Usually, in this post-case period, he very often suffered a mild depression but on occasion it was severe - depending on the intensity of the case just concluded. Now he felt he had a choice. He felt empowered to make the choice not to be depressed at all. Primarily, he put part of the change down to having resolved matters between himself and Gabbie. But that was not all. He was so very pleased about Maria coming into his life. They seemed to have nothing in common and, yet, they had everything in common. He wanted to see her happy and that was worth getting up for. He was beginning to depend on her and she on him. Also, there was Vane - and her friends. That was another reason to be up early. They would be in and around the set at six. He felt responsible for them and he liked that feeling. Today was their payday. He could not lie in bed when they could not. He made his choice and got up.

"So, like, we get the rest of the day off?" said Zack.

"That is so cool," said Mason.

"Here are your envelopes. All of you did good work. Thanks. I suggest you save some money for things that matter."

"Yo, Brent," said Zack. "It's been a blast, man. Anytime you need me just call. Here's your phone back."

"Keep it. You, too, Mason," said Brent.

"Hey, thanks. Come on, Zack. I'm outta here. You coming, Vane?"

"I'll see you guys later," answered Vane.

The two boys took off. They waved and were on their skateboards in seconds.

"I don't think I could do another week with those guys," said Vane.

"Is that so? And why would that be?"

"Like I said the other day, I'm moving on."

"I think that's good."

"Scares me a little, though. Other than you, I don't really know anyone outside of my own age group… I don't know what to expect."

"Maybe try not to look at it as scary - just different. You'll do fine. There's a lot of nice people around who will help you."

"I don't know. I have my waitressing jobs but they don't pay much. It's like it will take forever to get anywhere. I've got another three years of study. Can you put up with me for that long?"

"Vanessa…"

"Wow, this must be serious."

"It is. I'm with you for the long haul. Thirty years or sixty years, if I can make it that far - I will always be in your corner and on your side. As things change for you, I will be there if you need me. If you marry and have children I'll be old uncle Brent to them. If you don't marry, I'll still be your brother. There, I can't say more than that."

"You're so sweet to me and I don't deserve it." She hugged him.

When they disentangled themselves, Brent said, "I think it's about time you had a few driving lessons. Let's find a school near where you live and set something up. When you have a few lessons under your belt, we'll go out driving together so you can practise."

"That is amazing! I so want to get my licence."

"Then you should start by reading this that I picked up for you." He took a Driver's Handbook from his backpack and gave it to her. "You have to learn the rules of the road before you can get a learner's permit."

"You are so nice to me. I can't give anything back to you. I don't have anything."

"Yes, you can and you do. It pleases me to see you pleased. It warms my heart to see you try your best at things. I delight in seeing you mature and become a woman. You give more to me than I give to you."

"Well, so you say. It doesn't feel that way to me. It's like I'm in your debt and I can't repay it."

"There is no debt and there's nothing to repay. I tell you what, though, you buy me a coffee and we're quits."

"Okay! That sounds like a deal."

They left the movie set and headed towards the café. It was now eight o'clock. Brent explained what had happened in the case that morning and was not finished with his headline news until after they had sat down with their coffees. Vane made a few comments but was content to listen then to the whole story unfold.

"That is so sad," she said, when he had come to the end. "If it was just a story... I don't think that I'd blame Bobbie... not too much. But it's not a story and she killed someone like a cold-hearted killer. That's not right. This stuff must be hard on you sometimes. What are you going to do now the case is over?"

"Believe it or not, I've just taken on a housekeeper and it takes some getting used to."

"Housekeeper? What does a housekeeper do?"

"Looks after me, I hope, and keeps me in line. She does some cleaning and cooks the most amazing Italian dishes."

"You do need keeping in line sometimes." Vane sipped her coffee. "Do you know, I've never seen your new house?"

"That's right, you haven't. Then come over soon and meet Maria. I'll tell her you're coming and she'll have dinner with us."

"Okay... So, you don't trust yourself with me on your own?"

"Vane?"

"I'm teasing you... sort of. What are you going to do when I meet someone else? Will you get jealous?" said Vane.

"Very jealous. I will challenge him to a duel."

"I'd love that. Two men fighting over me, oh yes. Swords or pistols?"

"Pistols, I think. It would be over faster."

"Ha... With swords maybe you'd get an interesting scar."

"So, you'd want me to win?"

"I didn't say that... No, I'd never want to see you hurt. That's a bad idea."

"Okay. Instead, we would talk everything out like reasonable adults."

"That sounds awful... like there's no passion in it."

"It does, doesn't it? Best to live an uncomplicated life. Find the right person, Vane, and stick to him."

"I guess so. How's that going for you? You hinted at something the other day. Wanna talk about it?"

"Not today. Another time, though."

"Sure, whenever you like. Don't ever forget, I'm always here for you, Brent." Vane fluttered her eyelids at him.

"Oh, come on." Brent smiled.

It rained at the funeral. Brent had skipped going to the memorial service as he had no real part in it. He knew that comforting, pleasant things would be said about Kirby Mayo - words, poems, prayers, and songs that would celebrate the life of the departed. He had not wanted to hear the inevitable childhood reminiscences recounted by family and friends. Such stories would not help him feel sorry. He could not feel very sorry for Kirby.

The man had been torn from life, leaving a ragged hole where he used to exist, but Brent had never warmed to the man. If they had met, Brent surmised, they would not have been friends. Once, Kirby had probably been a decent man but he had changed. The Kirby that Brent had come to know was not decent but selfish to the point where no one around him mattered to him anymore. He certainly did not deserve death but neither did he deserve to be mourned by Brent, a stranger to him. He had come to show support to Rena and to bring to a close the final chapter of the case as far as he was concerned. He had come because he wanted to see the moment when Rena Mayo began to heal. It would be when the coffin was lowered into the ground.

The exact moment of interment was approaching as the rain beat down noisily on his umbrella. He stood apart from the people under the large tent. Nola Devon and Aunt Marjie were there. He saw Rena holding the hands of her two white-faced children. Rena looked better than he had expected. She cried - had been crying - but she was not going to collapse, he could see that. A man held an umbrella over her while she stood close to the grave as the coffin was lowered.

The cemetery was a cheerless world of wet green grass, dark, nearly bare trees and evergreens, grey sky, and people in black. It rained harder as the coffin sank down out of sight.

When it was over and the mourners began to disperse, he saw Galen Nash accompanied by Cooper Fisher. It surprised Brent that they had taken time out from the show's busy production schedule. Galen's presence was not so surprising but Cooper's was. Brent guessed that some species of guilt had brought him - though he did not presume to decide that it was so.

A thought struck him. Brent was astonished it had not occurred to him before. He looked carefully at the mourners and then about the cemetery. He looked behind him and saw a woman with an umbrella, standing by herself under a tree. She was veiled. It was Becki Kent. Brent went to her.

"Awful weather. Is there anything I can do for you?"

"No. Thank you for asking."

"I'm sorry for what has happened."

"Are you? I saw you had no choice in the matter... I did love him. Our daughter killed him. I've lost them both and I can't cry. I thought I would if I came here. Rena cried and I can't. Why is that?"

"Your time to cry will come. Try not to be alone too much. Is there anyone who can stay with you?"

"Yes.... I have some people. By the way, the police came to see me last night."

"How did that go?"

"I told them I had no idea that Bobbie had planned it. They insisted I knew something beforehand."

"You knew only because she told you afterwards."

"I said that Bobbie had been acting differently since the murder.... Oh, I don't care if they arrest me."

"You will if they do arrest you. Stick to your story because it's the truth. They may want to charge you with being an accessory after the fact but there's no real reason for them to do so. You didn't shield Bobbie or help her escape."

"I did shield her. After she told me I pretended like nothing had happened and it would all go away."

"She's your daughter. I would have done the same if I were in your place. We're human. Laws make sense most of the time but not all of the time. You only kept Bobbie's confidences to yourself."

"But she's a murderer."

"Then it shows how much you love her... She needs treatment, you realize?"

"It's out of my hands now."

"Then become an advocate for her so that she gets the help she needs. While you're at it, there are plenty of other people in prison who need help, as well as the families they leave on the outside. Think about getting involved and helping people. It would take your mind off your own troubles."

"Too early for that."

"I know. You have my number. If there's anything you think I can help you with give me a call.

Brent took delivery of the Porsche Macan. The car drove like a dream. He was more than pleased with the way it handled. After nearly an hour, Brent parked the car outside of Maria's house. They were going shopping and she would be driving.

Epilogue

$\mathcal{A}$t the police detective's invitation, Brent went to see Greg Darrow the following Monday to explain almost everything he had done in the case including the confronting of Becki and Bobbie.

"So you're telling me that Becki Kent really had nothing to do with it?" asked Greg.

"I wholeheartedly believe that."

"It's Schroeder. He thinks she was in on it and helped stage the murder."

"Can't you call him off?"

"Not exactly. He might be right and you might be wrong. Why should I believe your take on it over his?"

"Have you met Bobbie? Because if you haven't, you should do so. She is completely emotionless about killing her father. At the same time, there is no way that she would let her mother be at risk. She shot Mayo as soon as she could when her mother was safely out of the way. Had Becki not gone to talk to the Feinsteins, Bobbie would probably have shot Mayo publicly in the street or somewhere else. She chose the restaurant as the most fitting place to make a public display of his death. That is the act of a single, warped mind and not the plan of two people. Becki Kent did not have a monomania about killing Kirby. She had plenty of opportunity to do that over the years if she was so inclined. Why would she wait to see her daughter kill her father? A psychiatric assessment of her will demonstrate that she was not psychologically capable of this murder.

Look, Greg, if Becki's brought to trial as an accessory she'll be acquitted. You're wasting your time over her because even an average defence lawyer will shoot it down."

"Okay." Greg grimaced as he moved slightly in his seat. "I've got to get a new chair - this one's so uncomfortable. Yes, personally, I didn't think much of the mother-daughter angle. It looks plausible but, as you say, difficult to prove even if it's true. If I tell Schroeder that he's unlikely to get a conviction he'll back off. He won't want to waste his time."

The first thing Brent did upon leaving police headquarters was to order an extraordinarily expensive office chair for Greg. It was of the kind that has so many features, levers, and possible positions that it could serve as anything from a bed to a bar stool.

As it was a thank you gift, Brent was prudent enough to have it delivered as though it came from Greg's wife, Carrie - the police policy being to discourage officers from accepting free gifts from the public.

When the Darrow's finally sorted out the confusion about the chair, Greg called Brent. The most memorable line in their conversation was when Greg stated he wished to be buried in his new chair because it was so comfortable.

Later in the day, Brent went to Althorn Capital to give the partners an explanation of what he had done. He had written a summary report of his activities but there was much more he wanted to explain in person. Will Hutchinson's private life was kept out of the meeting.

"Hey, Brent! What do you want for dinner tonight?" Maria had one hand on the casing of the kitchen door while she called up to Brent who was in his office. It was two weeks after the case had ended and about ten-thirty in the morning.

"Spaghetti Bolognese, please." His voice was muffled by the distance.

"You had that last time. I want to cook something different."

There was nothing else for it when Maria bellowed; Brent had to come to her. She could hear his feet on the stairs and waited for him to appear.

"What do you want to cook?" asked Brent, as he walked towards her, smiling.

"I don't know. Anything you like, honey."

"But I don't want to put you to any trouble."

"Ah, it's no trouble. What do you want?"

"Um, I can't think of anything. I should look at a cookery book."

"I got a nice one. I'll bring it over next time and we can make a list."

"That's brilliant... I know, Chicken Francese. Like you did on that first dinner."

"Okay. I've got chicken, and ... let me see, yes ... oh-oh. We haven't got lemons. If you want Chicken Francese, you'll have to get some lemons. There are a few other things we need as well. I'll write them down for you."

Brent went to the supermarket. About ten minutes later, Eric arrived at the house, making his entrance through the patio door.

"Hello," he said to the surprised Maria. "I'm Eric. I do the gardening."

"Oh, hello. You made me jump."

"Sorry about that. You must be Maria."

"That's right." They shook hands.

"I came to see Brent. I'm a bit early. Is he about?"

"I just sent him to the supermarket. He should be back in half an hour."

"What's that nice smell? Are you cooking Italian food?"

"Yes. I'm making a soup. I like to get everything ready ahead of time. I hate to rush the preparation of a meal."

"Same with me and the garden. I like to get everything done early if I can." He paused to stare at what Maria was doing. "Italian, eh? You'll be wanting some fresh vegetables in season, won't you?"

"I don't know. Are you planting a vegetable garden?"

"Well, a small one. You'd want zucchini. Probably Black Beauty or Caserta... and Magda has a nice flavour to it."

"Yes. That sounds good. What about tomatoes?"

"We were only going to put in salad types but you'd want Roma, of course, then there's Pisanello. I've grown them before. What's the big one called?"

"Cuore di Buo? That's ox-heart."

"Yeah, that's the one. Would you like that one?"

"Oh, yes. You can grow all those?"

"Sure. Then there's peppers, artichokes, broccoli... we should put in some garlic. I'll sit down here and work it out. Oh, yes, Italian ladies like their herbs. What would you be wanting?"

Maria turned the heat down on the stove. They sat down at the table together. Eric had produced a dog-eared notebook and with the stub of a pencil was writing everything down.

"Rosemary, basil, sage, parsley, thyme, mint, oregano, bay, basil... I said that."

"Can't do bay. That's off a laurel tree. We can do all the others. If you think of anything else you're partial to let me know. I'll just draw this out."

She watched as he began a diagram of the garden.

"Would you like some coffee? Something to eat?"

"A coffee would be welcome."

They chatted a little. Eric planned, plotted, and sketched where everything would go. Coffee and cakes came out and were consumed. Eric had a second coffee because he declared the first to be so delicious.

"There. Done. We're putting most of it in raised beds so you don't have to stoop when you want something."

"That's so nice of you. It will be wonderful. All those fresh vegetables. I can't wait for summer to come. I'll can some of the produce."

"You do canning? I used to do that. There's just me now and so I don't hardly bother. It was different when my wife was alive. Maybe I can give you a hand with it."

"Of course. That would be so nice. There's plenty of room in the basement here to store everything."

"That's settled then. Brent's quite reasonable most of the time so there should be no problem. He's a bit late. I wonder where he's got to?"

No sooner had Eric finished speaking than Brent came in the front door and headed for the kitchen with a bag of shopping.

"Ah! Hello, Eric," said Brent.

"Morning, Brent."

"You wouldn't believe the line ups there today. They really should have more cashiers working."

"Let me take that," said Maria. She took hold of the bag and put the items away except for the bag of lemons.

"We need to discuss something," said Eric who stood up with notebook in hand.

"We do? What would that be?"

There was silence. Maria, standing in profile to Brent, was using a wooden spoon, seemingly to stir something slowly in a little saucepan. Eric stood like a statue facing him. He cleared his throat noisily before speaking.

"We have to re-arrange the garden. The vegetable patch we had planned is too small. Maria needs her vegetables."

In the tense silence that followed, Maria kept stirring.

"I know what you're going to say," continued Eric, "but we can move the rock garden you wanted somewhere else. It can go pretty much anywhere and be fine. It will be a bit of work but it will be fine. I'll do it for nothing."

Brent looked from one to the other of the pair of conspirators. Eric, in his seventies, could be his dad. Maria, nudging seventy, could be his mom. Lonely Eric, lonely Maria, and lonely son Brent. How could he disappoint them?

"Show me where the vegetable garden is going," said Brent.

"Here." Eric pointed at the diagram with his gnarled finger as he explained the intricacies of how everything would fit and where things would go.

When he had finished, Brent said, "I think that's an excellent idea. But Eric, no more talk about working for free, okay?"

"That's good of you. I knew you'd see it the right way."

Brent watched Maria. As soon as he had approved the vegetable patch, Maria smiled, left off stirring, and went out of the kitchen.

"Excuse me a moment. Maria might have left the heat on under that pan," said Brent to Eric.

He went to the stove to look in the saucepan that Maria had been using. There was nothing in it except a clean wooden spoon. She had been stirring nothing and had used the activity as a pretext to listen and not miss a word. Brent could not repress a laugh but gave Eric no explanation of it.

This little incident reminded him of the first day she came to do the cleaning. Brent had been present so that they could discuss further what needed to be done, where things were, and whether she required anything he did not already have. Brent had been downstairs and Maria was vacuuming upstairs. The vacuum cleaner was then switched off. There was a long silence lasting nearly fifteen minutes. Then the vacuum cleaner went on again. The silence had bothered Brent. He could not imagine what she had been doing. When she came down a little later he found out.

"Brent, how many suits do you have?"

"There are about fifteen upstairs."

"No, there are eighteen. Why do you have so many?"

"It's a habit of mine. I like suits. Did you go through my closets?"

"Sure. I've been through all of them. You could open a menswear store. How come you have so many clothes? I've never seen so many but they're beautiful."

"Oh, thanks … I like nice clothes."

"Would you do an old lady a favour?"

"What's that?"

"There's one suit I'd like you to put on. The green one."

"Green? Oh, I know which one you mean. You want me to model it for you?"

"Do you mind?"

"Um, er, no, I suppose not."

They both went upstairs. While Brent put the suit on in his room, Maria tidied the bathroom along the landing, even though it was not on her list of things to do. The suit was not exactly green but was a fine, dark, woollen weave of green, mauve, and black, that had an olive green cast to it. Brent carefully matched some smart black shoes and chose a dark tie. When he was ready, he called out to Maria.

"That's so beautiful. I never see a suit look so good on a man before. That must be expensive. How much?"

"This was eighteen hundred, I think."

"That's a lot of money but it looks like a million bucks on you."

The week following that episode, Maria began to ask why it was that Brent was not married. He could not come up with an answer that Maria found satisfactory.

"Are you gay?" she asked. Brent said, 'No.'

"Everything works?" Before he could answer, she said, "Sorry, that's rude of me and none of my business. It's just that there are, let me see, five, no six… no, she's too young. There are five girls in my family who would go out with you if you asked them. Wear the green suit to one of our family celebrations and a year later you'd be married."

"That's nice of you to say but it's not that easy, is it?"

"Maybe you're right. Brent, don't look for perfection. Look for someone you can live with. Believe me, I know. I was married for forty-six years."

Gabbie Wright posted on Facebook in short bursts each week. She had been travelling around Europe on her own, visiting friends and family. Brent did not post to her page very often.

GW: Took a side trip to Venice for three days. What a mistake! It did nothing but rain the whole time. I heard Venice was nice and quiet in November so I had hoped to visit a few museums, etc. Got to see those and they were great BUT couldn't do anything outside! Look at the pics!

JB: Gabbie, everyone knows it's Venice in the spring.....

PK: ..... The architecture is still beautiful. I'd love to have gone with you....

DM: .... Those are some seriously good photos. What camera did you use?.....

BU: .... How dare Venice pack away its romance for the season? I would have hammered on doors and shuttered windows until it produced for you a gleam of sunshine to restore its Venetian beauty for a few moments.

Your third photo of the Grand Canal is nearly identical to the painting I'll post below. That means you stood on the very spot where Canaletto stood and set up his easel to paint three hundred years earlier. The scene looks relatively unchanged - except for the rain!

Any thoughts on the project I mentioned?

GW: .... You always know the right thing to say. I would have knocked on doors alongside you. Love the tie in with Canaletto. That makes up for a lot.

The project. IDK, but the idea seems to be growing on me. Ask me in a month or two. It would need a real face-to-face discussion and I'm not sure I'm ready for that.

A few weeks passed by after this exchange between them. Brent gradually came to realize that Gabbie was gone for good and accepted it as a fact. He did draw some solace from their brief connection in so much as he found he was no longer paralyzed with fear at the thought of telling a woman he liked about his criminal past. It would never be easy for him but now it was not the insurmountable barrier it had once been.

After a month, Gabbie met someone. Tactfully, she softened the blow for Brent. He felt slightly wounded when the blow landed but, when he looked at it, he found it to be only a scratch which quickly healed. After that, Brent and Gabbie were always to remain friends.

Epi-Prologue

*I*t was now the twentieth of November, several weeks after the case had been concluded. Brent's life had returned to normal or, to be more precise, it had transformed into a new normal. His current work consisted of earning money through his stock portfolio. It kept him busy but only for the ten to fifteen hours he devoted to it each week. He had decided to give Althorn a tryout and had gone as far as to contact Kevin Jiang directly about the matter.

Kevin had been honest with him about Althorn and had recommended Brent wait a while. The partnership was continuing, a new deal would be in place, and Kevin was to become a junior partner. This was not likely to be finalized until after the middle of December at the earliest - the matter being kicked around between lawyers at present. Althorn, Kevin said, was doing well now that charges had been laid in the murder case. Clients remained loyal and a few more had been added because the company was continuing to return excellent profits to investors since Kirby's death. Kevin also said, after he had spoken to Nola Devon and Will Hutchinson, that Brent would not be charged any fees for the first year in recognition of the services he had provided.

The newness of Brent's current normalcy centred around Maria. Brent's empty house was filling up. Eric,

Maria, and even Monty provided regularity to his schedule and he liked the familiarity they all shared. He talked to the cat and Monty, having the habit of meowing back, acted as a sounding-board for Brent's thoughts, allowing Brent the semblance of sharing them.

He saw friends often enough, although he dropped out of the circle where he had met Linda Roberts. Nonetheless, he felt he was at a loose end. A couple of times it crossed his mind, in idle moments, to travel to Europe and surprise Gabbie. Then he would remember that she might be with someone else by now. He would laugh at the thought of what any new man-friend of hers would make of it if he suddenly turned up out of the blue. As time passed, though, thoughts of Gabbie were becoming less frequent. A whole day had recently elapsed when he had forgotten to think of her at all. He was slowly beginning to accept the situation - he was still alone, but he was no longer so lonely.

The trouble with Brent was that he had nothing challenging to do. He could fill in his time but not with anything that truly satisfied him or demanded much from him. In other words, he was bored. He read books and, when he paused for a moment, realized how bored he was. He loved his books but, being a young man brimming with health and energy, he needed also to be a man of action.

That morning of the twentieth, Brent opened a browser window to see what weather was forecast for the day. Apparently, snow was a possibility. He had a news feed running and noticed that a local police officer had been killed overnight. He followed the link.

The details were scant. A detective, whose name he did not recognize, had been shot while sitting in his car late the previous night. Joe Blaskett, 34, left behind his wife, Hayley, 32, and three children aged seven, four, and eighteen months. Brent, his naturally empathetic imagination fully engaged, felt bad as he read the details. Police were asking for witnesses and any camera footage to be sent to them. Currently, the police seemed to have no leads or description of the perpetrator. Brent felt sick over the callousness of the crime and the murder itself. His heart went out to the young family.

Zack sent Brent a video link. It was the opening theme music for the new show, Two-Way Street Beat. One shot was of Zack airborne like a bird on his skateboard with his hair streaming behind him. When he landed with a musical crash - the main title came up. Zack's brief note said, 'Thanks for making it happen.'

In the middle of the afternoon, Brent took his Jeep for an oil change appointment. He chatted for a while with the manager of the garage while the Jeep was being seen to. The manager got busy with other customers so Brent went for a walk outside. It was definitely colder than usual and he felt he would not be surprised if snow did fall overnight as the forecast had predicted. It was raw and damp so he went back inside to have a cup of the coffee provided by the garage for any customers who were kept waiting.

The music that was playing in the background was from a local radio station. Commercials came on and Brent learned he could replace his windows easily, replace his garage door using the best in the business, consolidate all his debts and never worry again, and, if necessary, have his hair replaced so that women could not tell if it was natural or not because he would have 'a head of hair to die for'. His own hair was thick and luxuriant and, he hoped, he would not need that last service for quite a while to come.

Breaking news interrupted the music with a loud fanfare. An arrest had been made in the case of the slain detective. Brent, staring out of the window at nothing in particular, was then given such a jolt that it caused him to spill some of his free coffee. Lieutenant Greg Darrow of the Newhampton Police Department had been arrested for the murder of Joe Blaskett.

OTHER TITLES IN THE BRENT UMBER SERIES

Death among the Vines
Death of a Detective,
Death at Hill Hall,
Death on the Slopes
+ Two more Brent Umber stories!
Coming soon - by the end of 2021.

NEWSLETTER + FREE STORY CYCLE

If you liked this story, a great choice is to sign up for the **monthly newsletter** and be automatically included in the **Free Story Cycle**.

The current cycle of novella length stories is entitled:

The Village of the Sevenfold Curse
- Murder Mystery through the ages

This new series of seven unpublished stories are free - exclusive only to newsletter subscribers. But it doesn't stop there. When one **Story Cycle** ends… another begins.

https://gjbellamy.com

Printed in Great Britain
by Amazon